Woodbourne Library
Washington-Centerville Public
Centerville, Ohio

W9-AEC-944

DISCARD

image comics presents

THE WALKING DEAD ™

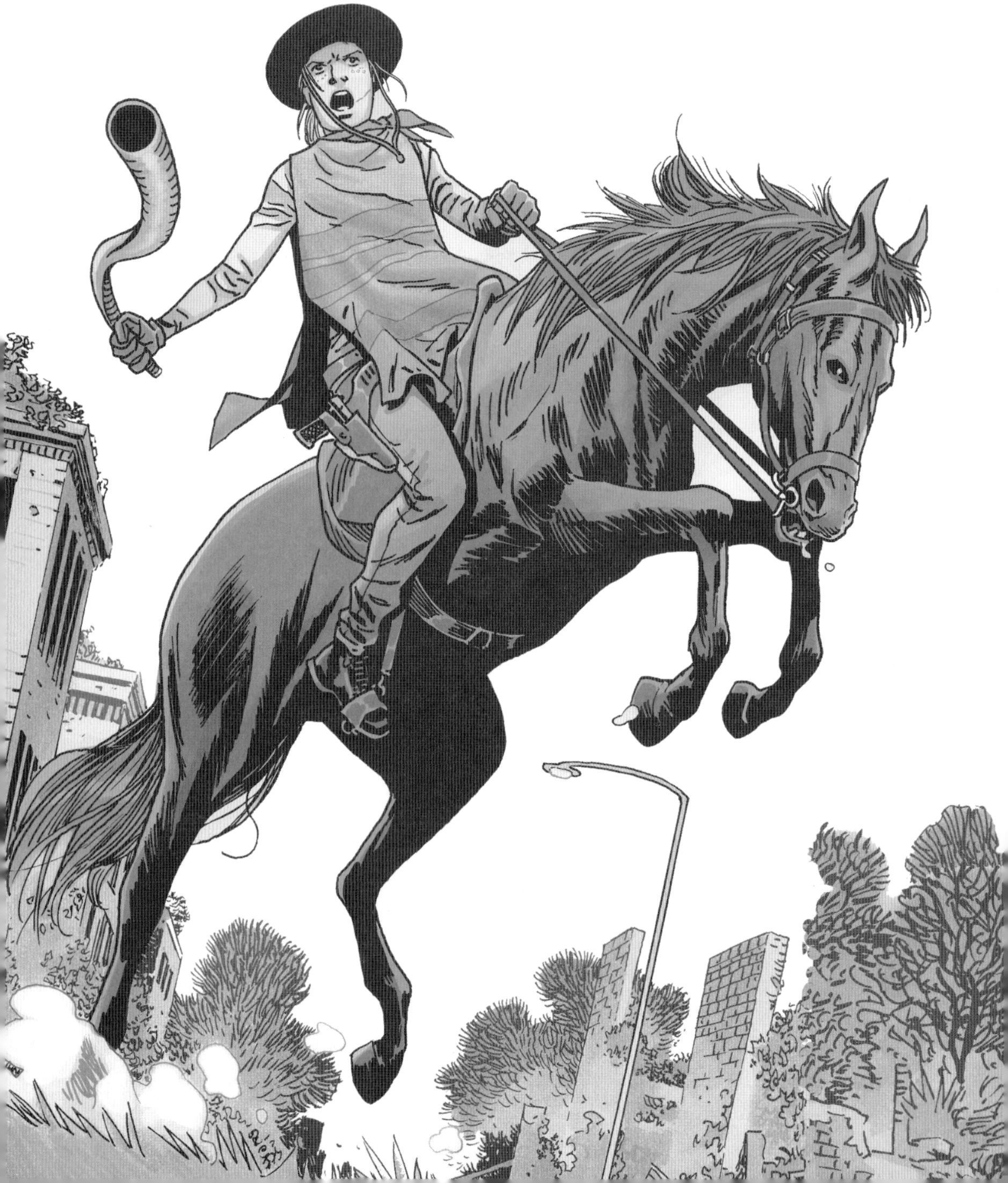

ROBERT KIRKMAN
CREATOR, WRITER

CHARLIE ADLARD
PENCILER

STEFANO GAUDIANO
INKER

CLIFF RATHBURN
GRAY TONES

RUS WOOTON
LETTERER

CHARLIE ADLARD
& DAVE STEWART
COVER

SEAN MACKIEWICZ
EDITOR

SKYBOUND™

For SKYBOUND ENTERTAINMENT
Robert Kirkman - Chairman
David Alpert - CEO
Sean Mackiewicz - SVP Editor-in-Chief
Shawn Kirkham - SVP Business Development
Brian Huntington - Online Editorial Director
June Alian - Publicity Director
Andres Juarez - Art Director
Jon Moisan - Editor
Arielle Basich - Assistant Editor
Carina Taylor - Production Artist
Paul Shin - Business Development Assistant
Johnny O'Dell - Online Editorial Assistant
Sally Jacka - Online Editorial Assistant
Dan Petersen - Director of Operations & Events
Nick Palmer - Operations Coordinator

International inquiries: ag@sequentialrights.com
Licensing inquiries: contact@skybound.com

WWW.SKYBOUND.COM

image ®

IMAGE COMICS, INC.
Robert Kirkman—Chief Operating Officer
Erik Larsen—Chief Financial Officer
Todd McFarlane—President
Marc Silvestri—Chief Executive Officer
Jim Valentino—Vice President

Eric Stephenson—Publisher
Corey Murphy—Director of Sales
Jeff Boison—Director of Publishing Planning & Book Trade Sales
Chris Ross—Director of Digital Sales
Jeff Stang—Director of Specialty Sales
Kat Salazar—Director of PR & Marketing
Branwyn Bigglestone—Controller
Kali Dugan—Senior Accounting Manager
Sue Korpela—Accounting & HR Manager
Drew Gill—Art Director
Heather Doornink—Production Director
Leigh Thomas—Print Manager
Tricia Ramos—Traffic Manager
Briah Skelly—Publicist
Aly Hoffman—Events & Conventions Coordinator
Sasha Head—Sales & Marketing Production Designer
David Brothers—Branding Manager
Melissa Gifford—Content Manager
Drew Fitzgerald—Publicity Assistant
Vincent Kukua—Production Artist
Erika Schnatz—Production Artist
Ryan Brewer—Production Artist
Shanna Matuszak—Production Artist
Carey Hall—Production Artist
Esther Kim—Direct Market Sales Representative
Emilio Bautista—Digital Sales Representative
Leanna Caunter—Accounting Analyst
Chloe Ramos-Peterson—Library Market Sales Representative
Maria Eizik—Administrative Assistant
IMAGECOMICS.COM

THE WALKING DEAD, VOL. 28: A CERTAIN DOOM. First Printing. ISBN: 978-1-5343-0244-0. Published by Image Comics, Inc. Office of publication: 2701 NW Vaughn St., Ste. 780, Portland, OR 97210. Copyright © 2017 Robert Kirkman, LLC. All rights reserved. Originally published in single magazine format as THE WALKING DEAD #163-168. THE WALKING DEAD™ (including all prominent characters featured in this issue), its logo and all character likenesses are trademarks of Robert Kirkman, LLC, unless otherwise noted. Image Comics® and its logos are registered trademarks and copyrights of Image Comics, Inc. All rights reserved. No part of this publication may be reproduced or transmitted, in any form or by any means (except for short excerpts for review purposes) without the express written permission of Image Comics, Inc. All names, characters, events and locales in this publication are entirely fictional. Any resemblance to actual persons (living and/or dead), events or places, without satiric intent, is coincidental. For information regarding the CPSIA on this printed material call: 203-595-3636 and provide reference # RICH – 756257. PRINTED IN THE USA

MY *GOD!* THEY'RE SO CLOSE YOU CAN *HEAR* THEM!

IS THAT? OH, GOD... I...IS *THAT* WHAT THAT IS?

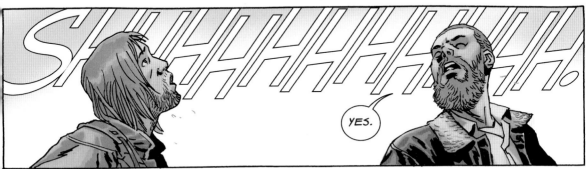

SHHHHHHHHHHHHH.

YES.

AN OCEAN OF THE DEAD.

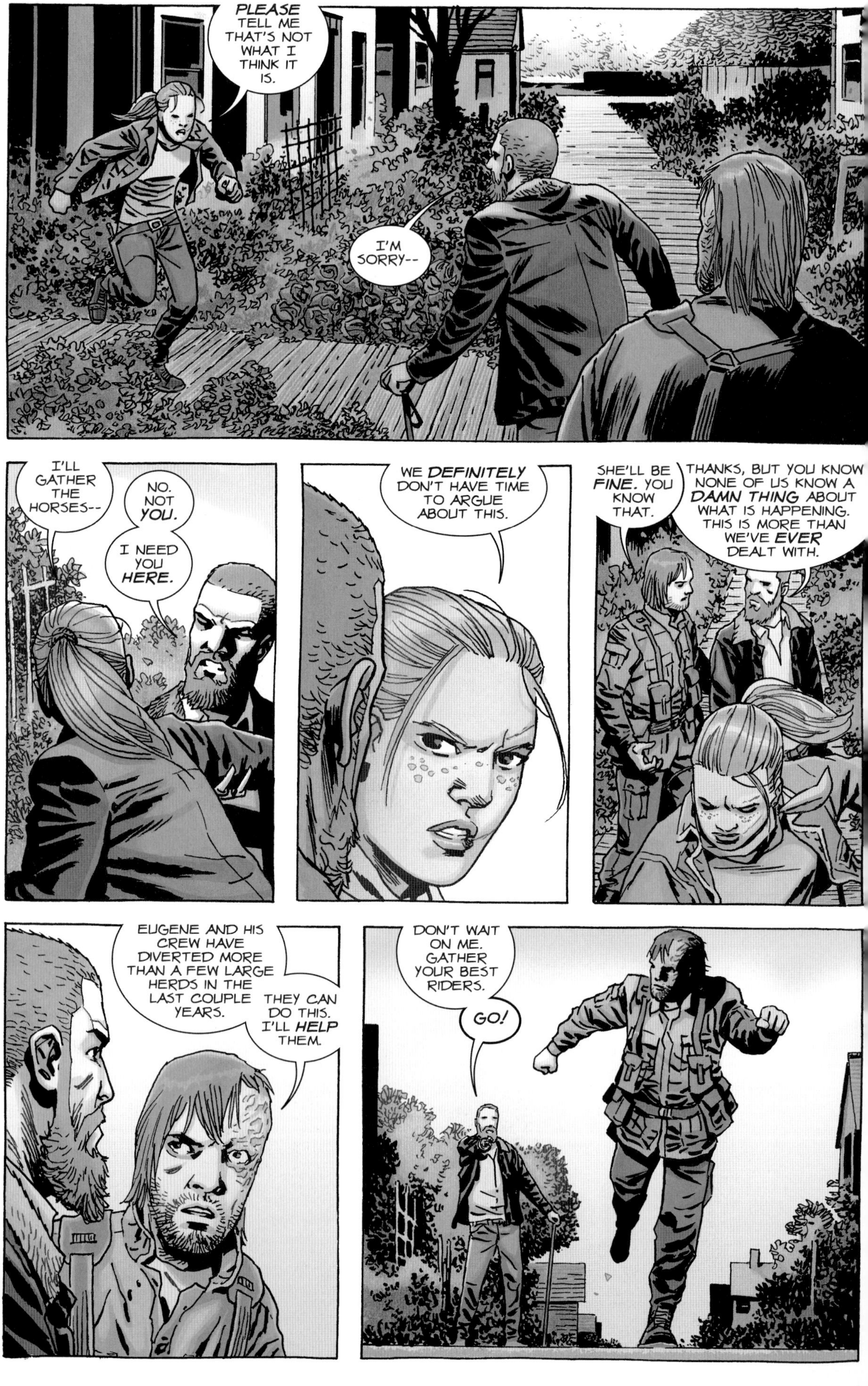
PLEASE TELL ME THAT'S NOT WHAT I THINK IT IS.
I'M SORRY--
I'LL GATHER THE HORSES--
NO. NOT YOU.
I NEED YOU HERE.
WE DEFINITELY DON'T HAVE TIME TO ARGUE ABOUT THIS.
SHE'LL BE FINE. YOU KNOW THAT.
THANKS, BUT YOU KNOW NONE OF US KNOW A DAMN THING ABOUT WHAT IS HAPPENING. THIS IS MORE THAN WE'VE EVER DEALT WITH.
EUGENE AND HIS CREW HAVE DIVERTED MORE THAN A FEW LARGE HERDS IN THE LAST COUPLE YEARS.
THEY CAN DO THIS. I'LL HELP THEM.
DON'T WAIT ON ME. GATHER YOUR BEST RIDERS.
GO!

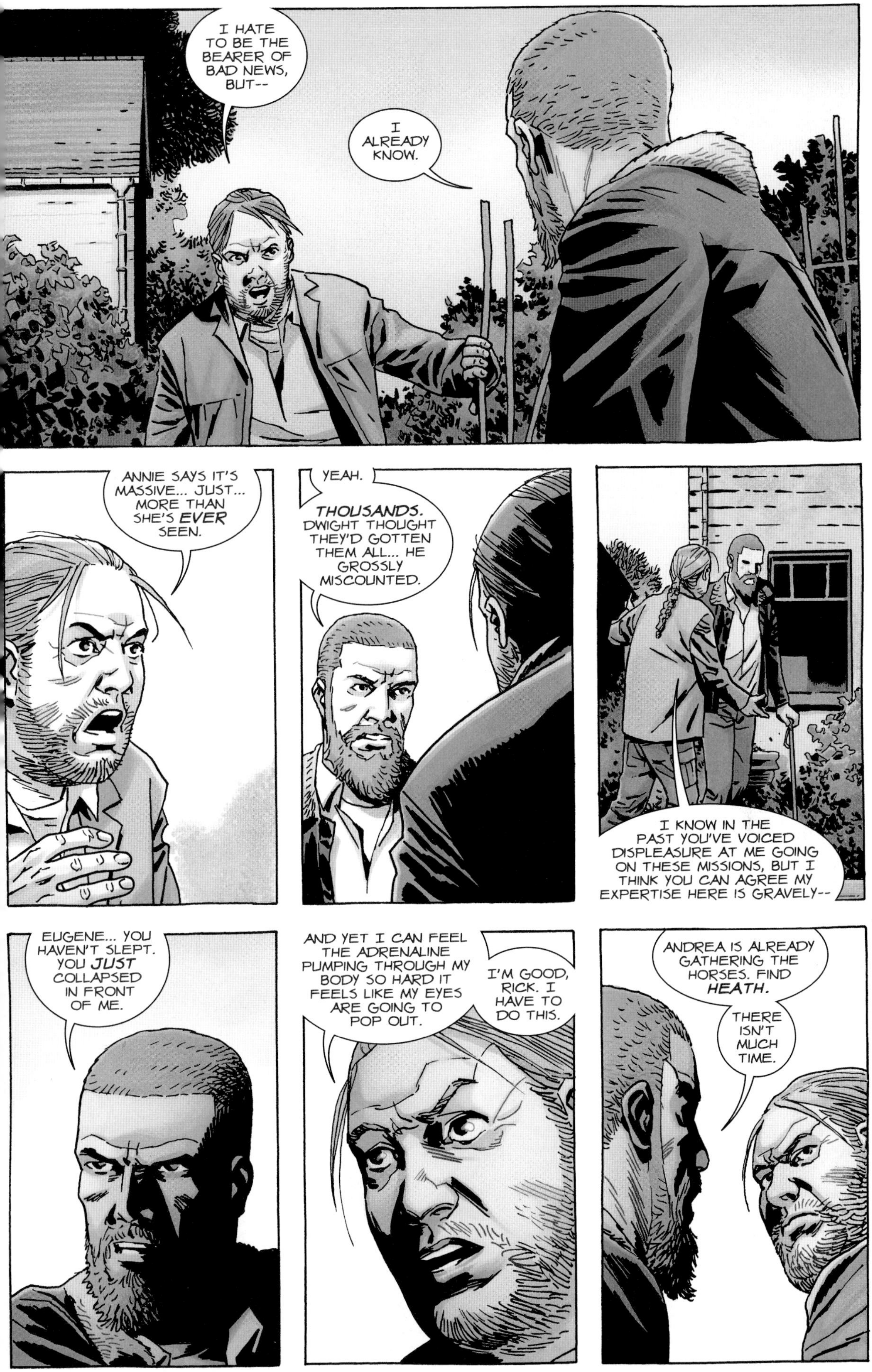
I HATE TO BE THE BEARER OF BAD NEWS, BUT--
I ALREADY KNOW.
ANNIE SAYS IT'S MASSIVE... JUST... MORE THAN SHE'S EVER SEEN.
YEAH.
THOUSANDS. DWIGHT THOUGHT THEY'D GOTTEN THEM ALL... HE GROSSLY MISCOUNTED.
I KNOW IN THE PAST YOU'VE VOICED DISPLEASURE AT ME GOING ON THESE MISSIONS, BUT I THINK YOU CAN AGREE MY EXPERTISE HERE IS GRAVELY--
EUGENE... YOU HAVEN'T SLEPT. YOU JUST COLLAPSED IN FRONT OF ME.
AND YET I CAN FEEL THE ADRENALINE PUMPING THROUGH MY BODY SO HARD IT FEELS LIKE MY EYES ARE GOING TO POP OUT.
I'M GOOD, RICK. I HAVE TO DO THIS.
ANDREA IS ALREADY GATHERING THE HORSES. FIND HEATH.
THERE ISN'T MUCH TIME.

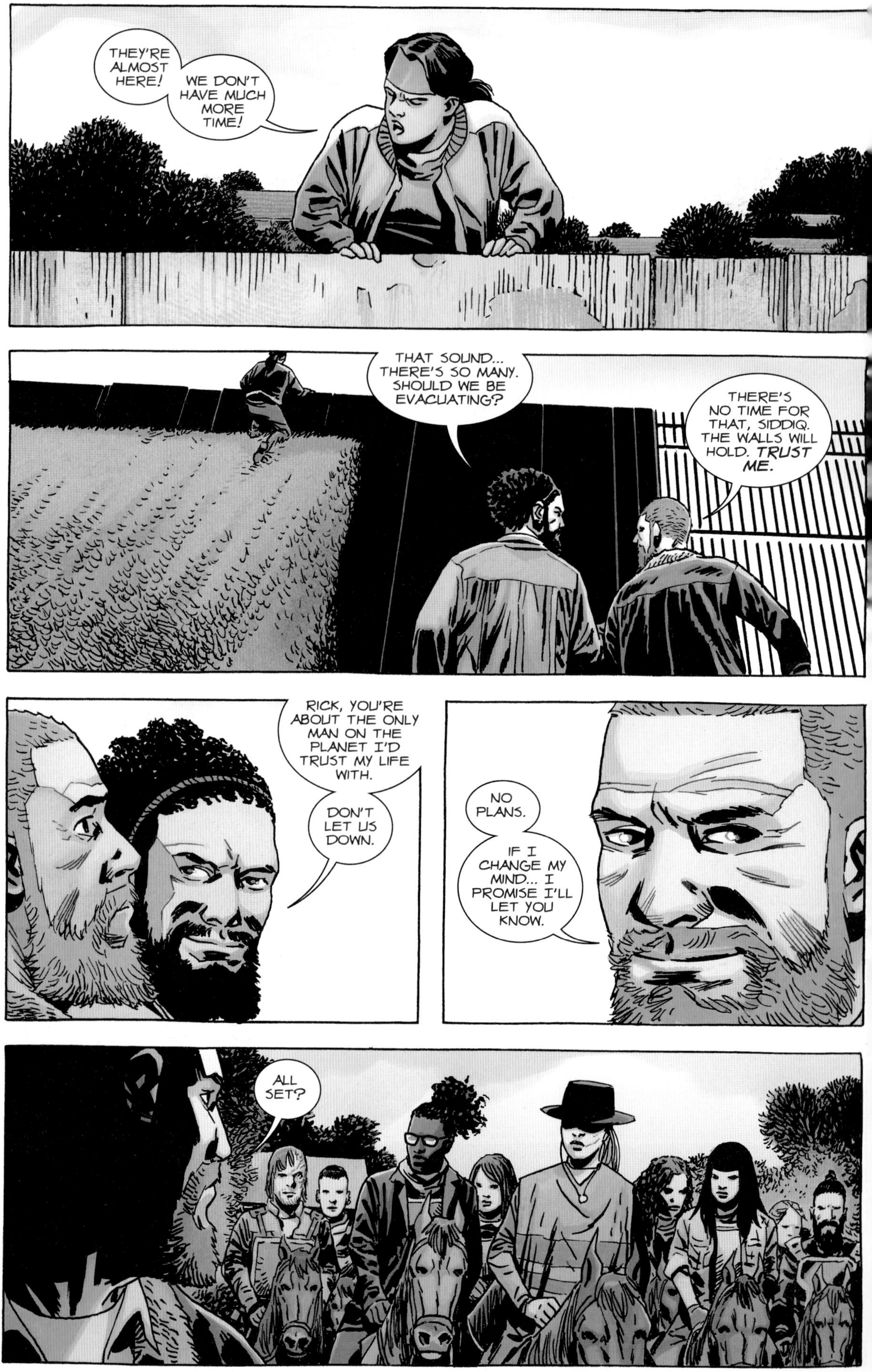
THEY'RE ALMOST HERE!
WE DON'T HAVE MUCH MORE TIME!
THAT SOUND... THERE'S SO MANY. SHOULD WE BE EVACUATING?
THERE'S NO TIME FOR THAT, SIDDIQ. THE WALLS WILL HOLD. TRUST ME.
RICK, YOU'RE ABOUT THE ONLY MAN ON THE PLANET I'D TRUST MY LIFE WITH.
DON'T LET US DOWN.
NO PLANS.
IF I CHANGE MY MIND... I PROMISE I'LL LET YOU KNOW.
ALL SET?

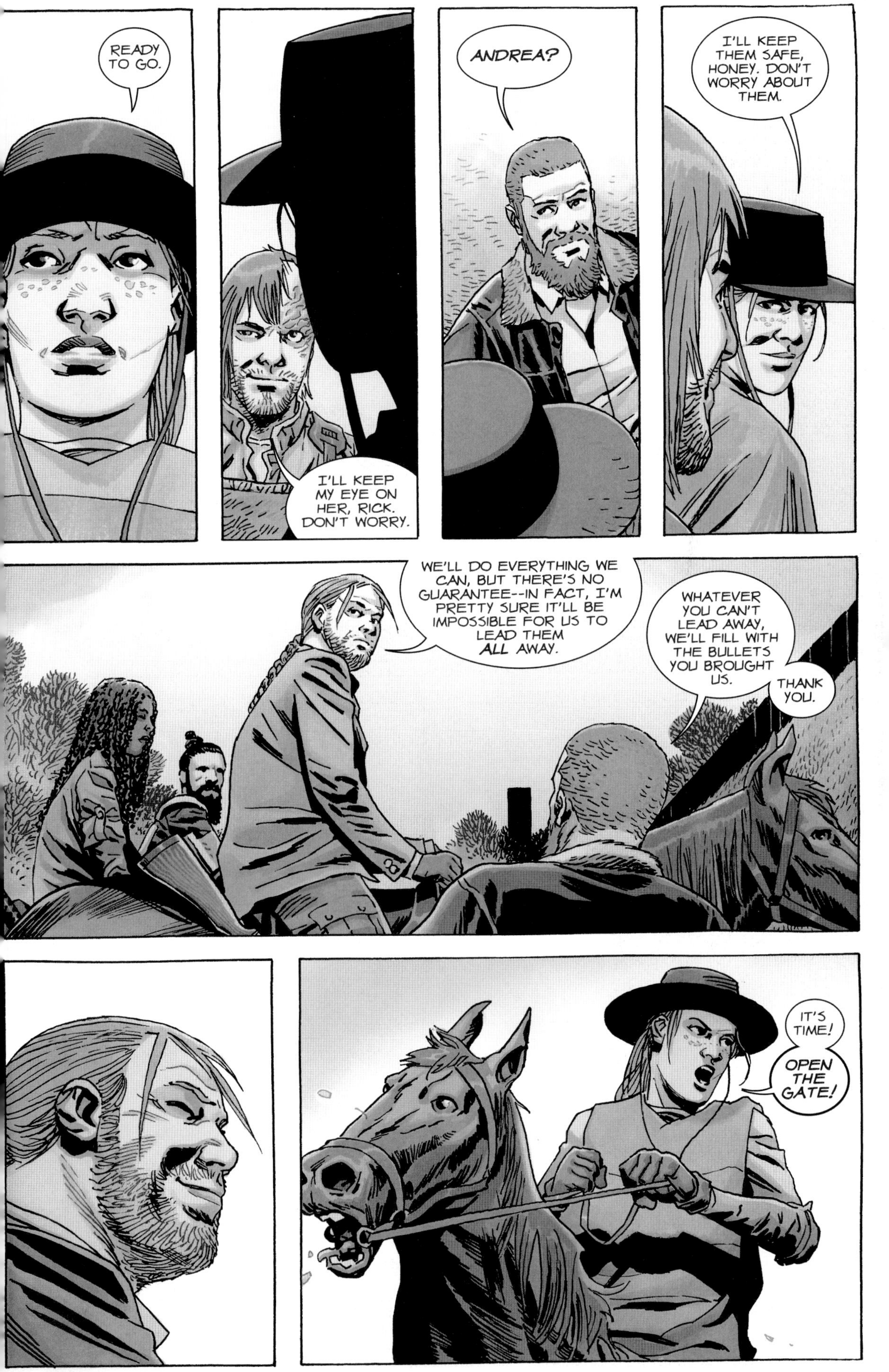
READY TO GO.
I'LL KEEP MY EYE ON HER, RICK. DON'T WORRY.
ANDREA?
I'LL KEEP THEM SAFE, HONEY. DON'T WORRY ABOUT THEM.
WE'LL DO EVERYTHING WE CAN, BUT THERE'S NO GUARANTEE--IN FACT, I'M PRETTY SURE IT'LL BE IMPOSSIBLE FOR US TO LEAD THEM ALL AWAY.
WHATEVER YOU CAN'T LEAD AWAY, WE'LL FILL WITH THE BULLETS YOU BROUGHT US.
THANK YOU.
IT'S TIME!
OPEN THE GATE!

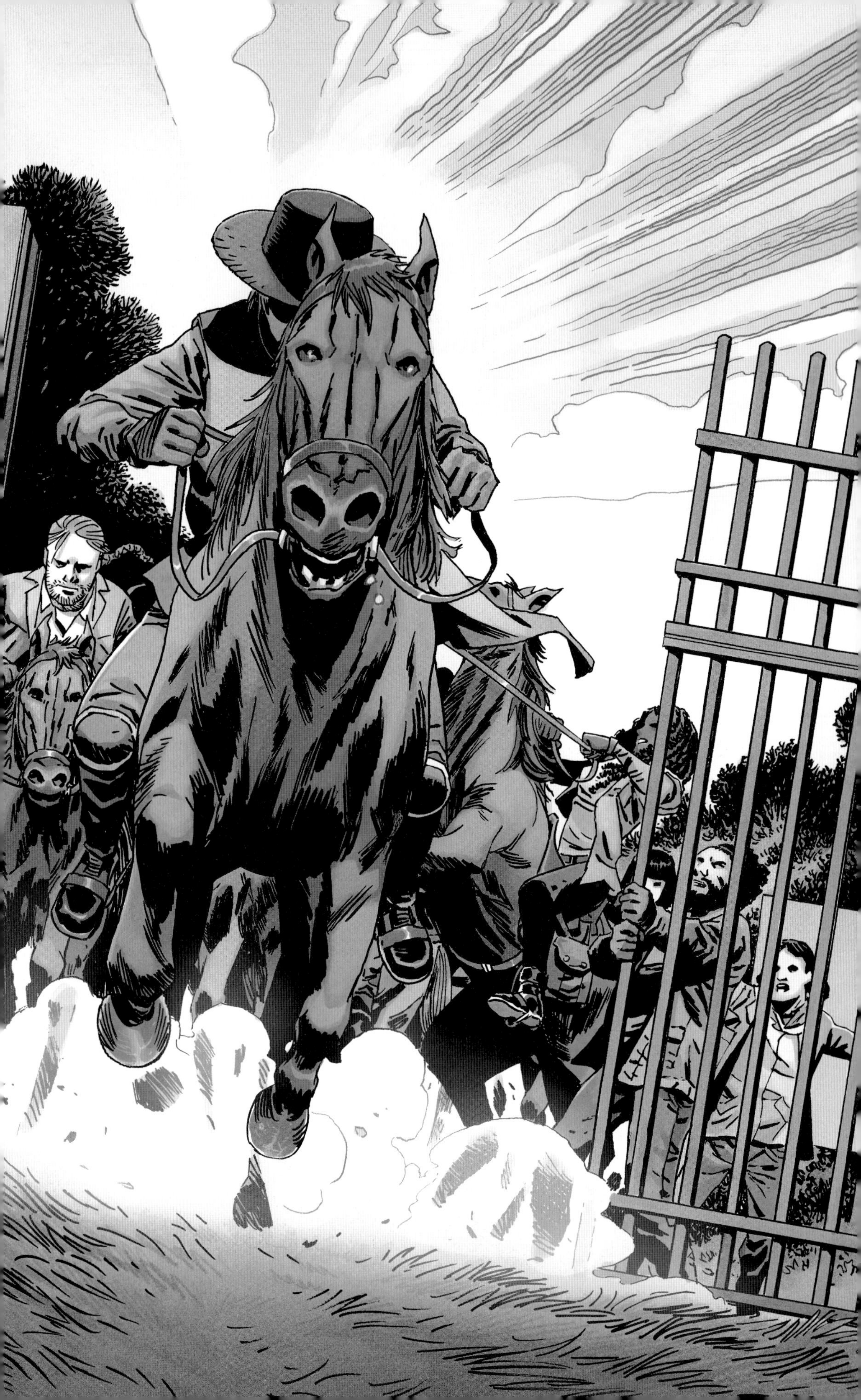

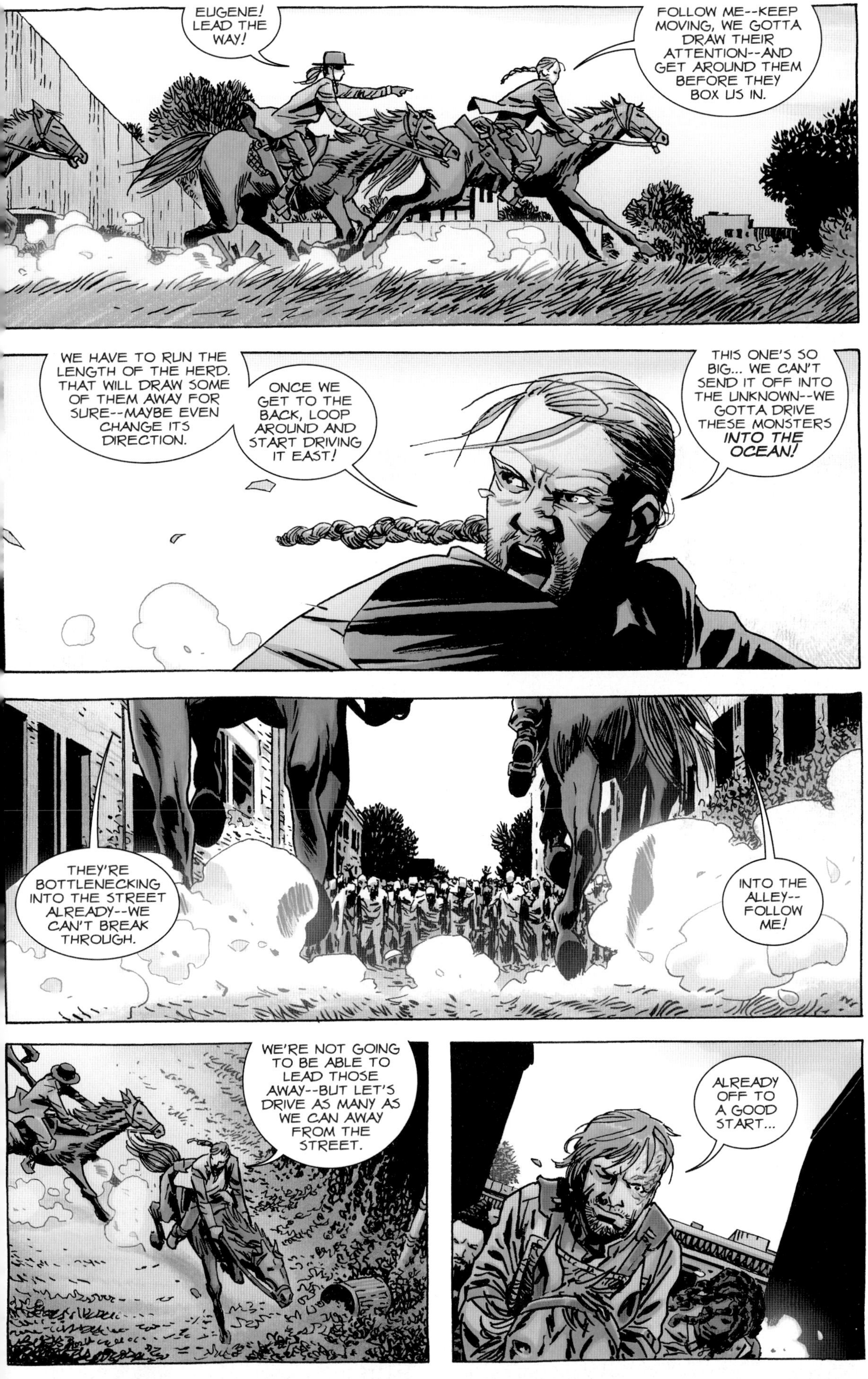
EUGENE! LEAD THE WAY!
FOLLOW ME--KEEP MOVING, WE GOTTA DRAW THEIR ATTENTION--AND GET AROUND THEM BEFORE THEY BOX US IN.
WE HAVE TO RUN THE LENGTH OF THE HERD. THAT WILL DRAW SOME OF THEM AWAY FOR SURE--MAYBE EVEN CHANGE ITS DIRECTION.
ONCE WE GET TO THE BACK, LOOP AROUND AND START DRIVING IT EAST!
THIS ONE'S SO BIG... WE CAN'T SEND IT OFF INTO THE UNKNOWN--WE GOTTA DRIVE THESE MONSTERS INTO THE OCEAN!
THEY'RE BOTTLENECKING INTO THE STREET ALREADY--WE CAN'T BREAK THROUGH.
INTO THE ALLEY--FOLLOW ME!
WE'RE NOT GOING TO BE ABLE TO LEAD THOSE AWAY--BUT LET'S DRIVE AS MANY AS WE CAN AWAY FROM THE STREET.
ALREADY OFF TO A GOOD START...

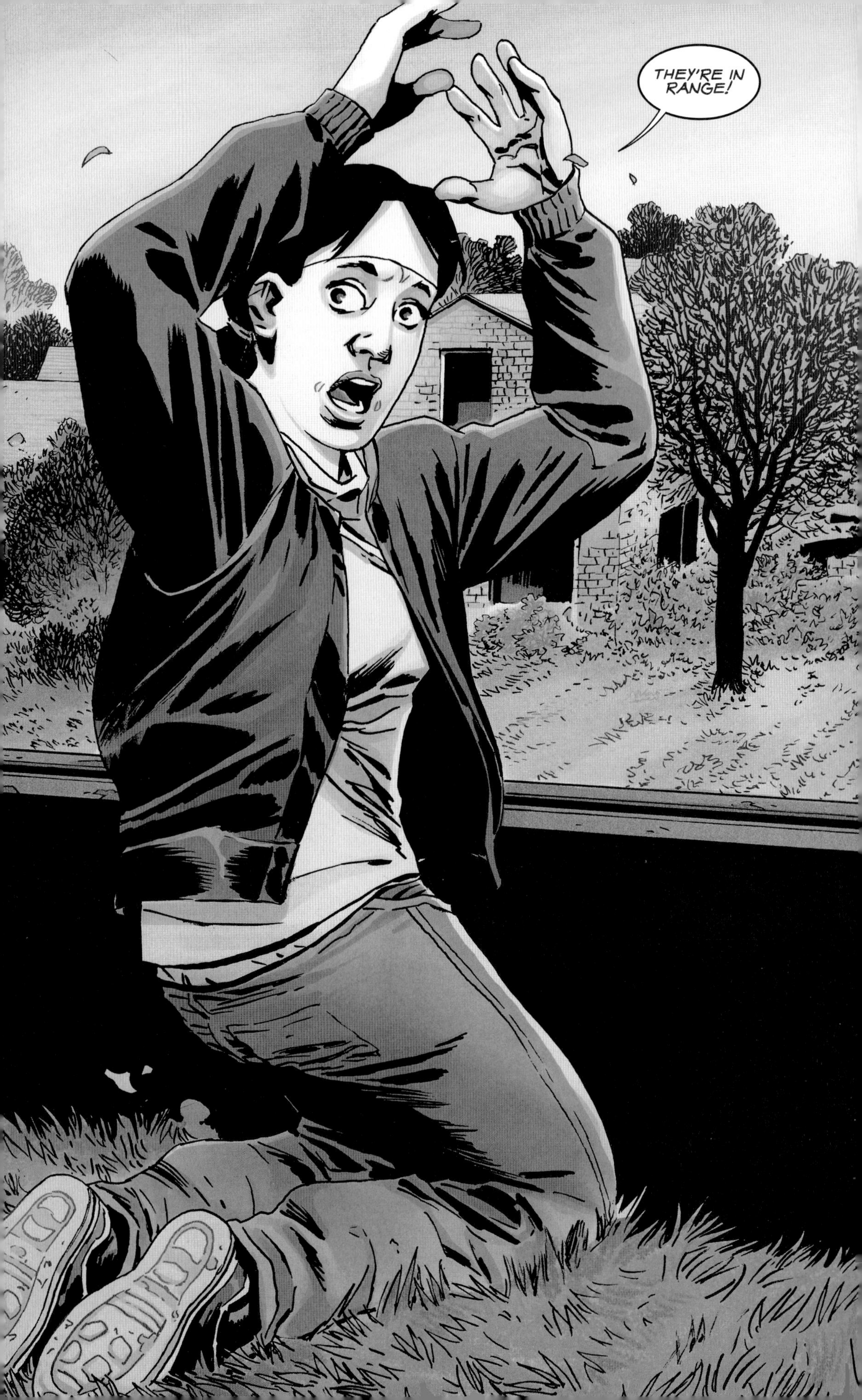
THEY'RE IN RANGE!

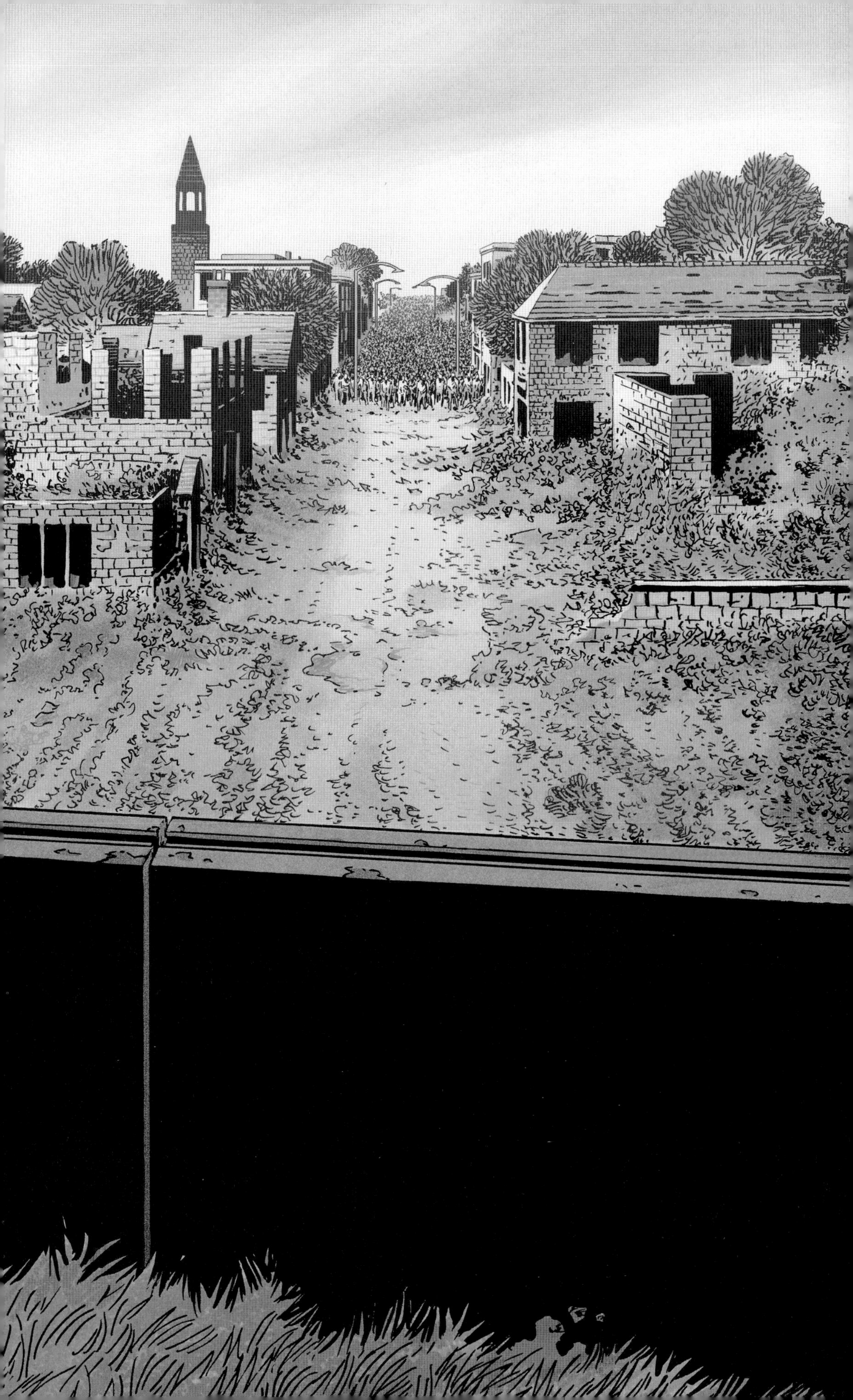

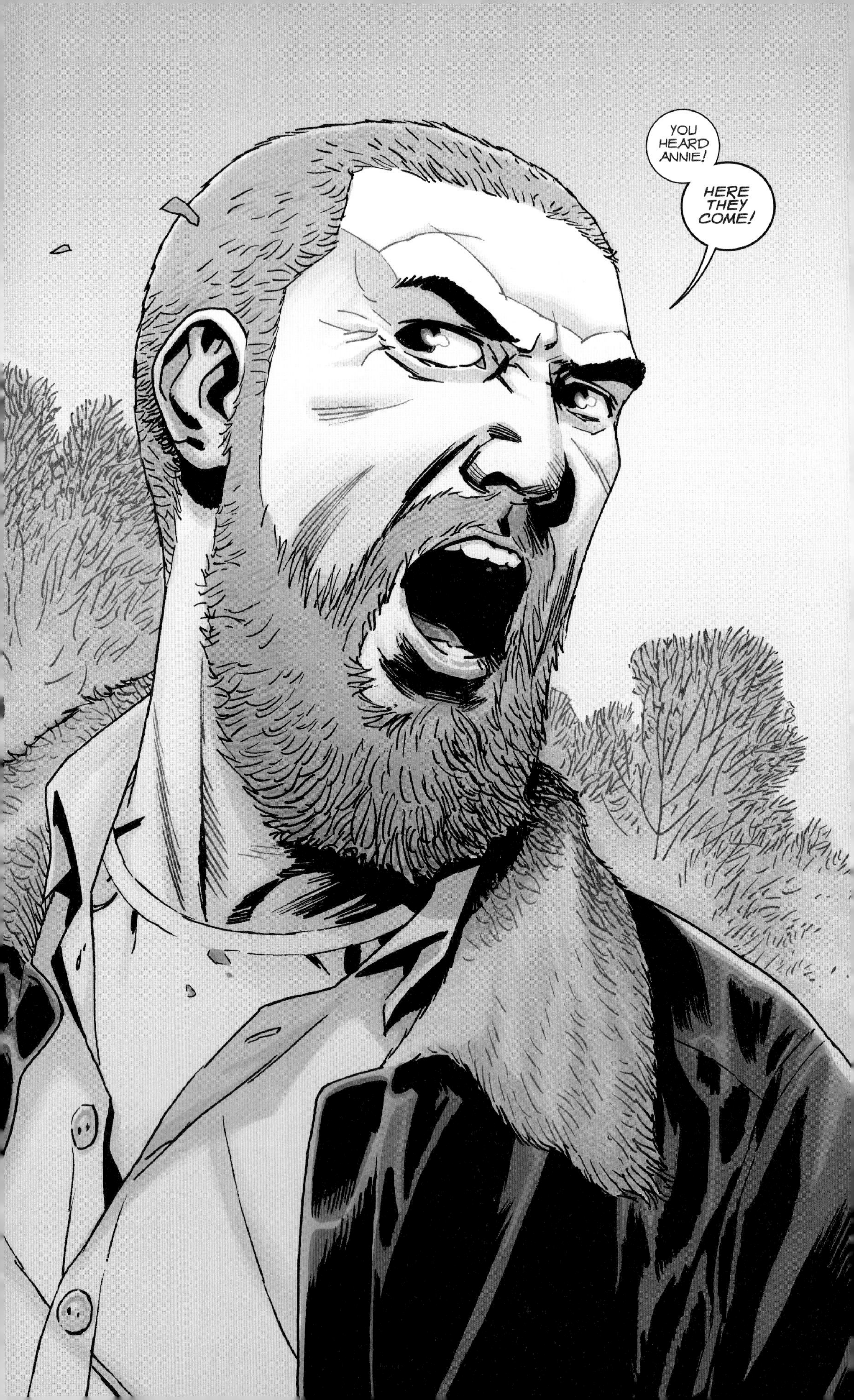
YOU HEARD ANNIE!
HERE THEY COME!

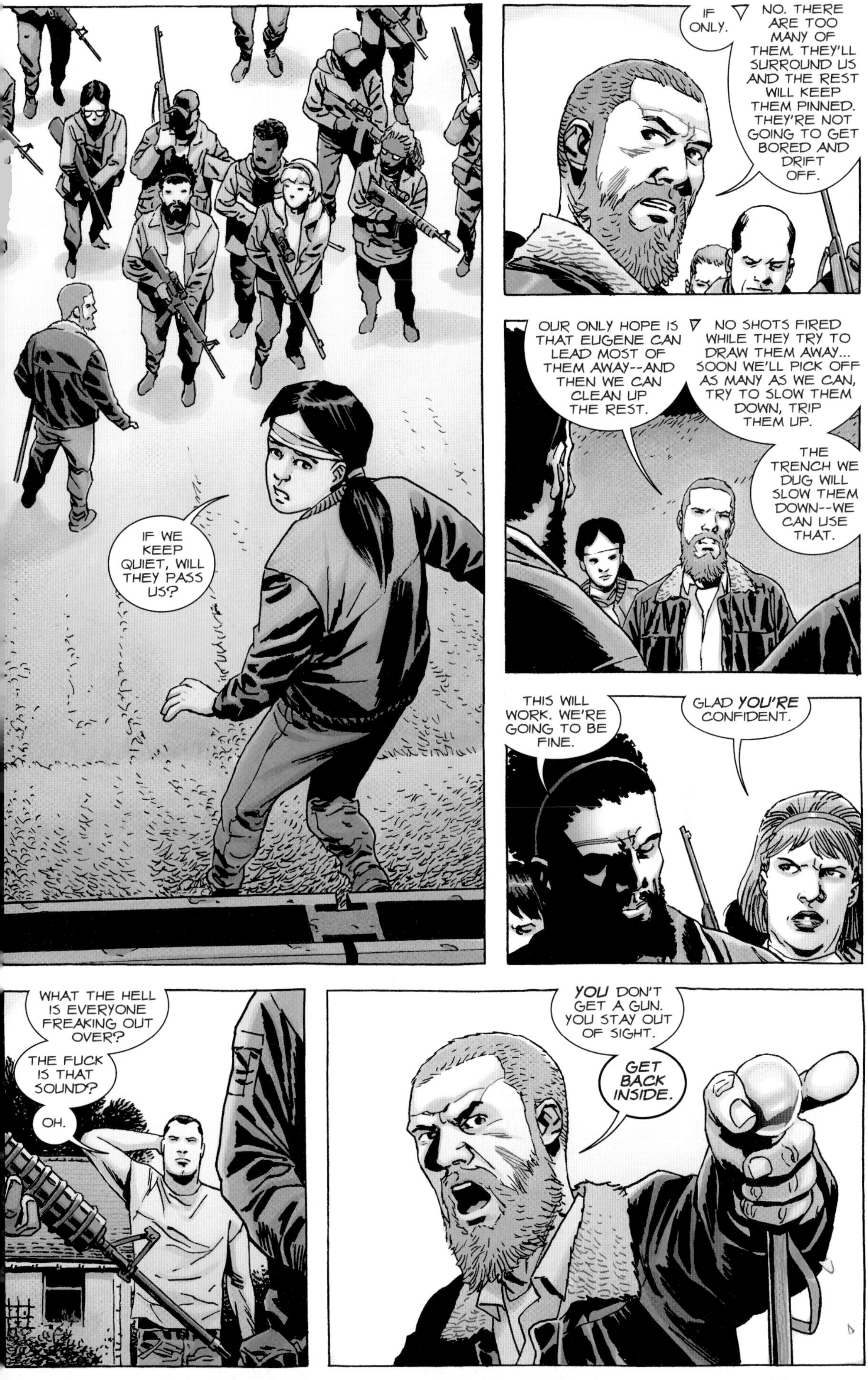

IF WE KEEP QUIET, WILL THEY PASS US?
IF ONLY.
NO. THERE ARE TOO MANY OF THEM. THEY'LL SURROUND US AND THE REST WILL KEEP THEM PINNED. THEY'RE NOT GOING TO GET BORED AND DRIFT OFF.
OUR ONLY HOPE IS THAT EUGENE CAN LEAD MOST OF THEM AWAY--AND THEN WE CAN CLEAN UP THE REST.
NO SHOTS FIRED WHILE THEY TRY TO DRAW THEM AWAY... SOON WE'LL PICK OFF AS MANY AS WE CAN, TRY TO SLOW THEM DOWN, TRIP THEM UP.
THE TRENCH WE DUG WILL SLOW THEM DOWN--WE CAN USE THAT.
THIS WILL WORK. WE'RE GOING TO BE FINE.
GLAD *YOU'RE* CONFIDENT.
WHAT THE HELL IS EVERYONE FREAKING OUT OVER?
THE FUCK IS THAT SOUND?
OH.
YOU DON'T GET A GUN. YOU STAY OUT OF SIGHT.
GET BACK INSIDE.

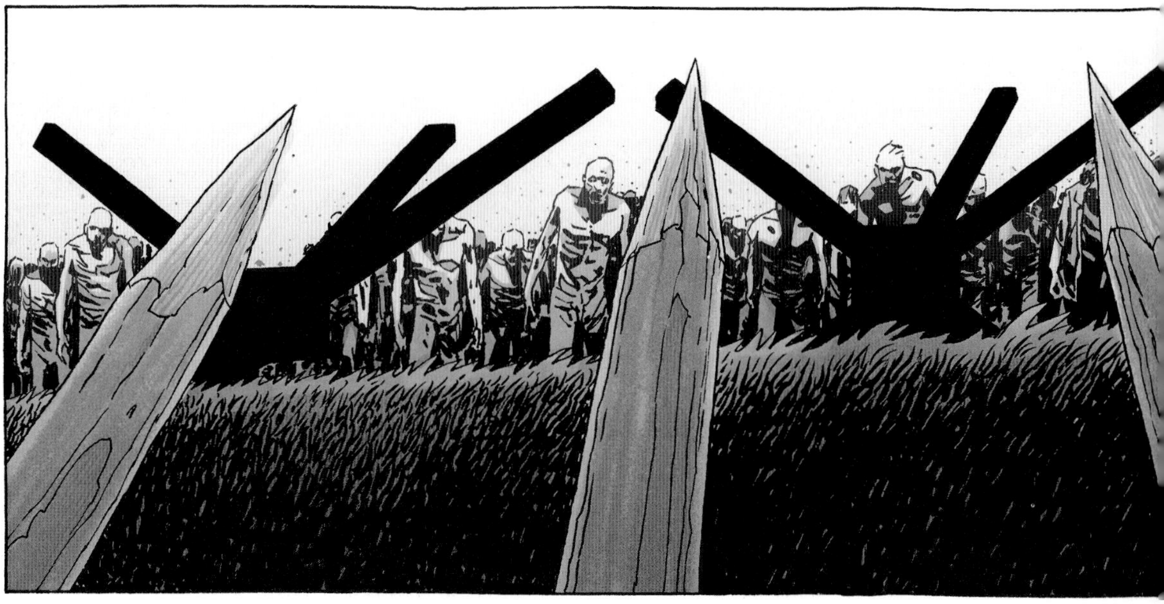
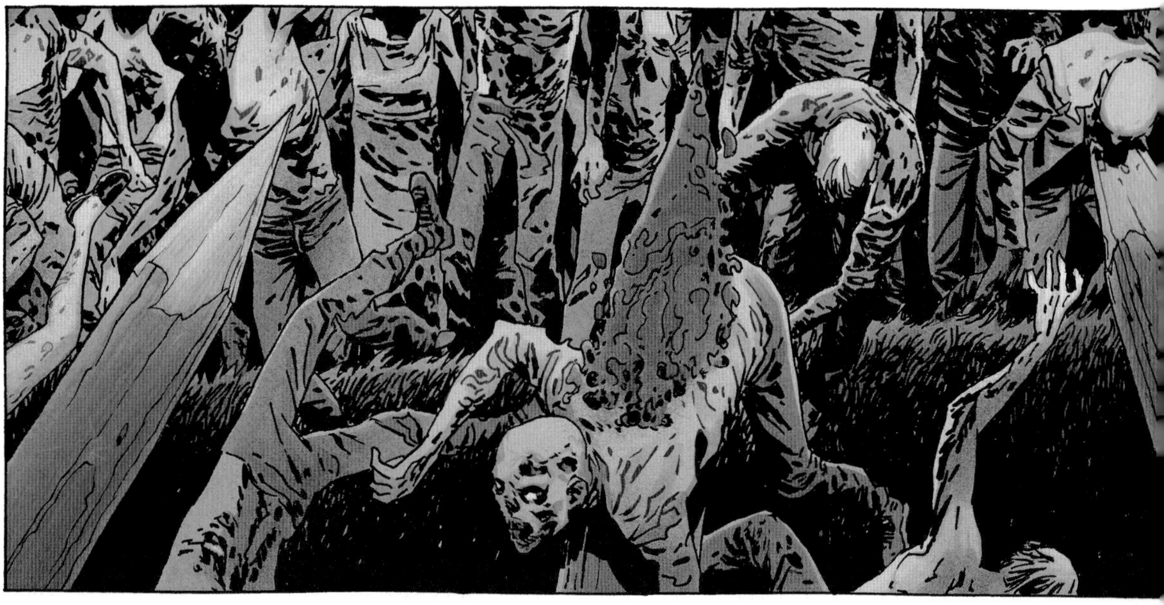
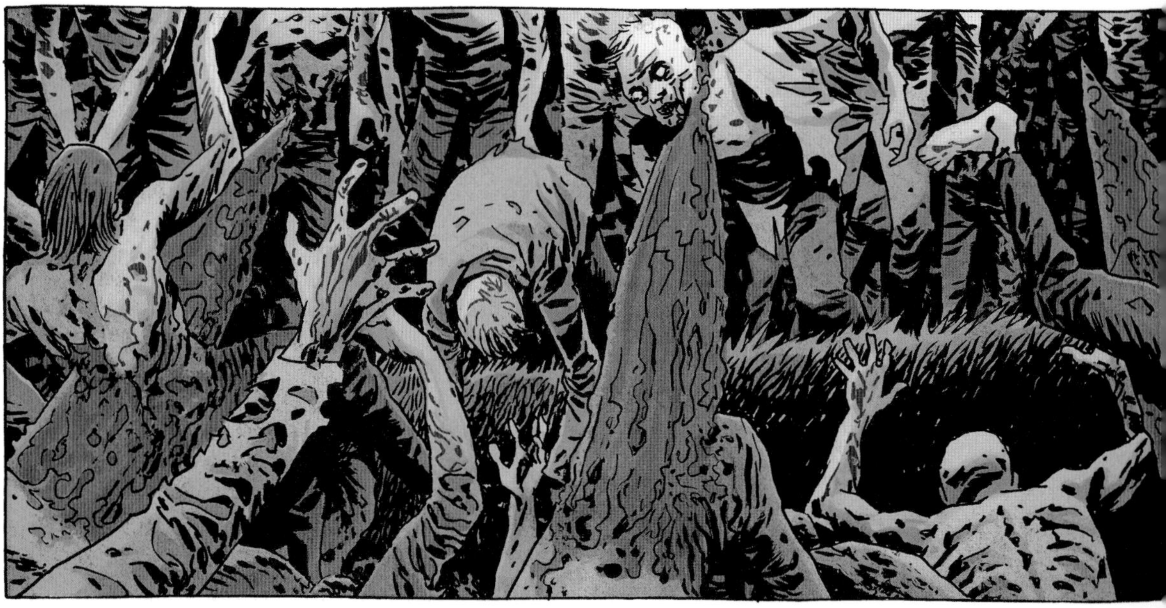

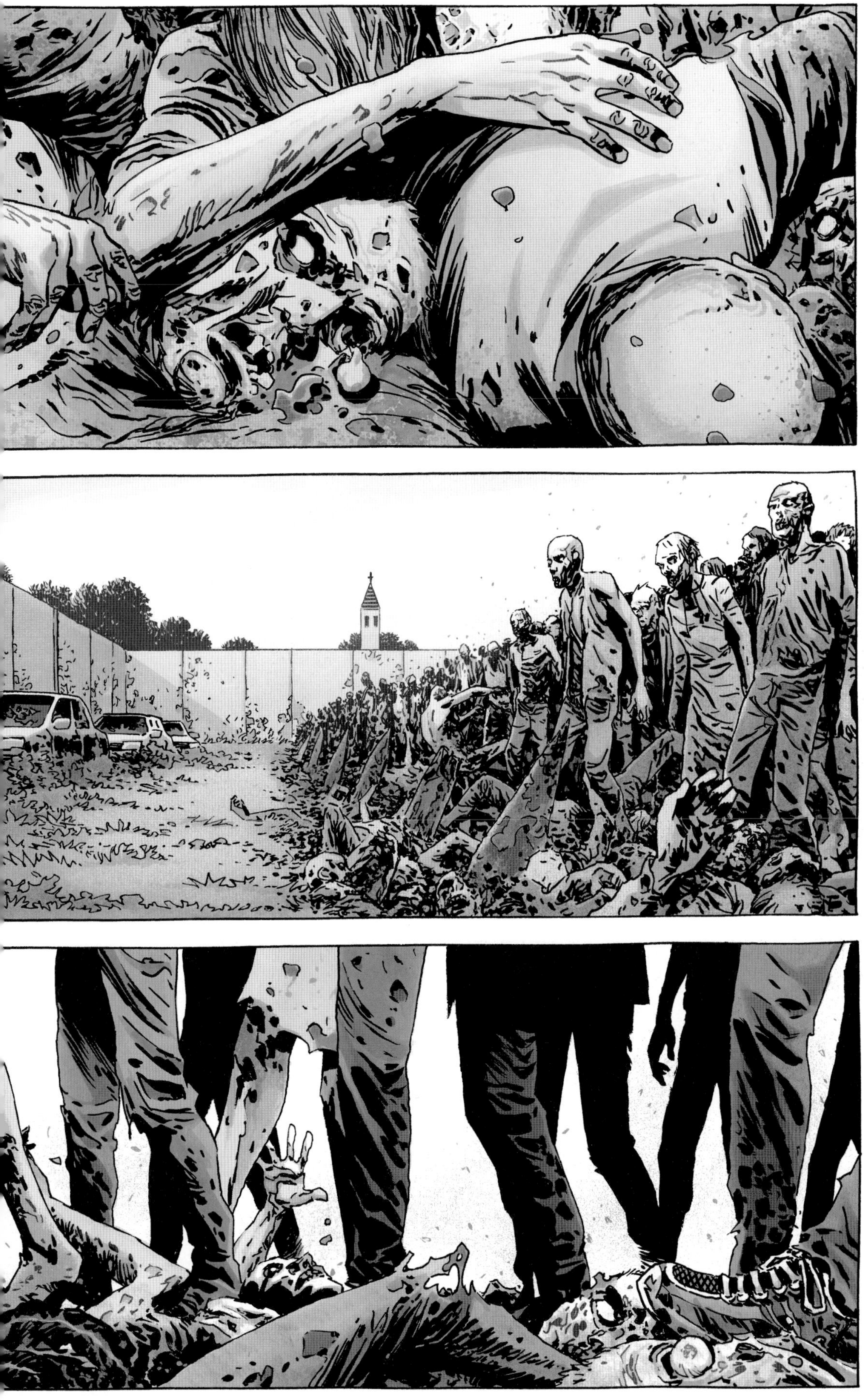

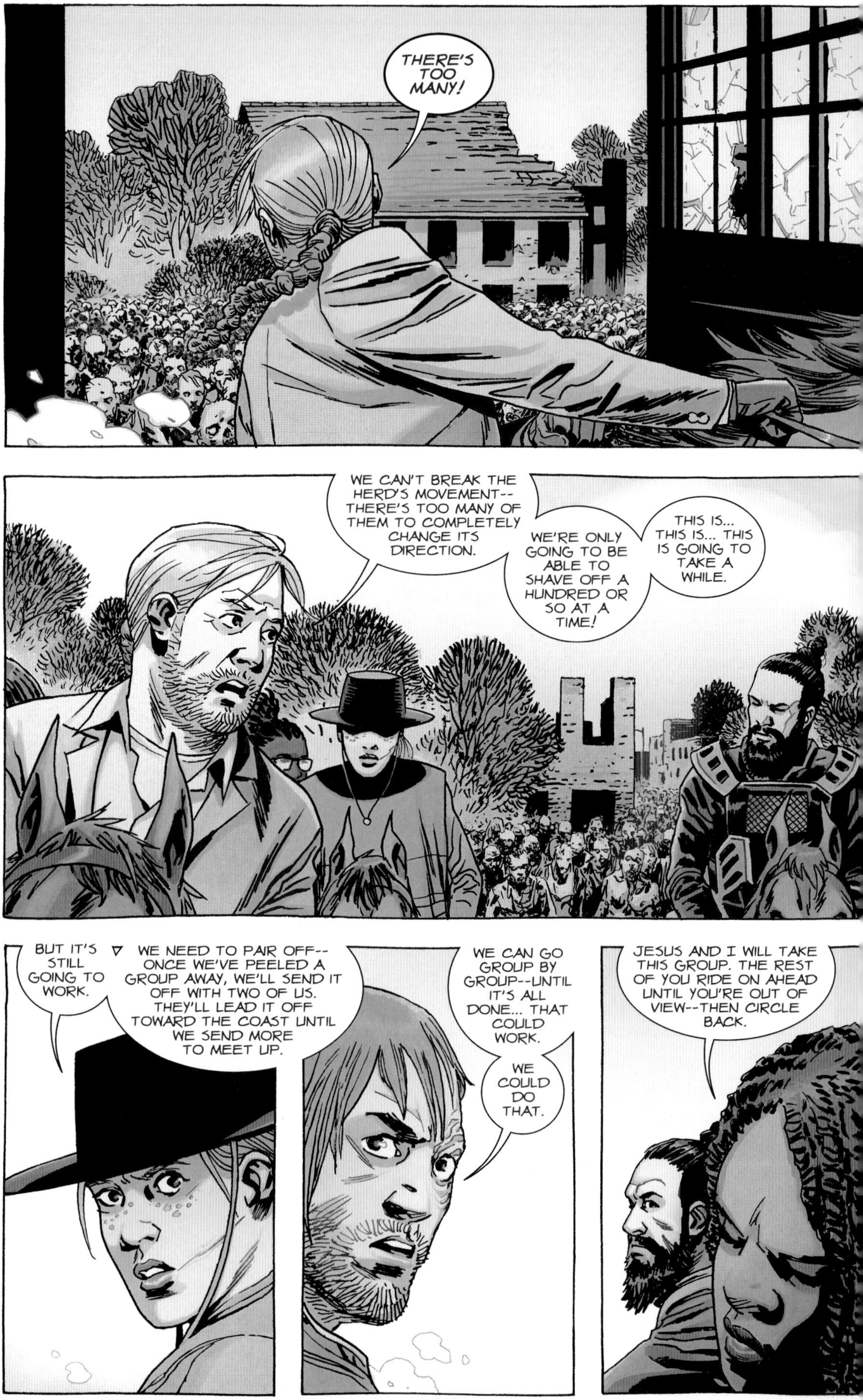
THERE'S TOO MANY!
WE CAN'T BREAK THE HERD'S MOVEMENT-- THERE'S TOO MANY OF THEM TO COMPLETELY CHANGE ITS DIRECTION.
WE'RE ONLY GOING TO BE ABLE TO SHAVE OFF A HUNDRED OR SO AT A TIME!
THIS IS... THIS IS... THIS IS GOING TO TAKE A WHILE.
BUT IT'S STILL GOING TO WORK.
WE NEED TO PAIR OFF-- ONCE WE'VE PEELED A GROUP AWAY, WE'LL SEND IT OFF WITH TWO OF US. THEY'LL LEAD IT OFF TOWARD THE COAST UNTIL WE SEND MORE TO MEET UP.
WE CAN GO GROUP BY GROUP--UNTIL IT'S ALL DONE... THAT COULD WORK.
WE COULD DO THAT.
JESUS AND I WILL TAKE THIS GROUP. THE REST OF YOU RIDE ON AHEAD UNTIL YOU'RE OUT OF VIEW--THEN CIRCLE BACK.

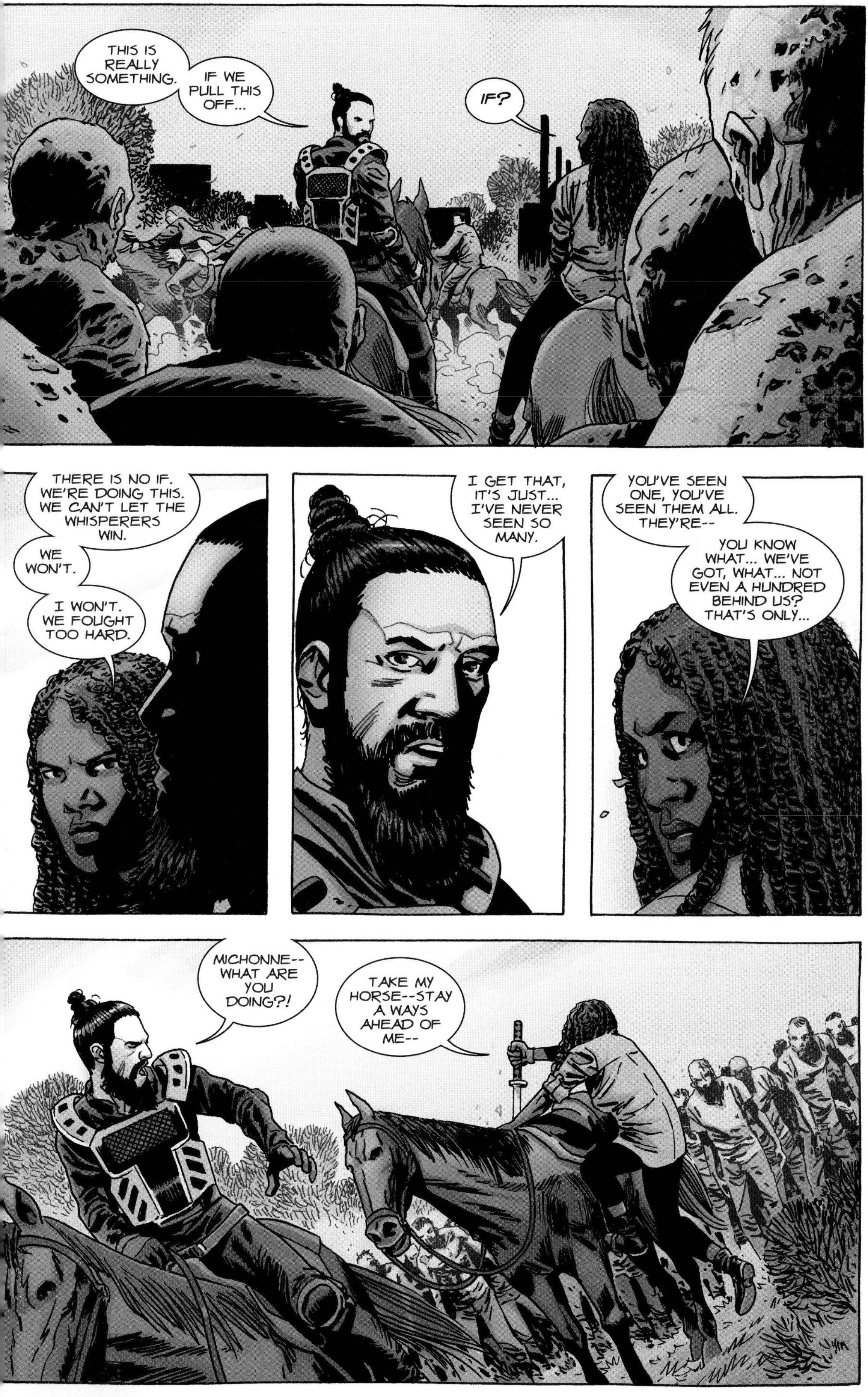

THIS IS REALLY SOMETHING.
IF WE PULL THIS OFF...
IF?
THERE IS NO IF. WE'RE DOING THIS. WE CAN'T LET THE WHISPERERS WIN.
WE WON'T.
I WON'T. WE FOUGHT TOO HARD.
I GET THAT, IT'S JUST... I'VE NEVER SEEN SO MANY.
YOU'VE SEEN ONE, YOU'VE SEEN THEM ALL. THEY'RE--
YOU KNOW WHAT... WE'VE GOT, WHAT... NOT EVEN A HUNDRED BEHIND US? THAT'S ONLY...
MICHONNE-- WHAT ARE YOU DOING?!
TAKE MY HORSE--STAY A WAYS AHEAD OF ME--

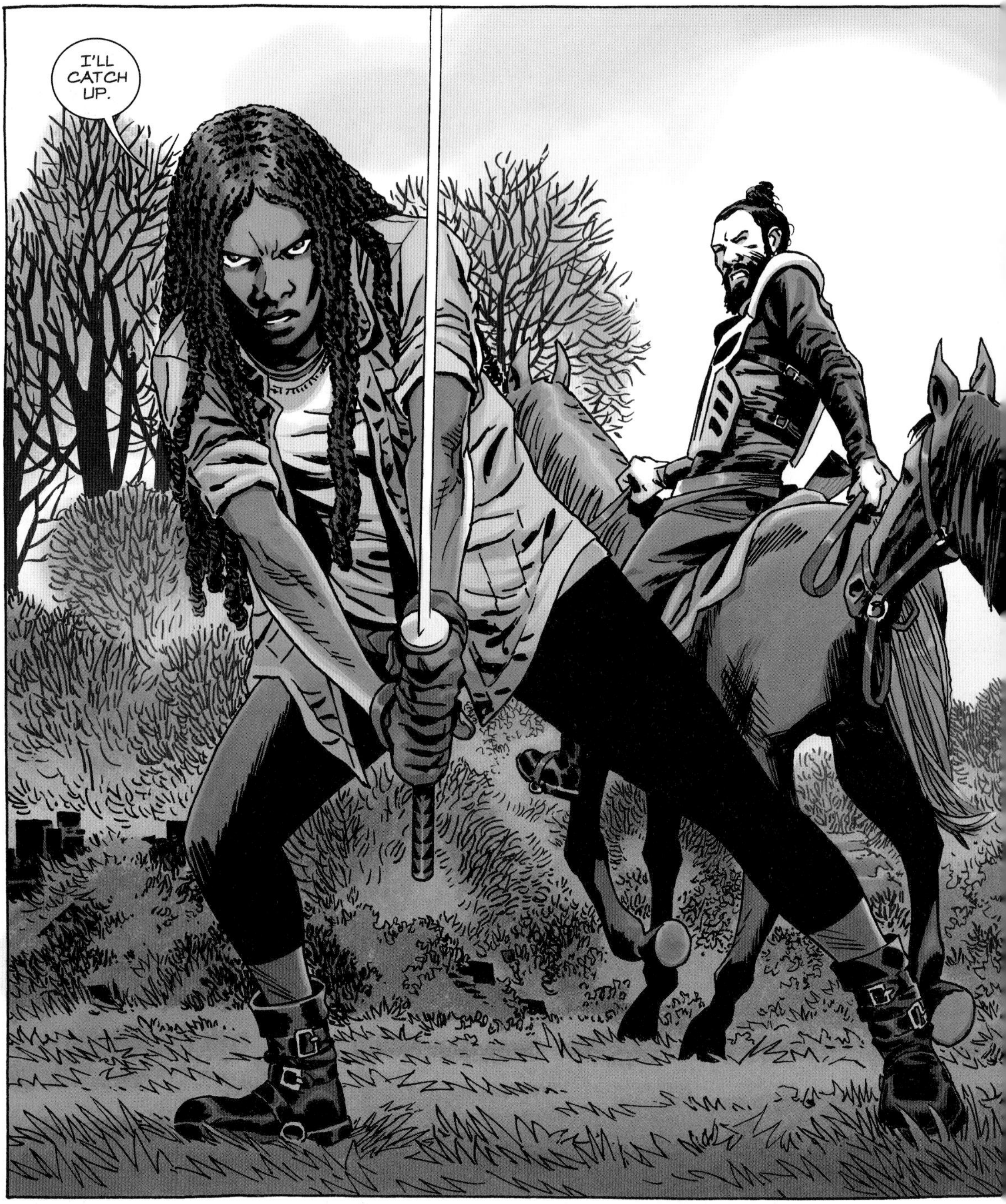
I'LL CATCH UP.

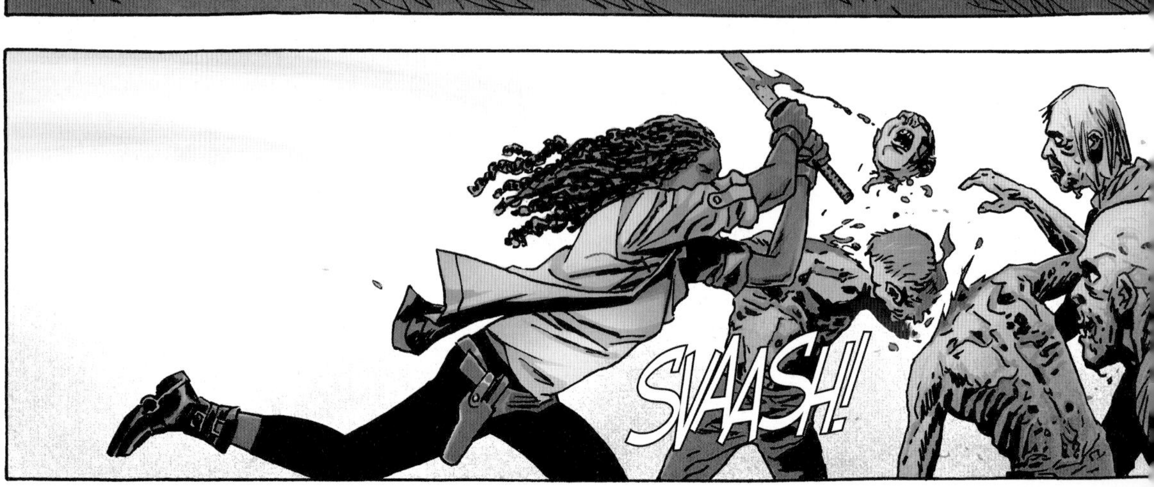
SVAASH!

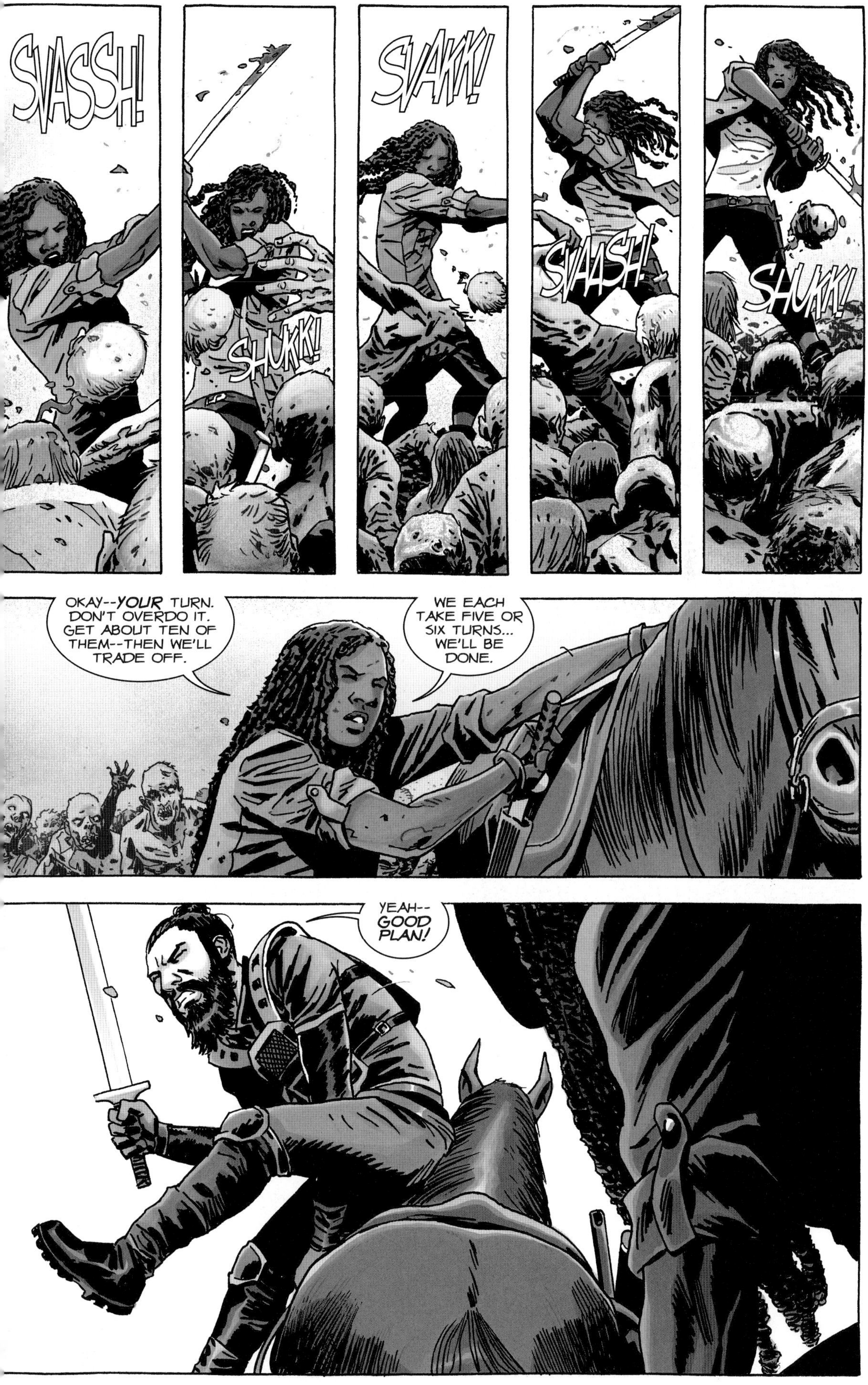
SVASSH!
SHUKK!
SVAKK!
SVAASH!
SHUKK!
OKAY--YOUR TURN. DON'T OVERDO IT. GET ABOUT TEN OF THEM--THEN WE'LL TRADE OFF.
WE EACH TAKE FIVE OR SIX TURNS... WE'LL BE DONE.
YEAH-- GOOD PLAN!

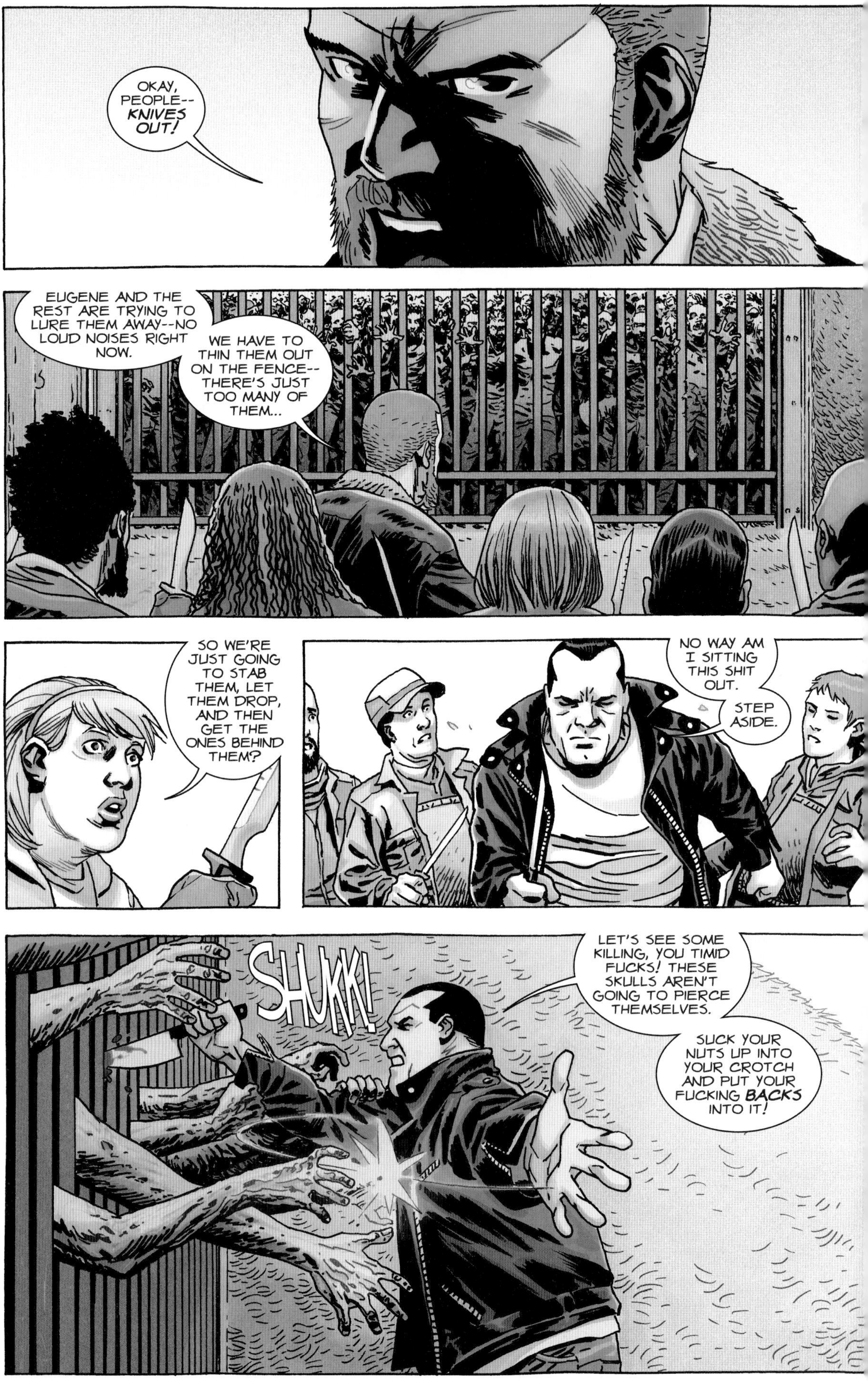
OKAY, PEOPLE-- KNIVES OUT!
EUGENE AND THE REST ARE TRYING TO LURE THEM AWAY--NO LOUD NOISES RIGHT NOW.
WE HAVE TO THIN THEM OUT ON THE FENCE-- THERE'S JUST TOO MANY OF THEM...
SO WE'RE JUST GOING TO STAB THEM, LET THEM DROP, AND THEN GET THE ONES BEHIND THEM?
NO WAY AM I SITTING THIS SHIT OUT.
STEP ASIDE.
SHUKK!
LET'S SEE SOME KILLING, YOU TIMID FUCKS! THESE SKULLS AREN'T GOING TO PIERCE THEMSELVES.
SUCK YOUR NUTS UP INTO YOUR CROTCH AND PUT YOUR FUCKING BACKS INTO IT!

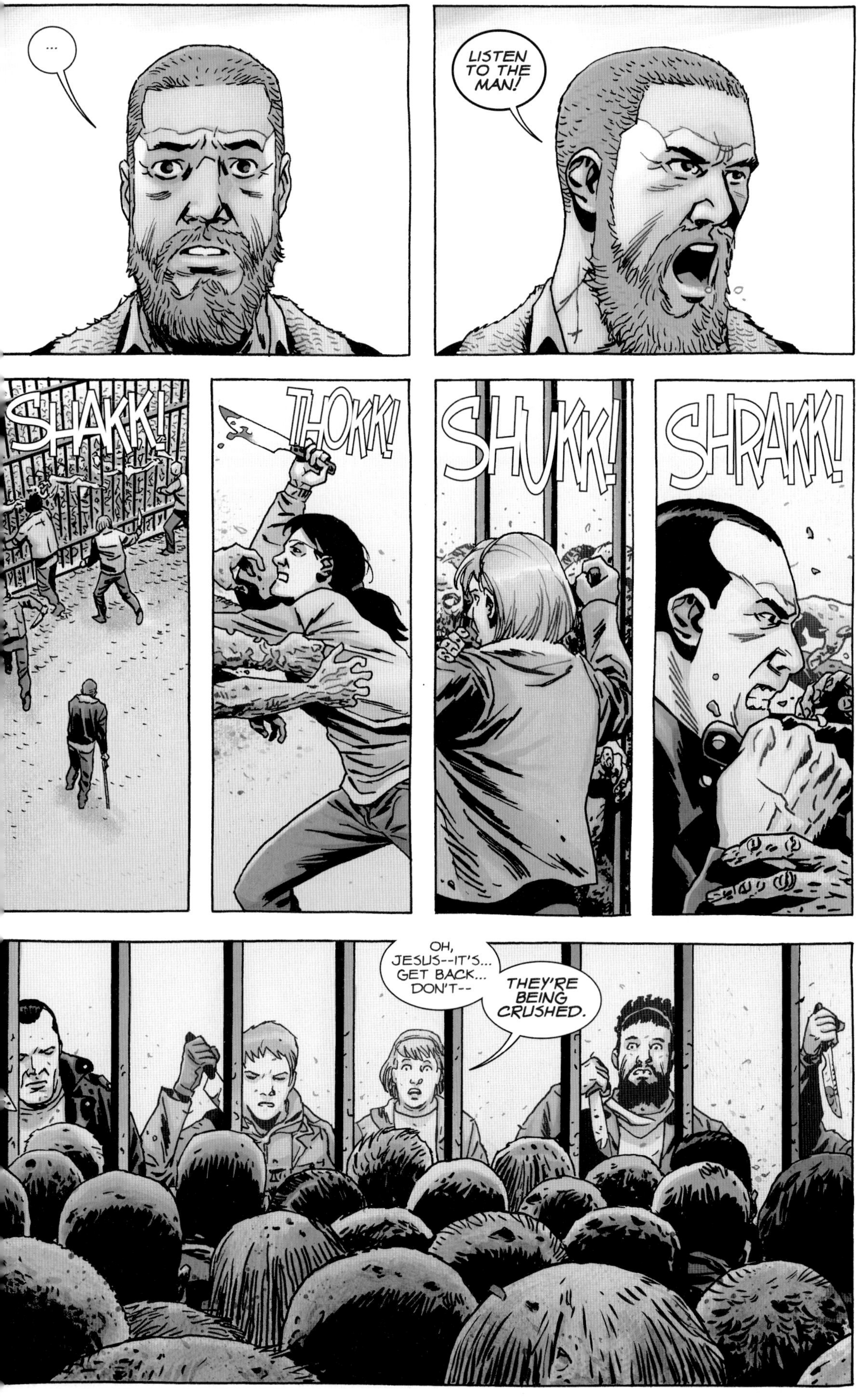
...
LISTEN TO THE MAN!
SHAKK!
THOKK!
SHUKK!
SHRAKK!
OH, JESUS--IT'S... GET BACK... DON'T--
THEY'RE BEING CRUSHED.

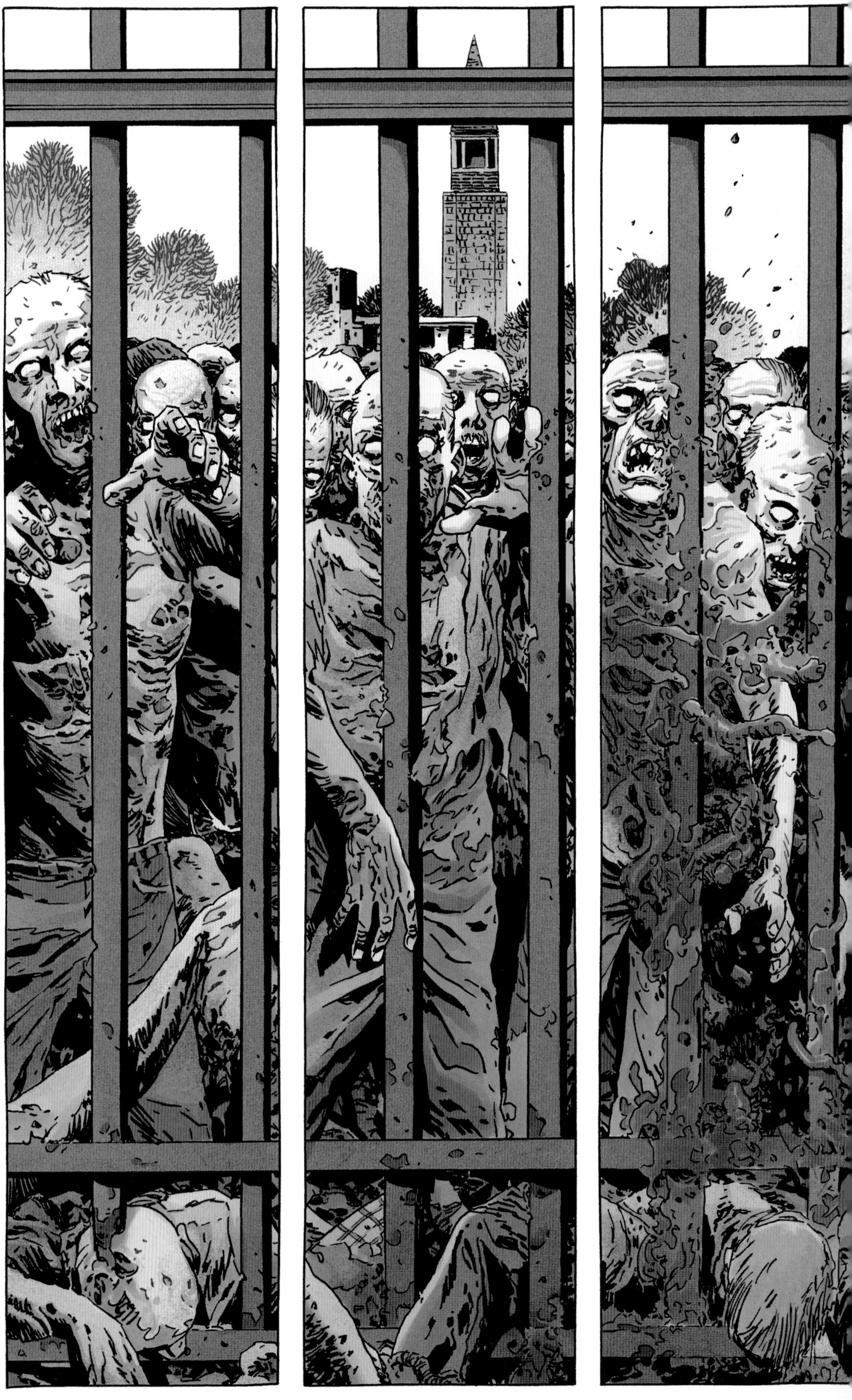

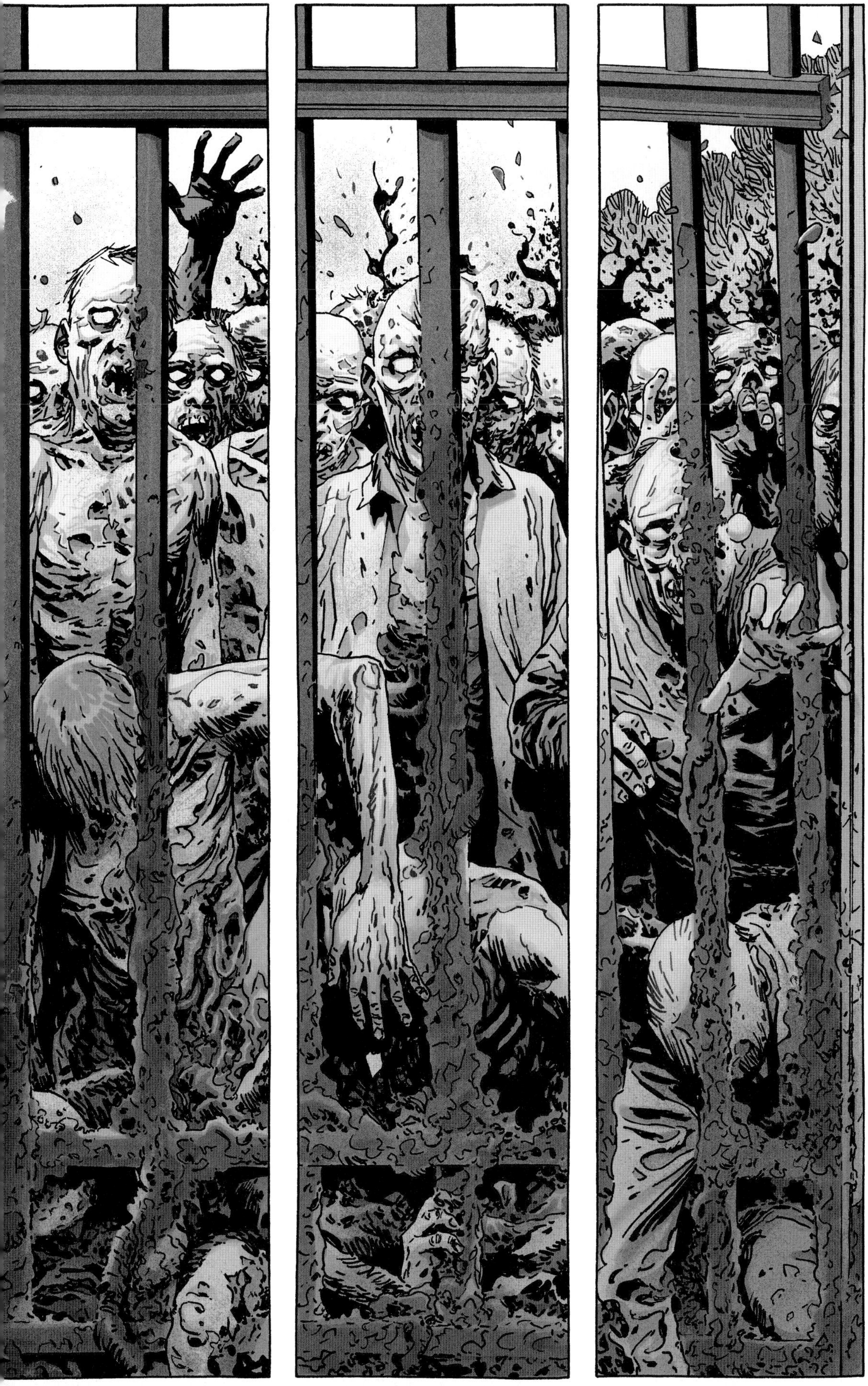

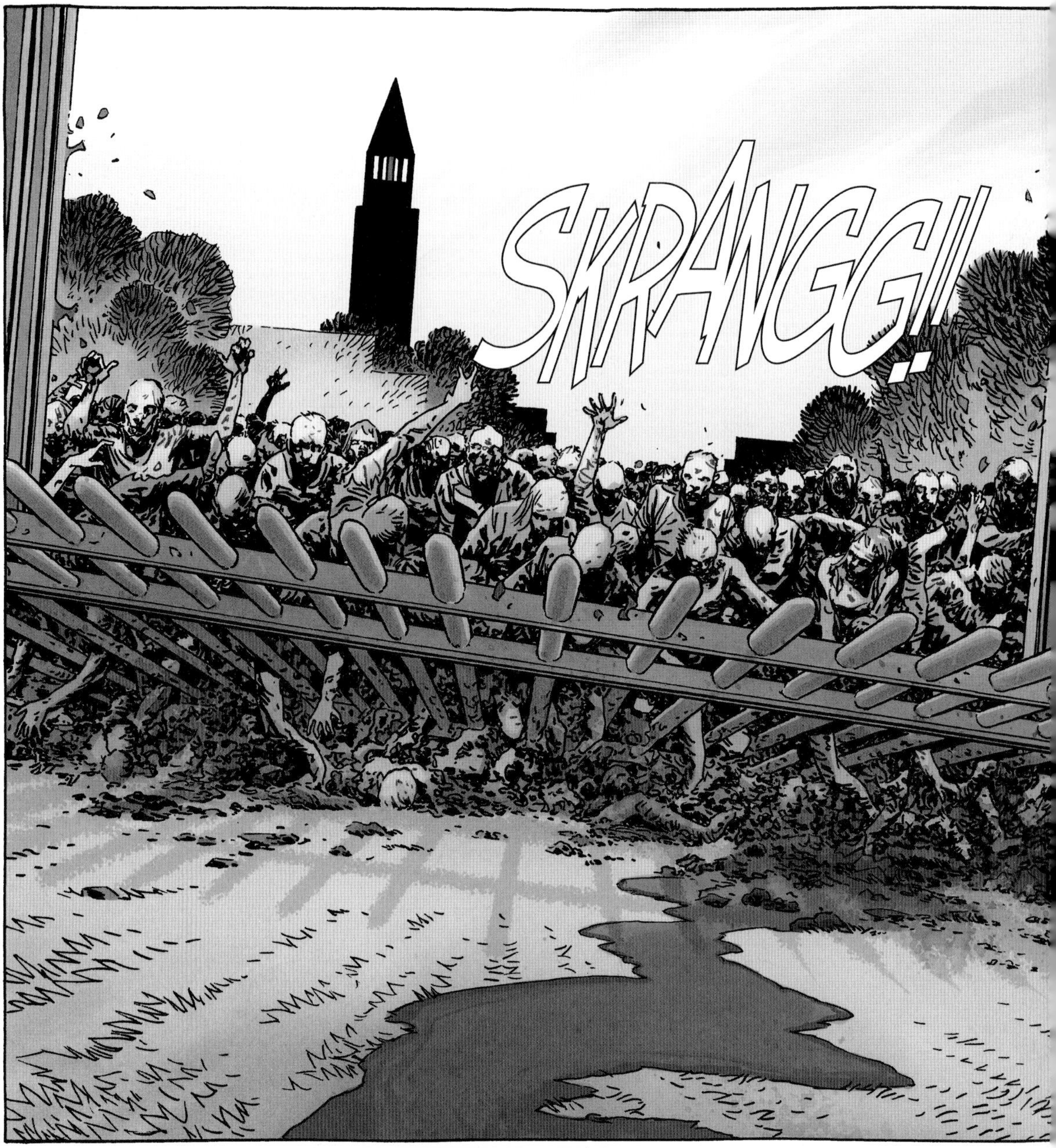
SKRANGG!!

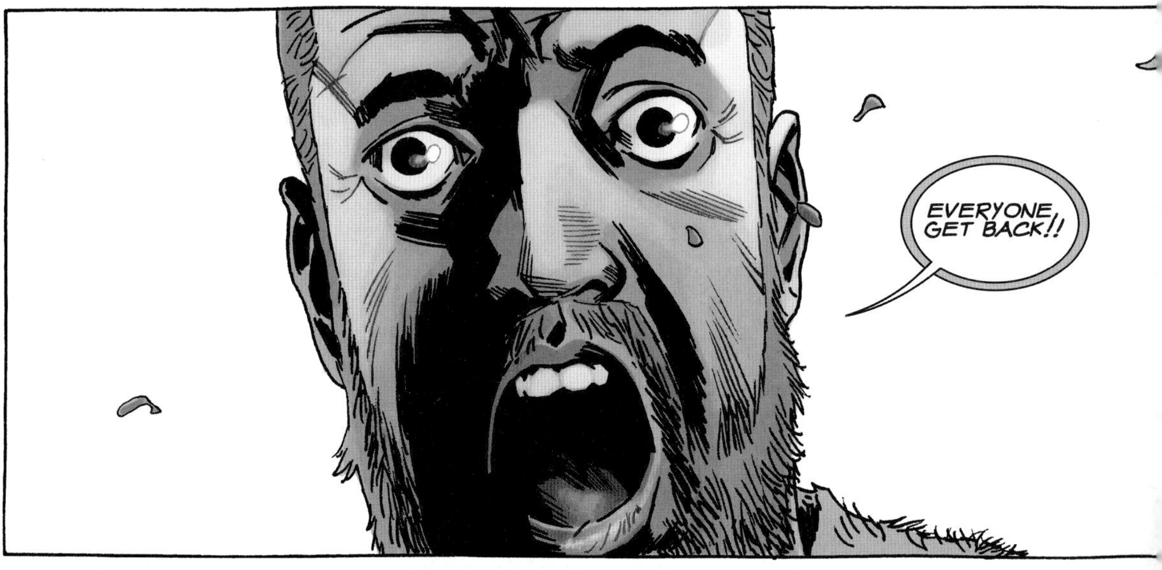
EVERYONE, GET BACK!!

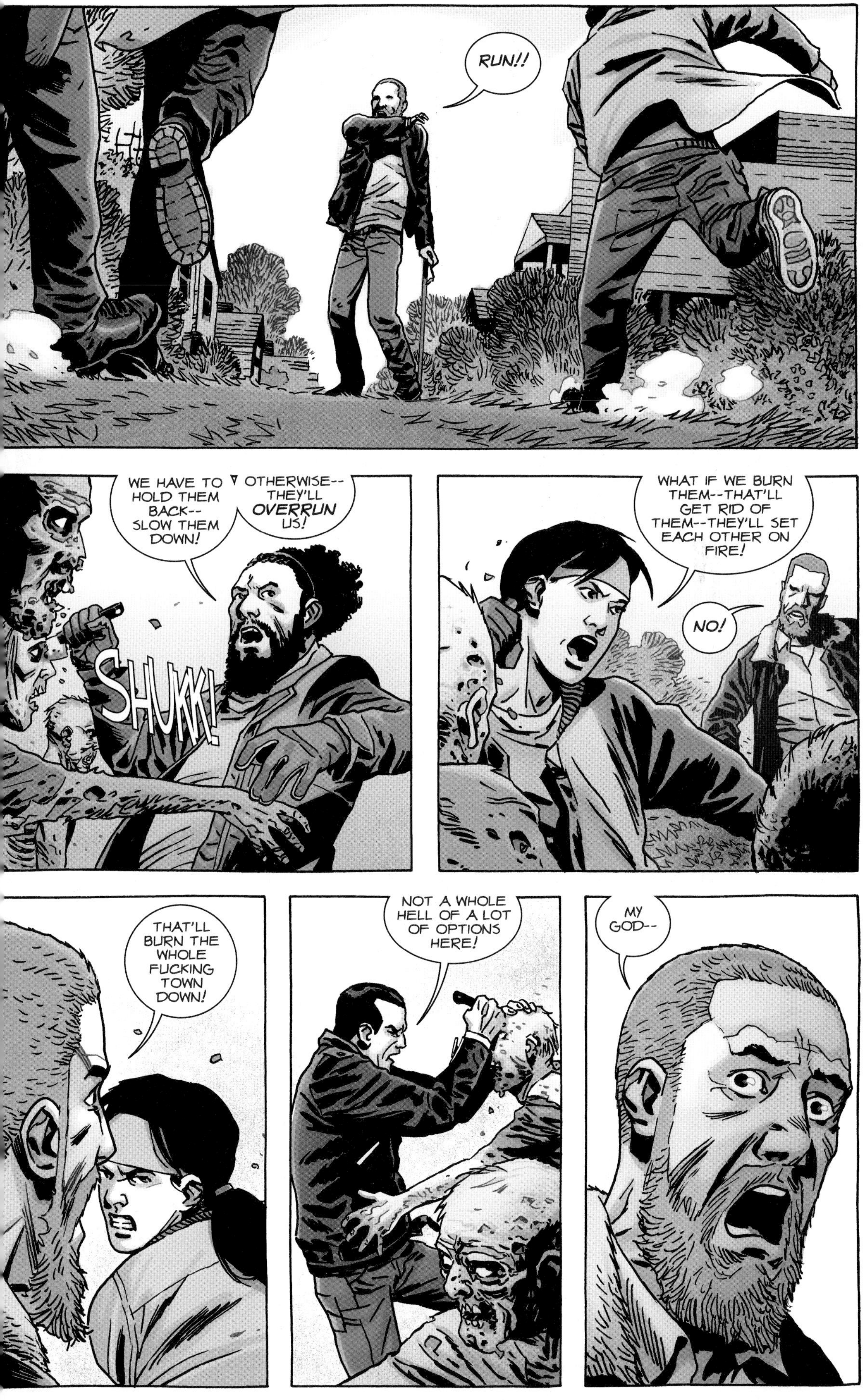
RUN!!
WE HAVE TO HOLD THEM BACK-- SLOW THEM DOWN!
OTHERWISE-- THEY'LL OVERRUN US!
SHUKK!
WHAT IF WE BURN THEM--THAT'LL GET RID OF THEM--THEY'LL SET EACH OTHER ON FIRE!
NO!
THAT'LL BURN THE WHOLE FUCKING TOWN DOWN!
NOT A WHOLE HELL OF A LOT OF OPTIONS HERE!
MY GOD--

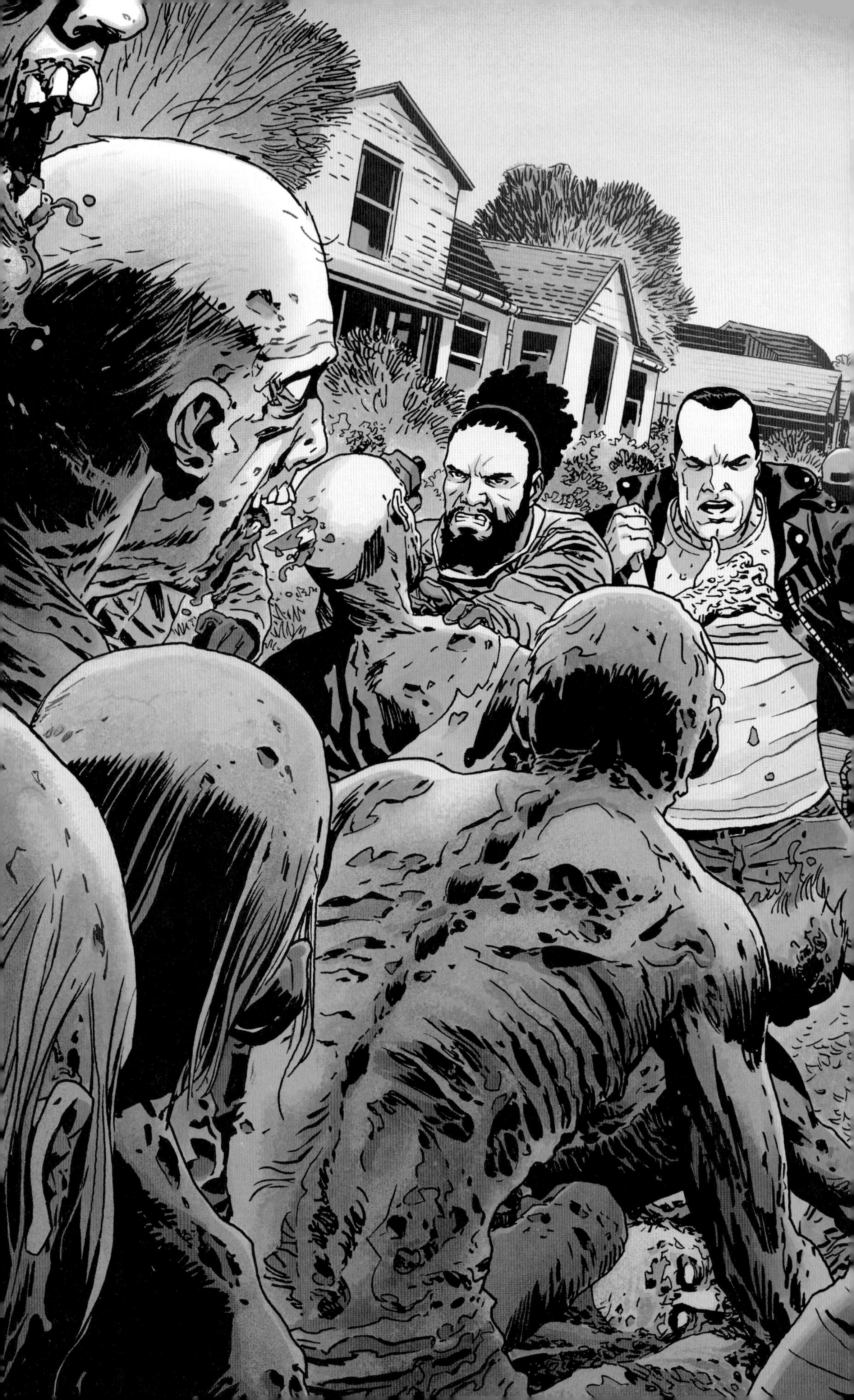

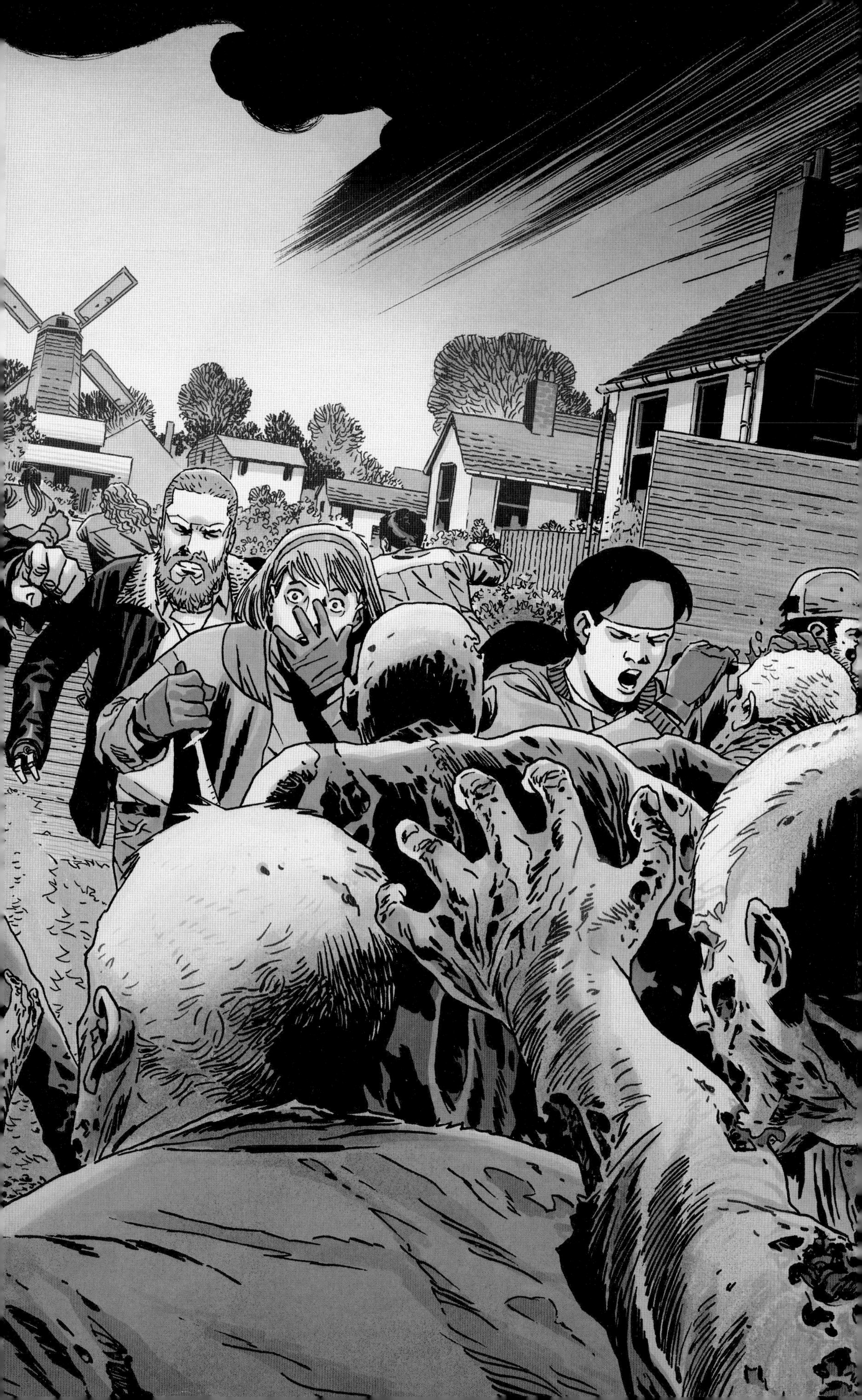

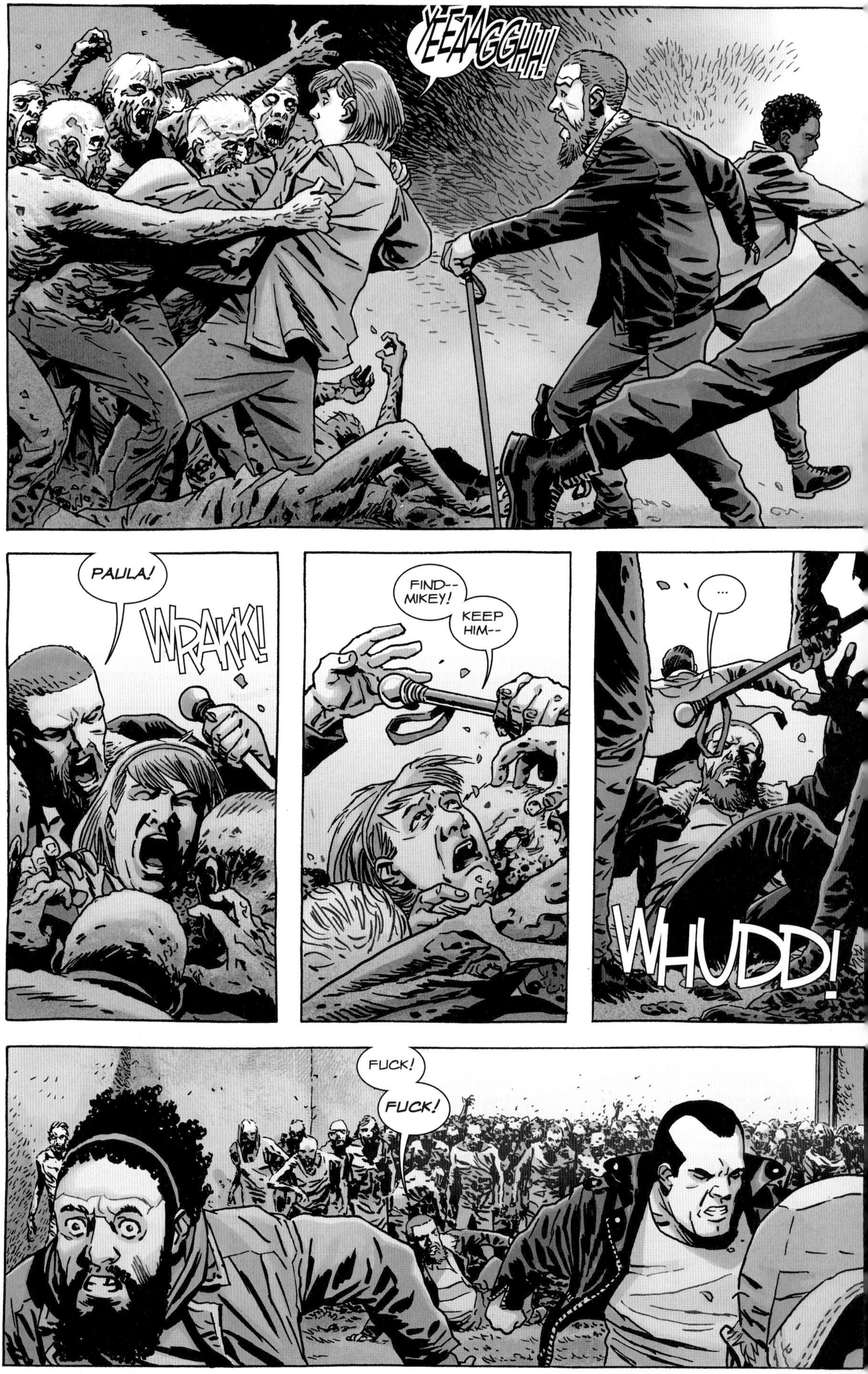
YEEAAGGHH!
PAULA!
WRAKK!
FIND-- MIKEY!
KEEP HIM--
...
WHUDD!
FUCK!
FUCK!

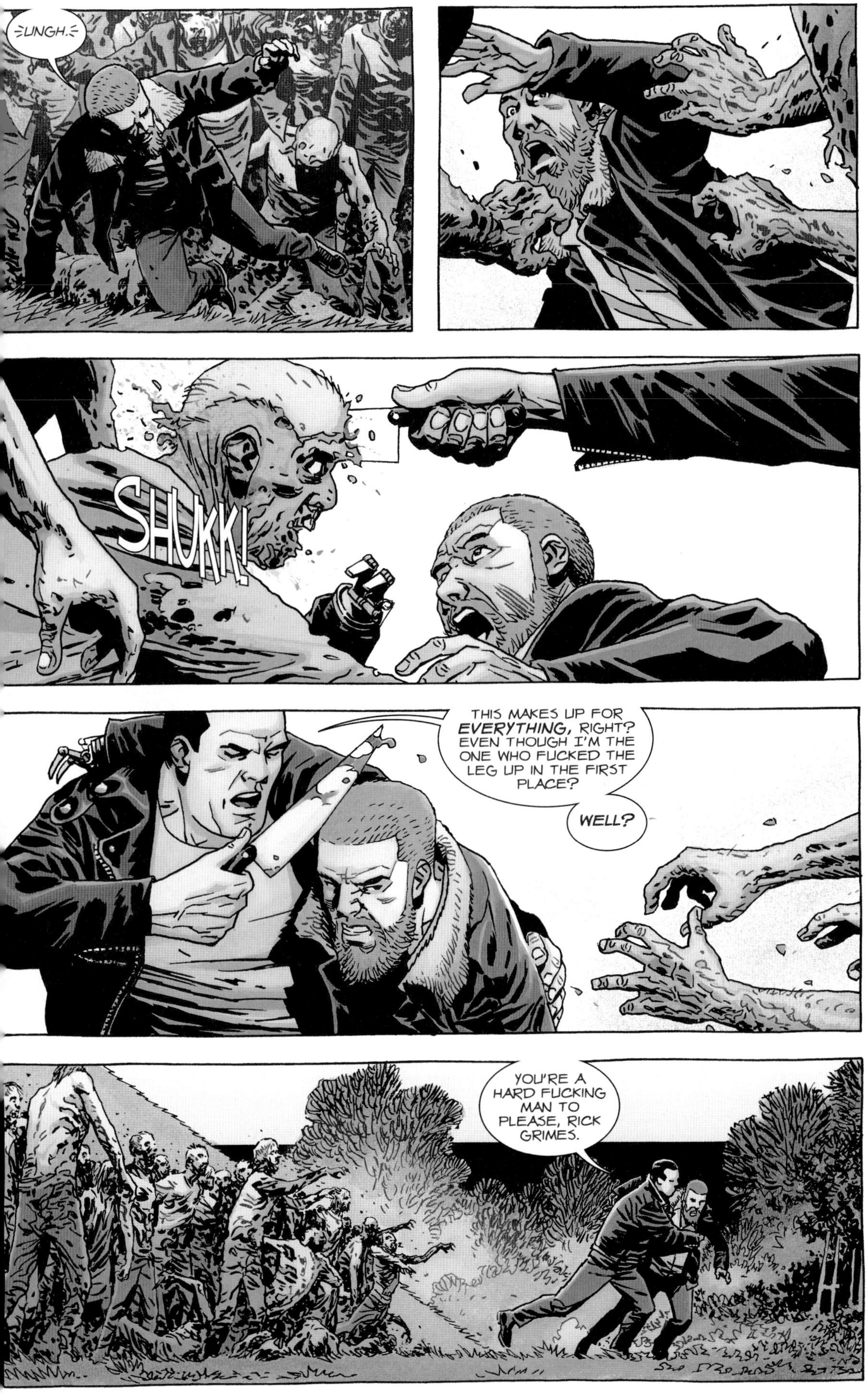
UNGH.
SHUKK!
THIS MAKES UP FOR EVERYTHING, RIGHT? EVEN THOUGH I'M THE ONE WHO FUCKED THE LEG UP IN THE FIRST PLACE?
WELL?
YOU'RE A HARD FUCKING MAN TO PLEASE, RICK GRIMES.

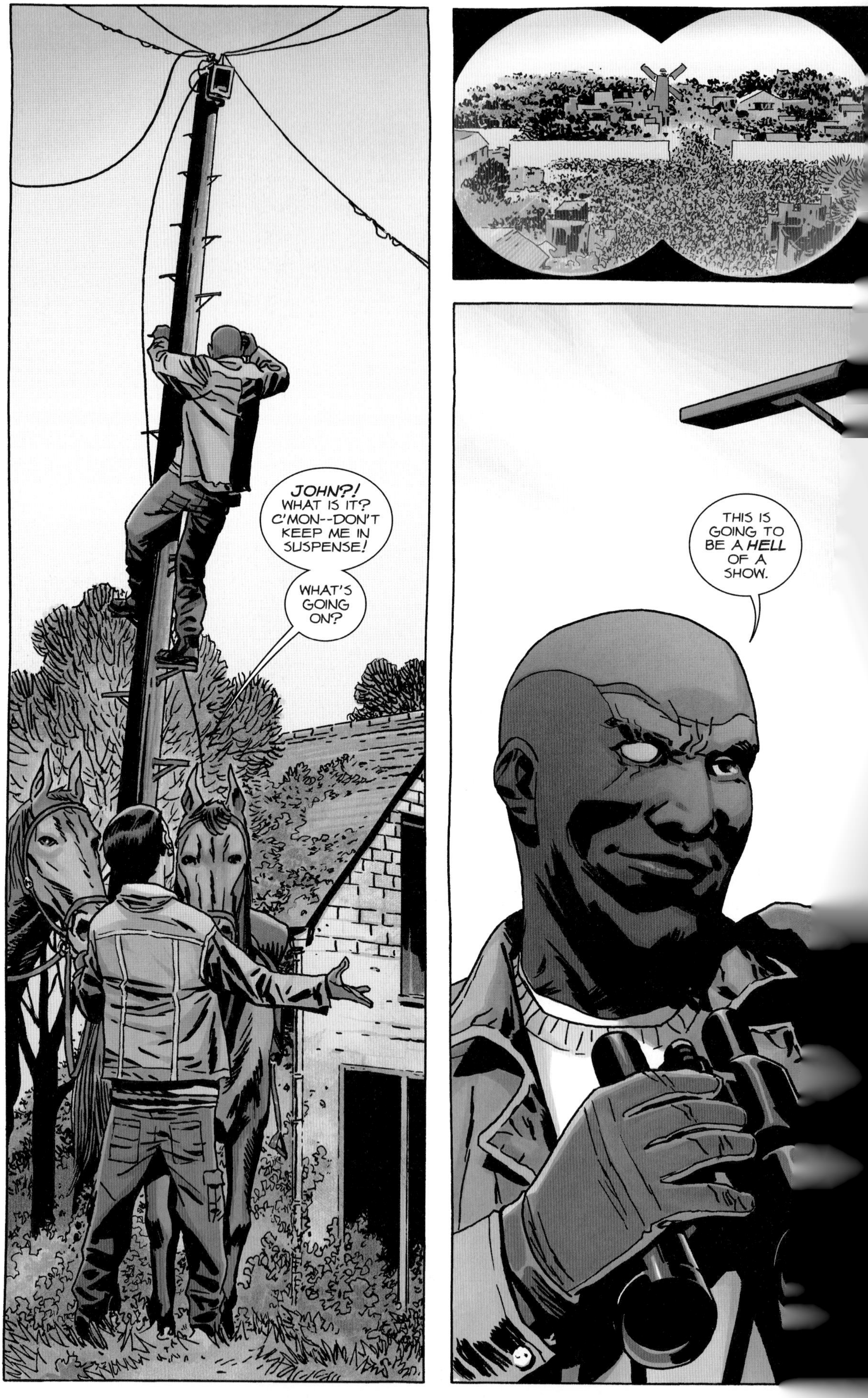

JOHN?! WHAT IS IT? C'MON--DON'T KEEP ME IN SUSPENSE!
WHAT'S GOING ON?
THIS IS GOING TO BE A HELL OF A SHOW.

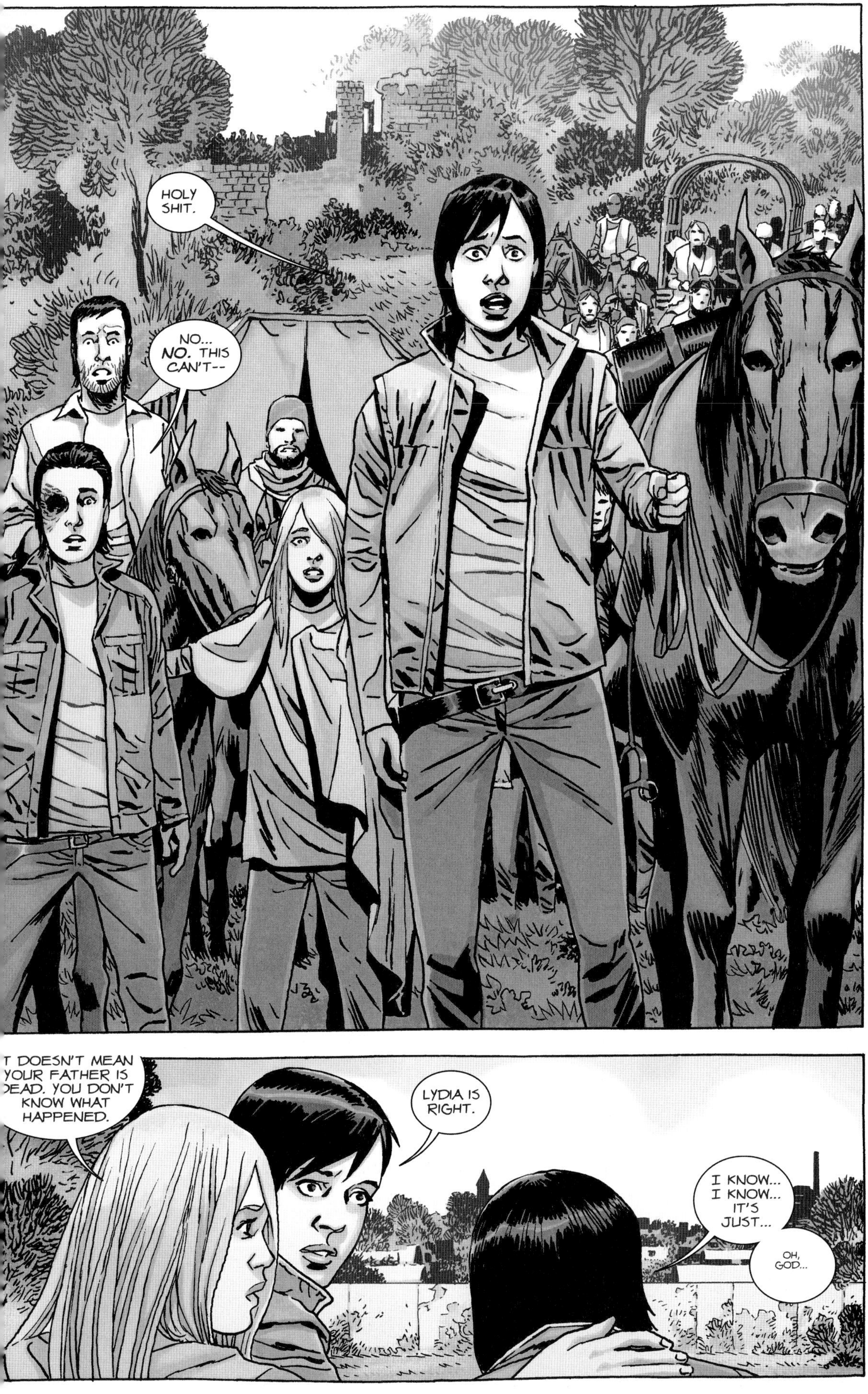
HOLY SHIT.
NO... NO. THIS CAN'T--
T DOESN'T MEAN YOUR FATHER IS EAD. YOU DON'T KNOW WHAT HAPPENED.
LYDIA IS RIGHT.
I KNOW... I KNOW... IT'S JUST...
OH, GOD...

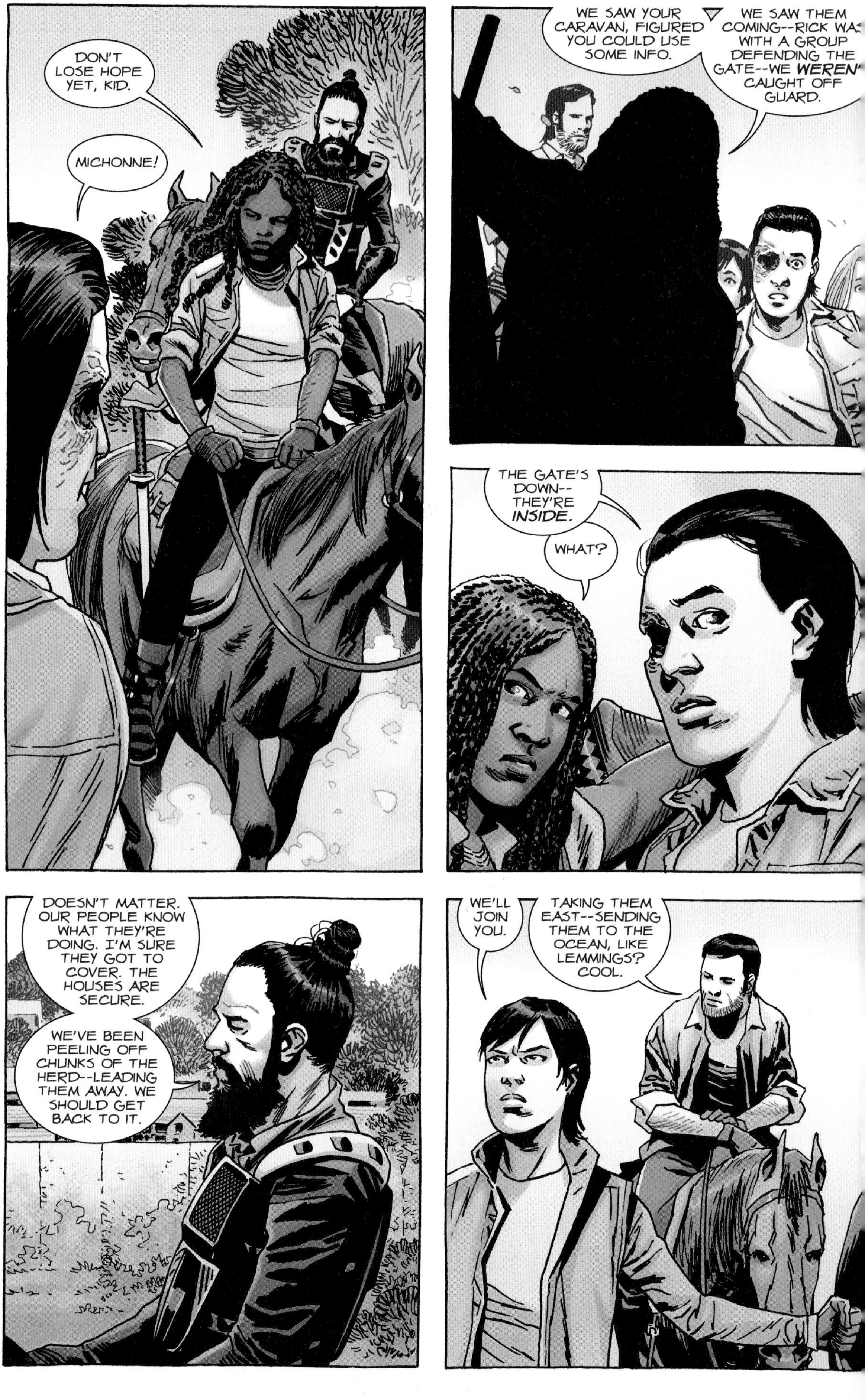
DON'T LOSE HOPE YET, KID.
MICHONNE!
WE SAW YOUR CARAVAN, FIGURED YOU COULD USE SOME INFO.
WE SAW THEM COMING--RICK WA WITH A GROUP DEFENDING THE GATE--WE *WEREN* CAUGHT OFF GUARD.
THE GATE'S DOWN--THEY'RE *INSIDE.*
WHAT?
DOESN'T MATTER. OUR PEOPLE KNOW WHAT THEY'RE DOING. I'M SURE THEY GOT TO COVER. THE HOUSES ARE SECURE.
WE'VE BEEN PEELING OFF CHUNKS OF THE HERD--LEADING THEM AWAY. WE SHOULD GET BACK TO IT.
WE'LL JOIN YOU.
TAKING THEM EAST--SENDING THEM TO THE OCEAN, LIKE LEMMINGS? COOL.

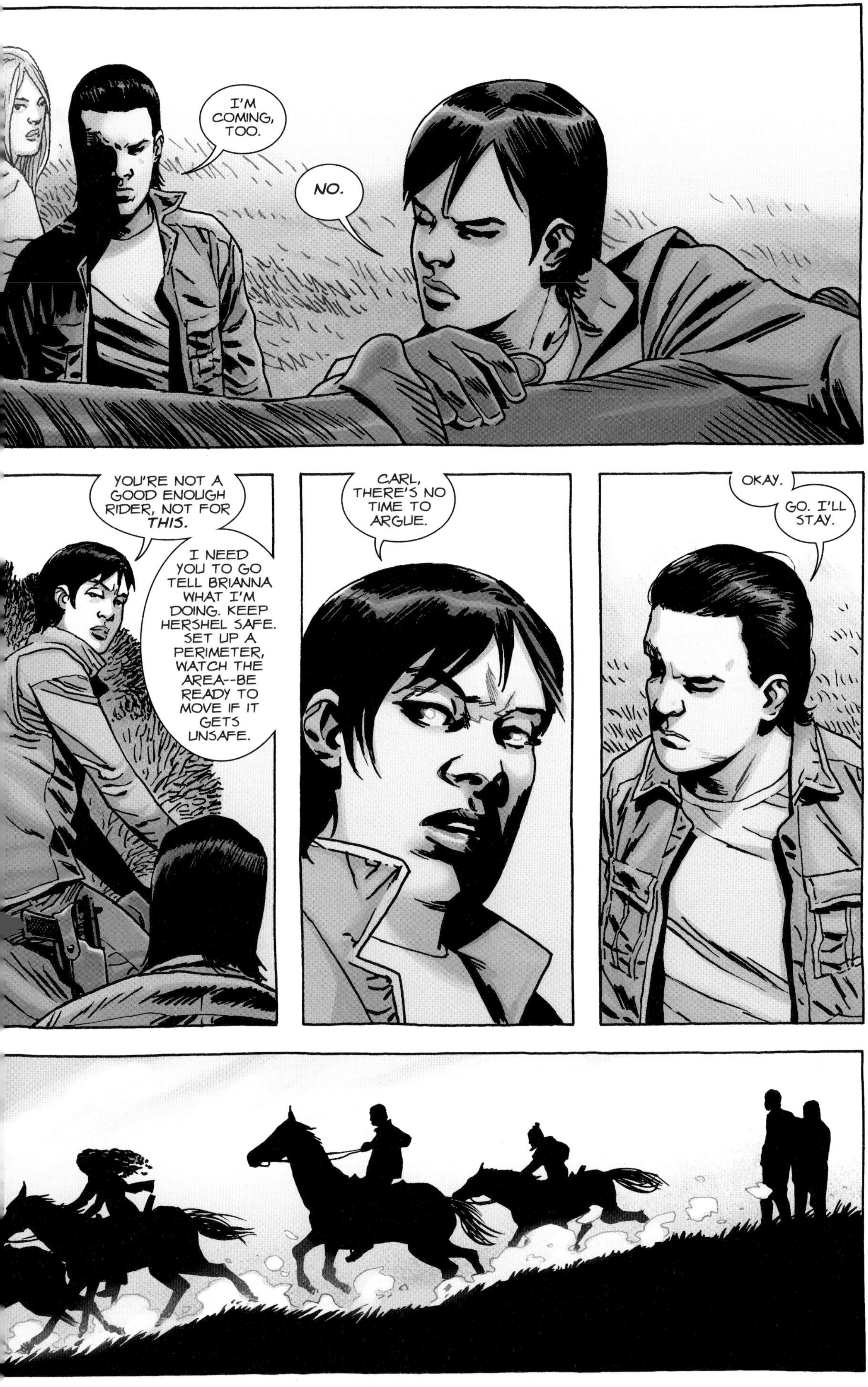
I'M COMING, TOO.
NO.
YOU'RE NOT A GOOD ENOUGH RIDER, NOT FOR *THIS.*
I NEED YOU TO GO TELL BRIANNA WHAT I'M DOING. KEEP HERSHEL SAFE. SET UP A PERIMETER, WATCH THE AREA--BE READY TO MOVE IF IT GETS UNSAFE.
CARL, THERE'S NO TIME TO ARGUE.
OKAY.
GO. I'LL STAY.

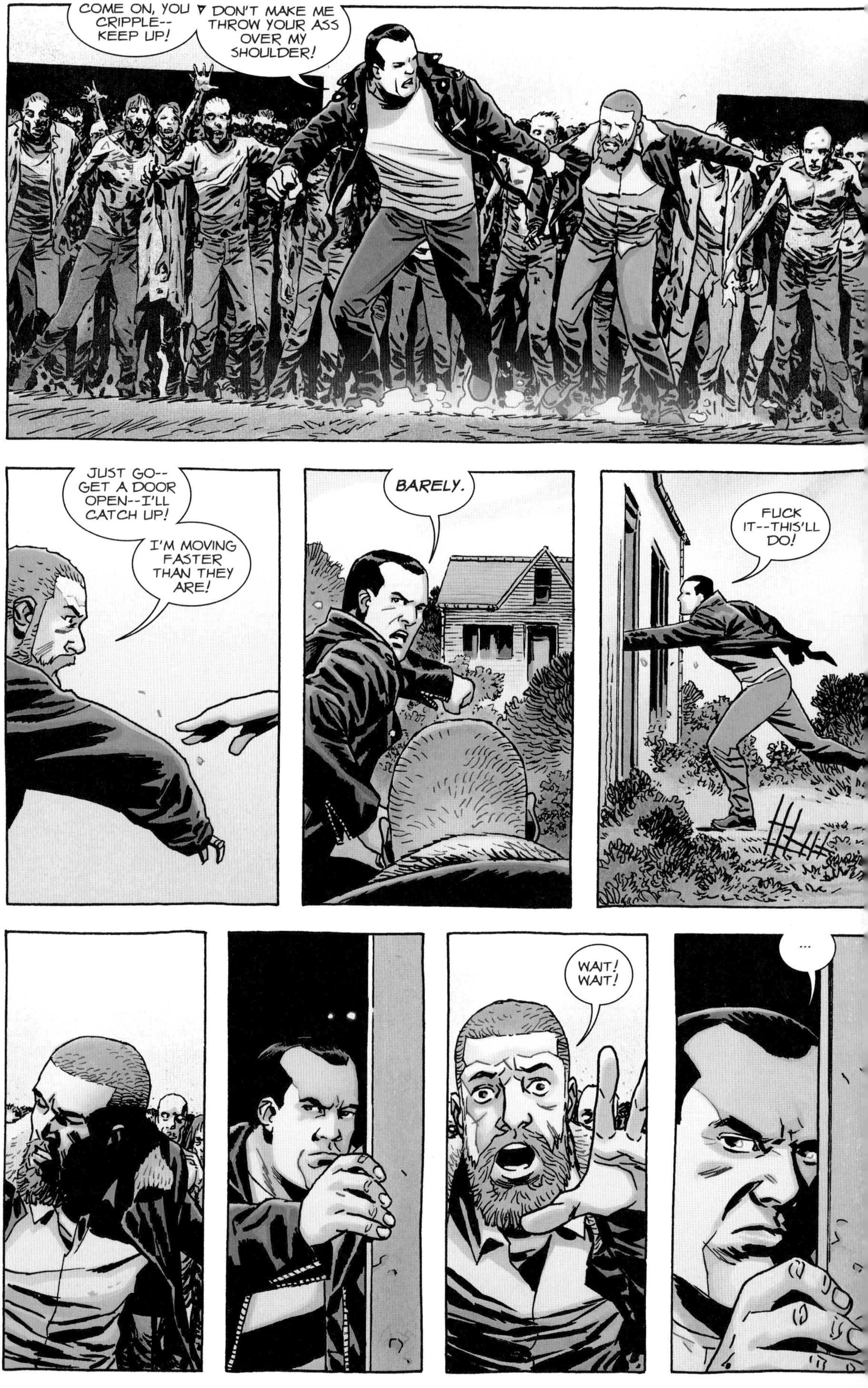

COME ON, YOU CRIPPLE-- KEEP UP!
DON'T MAKE ME THROW YOUR ASS OVER MY SHOULDER!
JUST GO-- GET A DOOR OPEN--I'LL CATCH UP!
I'M MOVING FASTER THAN THEY ARE!
BARELY.
FUCK IT--THIS'LL DO!
WAIT! WAIT!
...

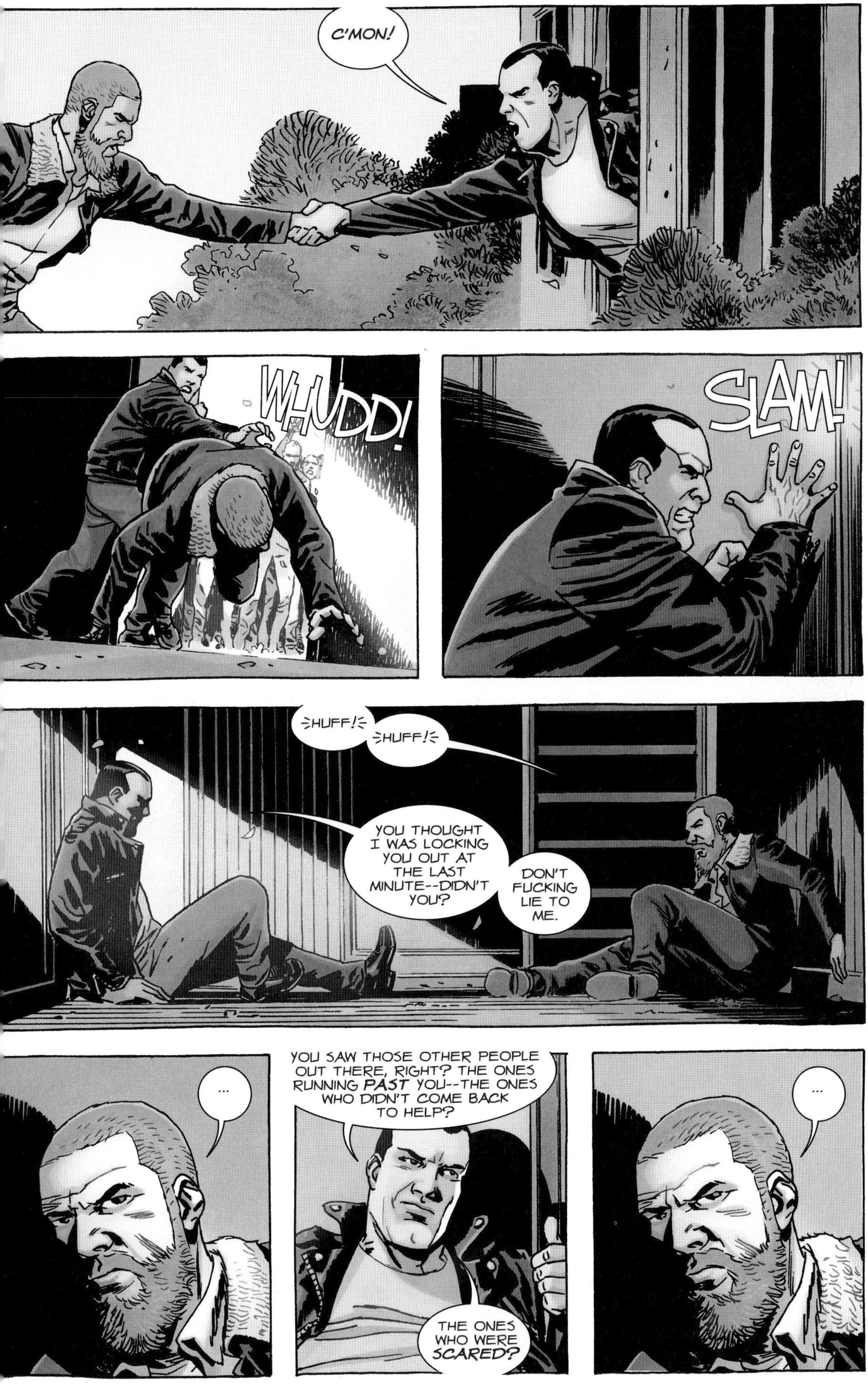
C'MON!
WHUDD!
SLAM!
HUFF!
HUFF!
YOU THOUGHT I WAS LOCKING YOU OUT AT THE LAST MINUTE--DIDN'T YOU?
DON'T FUCKING LIE TO ME.
...
YOU SAW THOSE OTHER PEOPLE OUT THERE, RIGHT? THE ONES RUNNING PAST YOU--THE ONES WHO DIDN'T COME BACK TO HELP?
THE ONES WHO WERE SCARED?
...

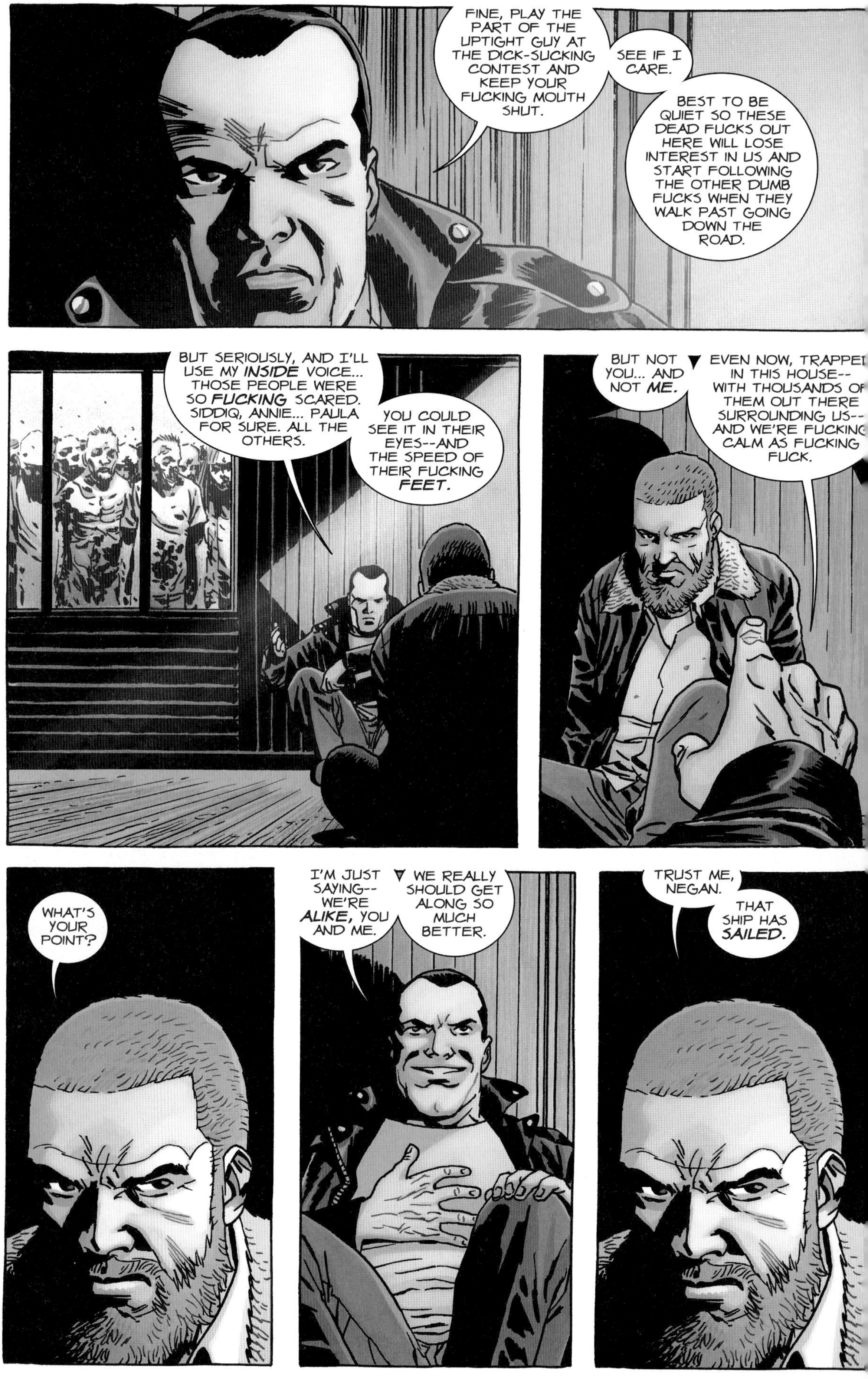
FINE, PLAY THE PART OF THE UPTIGHT GUY AT THE DICK-SUCKING CONTEST AND KEEP YOUR FUCKING MOUTH SHUT.
SEE IF I CARE.
BEST TO BE QUIET SO THESE DEAD FUCKS OUT HERE WILL LOSE INTEREST IN US AND START FOLLOWING THE OTHER DUMB FUCKS WHEN THEY WALK PAST GOING DOWN THE ROAD.
BUT SERIOUSLY, AND I'LL USE MY INSIDE VOICE... THOSE PEOPLE WERE SO FUCKING SCARED. SIDDIQ, ANNIE... PAULA FOR SURE. ALL THE OTHERS.
YOU COULD SEE IT IN THEIR EYES--AND THE SPEED OF THEIR FUCKING FEET.
BUT NOT YOU... AND NOT ME.
EVEN NOW, TRAPPE IN THIS HOUSE-- WITH THOUSANDS O THEM OUT THERE SURROUNDING US-- AND WE'RE FUCKIN CALM AS FUCKING FUCK.
WHAT'S YOUR POINT?
I'M JUST SAYING-- WE'RE ALIKE, YOU AND ME.
WE REALLY SHOULD GET ALONG SO MUCH BETTER.
TRUST ME, NEGAN.
THAT SHIP HAS SAILED.

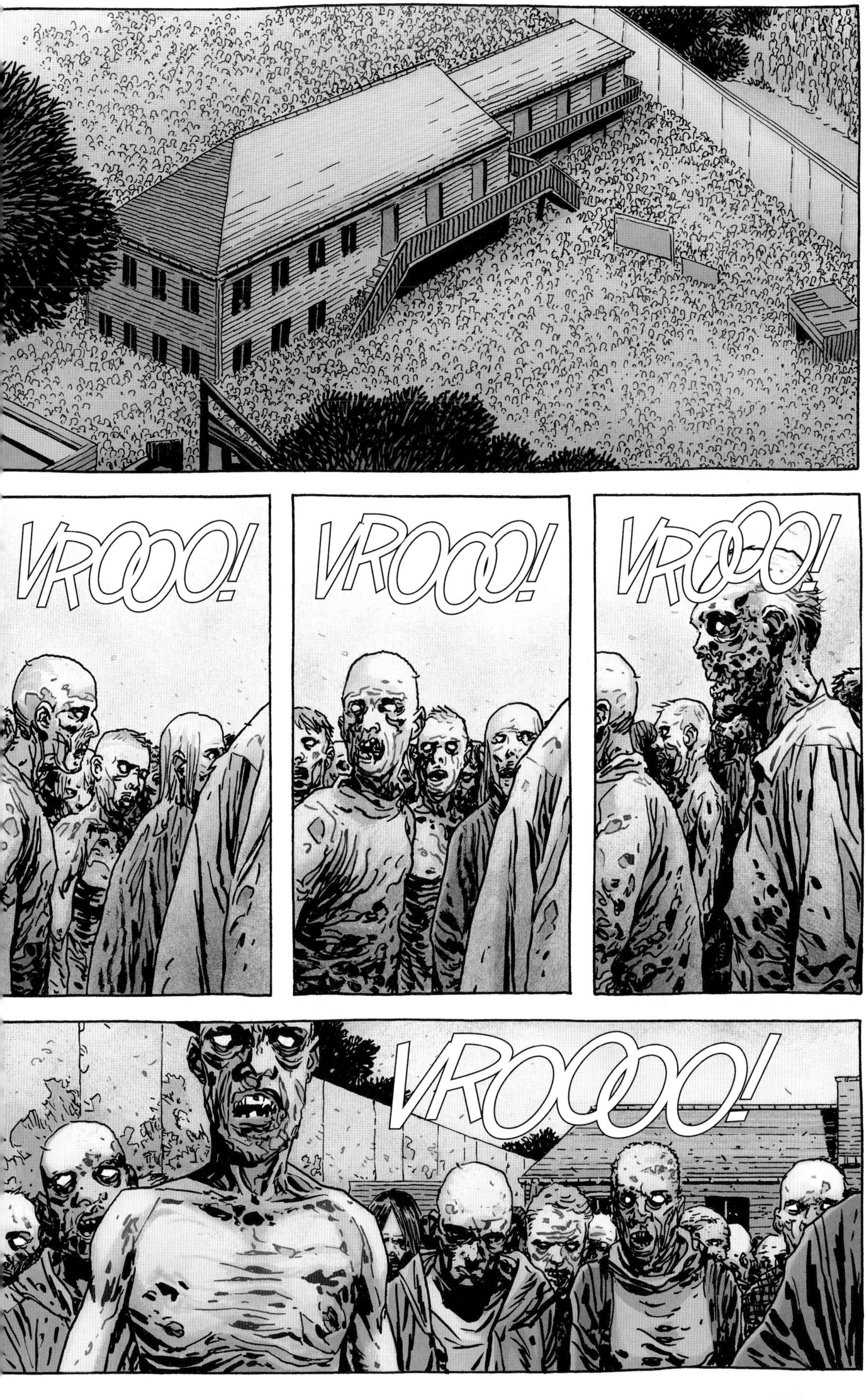
VROOO!
VROOOO!
VROOO!
VROOOO!

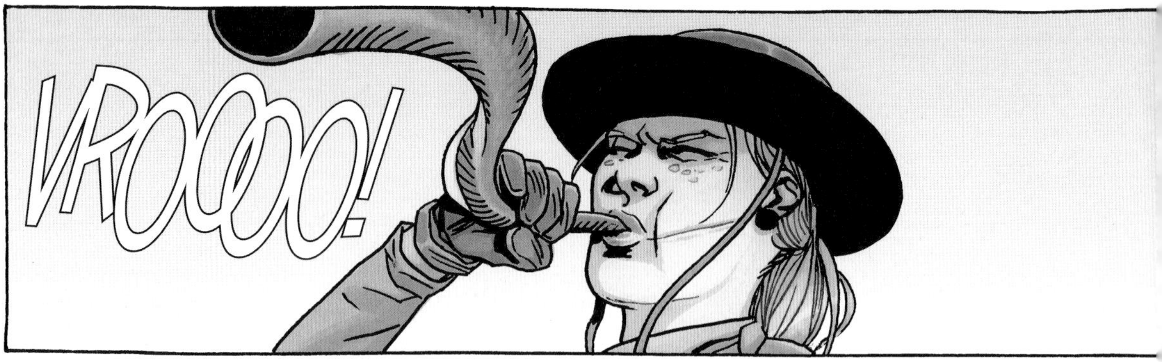
VROOOO!

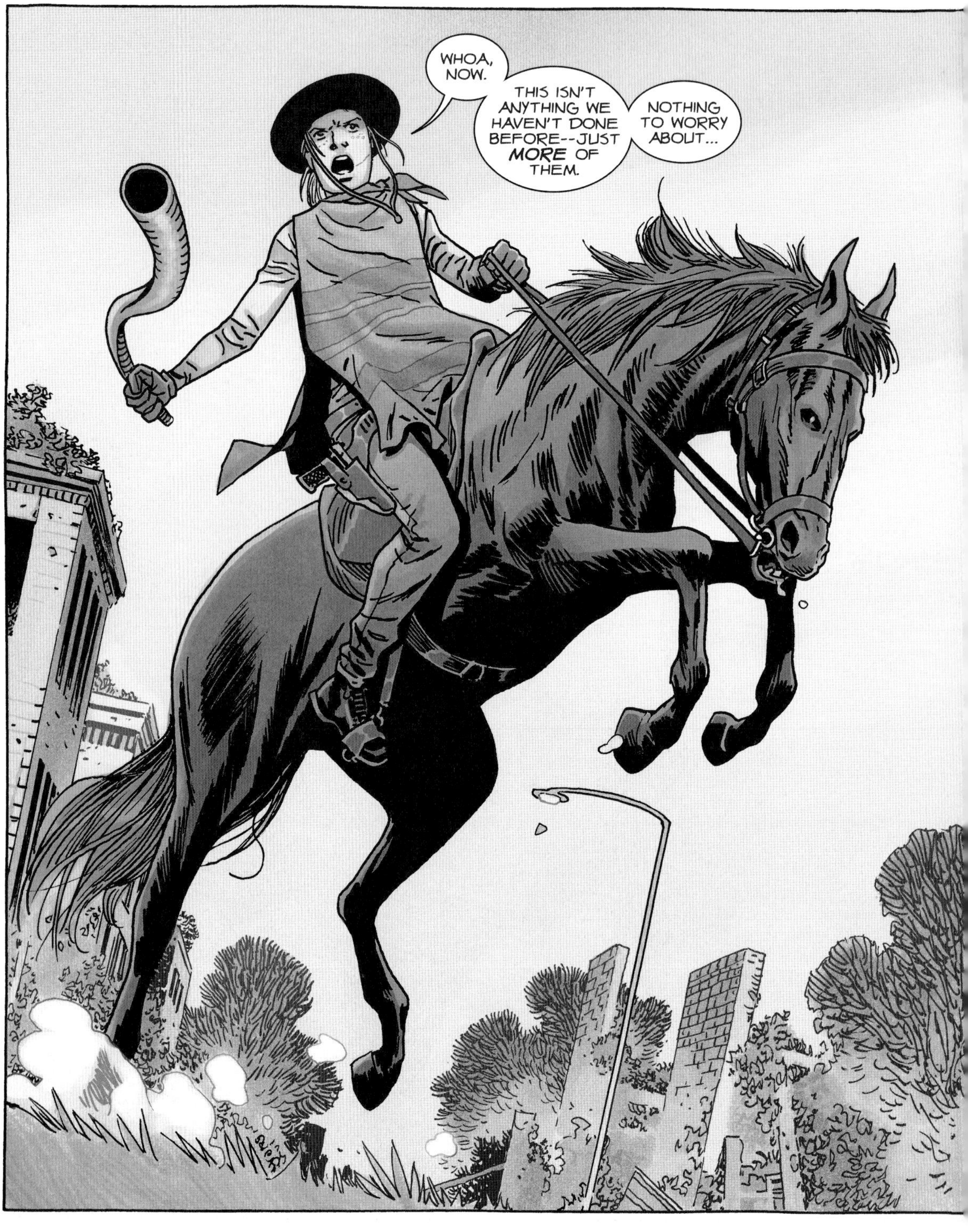
WHOA, NOW.
THIS ISN'T ANYTHING WE HAVEN'T DONE BEFORE--JUST MORE OF THEM.
NOTHING TO WORRY ABOUT...

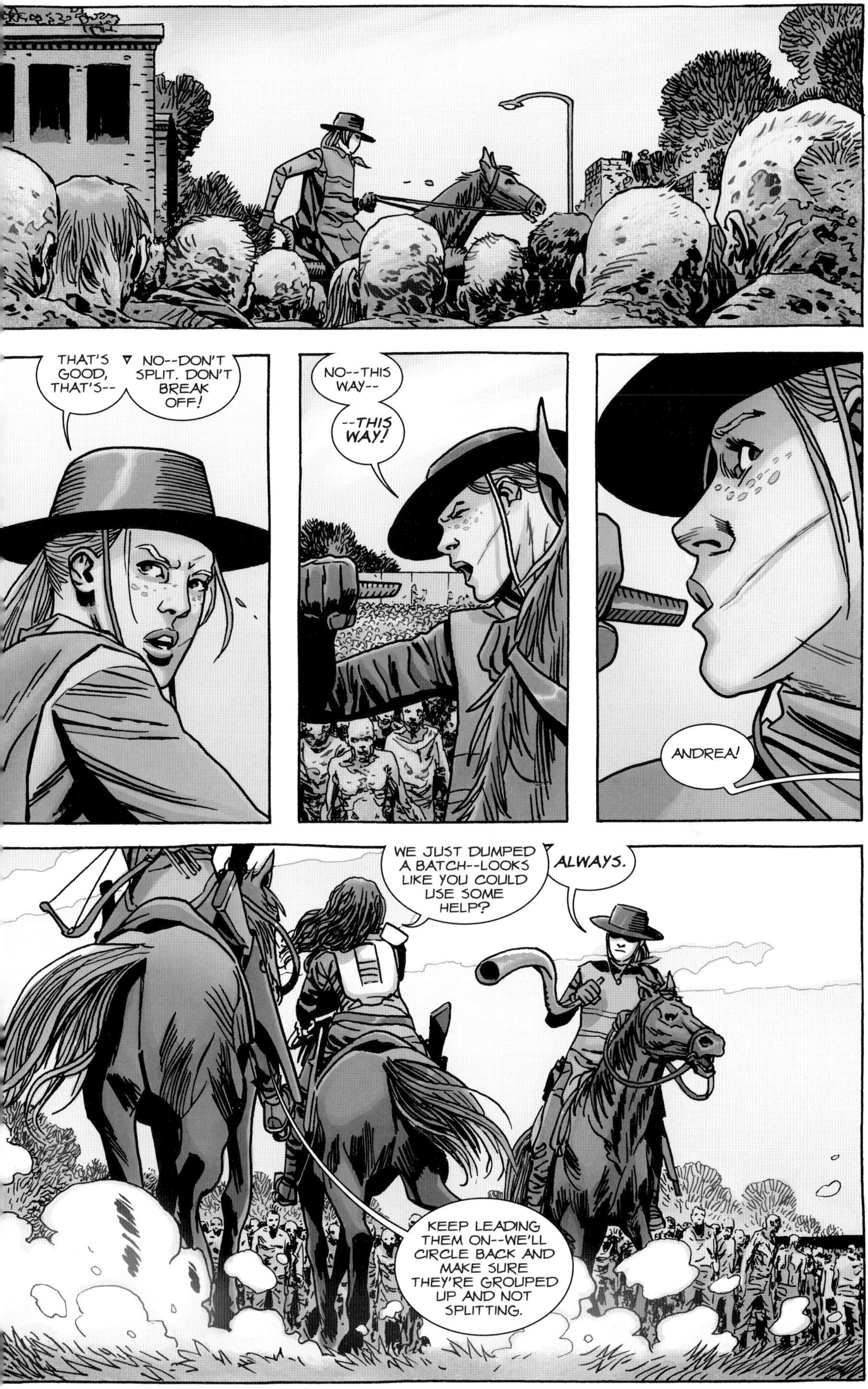
THAT'S GOOD, THAT'S--
NO--DON'T SPLIT. DON'T BREAK OFF!
NO--THIS WAY--
--THIS WAY!
ANDREA!
WE JUST DUMPED A BATCH--LOOKS LIKE YOU COULD USE SOME HELP?
ALWAYS.
KEEP LEADING THEM ON--WE'LL CIRCLE BACK AND MAKE SURE THEY'RE GROUPED UP AND NOT SPLITTING.

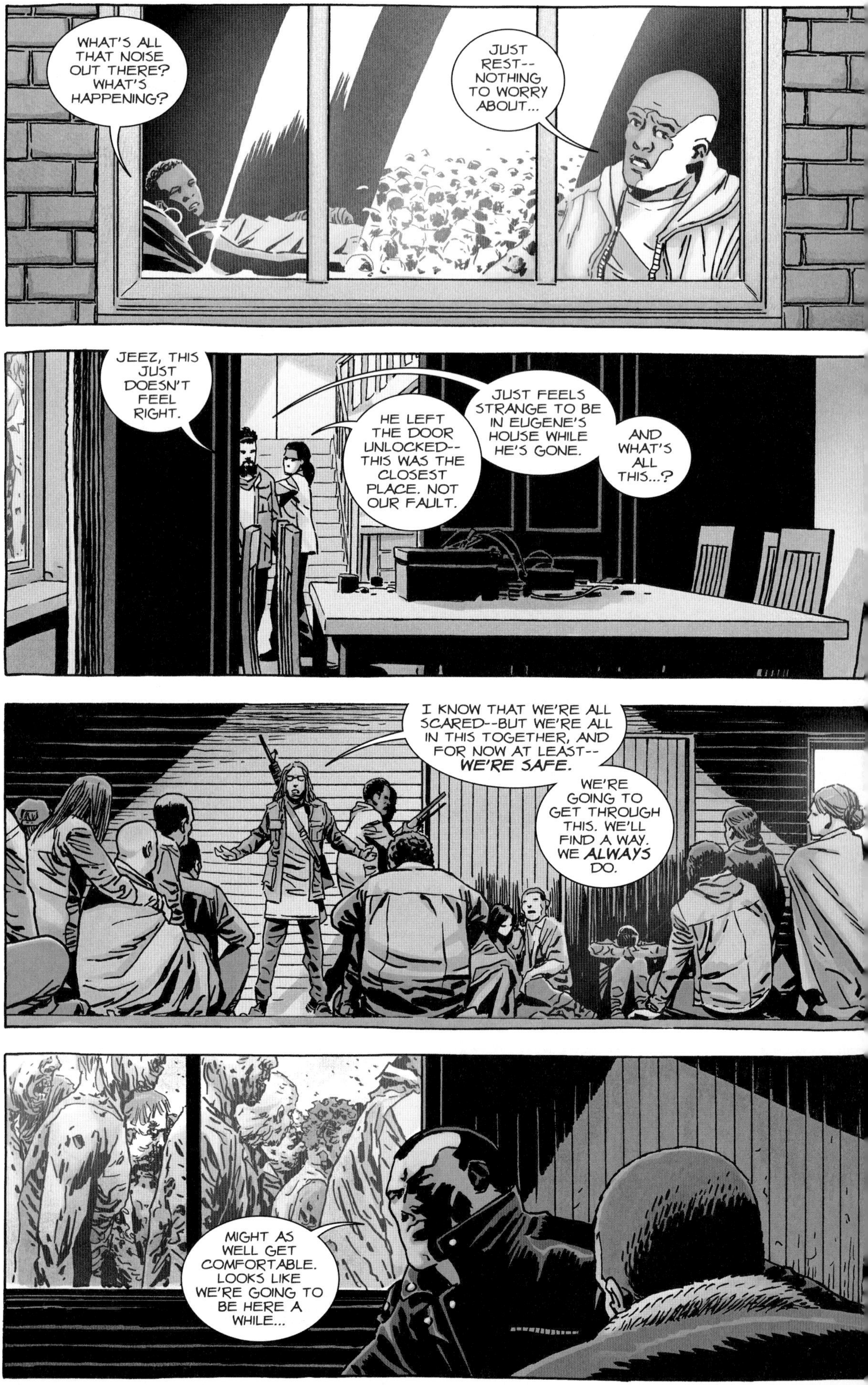
WHAT'S ALL THAT NOISE OUT THERE? WHAT'S HAPPENING?
JUST REST-- NOTHING TO WORRY ABOUT...
JEEZ, THIS JUST DOESN'T FEEL RIGHT.
JUST FEELS STRANGE TO BE IN EUGENE'S HOUSE WHILE HE'S GONE.
HE LEFT THE DOOR UNLOCKED-- THIS WAS THE CLOSEST PLACE. NOT OUR FAULT.
AND WHAT'S ALL THIS...?
I KNOW THAT WE'RE ALL SCARED--BUT WE'RE ALL IN THIS TOGETHER, AND FOR NOW AT LEAST-- WE'RE SAFE.
WE'RE GOING TO GET THROUGH THIS. WE'LL FIND A WAY. WE ALWAYS DO.
MIGHT AS WELL GET COMFORTABLE. LOOKS LIKE WE'RE GOING TO BE HERE A WHILE...

WHAT'S THE SINGLE **WORST** THING YOU'VE EVER DONE?

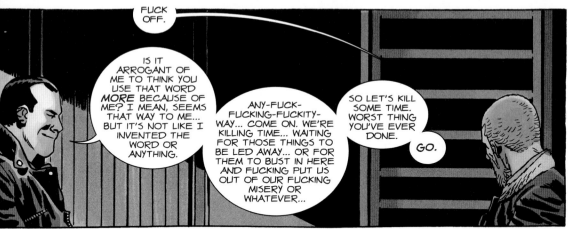

FUCK OFF.

IS IT ARROGANT OF ME TO THINK YOU USE THAT WORD **MORE** BECAUSE OF ME? I MEAN, SEEMS THAT WAY TO ME... BUT IT'S NOT LIKE I INVENTED THE WORD OR ANYTHING.

ANY-FUCK-FUCKING-FUCKITY-WAY... COME ON. WE'RE KILLING TIME... WAITING FOR THOSE THINGS TO BE LED AWAY... OR FOR THEM TO BUST IN HERE AND FUCKING PUT US OUT OF OUR FUCKING MISERY OR WHATEVER...

SO LET'S KILL SOME TIME. WORST THING YOU'VE EVER DONE.

GO.

IT ALL KIND OF RUNS TOGETHER AT THIS POINT...

...HARD TO NARROW IT DOWN. IT'S ONE SOLID BLOCK OF BAD ALL BOILING DOWN TO ONE THING...

THE WORST THING I EVER DID...

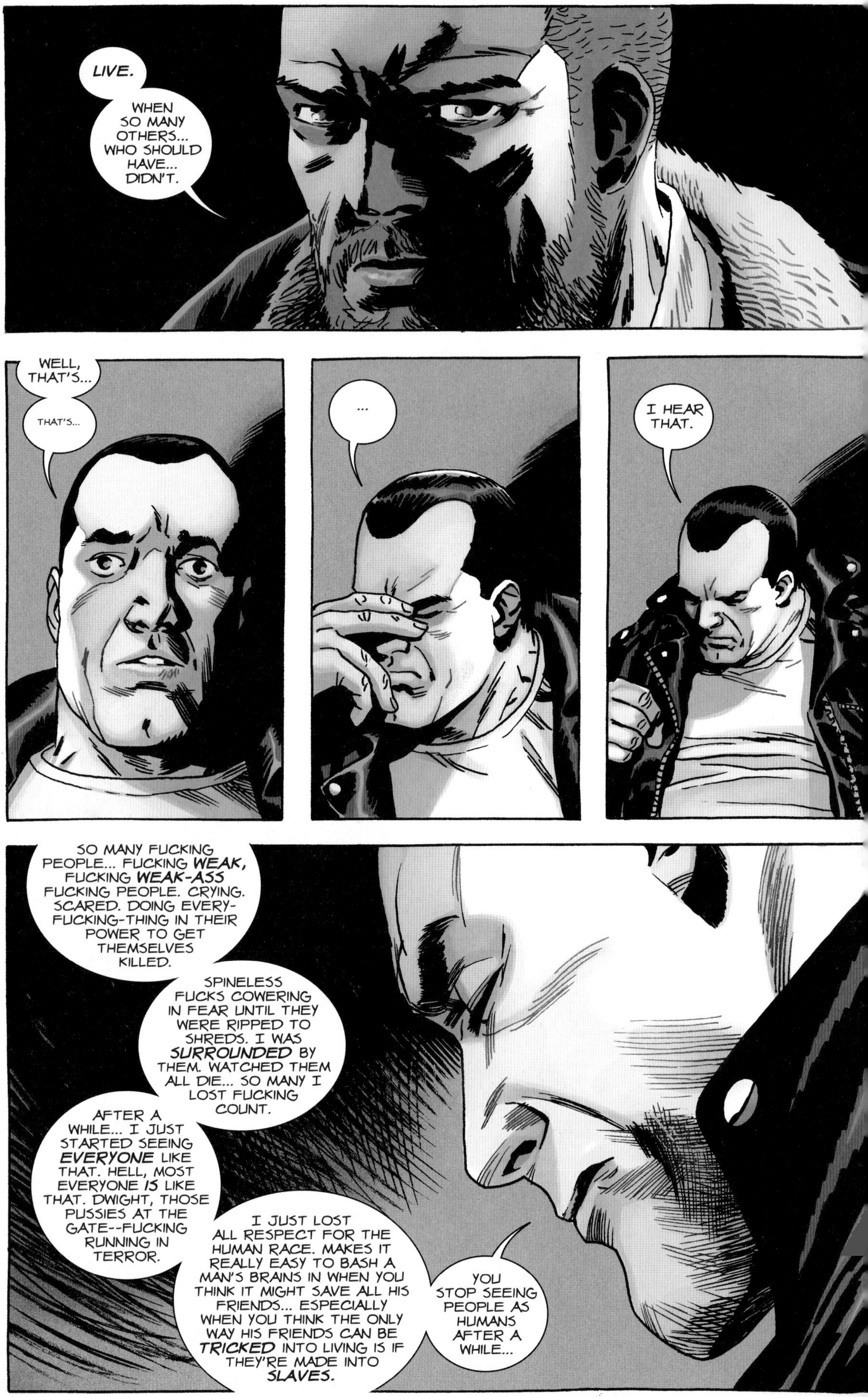
LIVE.
WHEN SO MANY OTHERS... WHO SHOULD HAVE... DIDN'T.
WELL, THAT'S...
THAT'S...
...
I HEAR THAT.
SO MANY FUCKING PEOPLE... FUCKING WEAK, FUCKING WEAK-ASS FUCKING PEOPLE. CRYING. SCARED. DOING EVERY-FUCKING-THING IN THEIR POWER TO GET THEMSELVES KILLED.
SPINELESS FUCKS COWERING IN FEAR UNTIL THEY WERE RIPPED TO SHREDS. I WAS SURROUNDED BY THEM. WATCHED THEM ALL DIE... SO MANY I LOST FUCKING COUNT.
AFTER A WHILE... I JUST STARTED SEEING EVERYONE LIKE THAT. HELL, MOST EVERYONE IS LIKE THAT. DWIGHT, THOSE PUSSIES AT THE GATE--FUCKING RUNNING IN TERROR.
I JUST LOST ALL RESPECT FOR THE HUMAN RACE. MAKES IT REALLY EASY TO BASH A MAN'S BRAINS IN WHEN YOU THINK IT MIGHT SAVE ALL HIS FRIENDS... ESPECIALLY WHEN YOU THINK THE ONLY WAY HIS FRIENDS CAN BE TRICKED INTO LIVING IS IF THEY'RE MADE INTO SLAVES.
YOU STOP SEEING PEOPLE AS HUMANS AFTER A WHILE...

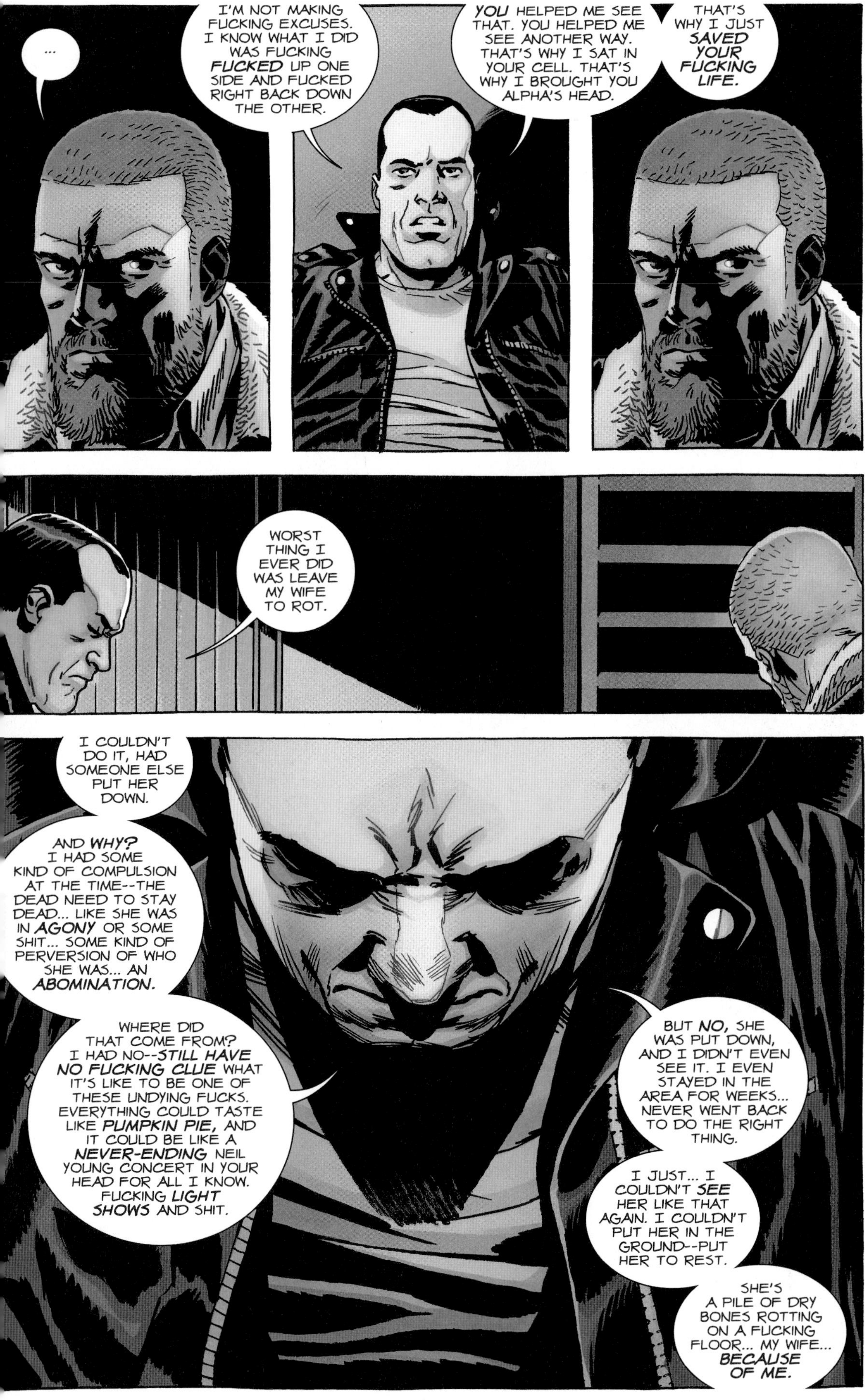
...
I'M NOT MAKING FUCKING EXCUSES. I KNOW WHAT I DID WAS FUCKING FUCKED UP ONE SIDE AND FUCKED RIGHT BACK DOWN THE OTHER.
YOU HELPED ME SEE THAT. YOU HELPED ME SEE ANOTHER WAY. THAT'S WHY I SAT IN YOUR CELL. THAT'S WHY I BROUGHT YOU ALPHA'S HEAD.
THAT'S WHY I JUST SAVED YOUR FUCKING LIFE.
WORST THING I EVER DID WAS LEAVE MY WIFE TO ROT.
I COULDN'T DO IT, HAD SOMEONE ELSE PUT HER DOWN.
AND WHY? I HAD SOME KIND OF COMPULSION AT THE TIME--THE DEAD NEED TO STAY DEAD... LIKE SHE WAS IN AGONY OR SOME SHIT... SOME KIND OF PERVERSION OF WHO SHE WAS... AN ABOMINATION.
WHERE DID THAT COME FROM? I HAD NO--STILL HAVE NO FUCKING CLUE WHAT IT'S LIKE TO BE ONE OF THESE UNDYING FUCKS. EVERYTHING COULD TASTE LIKE PUMPKIN PIE, AND IT COULD BE LIKE A NEVER-ENDING NEIL YOUNG CONCERT IN YOUR HEAD FOR ALL I KNOW. FUCKING LIGHT SHOWS AND SHIT.
BUT NO, SHE WAS PUT DOWN, AND I DIDN'T EVEN SEE IT. I EVEN STAYED IN THE AREA FOR WEEKS... NEVER WENT BACK TO DO THE RIGHT THING.
I JUST... I COULDN'T SEE HER LIKE THAT AGAIN. I COULDN'T PUT HER IN THE GROUND--PUT HER TO REST.
SHE'S A PILE OF DRY BONES ROTTING ON A FUCKING FLOOR... MY WIFE... BECAUSE OF ME.

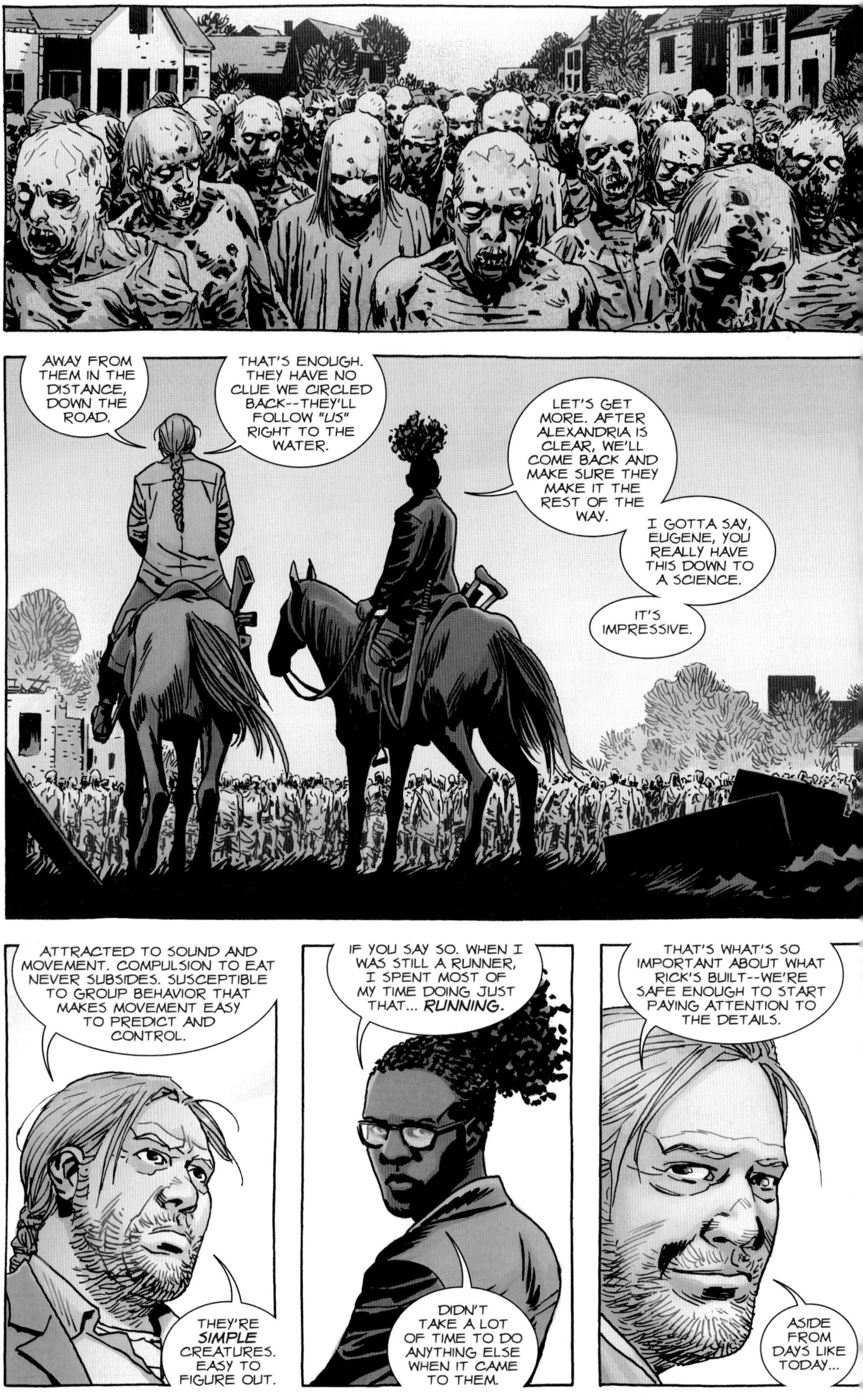
AWAY FROM THEM IN THE DISTANCE, DOWN THE ROAD.
THAT'S ENOUGH. THEY HAVE NO CLUE WE CIRCLED BACK--THEY'LL FOLLOW "US" RIGHT TO THE WATER.
LET'S GET MORE. AFTER ALEXANDRIA IS CLEAR, WE'LL COME BACK AND MAKE SURE THEY MAKE IT THE REST OF THE WAY.
I GOTTA SAY, EUGENE, YOU REALLY HAVE THIS DOWN TO A SCIENCE.
IT'S IMPRESSIVE.
ATTRACTED TO SOUND AND MOVEMENT. COMPULSION TO EAT NEVER SUBSIDES. SUSCEPTIBLE TO GROUP BEHAVIOR THAT MAKES MOVEMENT EASY TO PREDICT AND CONTROL.
THEY'RE *SIMPLE* CREATURES. EASY TO FIGURE OUT.
IF YOU SAY SO. WHEN I WAS STILL A RUNNER, I SPENT MOST OF MY TIME DOING JUST THAT... *RUNNING.*
DIDN'T TAKE A LOT OF TIME TO DO ANYTHING ELSE WHEN IT CAME TO THEM.
THAT'S WHAT'S SO IMPORTANT ABOUT WHAT RICK'S BUILT--WE'RE SAFE ENOUGH TO START PAYING ATTENTION TO THE DETAILS.
ASIDE FROM DAYS LIKE TODAY...

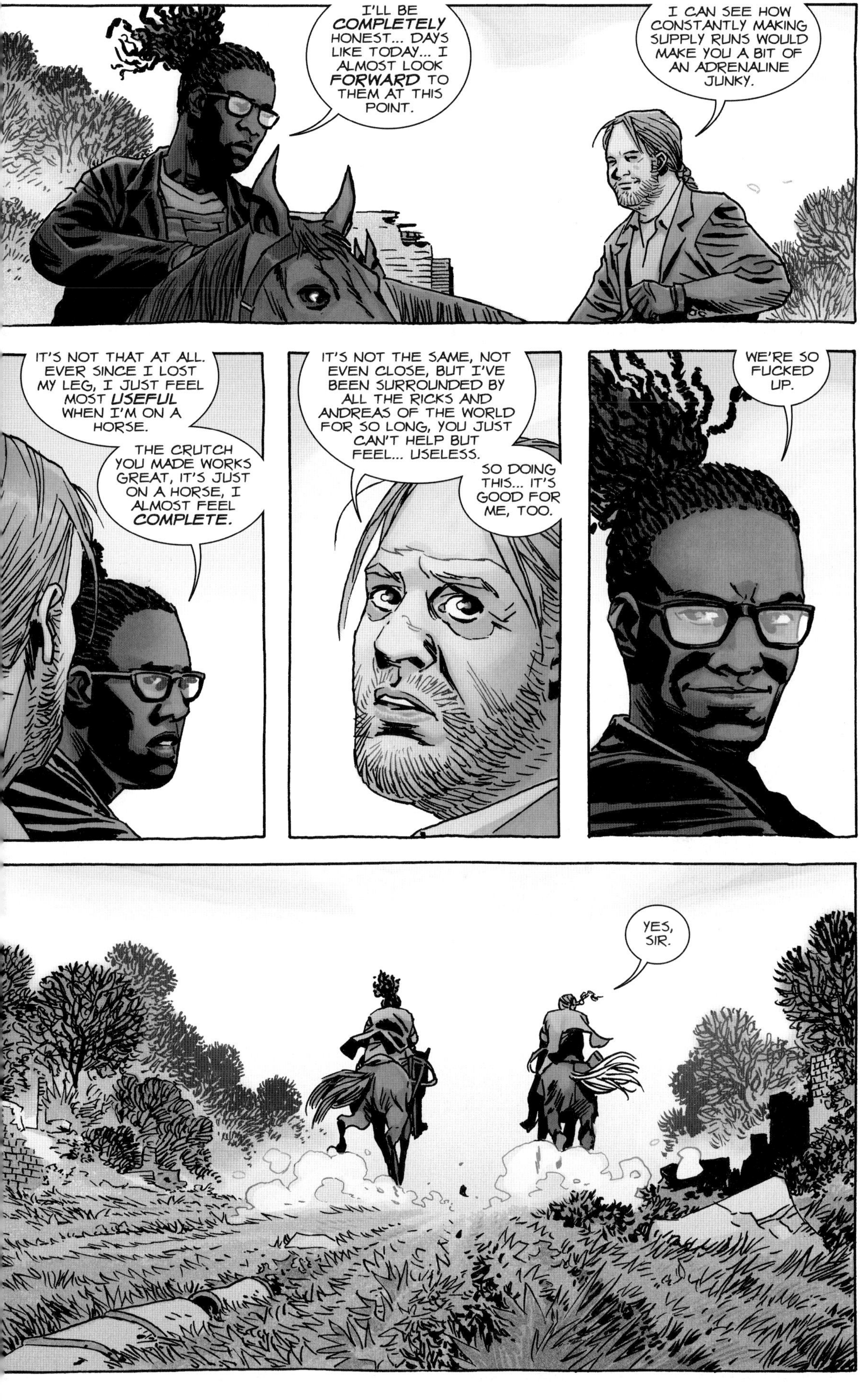
I'LL BE COMPLETELY HONEST... DAYS LIKE TODAY... I ALMOST LOOK FORWARD TO THEM AT THIS POINT.
I CAN SEE HOW CONSTANTLY MAKING SUPPLY RUNS WOULD MAKE YOU A BIT OF AN ADRENALINE JUNKY.
IT'S NOT THAT AT ALL. EVER SINCE I LOST MY LEG, I JUST FEEL MOST USEFUL WHEN I'M ON A HORSE.
THE CRUTCH YOU MADE WORKS GREAT, IT'S JUST ON A HORSE, I ALMOST FEEL COMPLETE.
IT'S NOT THE SAME, NOT EVEN CLOSE, BUT I'VE BEEN SURROUNDED BY ALL THE RICKS AND ANDREAS OF THE WORLD FOR SO LONG, YOU JUST CAN'T HELP BUT FEEL... USELESS.
SO DOING THIS... IT'S GOOD FOR ME, TOO.
WE'RE SO FUCKED UP.
YES, SIR.

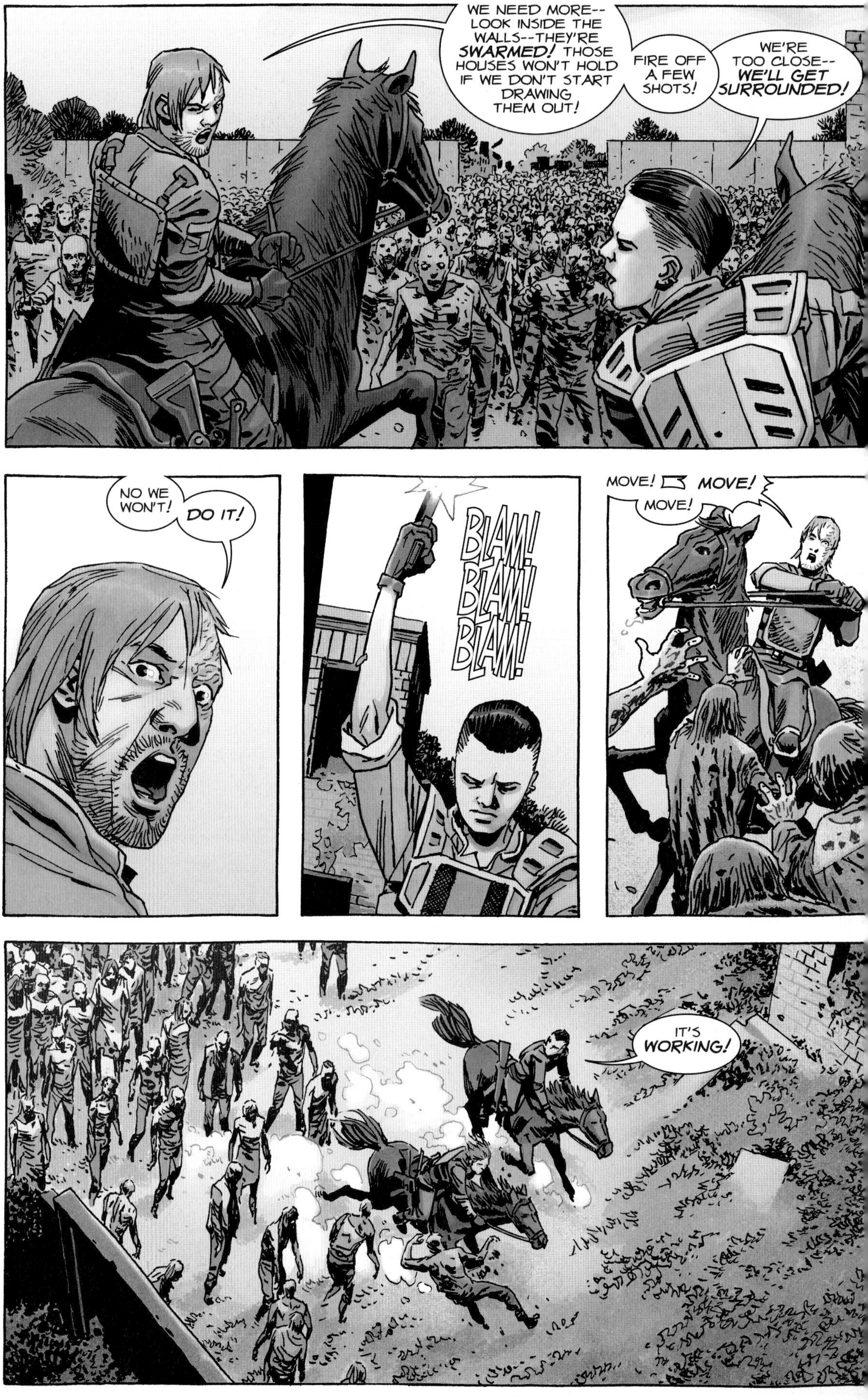
WE NEED MORE-- LOOK INSIDE THE WALLS--THEY'RE **SWARMED!** THOSE HOUSES WON'T HOLD IF WE DON'T START DRAWING THEM OUT!
FIRE OFF A FEW SHOTS!
WE'RE TOO CLOSE-- **WE'LL GET SURROUNDED!**
NO WE WON'T!
DO IT!
BLAM! BLAM! BLAM! BLAM!
MOVE!
MOVE!
MOVE!
IT'S **WORKING!**

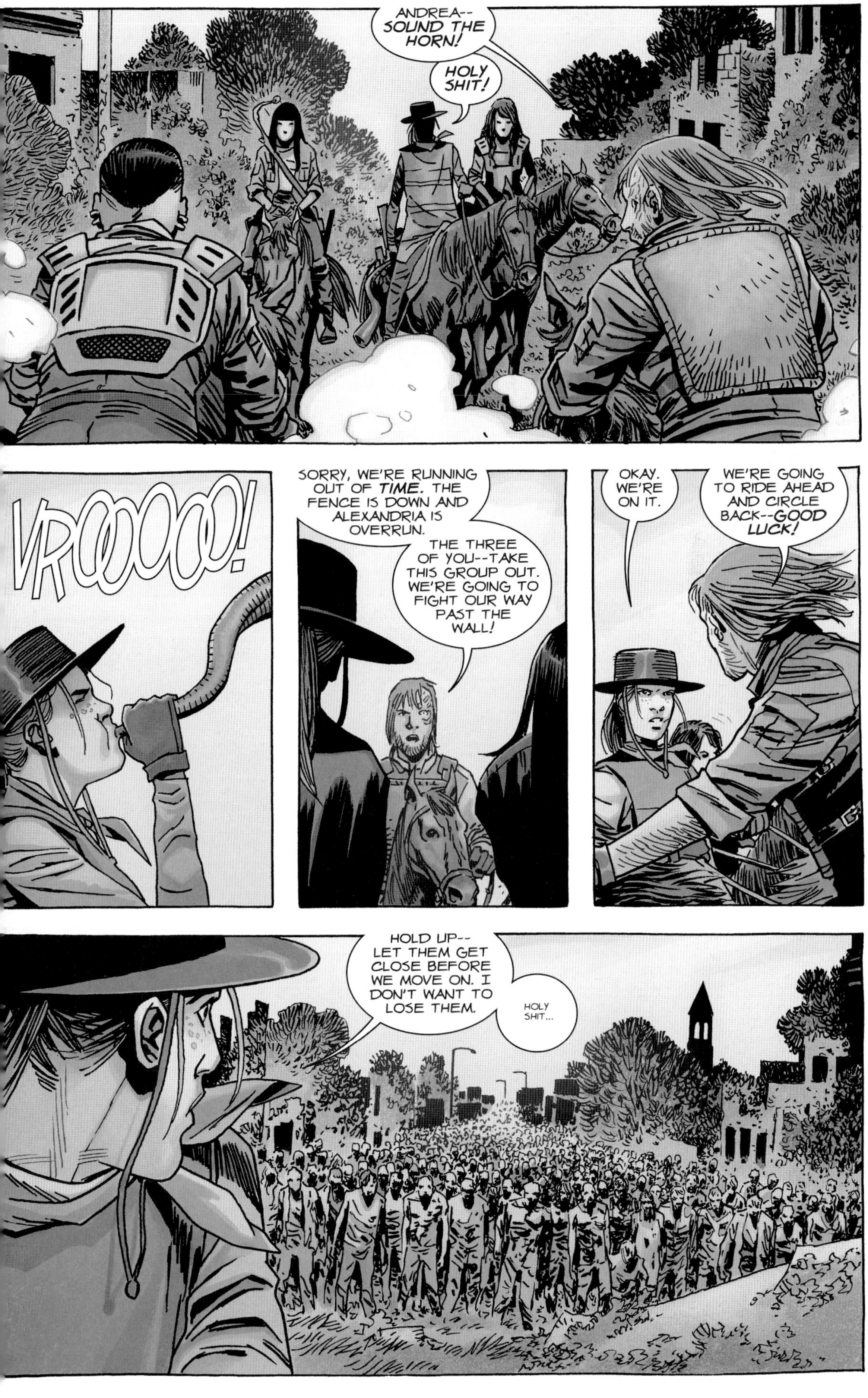
ANDREA-- SOUND THE HORN!
HOLY SHIT!
VROOOOO!
SORRY, WE'RE RUNNING OUT OF TIME. THE FENCE IS DOWN AND ALEXANDRIA IS OVERRUN.
THE THREE OF YOU--TAKE THIS GROUP OUT. WE'RE GOING TO FIGHT OUR WAY PAST THE WALL!
OKAY. WE'RE ON IT.
WE'RE GOING TO RIDE AHEAD AND CIRCLE BACK--GOOD LUCK!
HOLD UP-- LET THEM GET CLOSE BEFORE WE MOVE ON. I DON'T WANT TO LOSE THEM.
HOLY SHIT...

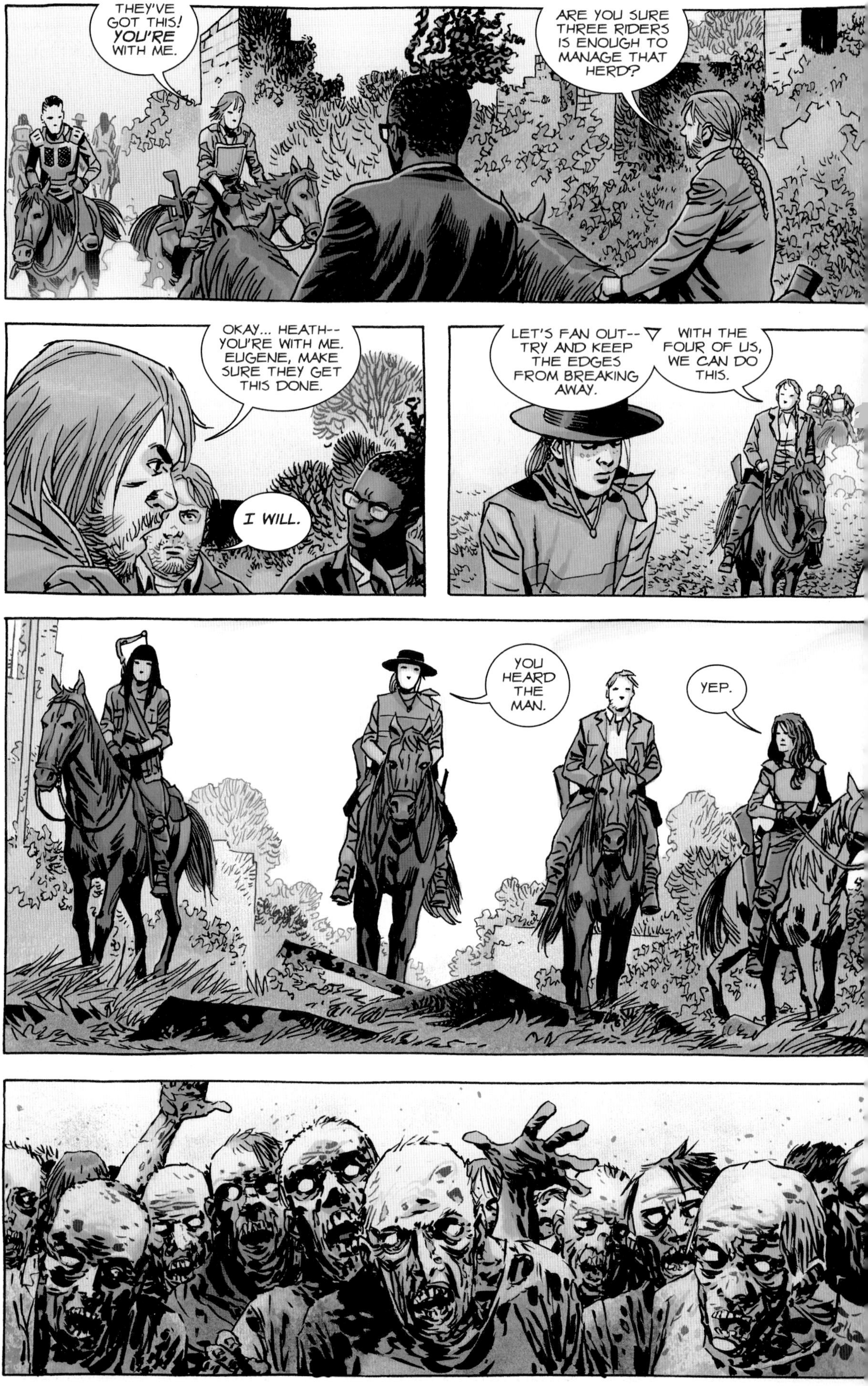
THEY'VE GOT THIS! YOU'RE WITH ME.
ARE YOU SURE THREE RIDERS IS ENOUGH TO MANAGE THAT HERD?
OKAY... HEATH-- YOU'RE WITH ME. EUGENE, MAKE SURE THEY GET THIS DONE.
I WILL.
LET'S FAN OUT-- TRY AND KEEP THE EDGES FROM BREAKING AWAY.
WITH THE FOUR OF US, WE CAN DO THIS.
YOU HEARD THE MAN.
YEP.

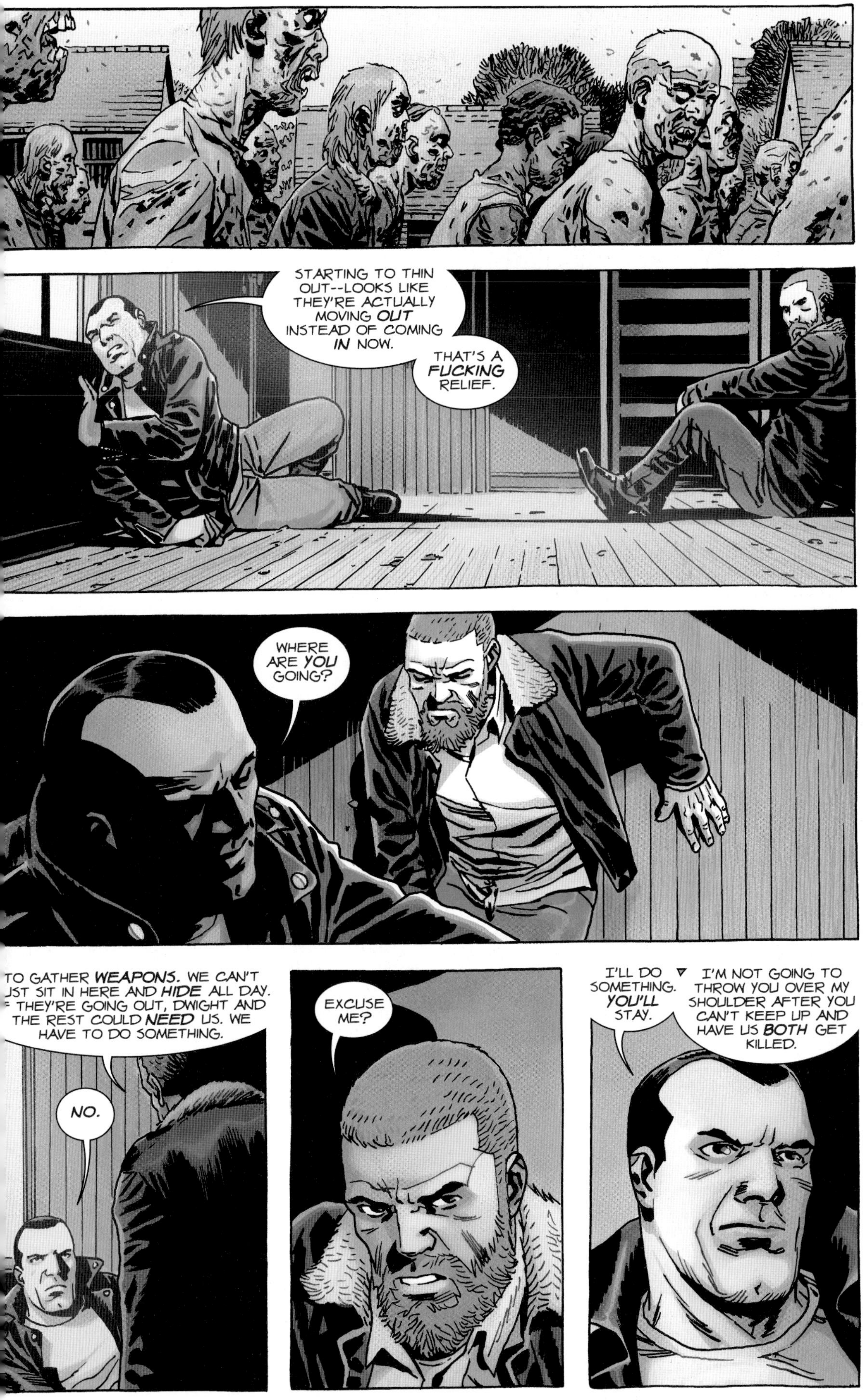

STARTING TO THIN OUT--LOOKS LIKE THEY'RE ACTUALLY MOVING OUT INSTEAD OF COMING IN NOW.
THAT'S A FUCKING RELIEF.
WHERE ARE YOU GOING?
TO GATHER WEAPONS. WE CAN'T JST SIT IN HERE AND HIDE ALL DAY. F THEY'RE GOING OUT, DWIGHT AND THE REST COULD NEED US. WE HAVE TO DO SOMETHING.
NO.
EXCUSE ME?
I'LL DO SOMETHING. YOU'LL STAY.
I'M NOT GOING TO THROW YOU OVER MY SHOULDER AFTER YOU CAN'T KEEP UP AND HAVE US BOTH GET KILLED.

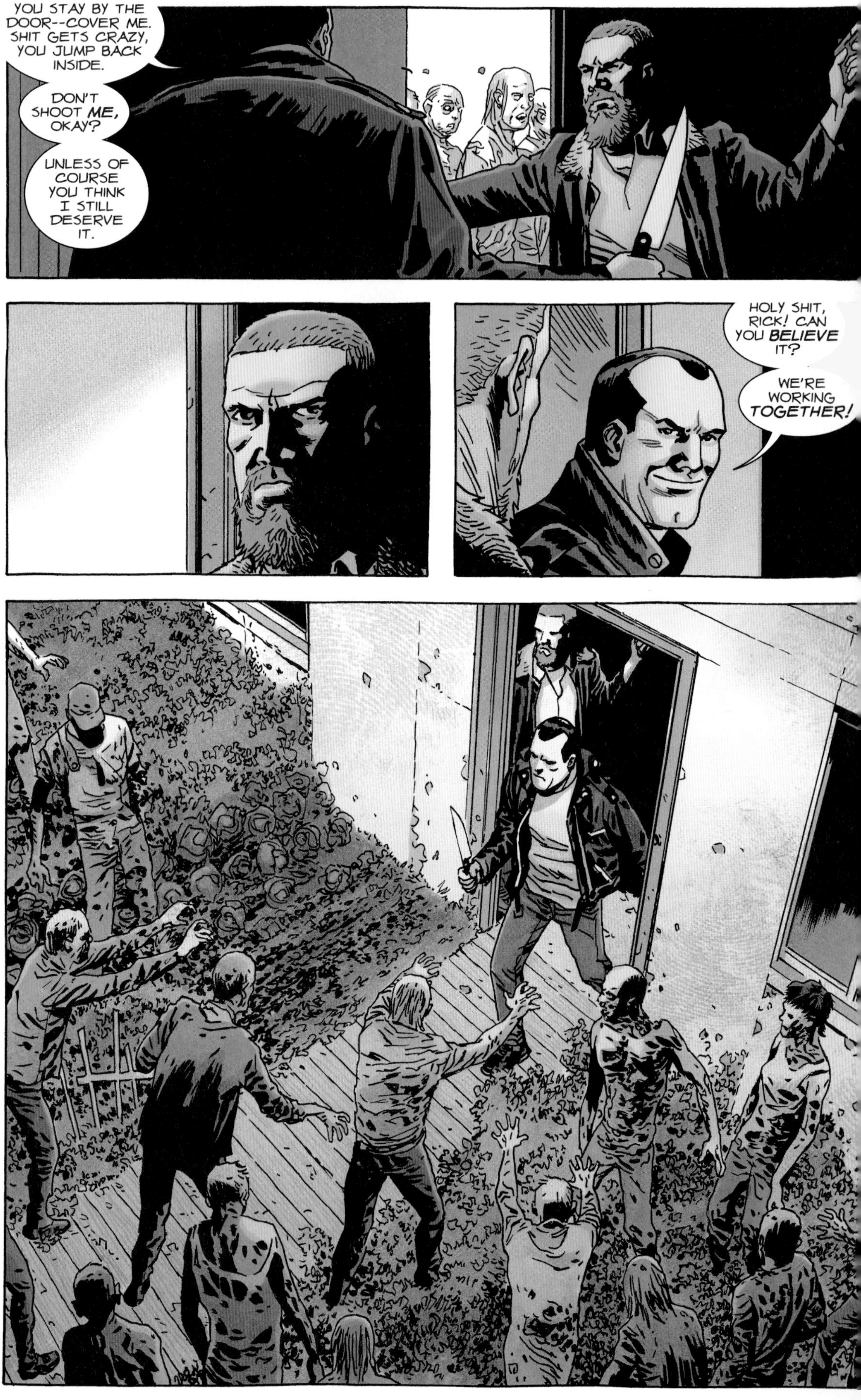
YOU STAY BY THE DOOR--COVER ME. SHIT GETS CRAZY, YOU JUMP BACK INSIDE.
DON'T SHOOT *ME,* OKAY?
UNLESS OF COURSE YOU THINK I STILL DESERVE IT.
HOLY SHIT, RICK! CAN YOU *BELIEVE* IT?
WE'RE WORKING *TOGETHER!*

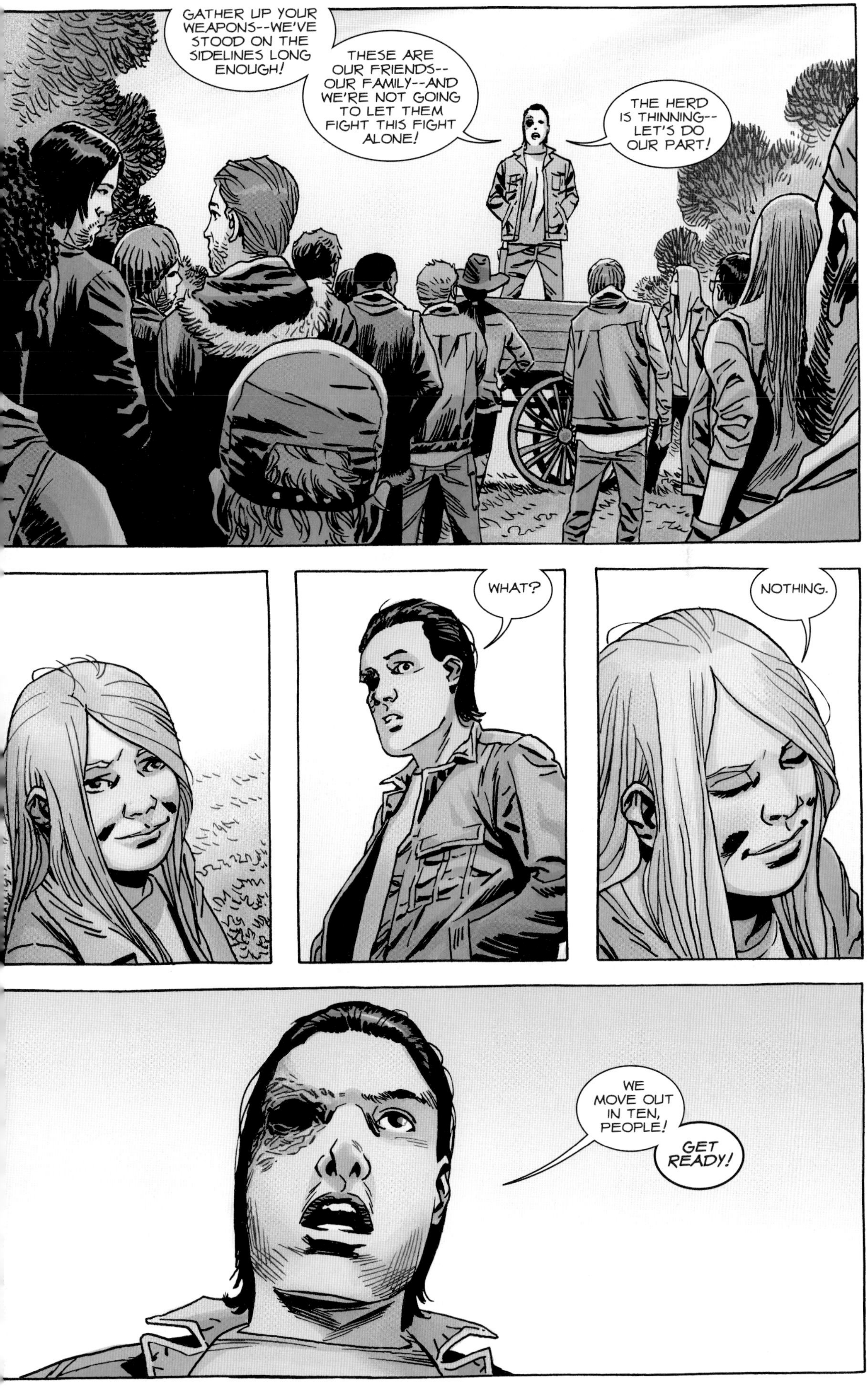
GATHER UP YOUR WEAPONS--WE'VE STOOD ON THE SIDELINES LONG ENOUGH!
THESE ARE OUR FRIENDS--OUR FAMILY--AND WE'RE NOT GOING TO LET THEM FIGHT THIS FIGHT ALONE!
THE HERD IS THINNING--LET'S DO OUR PART!
WHAT?
NOTHING.
WE MOVE OUT IN TEN, PEOPLE!
GET READY!

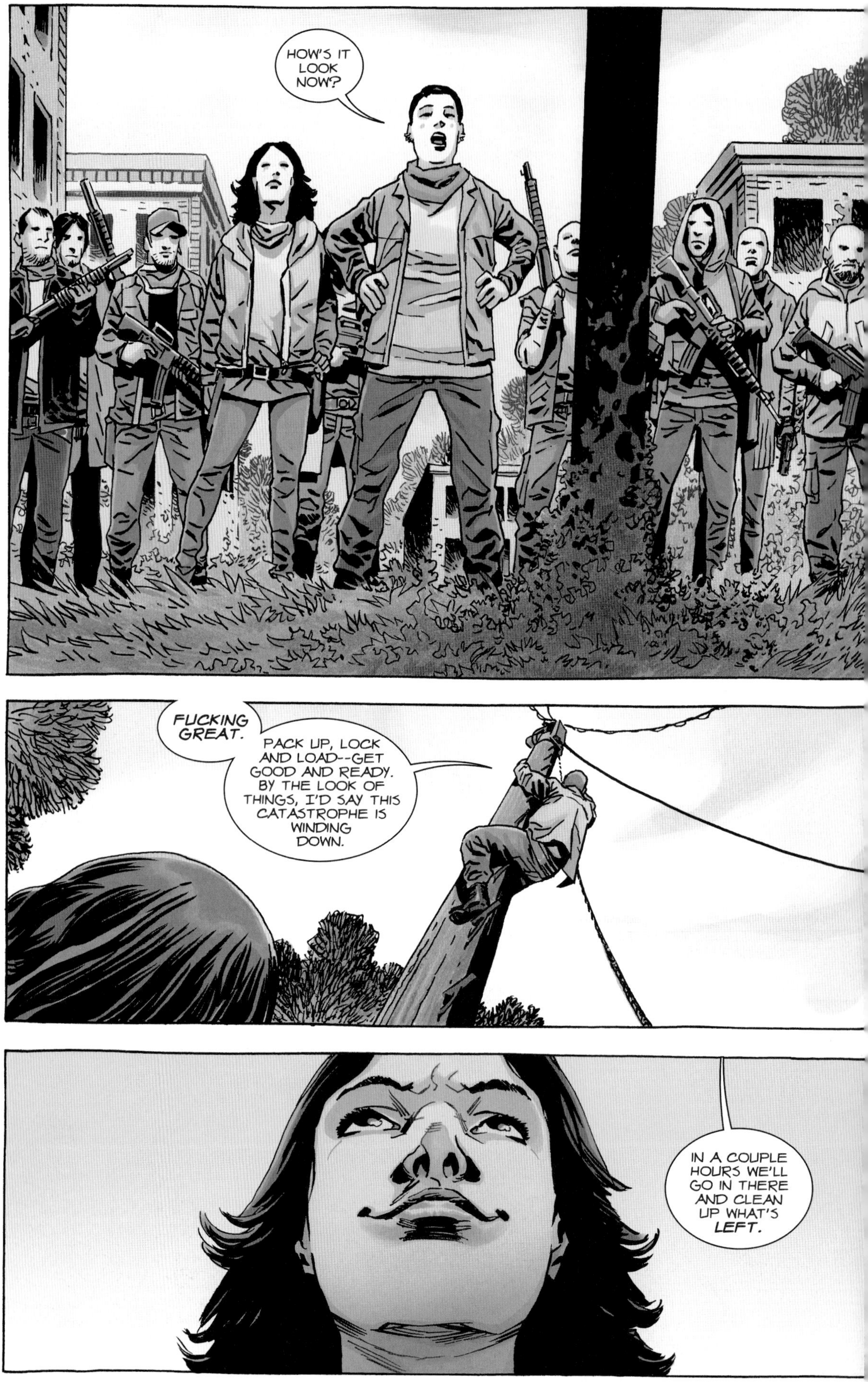
HOW'S IT LOOK NOW?
FUCKING GREAT.
PACK UP, LOCK AND LOAD--GET GOOD AND READY. BY THE LOOK OF THINGS, I'D SAY THIS CATASTROPHE IS WINDING DOWN.
IN A COUPLE HOURS WE'LL GO IN THERE AND CLEAN UP WHAT'S LEFT.

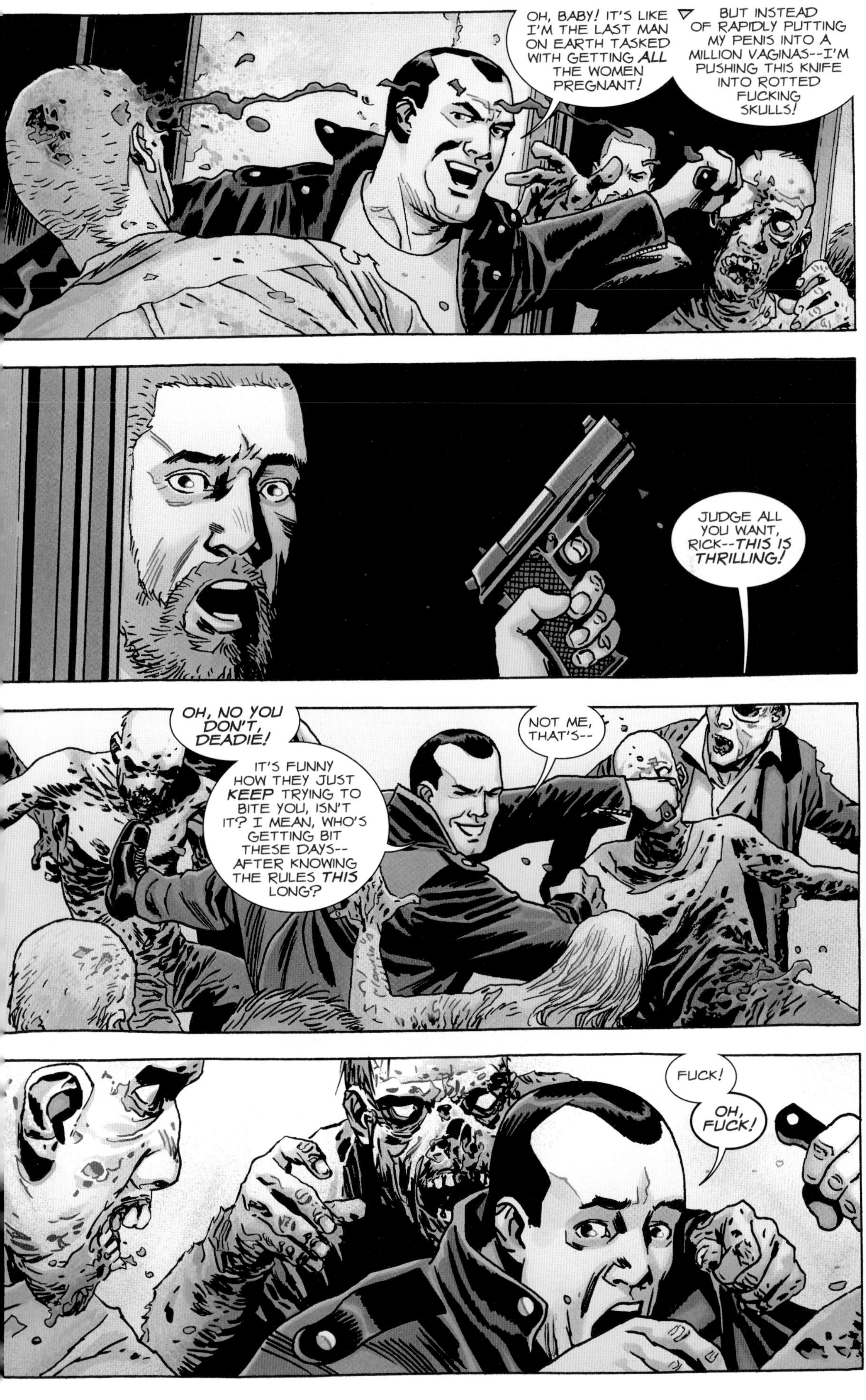
OH, BABY! IT'S LIKE I'M THE LAST MAN ON EARTH TASKED WITH GETTING ALL THE WOMEN PREGNANT!
BUT INSTEAD OF RAPIDLY PUTTING MY PENIS INTO A MILLION VAGINAS--I'M PUSHING THIS KNIFE INTO ROTTED FUCKING SKULLS!
JUDGE ALL YOU WANT, RICK--THIS IS THRILLING!
OH, NO YOU DON'T, DEADIE!
IT'S FUNNY HOW THEY JUST KEEP TRYING TO BITE YOU, ISN'T IT? I MEAN, WHO'S GETTING BIT THESE DAYS--AFTER KNOWING THE RULES THIS LONG?
NOT ME, THAT'S--
FUCK!
OH, FUCK!

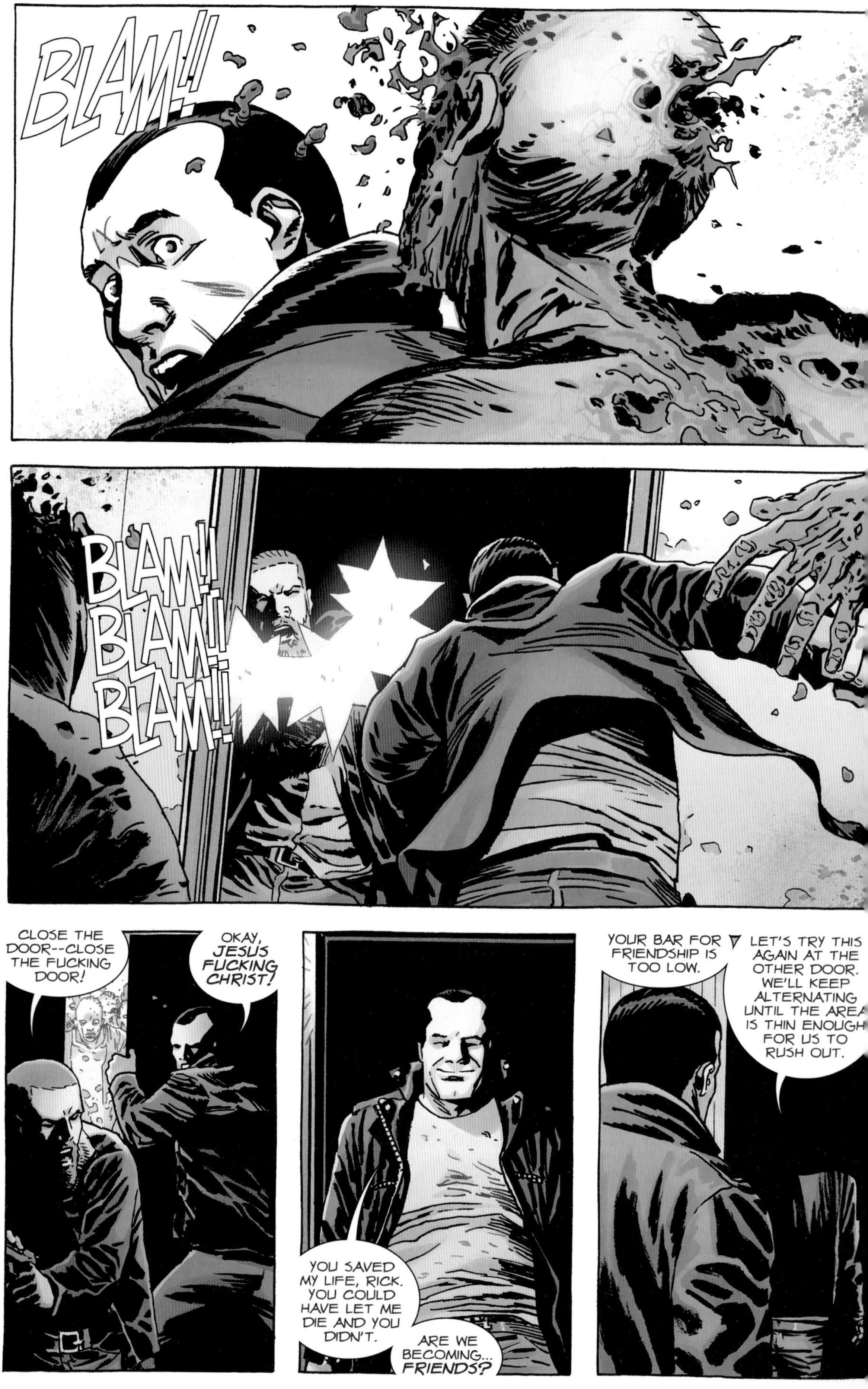
BLAM!!
BLAM!!
BLAM!!
BLAM!!
CLOSE THE DOOR--CLOSE THE FUCKING DOOR!
OKAY, JESUS FUCKING CHRIST!
YOU SAVED MY LIFE, RICK. YOU COULD HAVE LET ME DIE AND YOU DIDN'T.
ARE WE BECOMING... FRIENDS?
YOUR BAR FOR FRIENDSHIP IS TOO LOW.
LET'S TRY THIS AGAIN AT THE OTHER DOOR. WE'LL KEEP ALTERNATING UNTIL THE AREA IS THIN ENOUGH FOR US TO RUSH OUT.

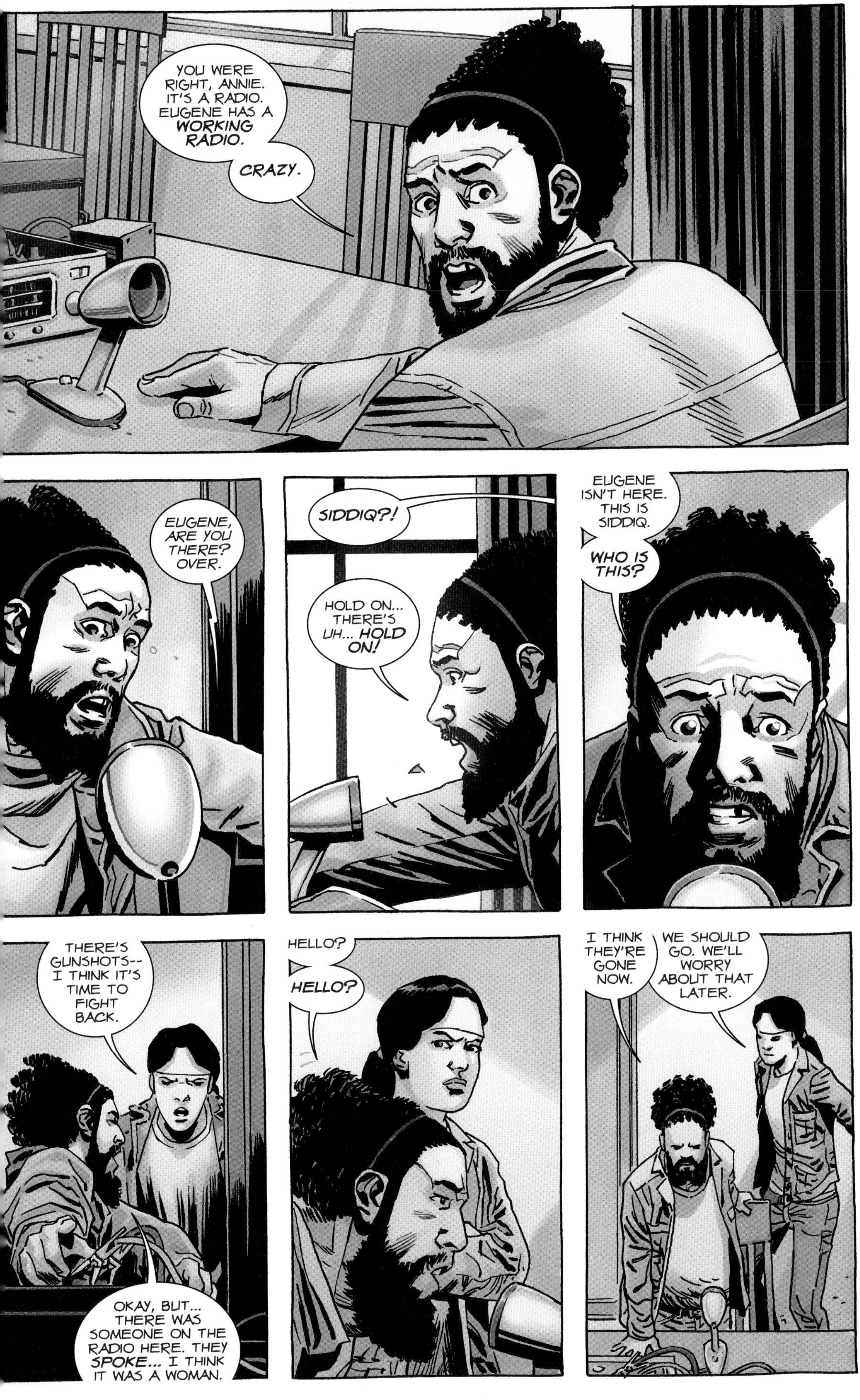
YOU WERE RIGHT, ANNIE. IT'S A RADIO. EUGENE HAS A WORKING RADIO.
CRAZY.
EUGENE, ARE YOU THERE? OVER.
SIDDIQ?!
HOLD ON... THERE'S UH... HOLD ON!
EUGENE ISN'T HERE. THIS IS SIDDIQ.
WHO IS THIS?
THERE'S GUNSHOTS-- I THINK IT'S TIME TO FIGHT BACK.
OKAY, BUT... THERE WAS SOMEONE ON THE RADIO HERE. THEY SPOKE... I THINK IT WAS A WOMAN.
HELLO?
HELLO?
I THINK THEY'RE GONE NOW.
WE SHOULD GO. WE'LL WORRY ABOUT THAT LATER.

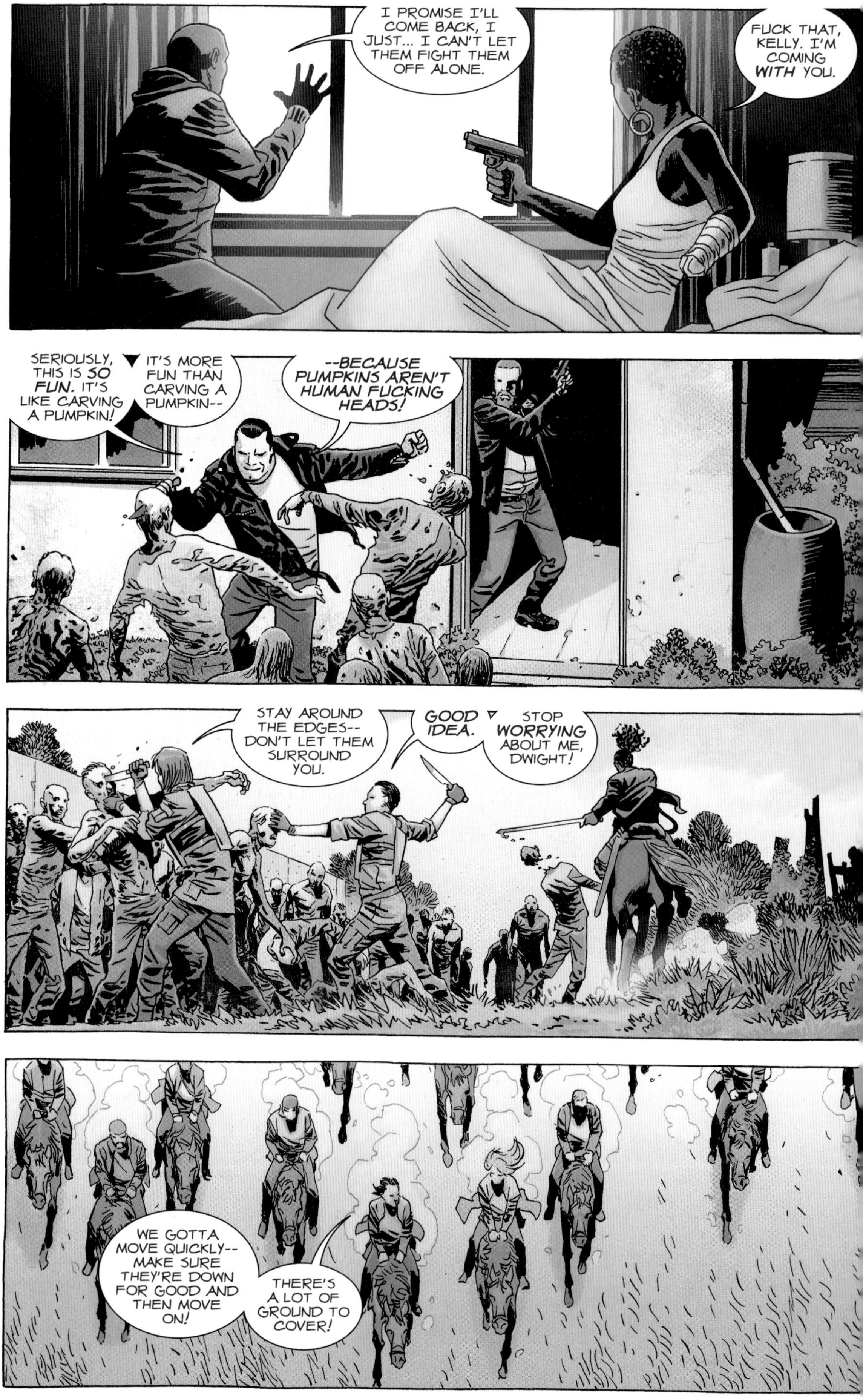
I PROMISE I'LL COME BACK, I JUST... I CAN'T LET THEM FIGHT THEM OFF ALONE.
FUCK THAT, KELLY. I'M COMING WITH YOU.
SERIOUSLY, THIS IS SO FUN. IT'S LIKE CARVING A PUMPKIN!
IT'S MORE FUN THAN CARVING A PUMPKIN--
--BECAUSE PUMPKINS AREN'T HUMAN FUCKING HEADS!
STAY AROUND THE EDGES-- DON'T LET THEM SURROUND YOU.
GOOD IDEA.
STOP WORRYING ABOUT ME, DWIGHT!
WE GOTTA MOVE QUICKLY-- MAKE SURE THEY'RE DOWN FOR GOOD AND THEN MOVE ON!
THERE'S A LOT OF GROUND TO COVER!

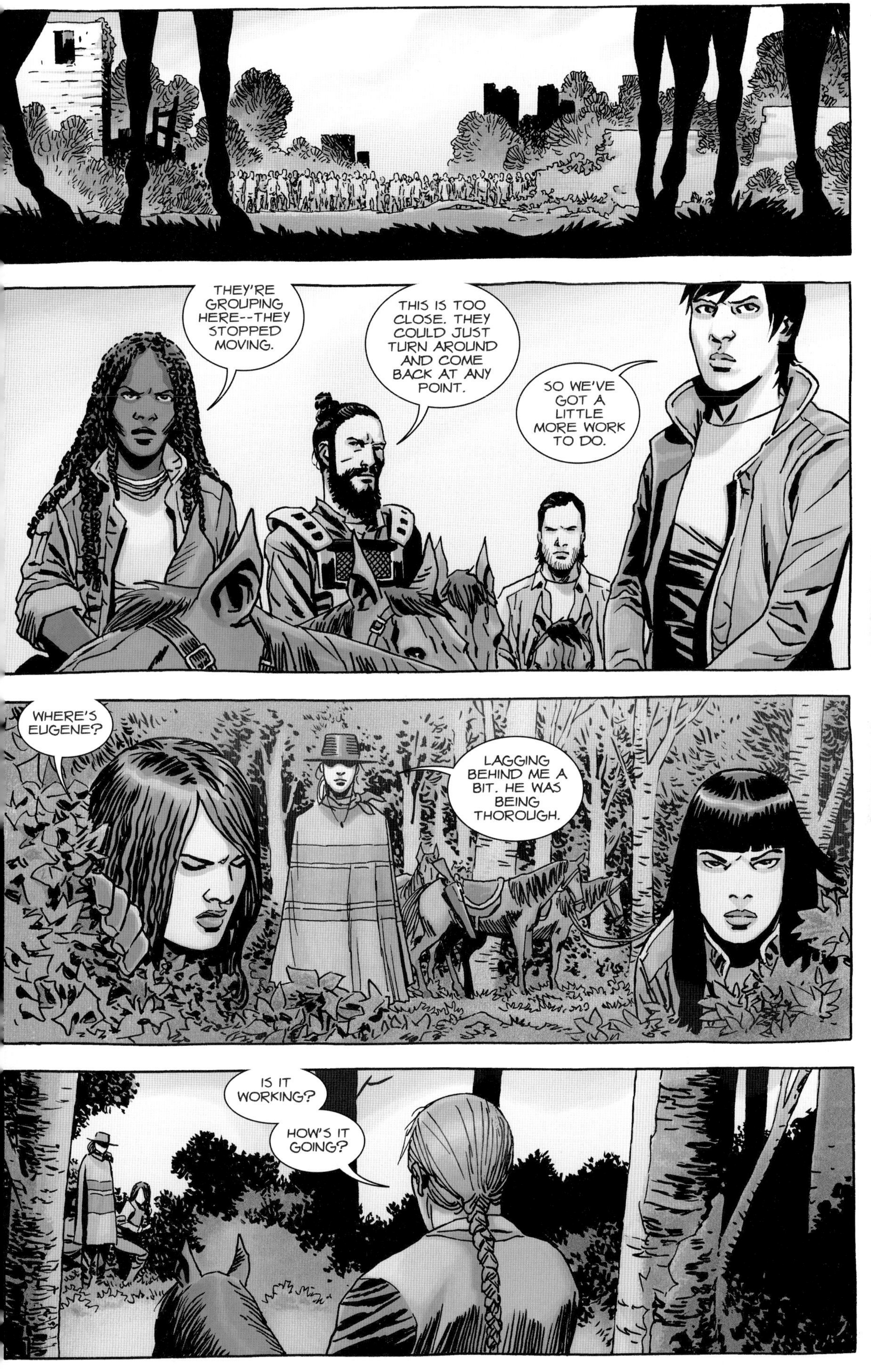
THEY'RE GROUPING HERE--THEY STOPPED MOVING.
THIS IS TOO CLOSE. THEY COULD JUST TURN AROUND AND COME BACK AT ANY POINT.
SO WE'VE GOT A LITTLE MORE WORK TO DO.
WHERE'S EUGENE?
LAGGING BEHIND ME A BIT. HE WAS BEING THOROUGH.
IS IT WORKING?
HOW'S IT GOING?

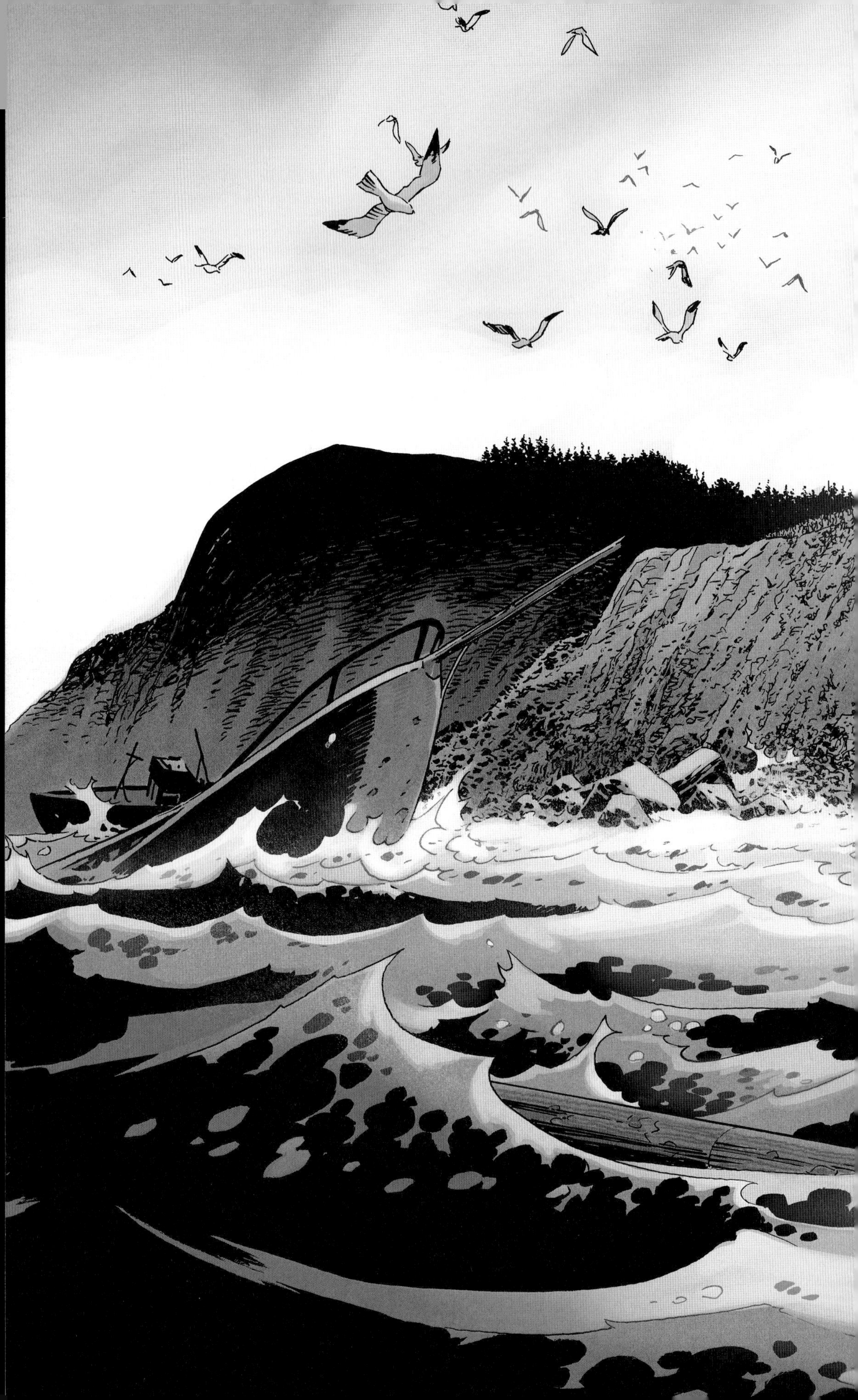

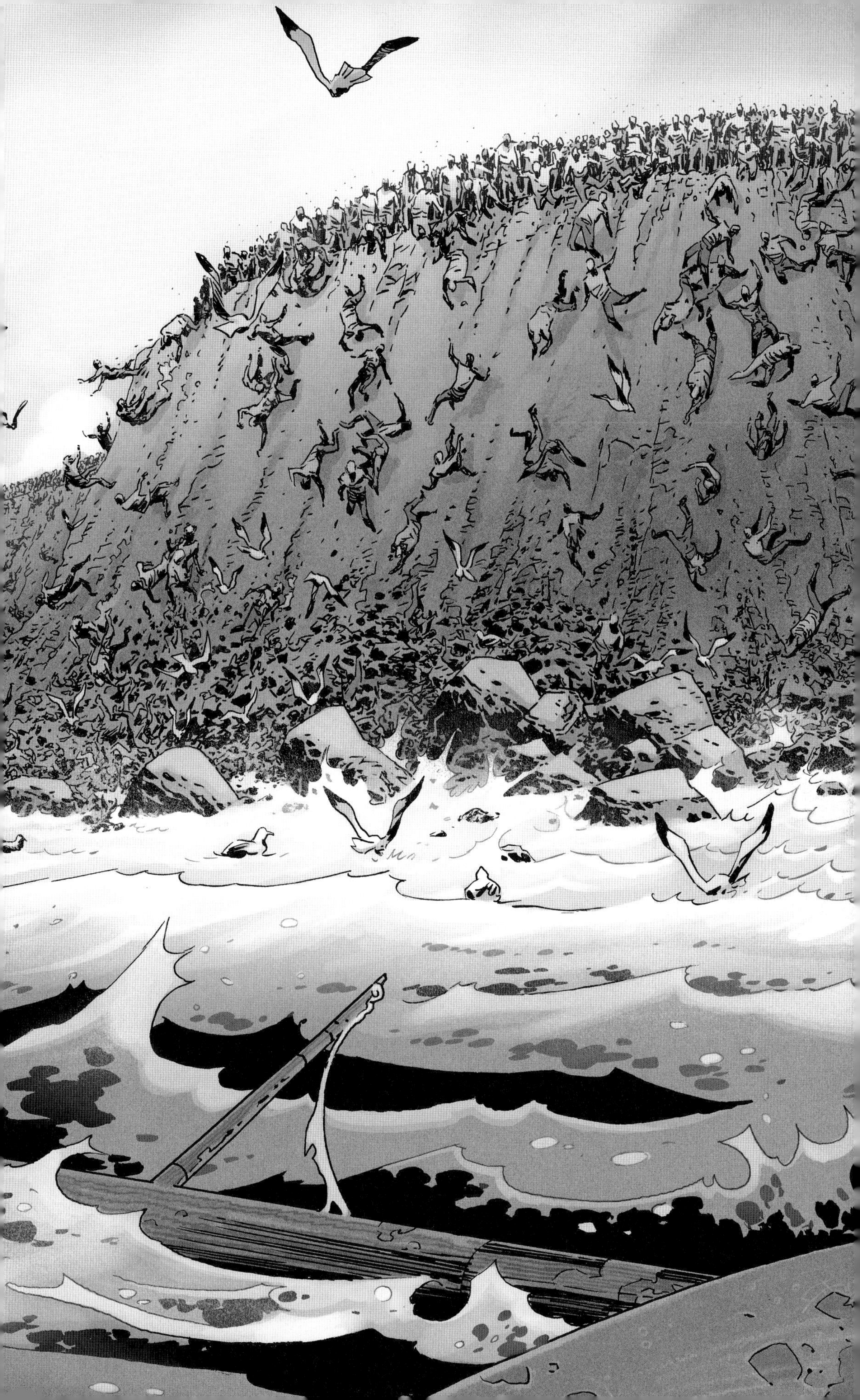

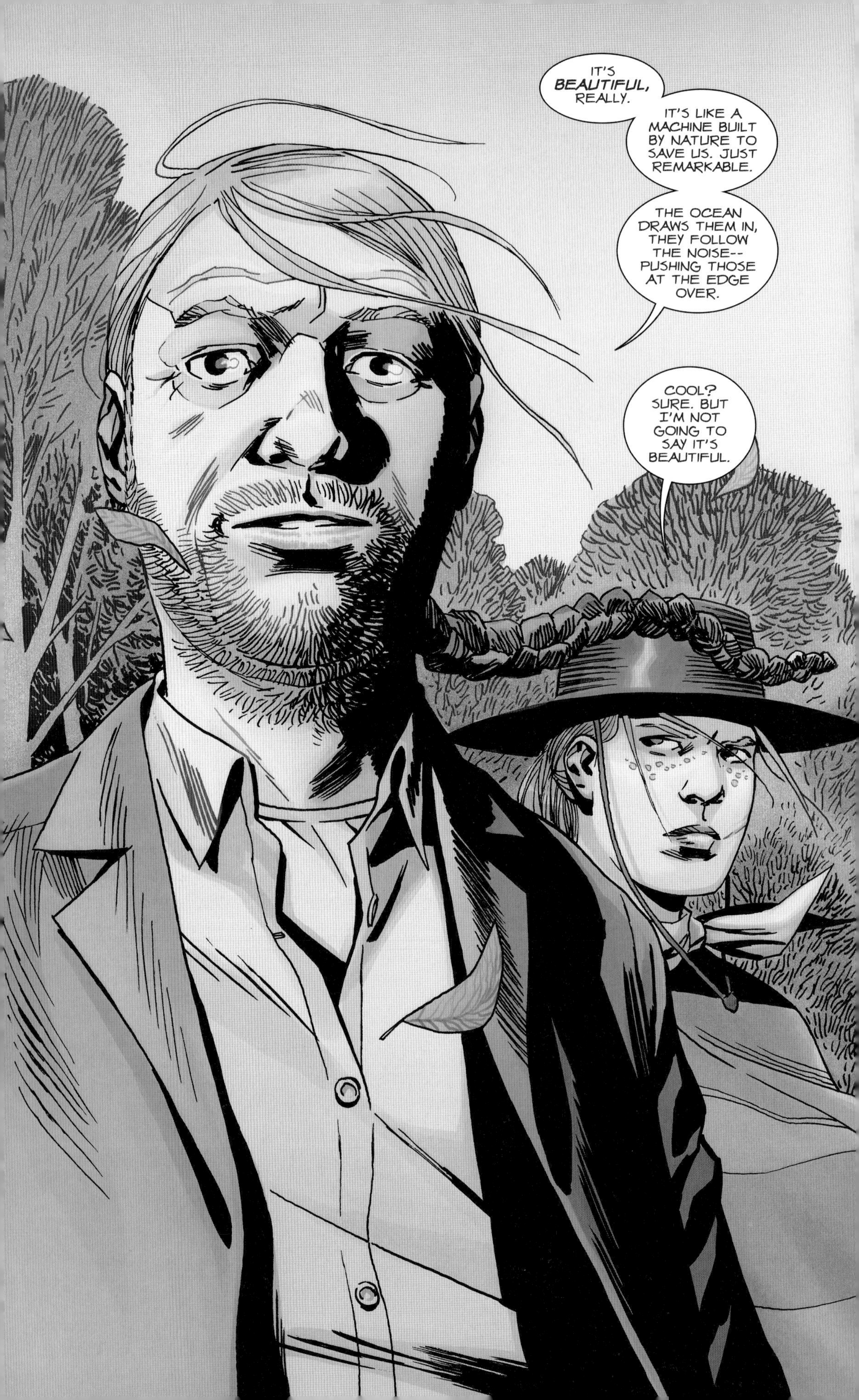
IT'S BEAUTIFUL, REALLY.
IT'S LIKE A MACHINE BUILT BY NATURE TO SAVE US. JUST REMARKABLE.
THE OCEAN DRAWS THEM IN, THEY FOLLOW THE NOISE-- PUSHING THOSE AT THE EDGE OVER.
COOL? SURE. BUT I'M NOT GOING TO SAY IT'S BEAUTIFUL.

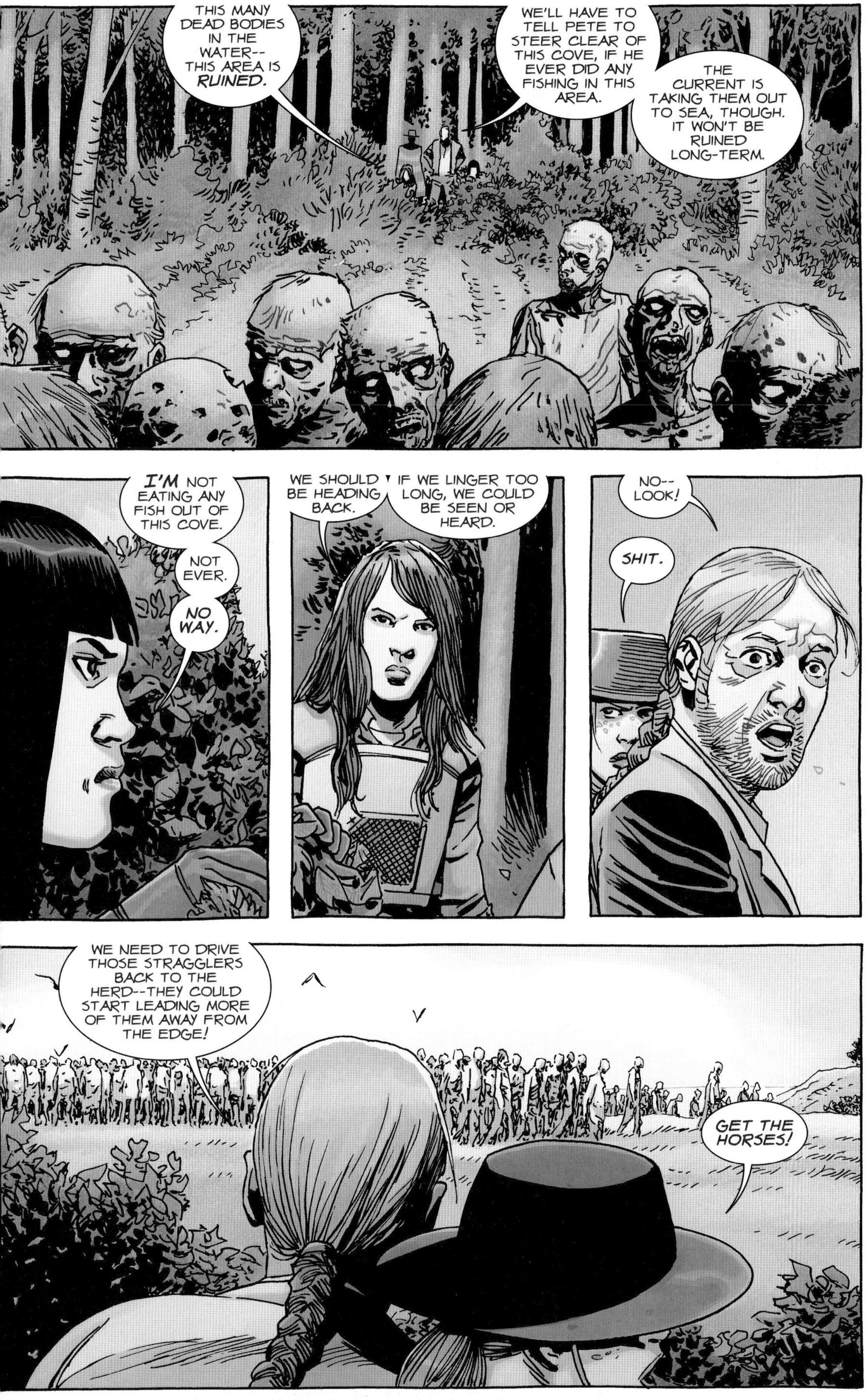
THIS MANY DEAD BODIES IN THE WATER-- THIS AREA IS RUINED.
WE'LL HAVE TO TELL PETE TO STEER CLEAR OF THIS COVE, IF HE EVER DID ANY FISHING IN THIS AREA.
THE CURRENT IS TAKING THEM OUT TO SEA, THOUGH. IT WON'T BE RUINED LONG-TERM.
I'M NOT EATING ANY FISH OUT OF THIS COVE.
NOT EVER.
NO WAY.
WE SHOULD BE HEADING BACK.
IF WE LINGER TOO LONG, WE COULD BE SEEN OR HEARD.
NO-- LOOK!
SHIT.
WE NEED TO DRIVE THOSE STRAGGLERS BACK TO THE HERD--THEY COULD START LEADING MORE OF THEM AWAY FROM THE EDGE!
GET THE HORSES!

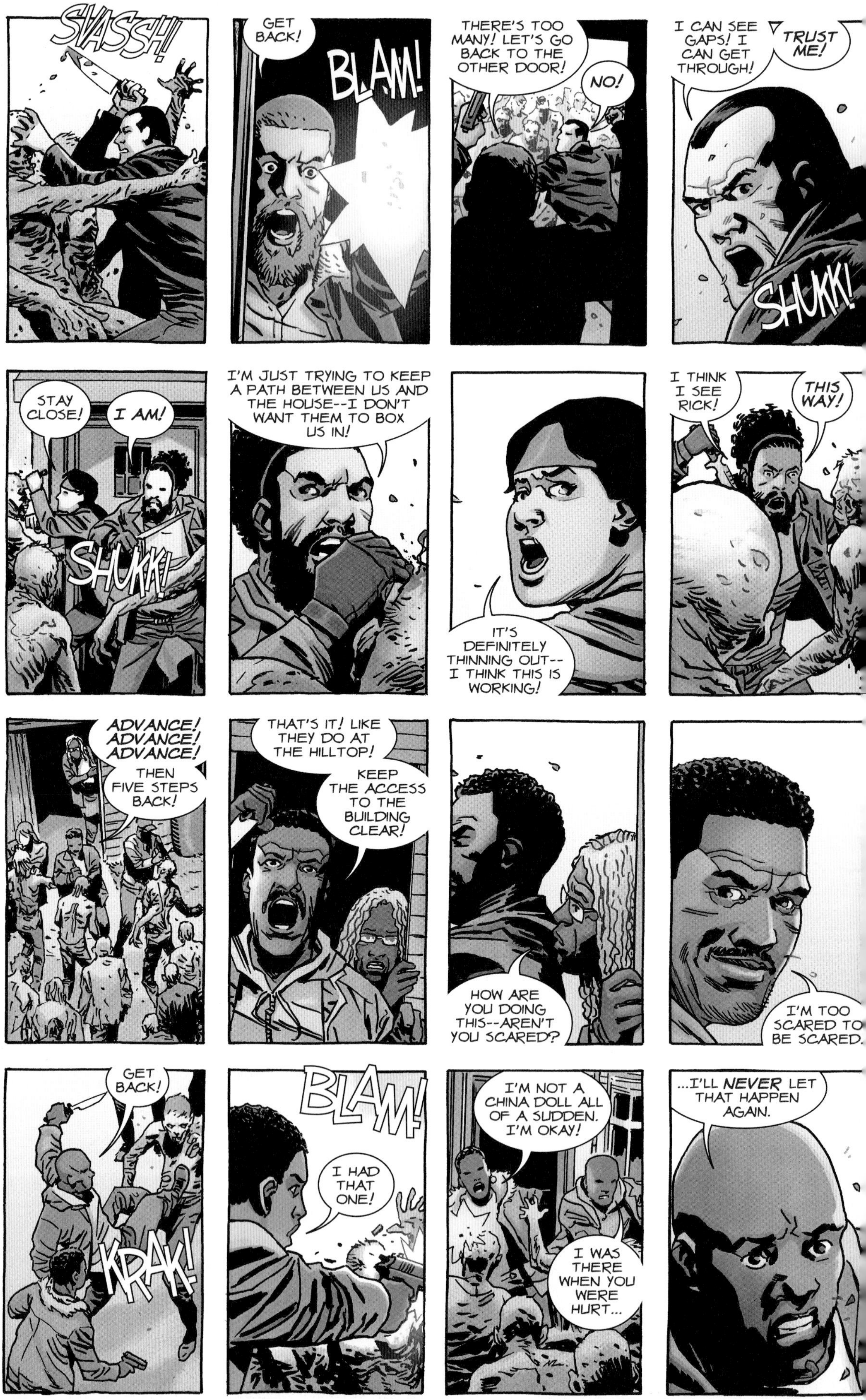
SVASSH!
GET BACK!
BLAM!
THERE'S TOO MANY! LET'S GO BACK TO THE OTHER DOOR!
NO!
I CAN SEE GAPS! I CAN GET THROUGH!
TRUST ME!
SHUKK!
STAY CLOSE!
I AM!
SHUKK!
I'M JUST TRYING TO KEEP A PATH BETWEEN US AND THE HOUSE--I DON'T WANT THEM TO BOX US IN!
IT'S DEFINITELY THINNING OUT-- I THINK THIS IS WORKING!
I THINK I SEE RICK!
THIS WAY!
ADVANCE! ADVANCE! ADVANCE!
THEN FIVE STEPS BACK!
THAT'S IT! LIKE THEY DO AT THE HILLTOP!
KEEP THE ACCESS TO THE BUILDING CLEAR!
HOW ARE YOU DOING THIS--AREN'T YOU SCARED?
I'M TOO SCARED TO BE SCARED.
GET BACK!
KRAK!
BLAM!
I HAD THAT ONE!
I'M NOT A CHINA DOLL ALL OF A SUDDEN. I'M OKAY!
I WAS THERE WHEN YOU WERE HURT...
...I'LL NEVER LET THAT HAPPEN AGAIN.

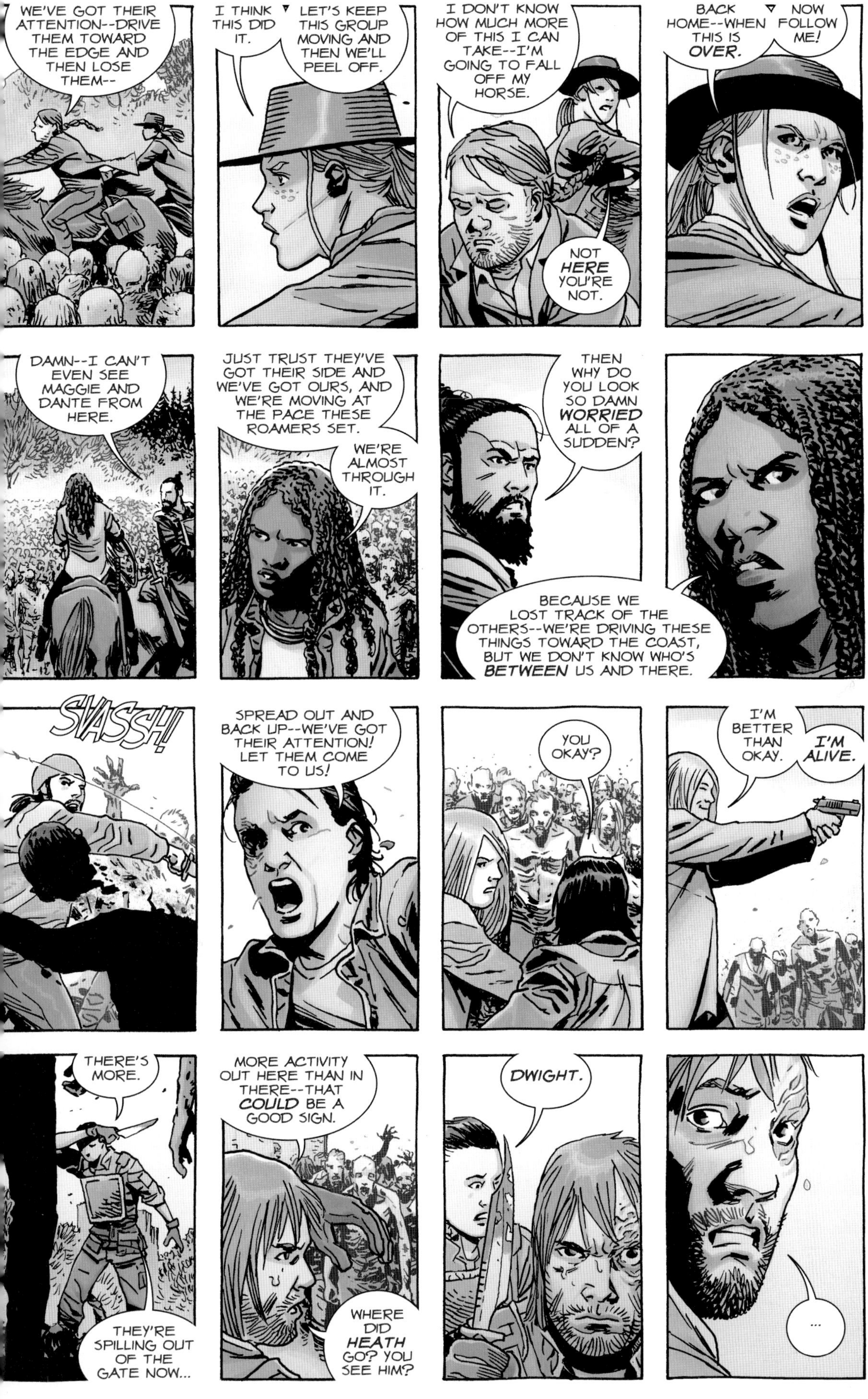
WE'VE GOT THEIR ATTENTION--DRIVE THEM TOWARD THE EDGE AND THEN LOSE THEM--
I THINK THIS DID IT.
LET'S KEEP THIS GROUP MOVING AND THEN WE'LL PEEL OFF.
I DON'T KNOW HOW MUCH MORE OF THIS I CAN TAKE--I'M GOING TO FALL OFF MY HORSE.
NOT HERE YOU'RE NOT.
BACK HOME--WHEN THIS IS OVER.
NOW FOLLOW ME!
DAMN--I CAN'T EVEN SEE MAGGIE AND DANTE FROM HERE.
JUST TRUST THEY'VE GOT THEIR SIDE AND WE'VE GOT OURS, AND WE'RE MOVING AT THE PACE THESE ROAMERS SET.
WE'RE ALMOST THROUGH IT.
THEN WHY DO YOU LOOK SO DAMN WORRIED ALL OF A SUDDEN?
BECAUSE WE LOST TRACK OF THE OTHERS--WE'RE DRIVING THESE THINGS TOWARD THE COAST, BUT WE DON'T KNOW WHO'S BETWEEN US AND THERE.
SVASSH!
SPREAD OUT AND BACK UP--WE'VE GOT THEIR ATTENTION! LET THEM COME TO US!
YOU OKAY?
I'M BETTER THAN OKAY.
I'M ALIVE.
THERE'S MORE.
THEY'RE SPILLING OUT OF THE GATE NOW...
MORE ACTIVITY OUT HERE THAN IN THERE--THAT COULD BE A GOOD SIGN.
WHERE DID HEATH GO? YOU SEE HIM?
DWIGHT.
...

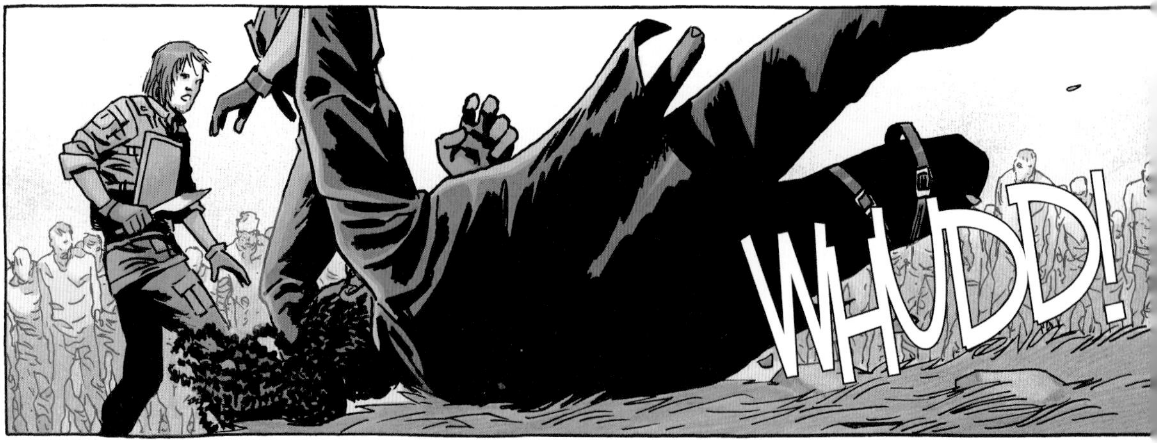
WHUDD!

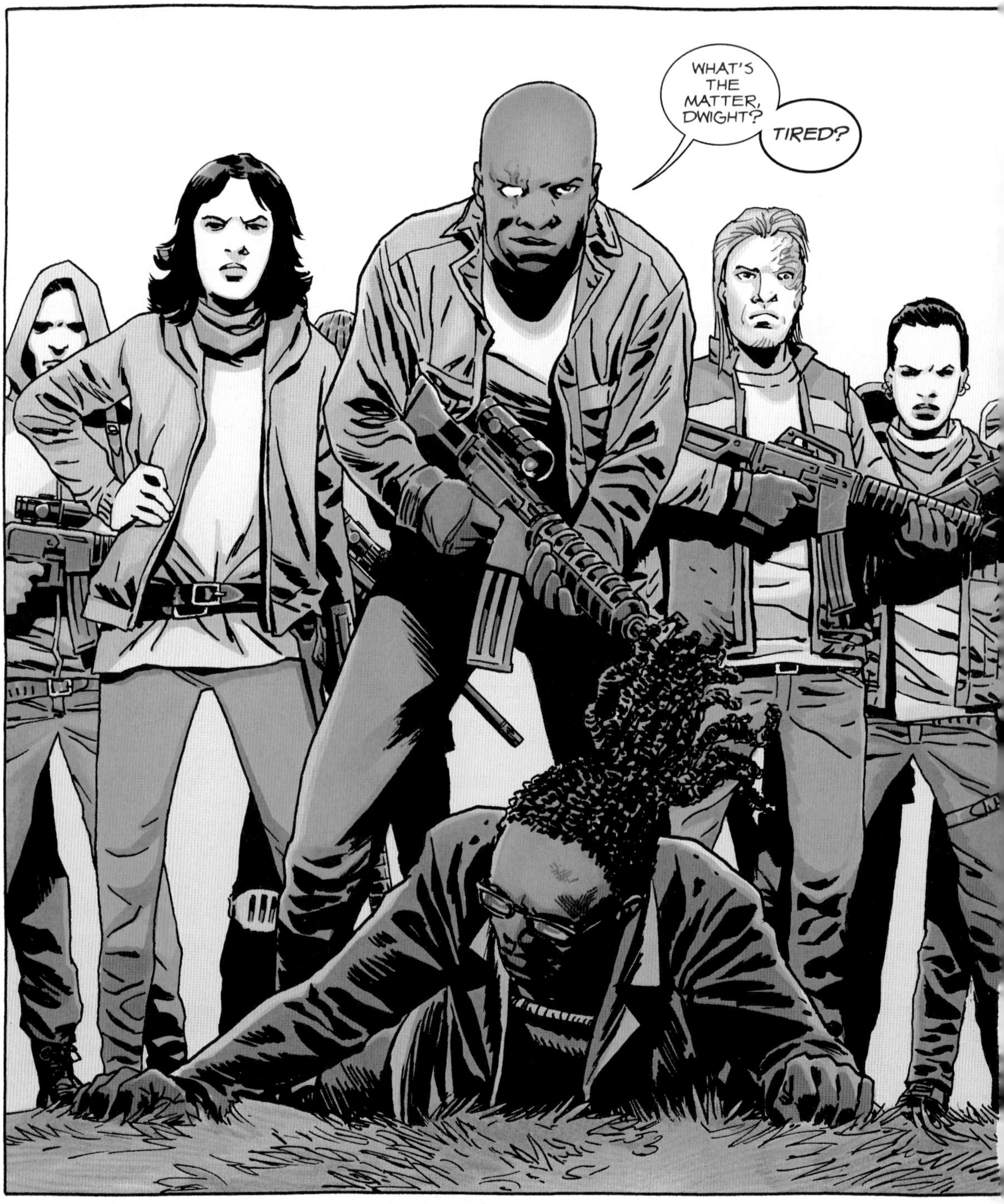
WHAT'S THE MATTER, DWIGHT?
TIRED?

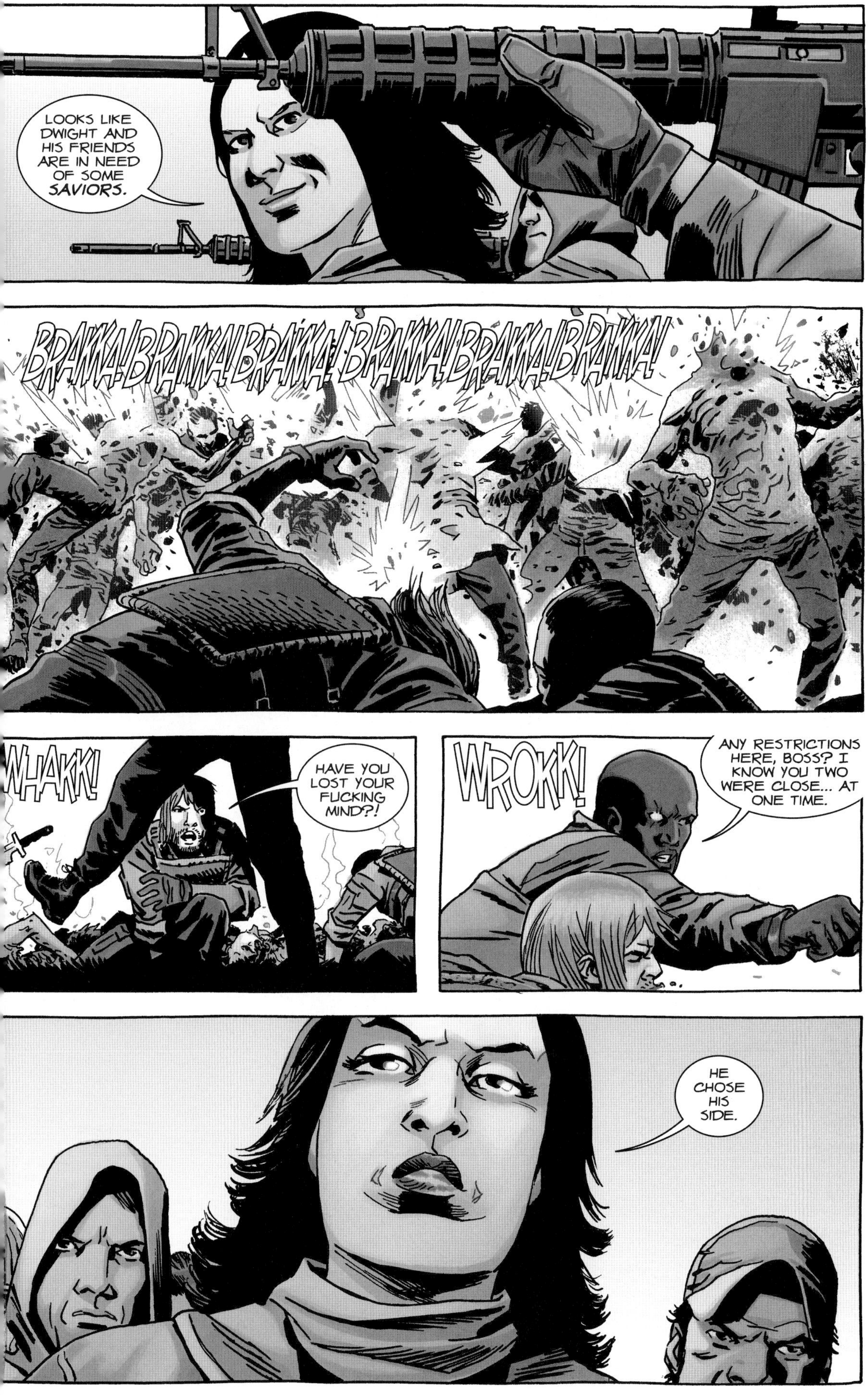

LOOKS LIKE DWIGHT AND HIS FRIENDS ARE IN NEED OF SOME SAVIORS.
BRAKKA! BRAKKA! BRAKKA! BRAKKA! BRAKKA! BRAKKA!
WHAKK!
HAVE YOU LOST YOUR FUCKING MIND?!
WROKK!
ANY RESTRICTIONS HERE, BOSS? I KNOW YOU TWO WERE CLOSE... AT ONE TIME.
HE CHOSE HIS SIDE.

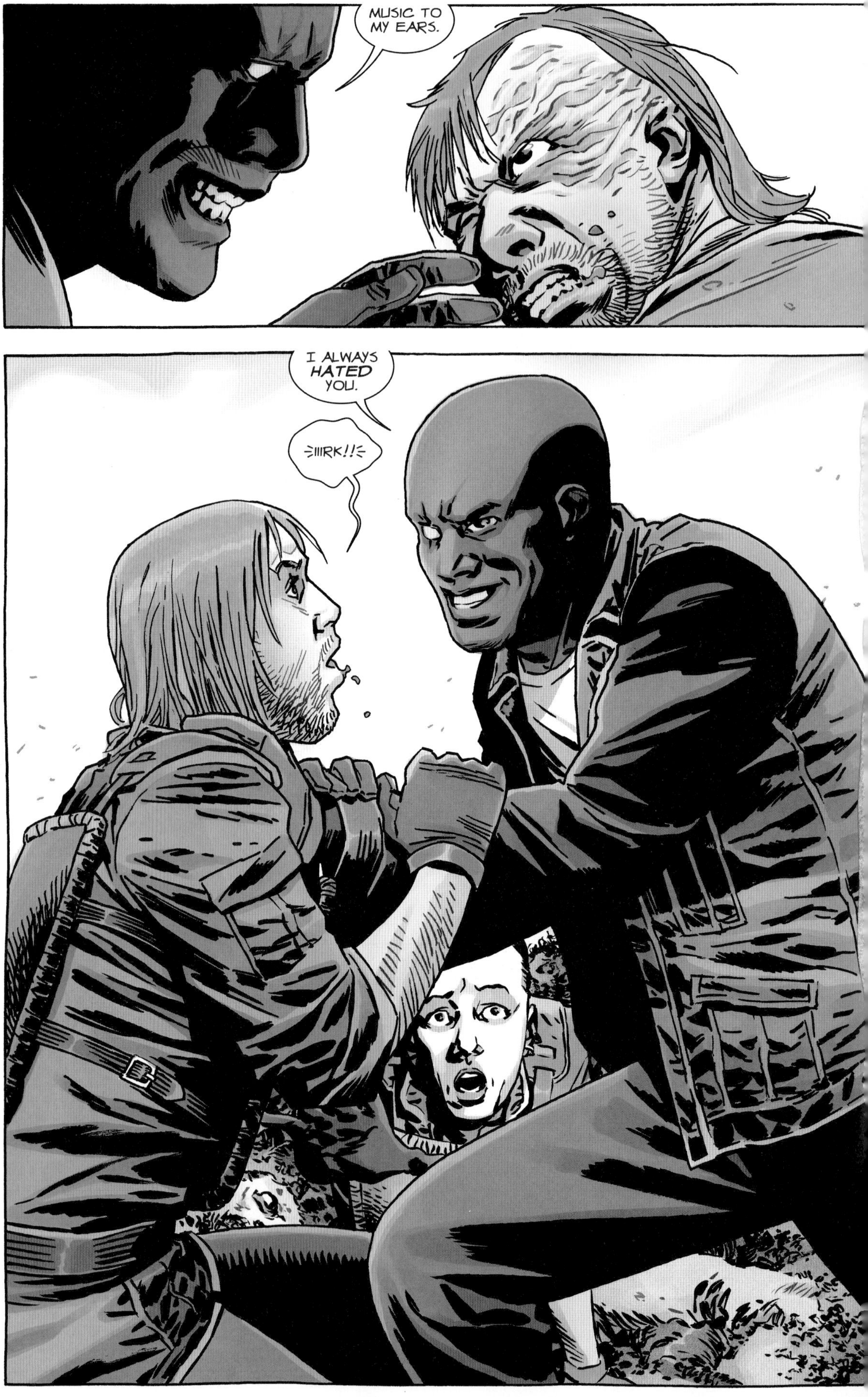
MUSIC TO MY EARS.
I ALWAYS HATED YOU.
IIIRK!!

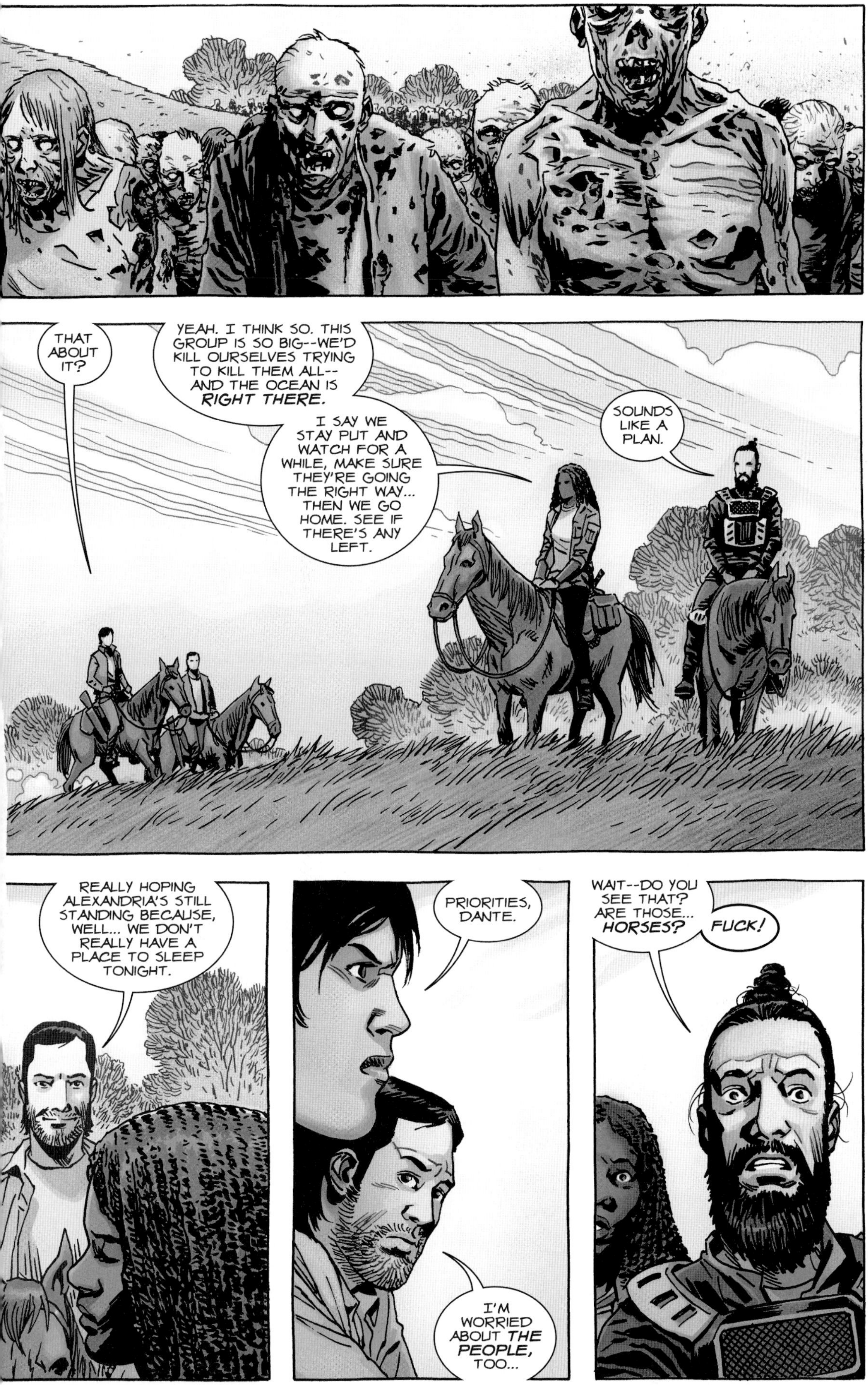
THAT ABOUT IT?
YEAH. I THINK SO. THIS GROUP IS SO BIG--WE'D KILL OURSELVES TRYING TO KILL THEM ALL-- AND THE OCEAN IS RIGHT THERE.
I SAY WE STAY PUT AND WATCH FOR A WHILE, MAKE SURE THEY'RE GOING THE RIGHT WAY... THEN WE GO HOME. SEE IF THERE'S ANY LEFT.
SOUNDS LIKE A PLAN.
REALLY HOPING ALEXANDRIA'S STILL STANDING BECAUSE, WELL... WE DON'T REALLY HAVE A PLACE TO SLEEP TONIGHT.
PRIORITIES, DANTE.
I'M WORRIED ABOUT THE PEOPLE, TOO...
WAIT--DO YOU SEE THAT? ARE THOSE... HORSES?
FUCK!

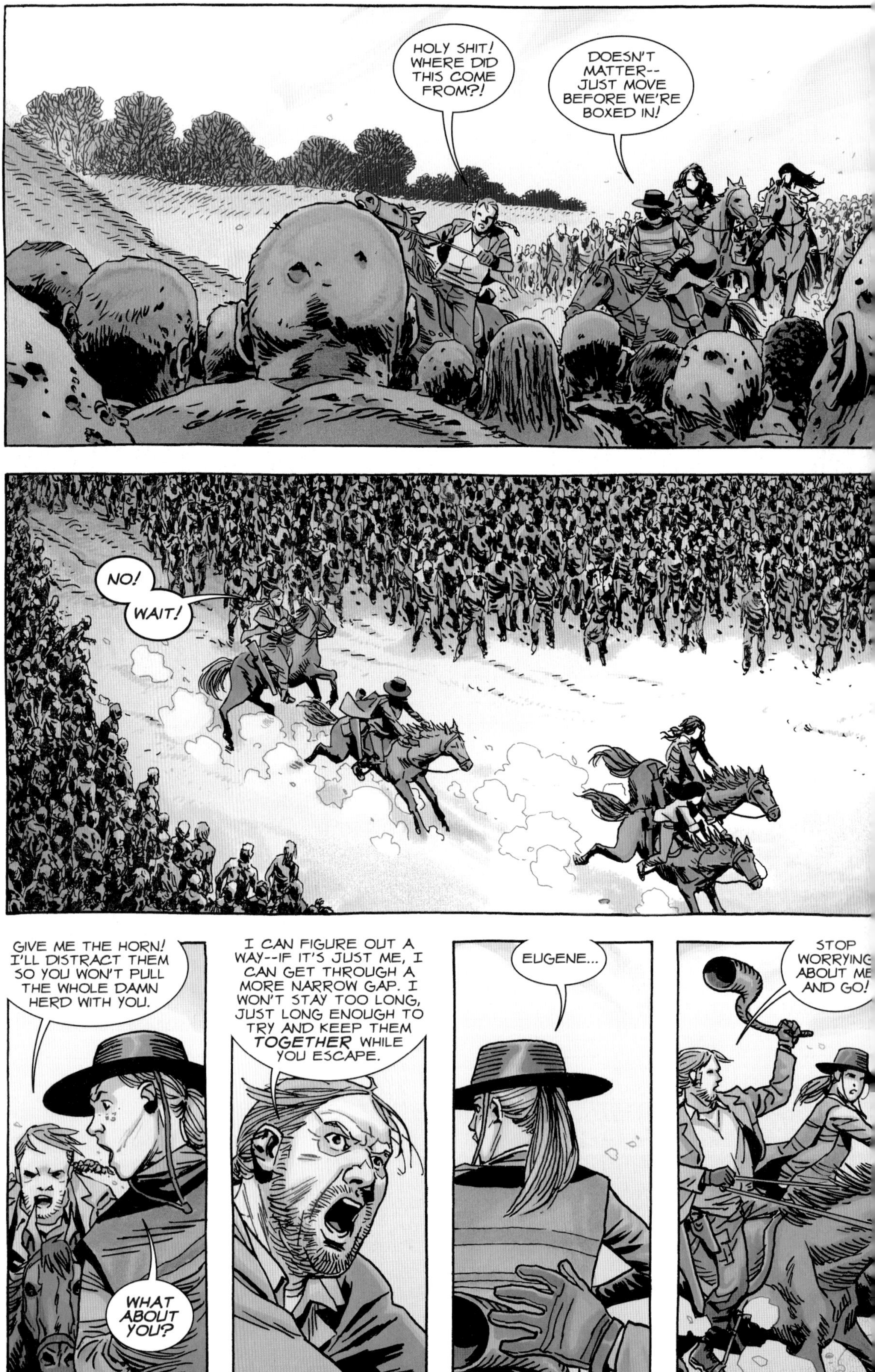
HOLY SHIT! WHERE DID THIS COME FROM?!
DOESN'T MATTER-- JUST MOVE BEFORE WE'RE BOXED IN!
NO!
WAIT!
GIVE ME THE HORN! I'LL DISTRACT THEM SO YOU WON'T PULL THE WHOLE DAMN HERD WITH YOU.
WHAT ABOUT YOU?
I CAN FIGURE OUT A WAY--IF IT'S JUST ME, I CAN GET THROUGH A MORE NARROW GAP. I WON'T STAY TOO LONG, JUST LONG ENOUGH TO TRY AND KEEP THEM TOGETHER WHILE YOU ESCAPE.
EUGENE...
STOP WORRYING ABOUT ME AND GO!

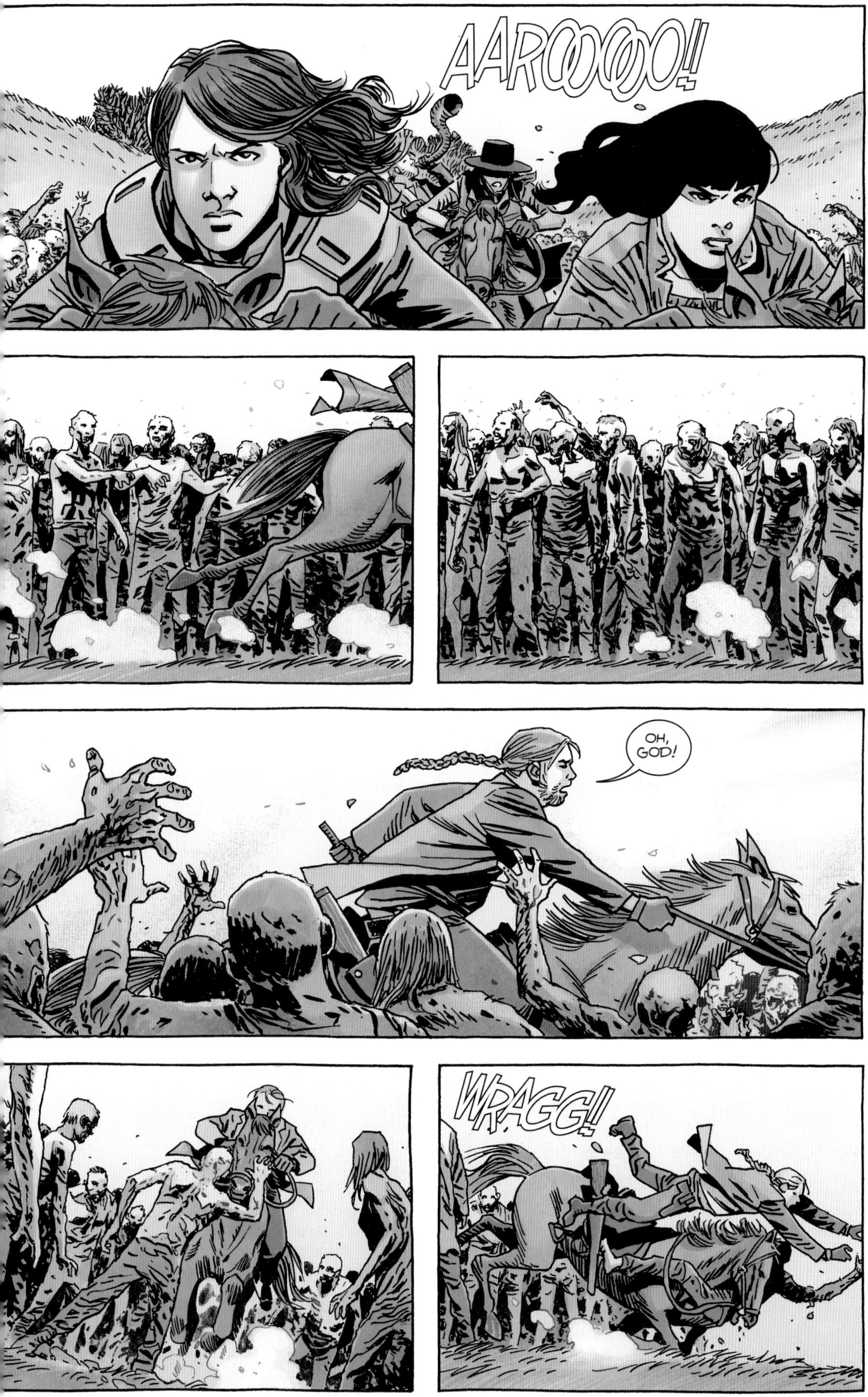
AARGOOOO!!
OH, GOD!
WRAGG!!

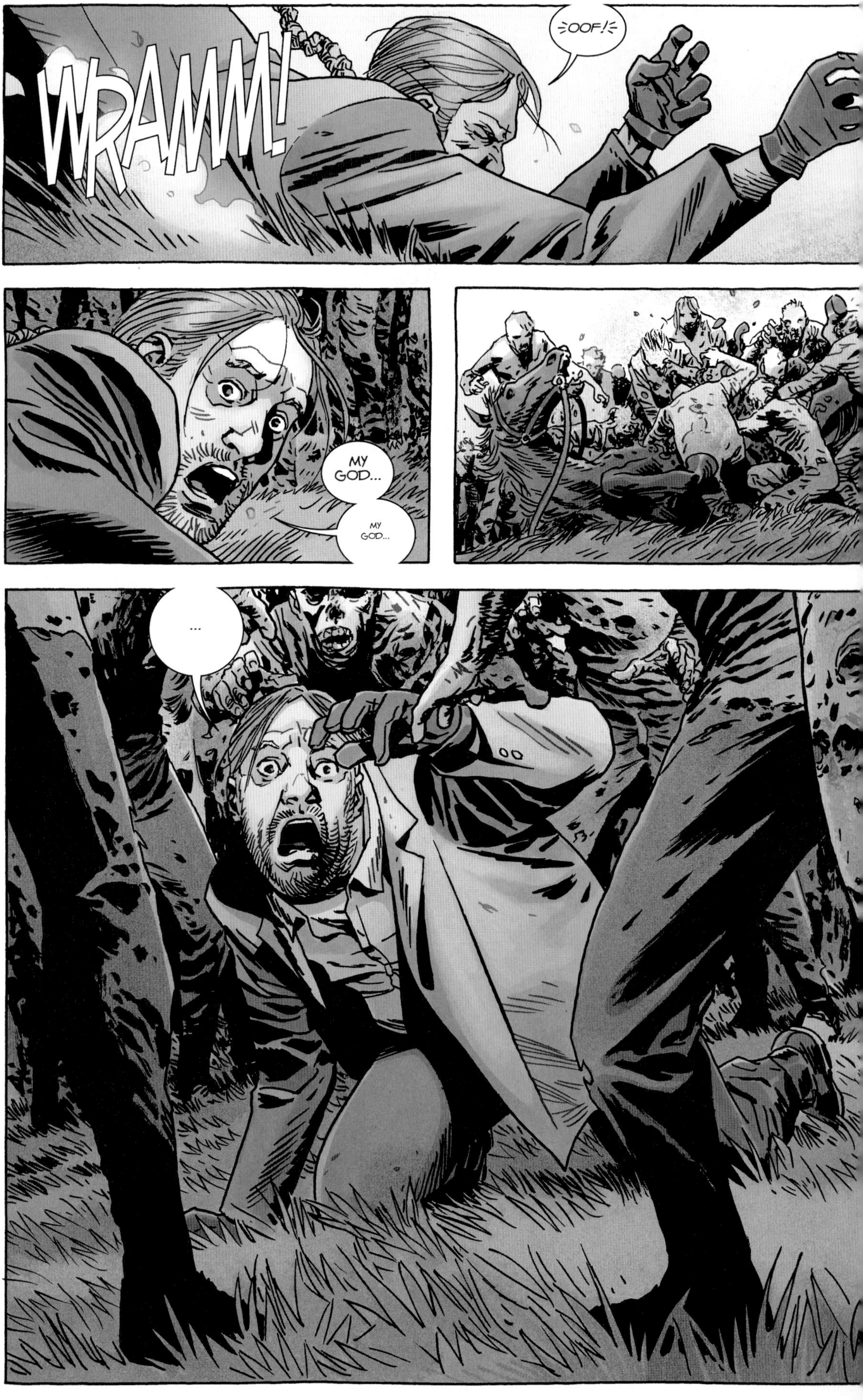

WRAMM!
OOF!
MY GOD...
MY GOD...
...

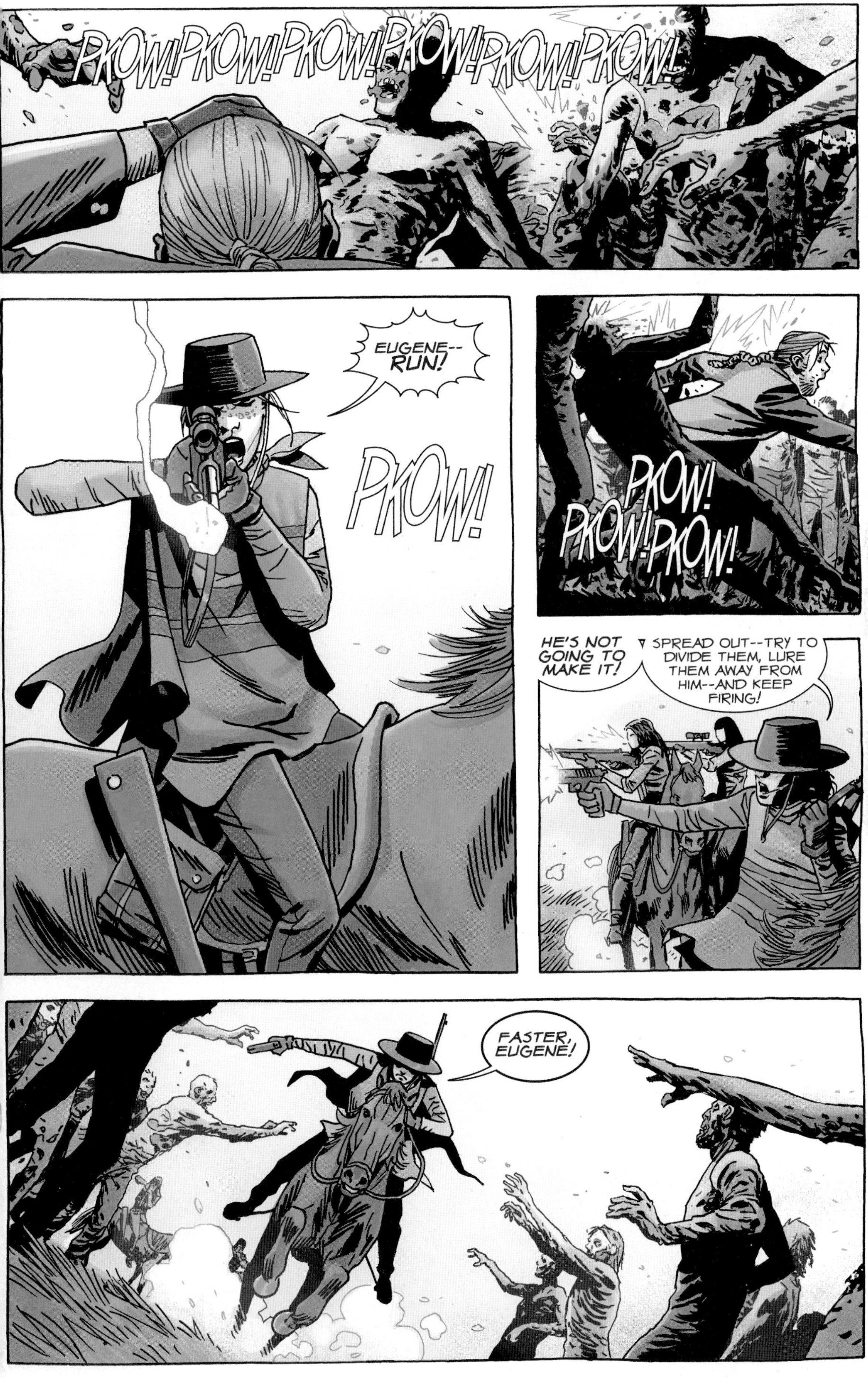
PKOW! PKOW! PKOW! PKOW! PKOW! PKOW!
EUGENE-- RUN!
PKOW!
PKOW! PKOW! PKOW!
HE'S NOT GOING TO MAKE IT!
SPREAD OUT--TRY TO DIVIDE THEM, LURE THEM AWAY FROM HIM--AND KEEP FIRING!
FASTER, EUGENE!

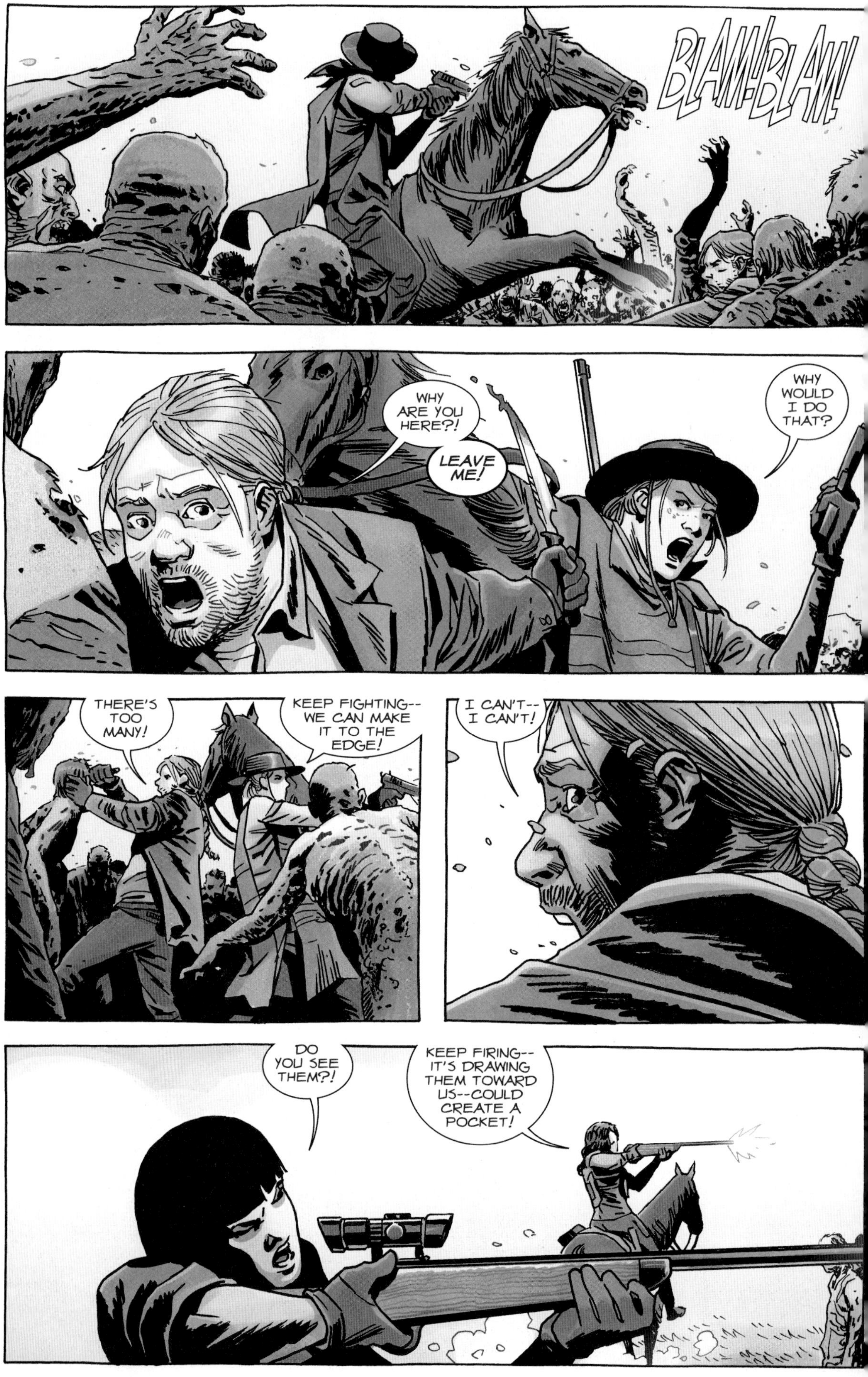
BLAM-BLAM!
WHY ARE YOU HERE?!
LEAVE ME!
WHY WOULD I DO THAT?
THERE'S TOO MANY!
KEEP FIGHTING-- WE CAN MAKE IT TO THE EDGE!
I CAN'T-- I CAN'T!
DO YOU SEE THEM?!
KEEP FIRING-- IT'S DRAWING THEM TOWARD US--COULD CREATE A POCKET!

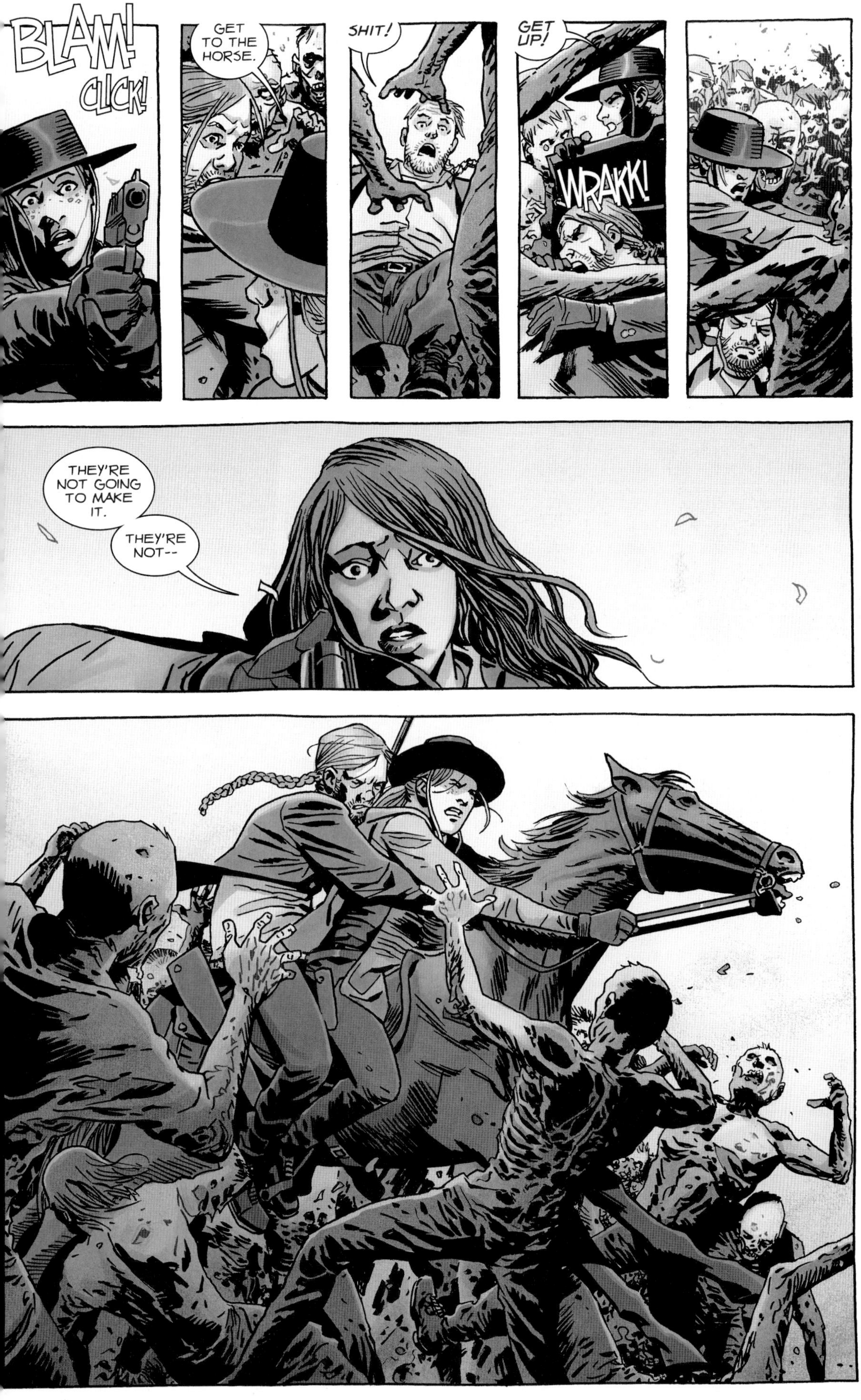
BLAM!
CLICK!
GET TO THE HORSE.
SHIT!
GET UP!
WRAKK!
THEY'RE NOT GOING TO MAKE IT.
THEY'RE NOT--

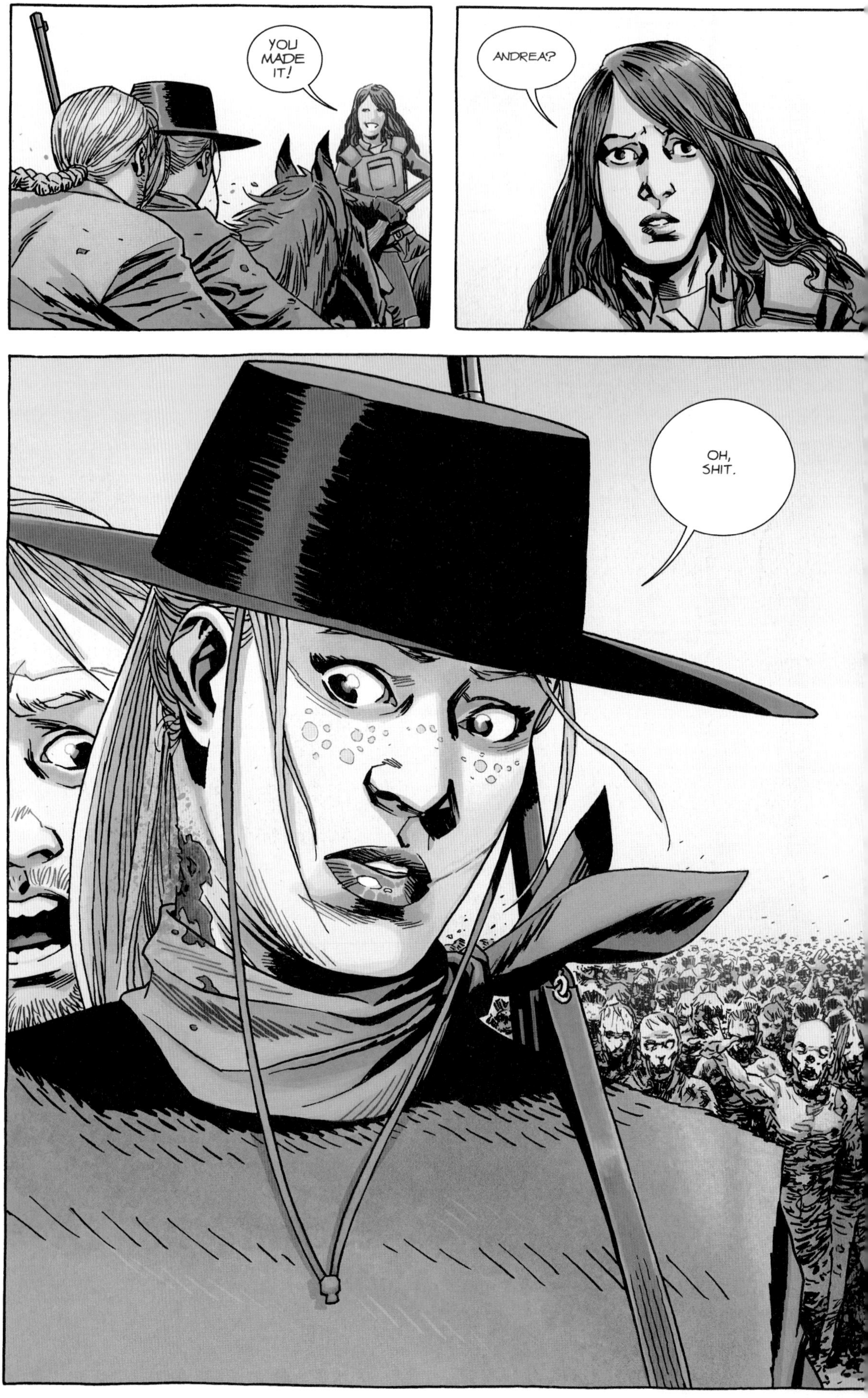
YOU MADE IT!
ANDREA?
OH, SHIT.

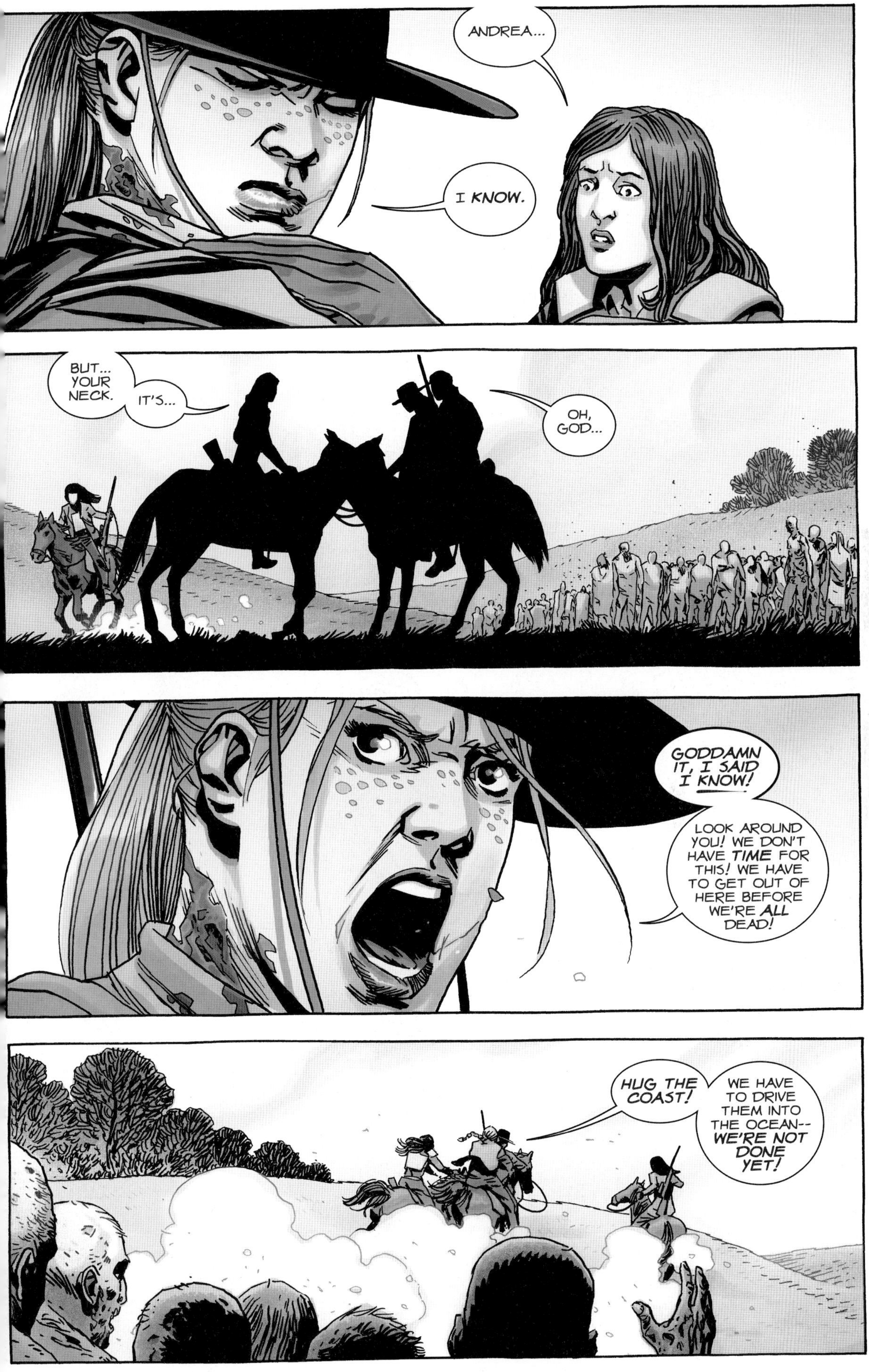
ANDREA...
I KNOW.
BUT... YOUR NECK.
IT'S...
OH, GOD...
GODDAMN IT, I SAID I KNOW!
LOOK AROUND YOU! WE DON'T HAVE TIME FOR THIS! WE HAVE TO GET OUT OF HERE BEFORE WE'RE ALL DEAD!
HUG THE COAST!
WE HAVE TO DRIVE THEM INTO THE OCEAN-- WE'RE NOT DONE YET!

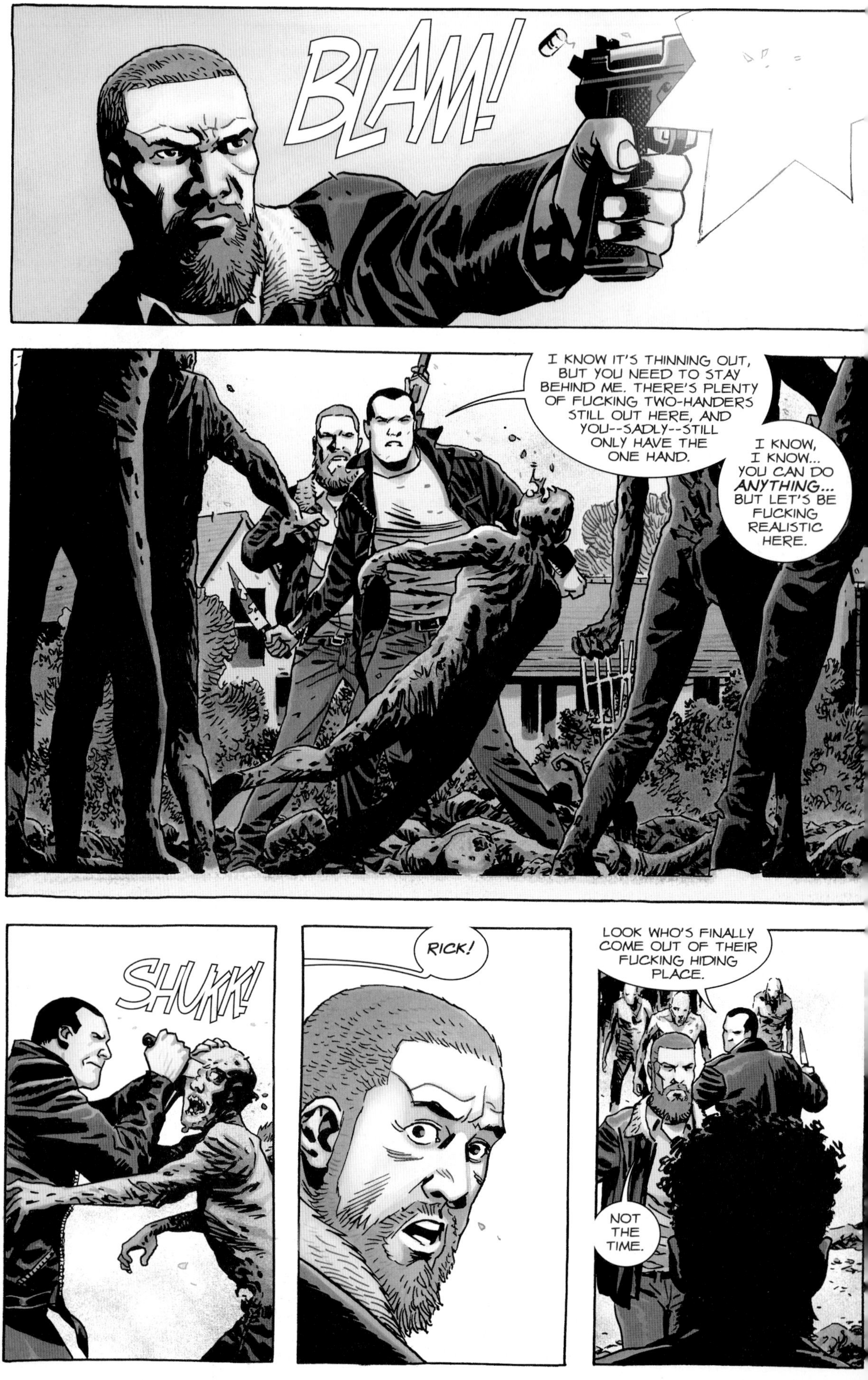
BLAM!
I KNOW IT'S THINNING OUT, BUT YOU NEED TO STAY BEHIND ME. THERE'S PLENTY OF FUCKING TWO-HANDERS STILL OUT HERE, AND YOU--SADLY--STILL ONLY HAVE THE ONE HAND.
I KNOW, I KNOW... YOU CAN DO ANYTHING... BUT LET'S BE FUCKING REALISTIC HERE.
SHUKK!
RICK!
LOOK WHO'S FINALLY COME OUT OF THEIR FUCKING HIDING PLACE.
NOT THE TIME.

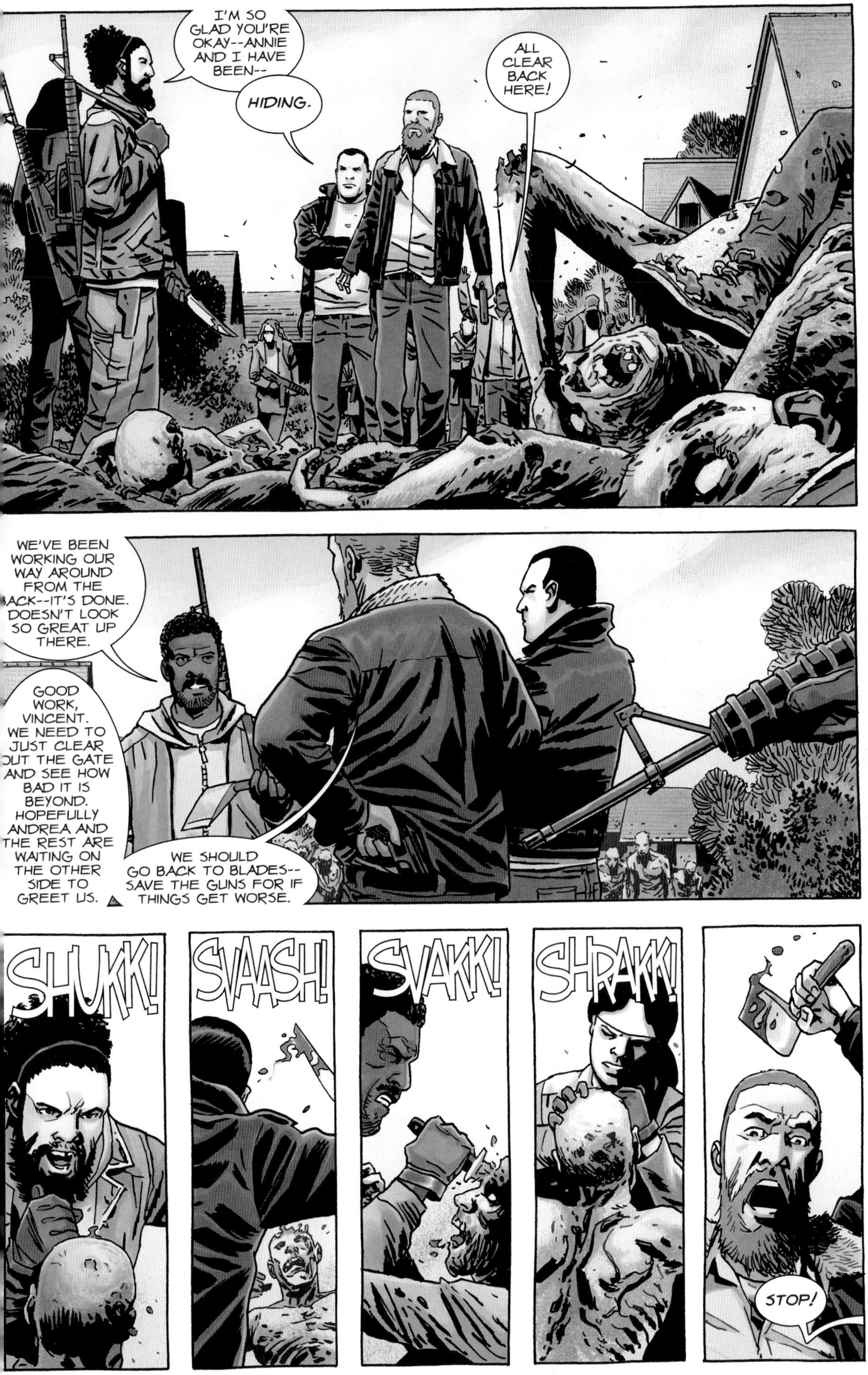
I'M SO GLAD YOU'RE OKAY--ANNIE AND I HAVE BEEN--
HIDING.
ALL CLEAR BACK HERE!
WE'VE BEEN WORKING OUR WAY AROUND FROM THE BACK--IT'S DONE. DOESN'T LOOK SO GREAT UP THERE.
GOOD WORK, VINCENT. WE NEED TO JUST CLEAR OUT THE GATE AND SEE HOW BAD IT IS BEYOND. HOPEFULLY ANDREA AND THE REST ARE WAITING ON THE OTHER SIDE TO GREET US.
WE SHOULD GO BACK TO BLADES-- SAVE THE GUNS FOR IF THINGS GET WORSE.
SHUKK!
SVAASH!
SVAKK!
SHRAKK!
STOP!

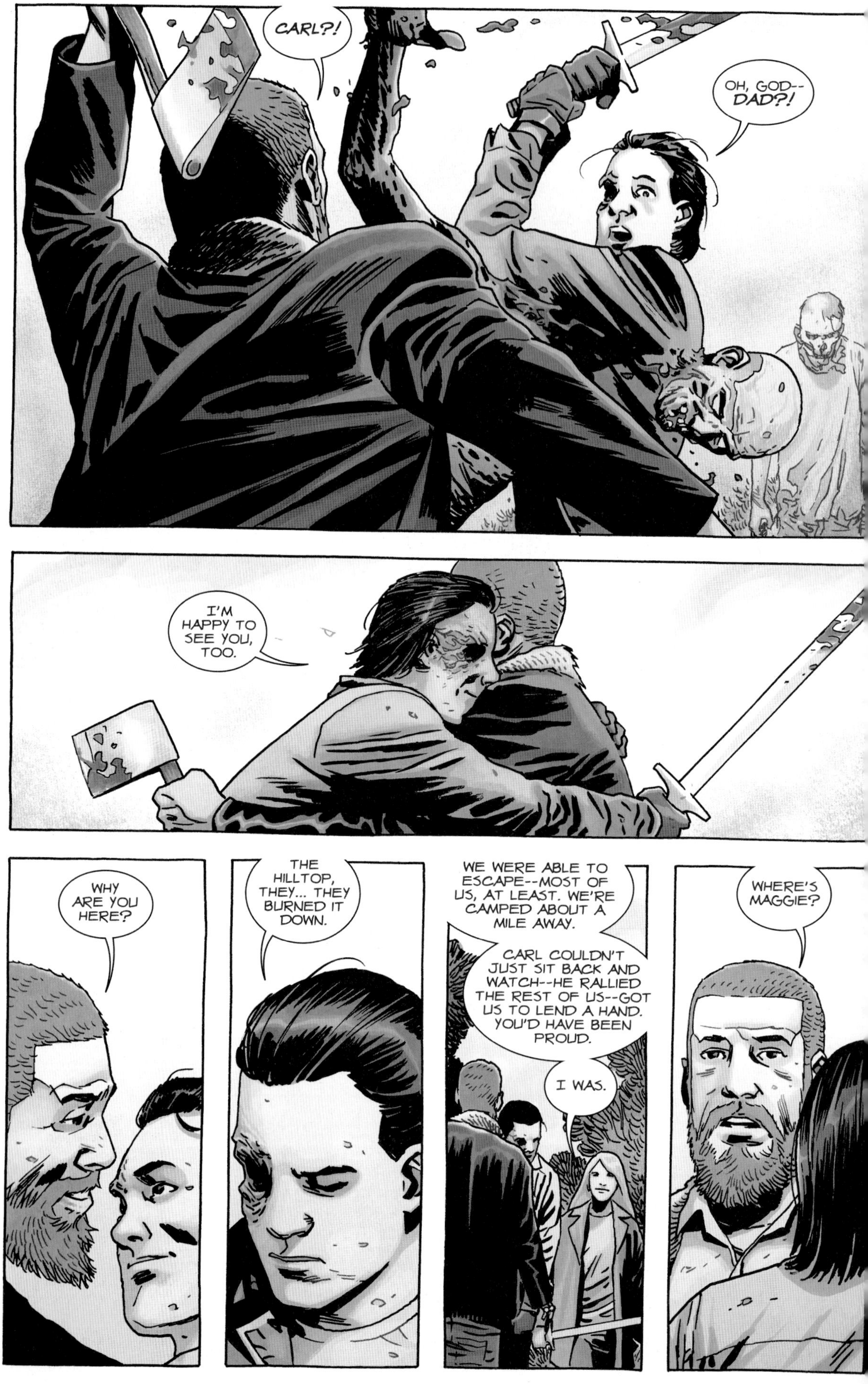
CARL?!
OH, GOD-- DAD?!
I'M HAPPY TO SEE YOU, TOO.
WHY ARE YOU HERE?
THE HILLTOP, THEY... THEY BURNED IT DOWN.
WE WERE ABLE TO ESCAPE--MOST OF US, AT LEAST. WE'RE CAMPED ABOUT A MILE AWAY.
CARL COULDN'T JUST SIT BACK AND WATCH--HE RALLIED THE REST OF US--GOT US TO LEND A HAND. YOU'D HAVE BEEN PROUD.
I WAS.
WHERE'S MAGGIE?

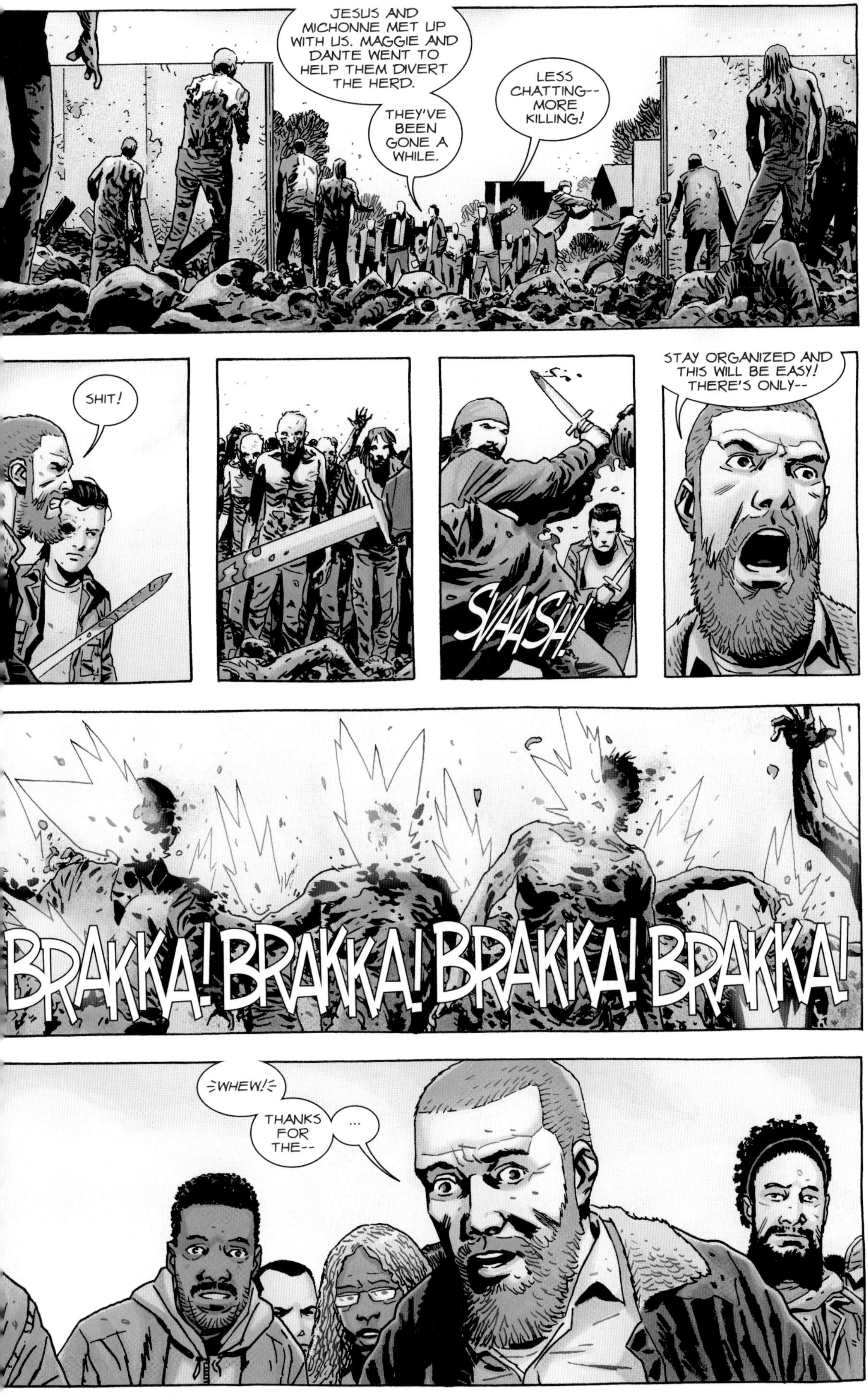
JESUS AND MICHONNE MET UP WITH US. MAGGIE AND DANTE WENT TO HELP THEM DIVERT THE HERD.
THEY'VE BEEN GONE A WHILE.
LESS CHATTING-- MORE KILLING!
SHIT!
SVAASH!
STAY ORGANIZED AND THIS WILL BE EASY! THERE'S ONLY--
BRAKKA! BRAKKA! BRAKKA! BRAKKA!
WHEW!
THANKS FOR THE--
...

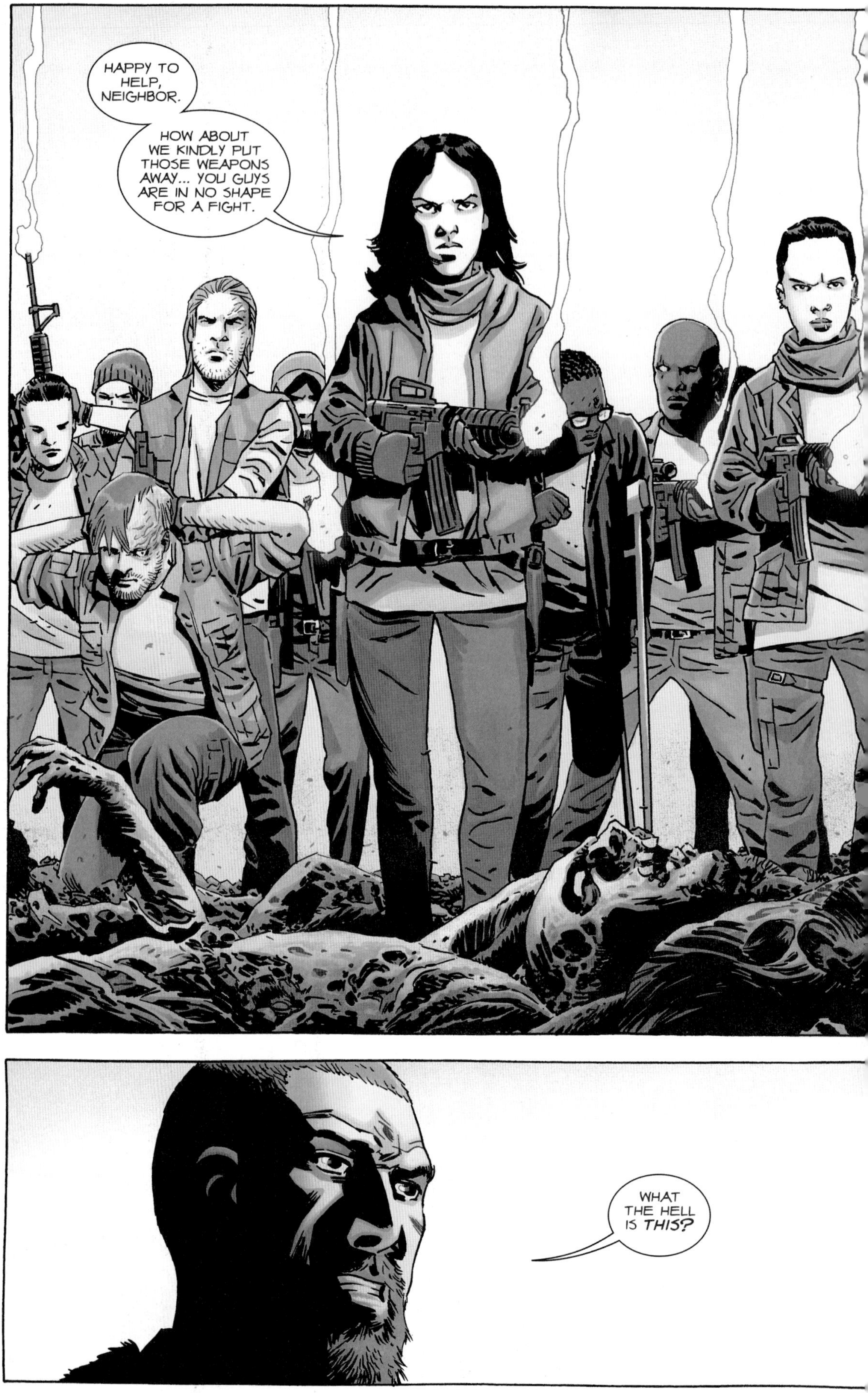
HAPPY TO HELP, NEIGHBOR.
HOW ABOUT WE KINDLY PUT THOSE WEAPONS AWAY... YOU GUYS ARE IN NO SHAPE FOR A FIGHT.
WHAT THE HELL IS *THIS?*

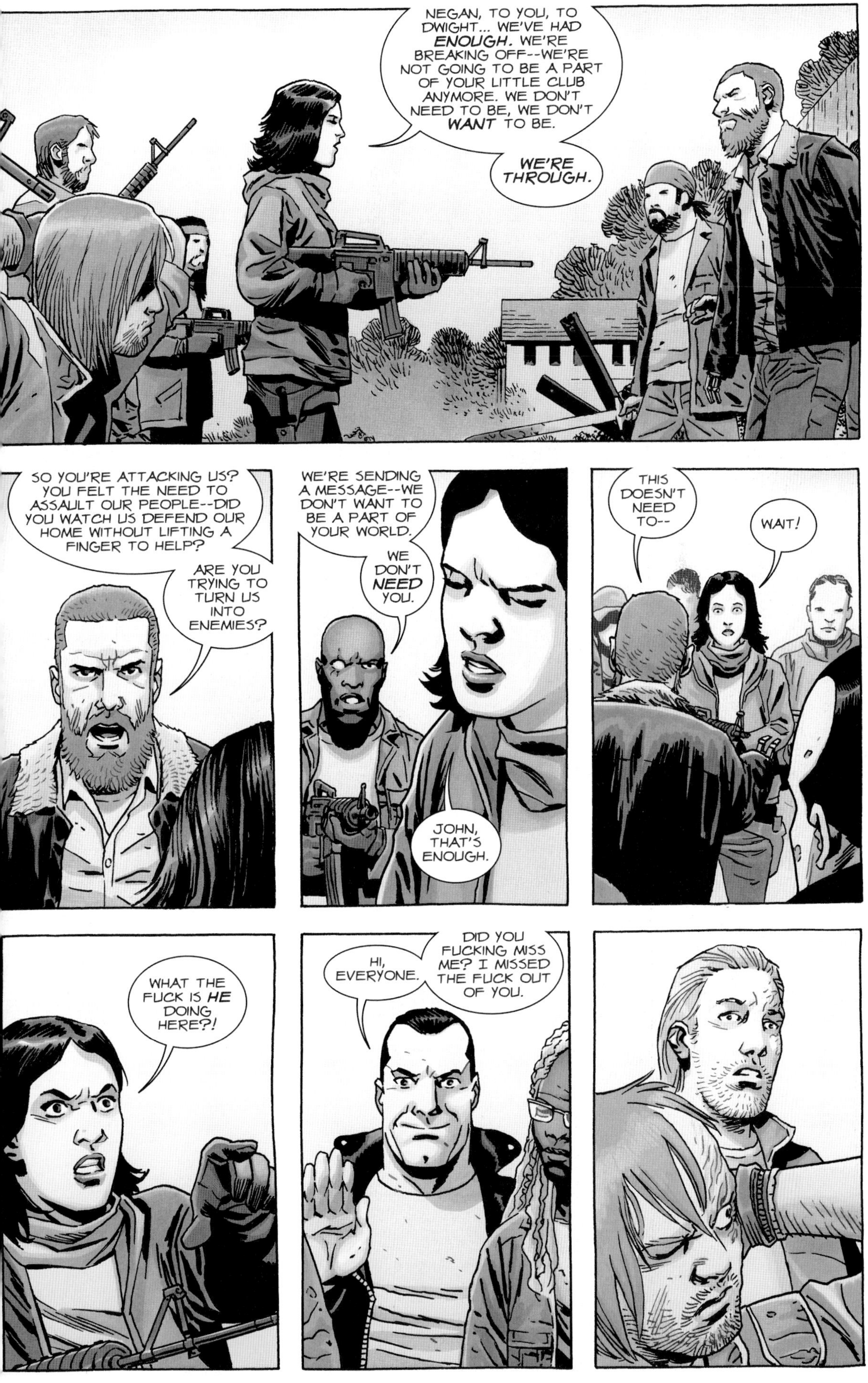
NEGAN, TO YOU, TO DWIGHT... WE'VE HAD ENOUGH. WE'RE BREAKING OFF--WE'RE NOT GOING TO BE A PART OF YOUR LITTLE CLUB ANYMORE. WE DON'T NEED TO BE, WE DON'T WANT TO BE.
WE'RE THROUGH.
SO YOU'RE ATTACKING US? YOU FELT THE NEED TO ASSAULT OUR PEOPLE--DID YOU WATCH US DEFEND OUR HOME WITHOUT LIFTING A FINGER TO HELP?
ARE YOU TRYING TO TURN US INTO ENEMIES?
WE'RE SENDING A MESSAGE--WE DON'T WANT TO BE A PART OF YOUR WORLD.
WE DON'T NEED YOU.
JOHN, THAT'S ENOUGH.
THIS DOESN'T NEED TO--
WAIT!
WHAT THE FUCK IS HE DOING HERE?!
HI, EVERYONE.
DID YOU FUCKING MISS ME? I MISSED THE FUCK OUT OF YOU.

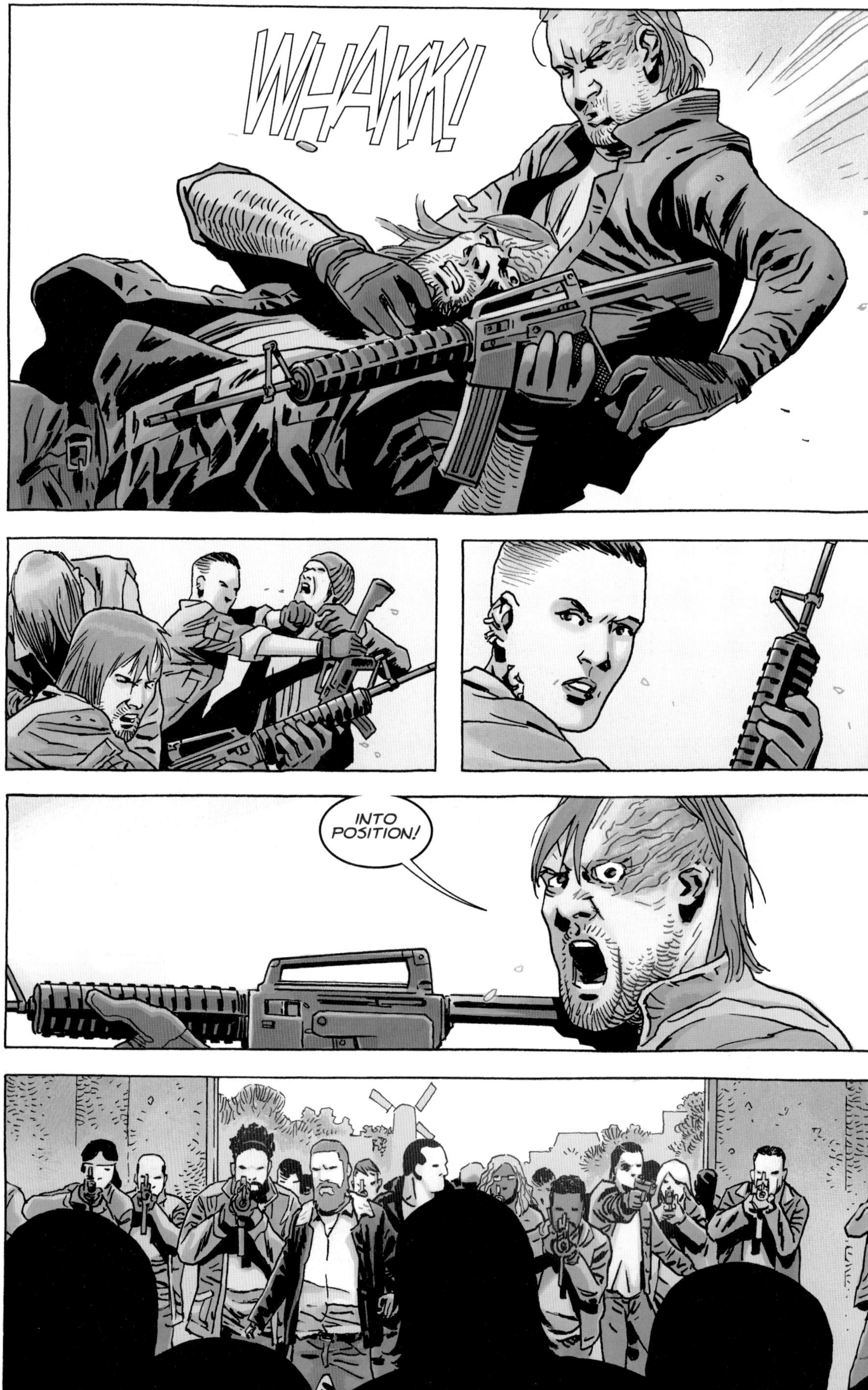
WHAKK!
INTO POSITION!

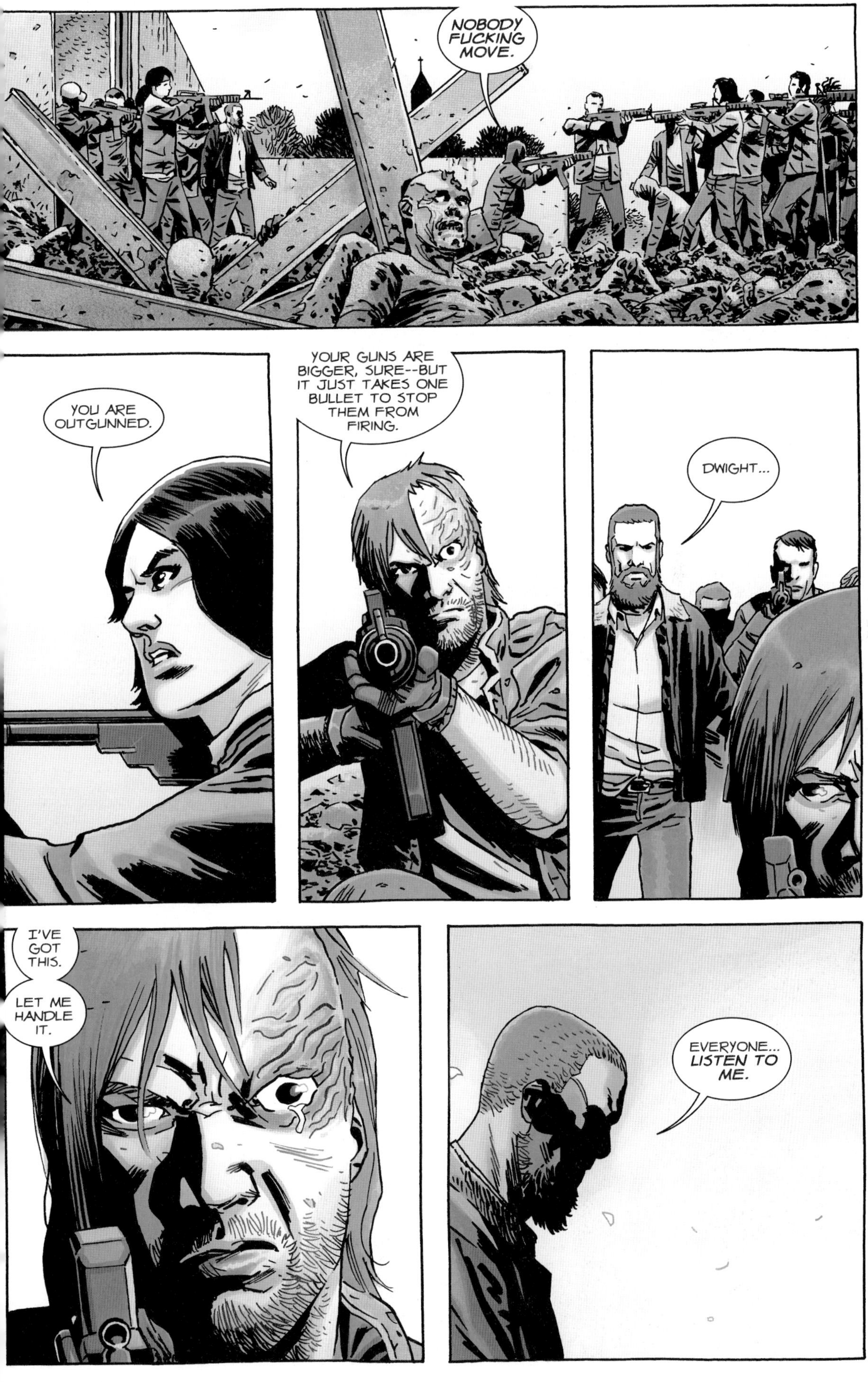
NOBODY FUCKING MOVE.
YOU ARE OUTGUNNED.
YOUR GUNS ARE BIGGER, SURE--BUT IT JUST TAKES ONE BULLET TO STOP THEM FROM FIRING.
DWIGHT...
I'VE GOT THIS.
LET ME HANDLE IT.
EVERYONE... LISTEN TO ME.

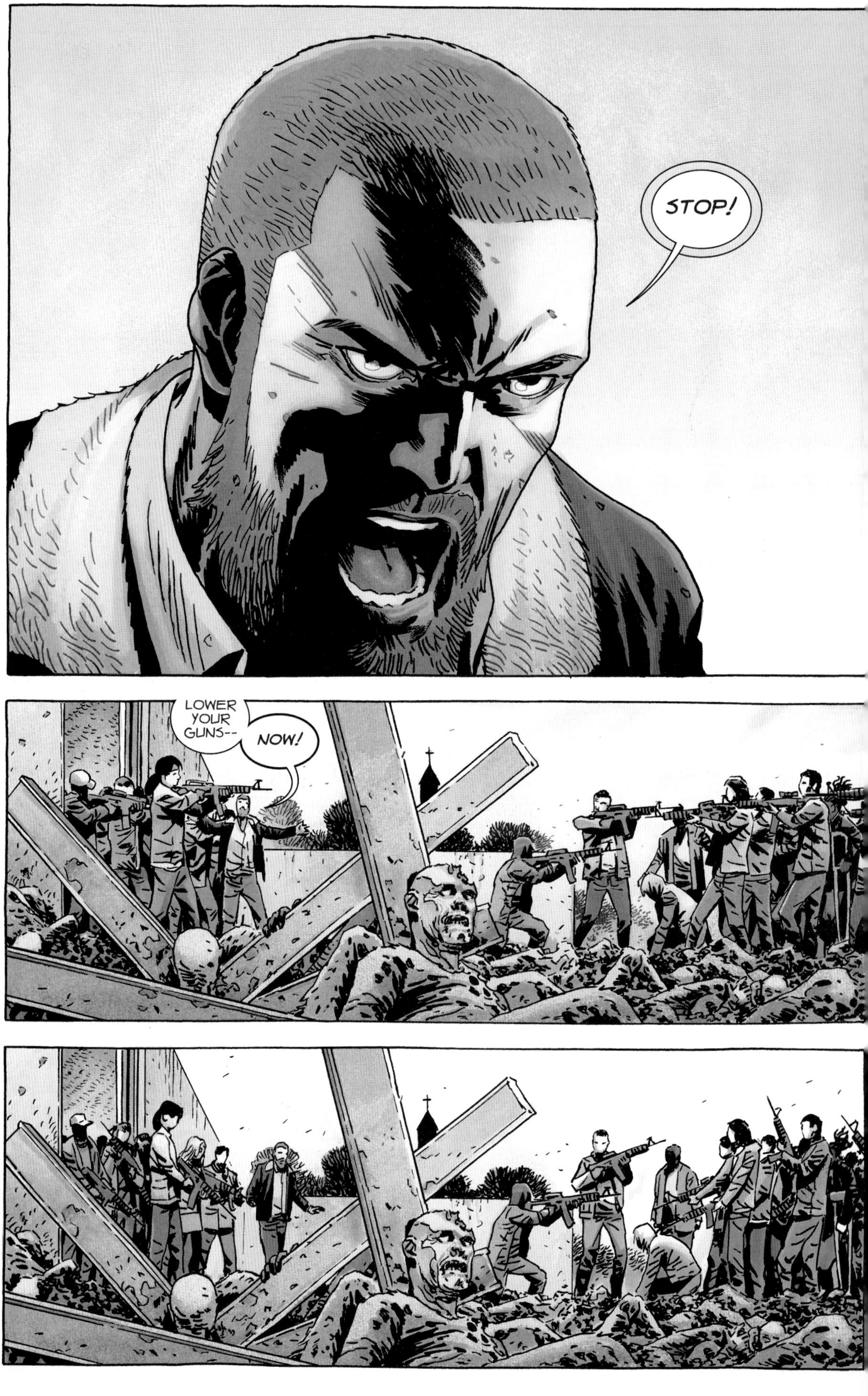
STOP!
LOWER YOUR GUNS--
NOW!

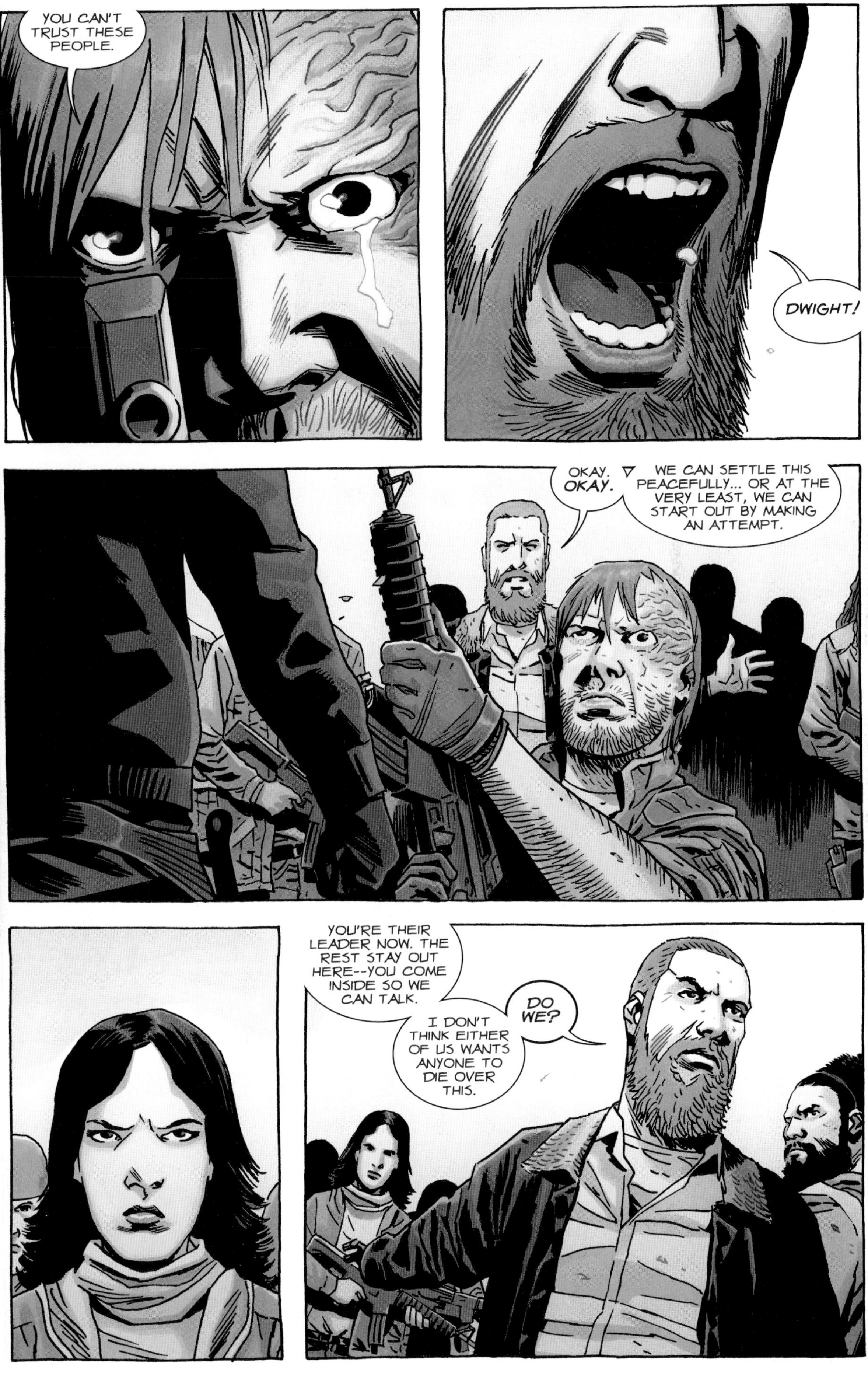
YOU CAN'T TRUST THESE PEOPLE.
DWIGHT!
OKAY. OKAY.
WE CAN SETTLE THIS PEACEFULLY... OR AT THE VERY LEAST, WE CAN START OUT BY MAKING AN ATTEMPT.
YOU'RE THEIR LEADER NOW. THE REST STAY OUT HERE--YOU COME INSIDE SO WE CAN TALK.
I DON'T THINK EITHER OF US WANTS ANYONE TO DIE OVER THIS.
DO WE?

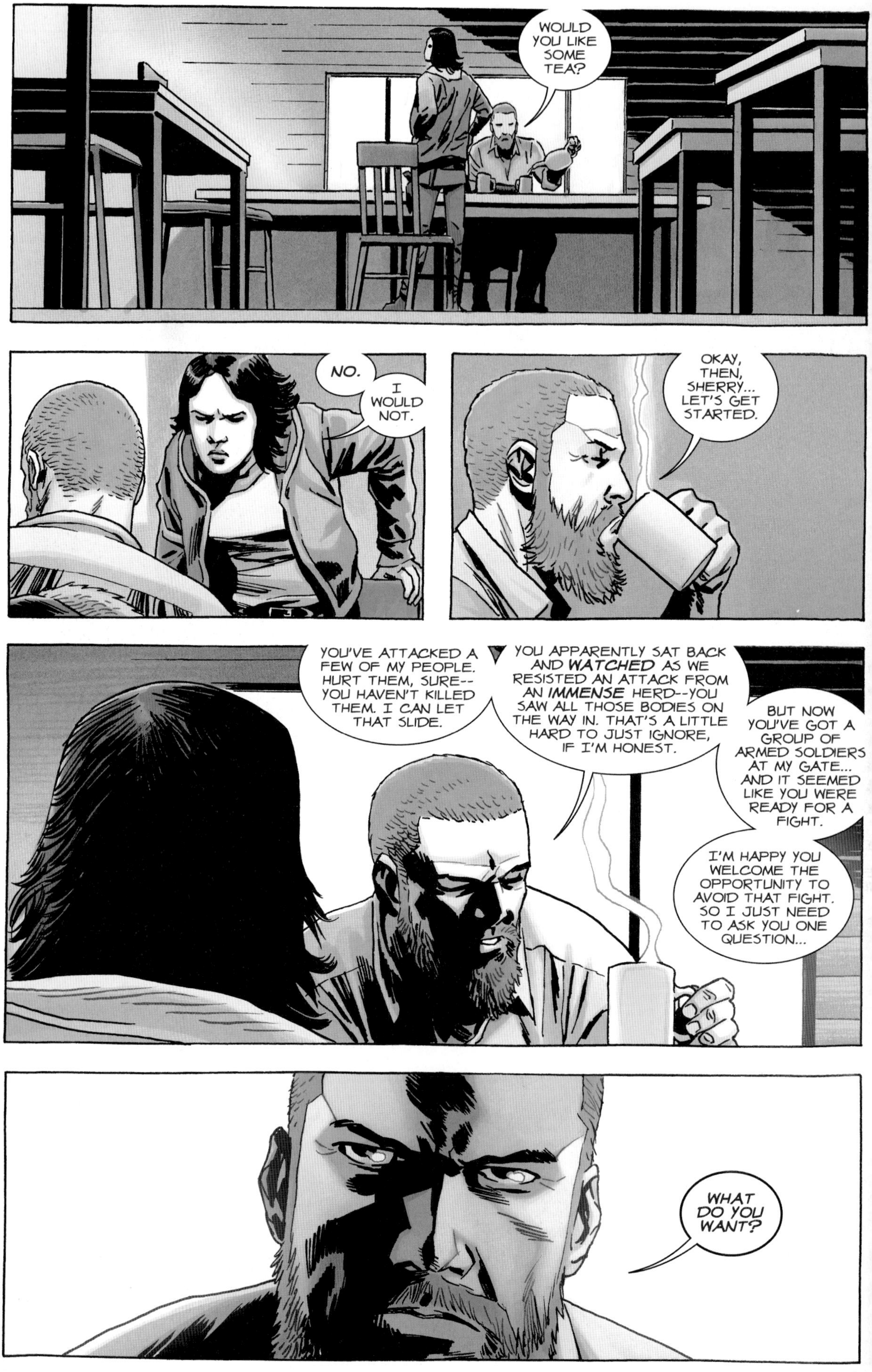
WOULD YOU LIKE SOME TEA?
NO.
I WOULD NOT.
OKAY, THEN, SHERRY... LET'S GET STARTED.
YOU'VE ATTACKED A FEW OF MY PEOPLE. HURT THEM, SURE-- YOU HAVEN'T KILLED THEM. I CAN LET THAT SLIDE.
YOU APPARENTLY SAT BACK AND WATCHED AS WE RESISTED AN ATTACK FROM AN IMMENSE HERD--YOU SAW ALL THOSE BODIES ON THE WAY IN. THAT'S A LITTLE HARD TO JUST IGNORE, IF I'M HONEST.
BUT NOW YOU'VE GOT A GROUP OF ARMED SOLDIERS AT MY GATE... AND IT SEEMED LIKE YOU WERE READY FOR A FIGHT.
I'M HAPPY YOU WELCOME THE OPPORTUNITY TO AVOID THAT FIGHT. SO I JUST NEED TO ASK YOU ONE QUESTION...
WHAT DO YOU WANT?

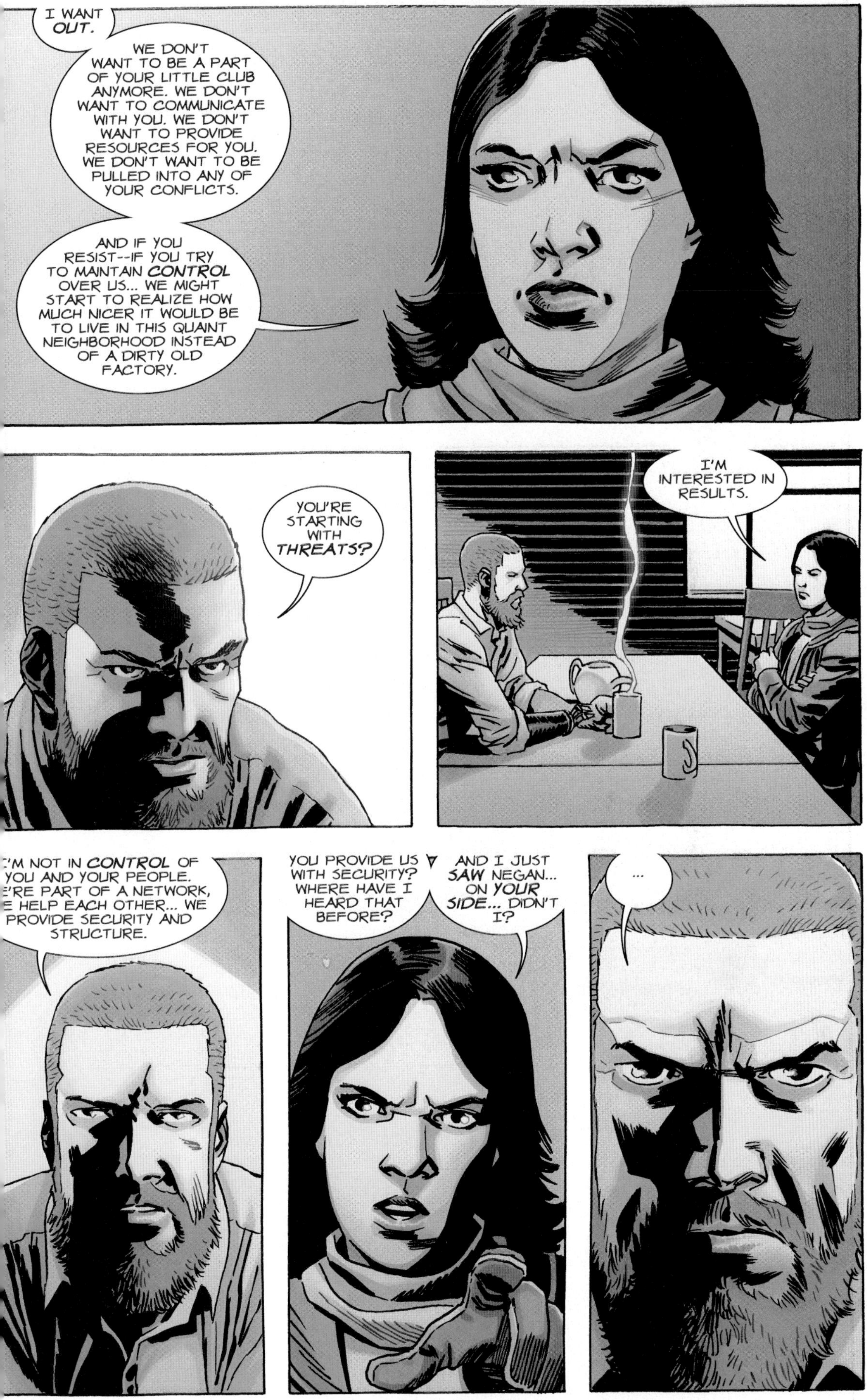
I WANT OUT.
WE DON'T WANT TO BE A PART OF YOUR LITTLE CLUB ANYMORE. WE DON'T WANT TO COMMUNICATE WITH YOU. WE DON'T WANT TO PROVIDE RESOURCES FOR YOU. WE DON'T WANT TO BE PULLED INTO ANY OF YOUR CONFLICTS.
AND IF YOU RESIST--IF YOU TRY TO MAINTAIN CONTROL OVER US... WE MIGHT START TO REALIZE HOW MUCH NICER IT WOULD BE TO LIVE IN THIS QUAINT NEIGHBORHOOD INSTEAD OF A DIRTY OLD FACTORY.
YOU'RE STARTING WITH THREATS?
I'M INTERESTED IN RESULTS.
'M NOT IN CONTROL OF YOU AND YOUR PEOPLE. E'RE PART OF A NETWORK, E HELP EACH OTHER... WE PROVIDE SECURITY AND STRUCTURE.
YOU PROVIDE US WITH SECURITY? WHERE HAVE I HEARD THAT BEFORE?
AND I JUST SAW NEGAN... ON YOUR SIDE... DIDN'T I?
...

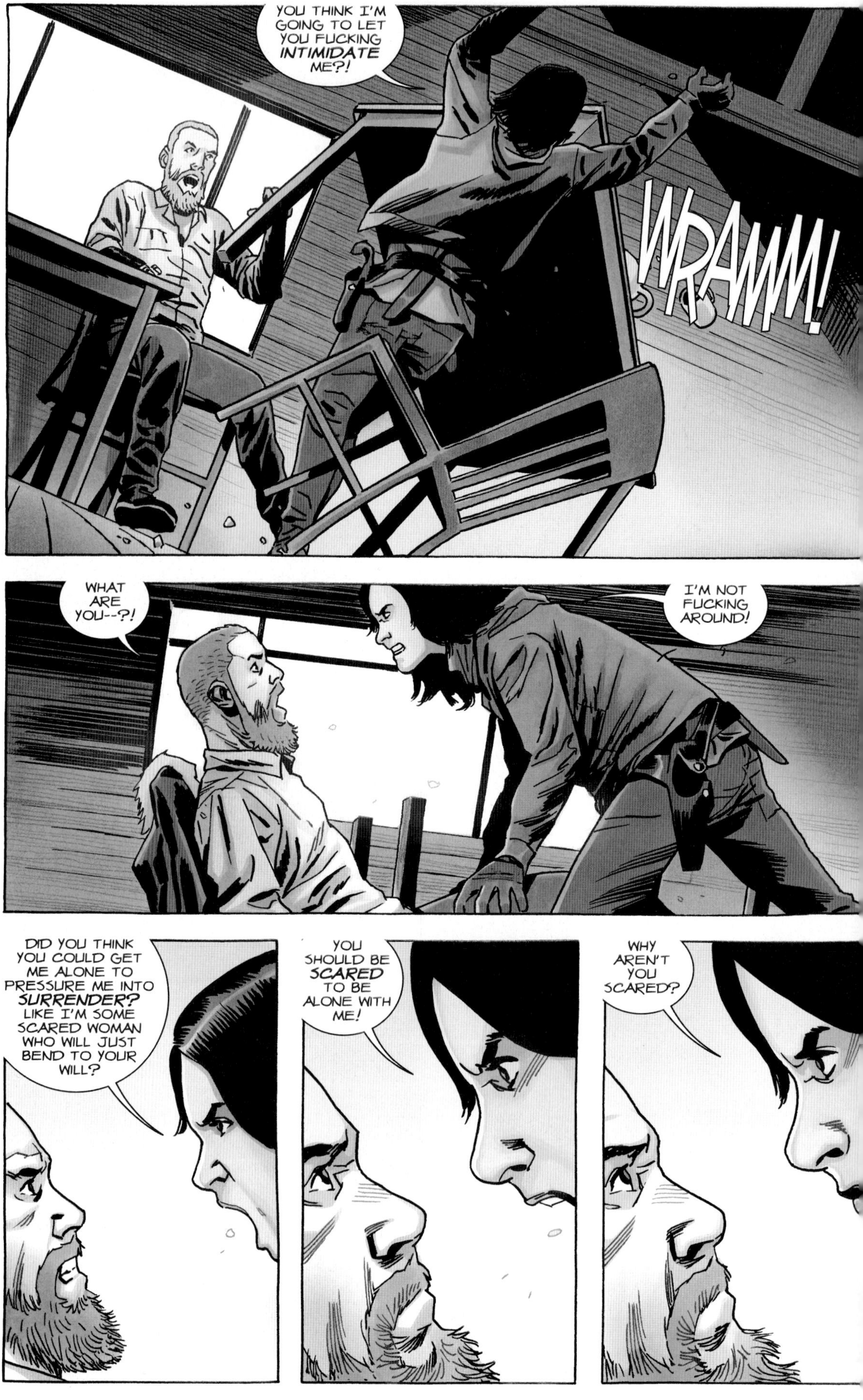
YOU THINK I'M GOING TO LET YOU FUCKING INTIMIDATE ME?!
WRAMM!
WHAT ARE YOU--?!
I'M NOT FUCKING AROUND!
DID YOU THINK YOU COULD GET ME ALONE TO PRESSURE ME INTO SURRENDER? LIKE I'M SOME SCARED WOMAN WHO WILL JUST BEND TO YOUR WILL?
YOU SHOULD BE SCARED TO BE ALONE WITH ME!
WHY AREN'T YOU SCARED?

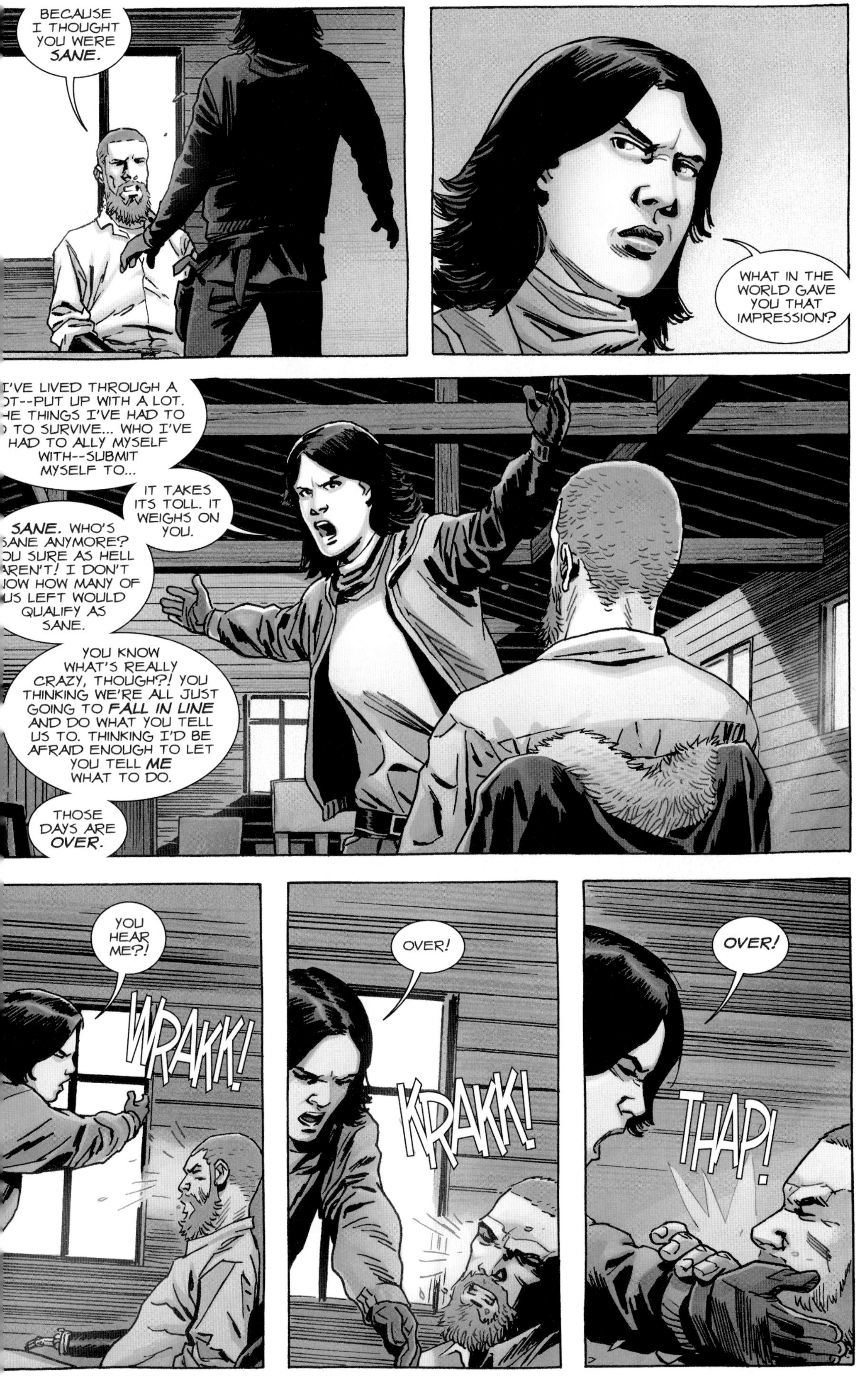

BECAUSE I THOUGHT YOU WERE SANE.
WHAT IN THE WORLD GAVE YOU THAT IMPRESSION?
I'VE LIVED THROUGH A OT--PUT UP WITH A LOT. HE THINGS I'VE HAD TO O TO SURVIVE... WHO I'VE HAD TO ALLY MYSELF WITH--SUBMIT MYSELF TO...
IT TAKES ITS TOLL. IT WEIGHS ON YOU.
SANE. WHO'S SANE ANYMORE? OU SURE AS HELL AREN'T! I DON'T NOW HOW MANY OF US LEFT WOULD QUALIFY AS SANE.
YOU KNOW WHAT'S REALLY CRAZY, THOUGH?! YOU THINKING WE'RE ALL JUST GOING TO FALL IN LINE AND DO WHAT YOU TELL US TO. THINKING I'D BE AFRAID ENOUGH TO LET YOU TELL ME WHAT TO DO.
THOSE DAYS ARE OVER.
YOU HEAR ME?!
WRAKK!
OVER!
KRAKK!
OVER!
THAP!

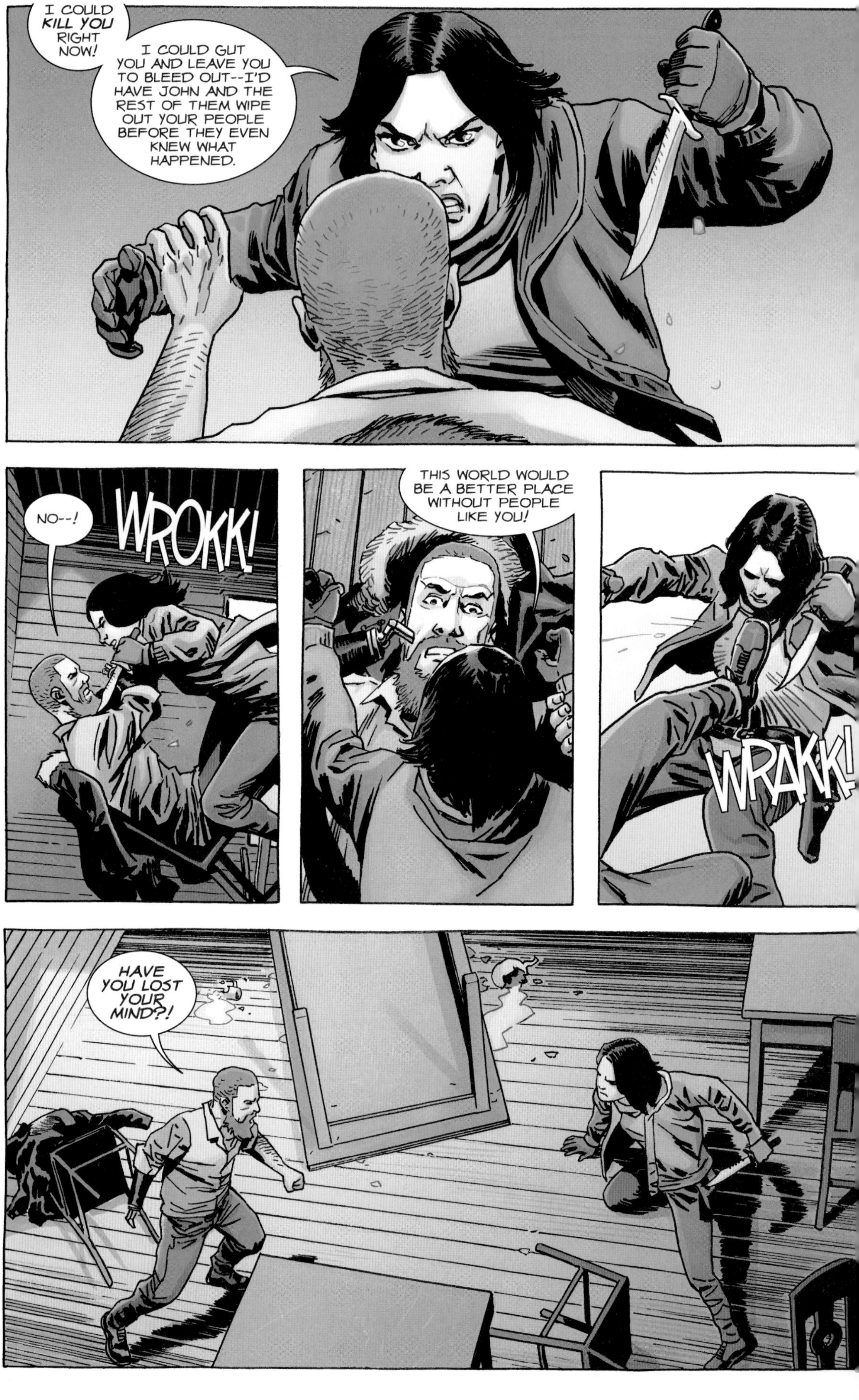
I COULD KILL YOU RIGHT NOW!
I COULD GUT YOU AND LEAVE YOU TO BLEED OUT--I'D HAVE JOHN AND THE REST OF THEM WIPE OUT YOUR PEOPLE BEFORE THEY EVEN KNEW WHAT HAPPENED.
NO--!
WROKK!
THIS WORLD WOULD BE A BETTER PLACE WITHOUT PEOPLE LIKE YOU!
WRAKK!
HAVE YOU LOST YOUR MIND?!

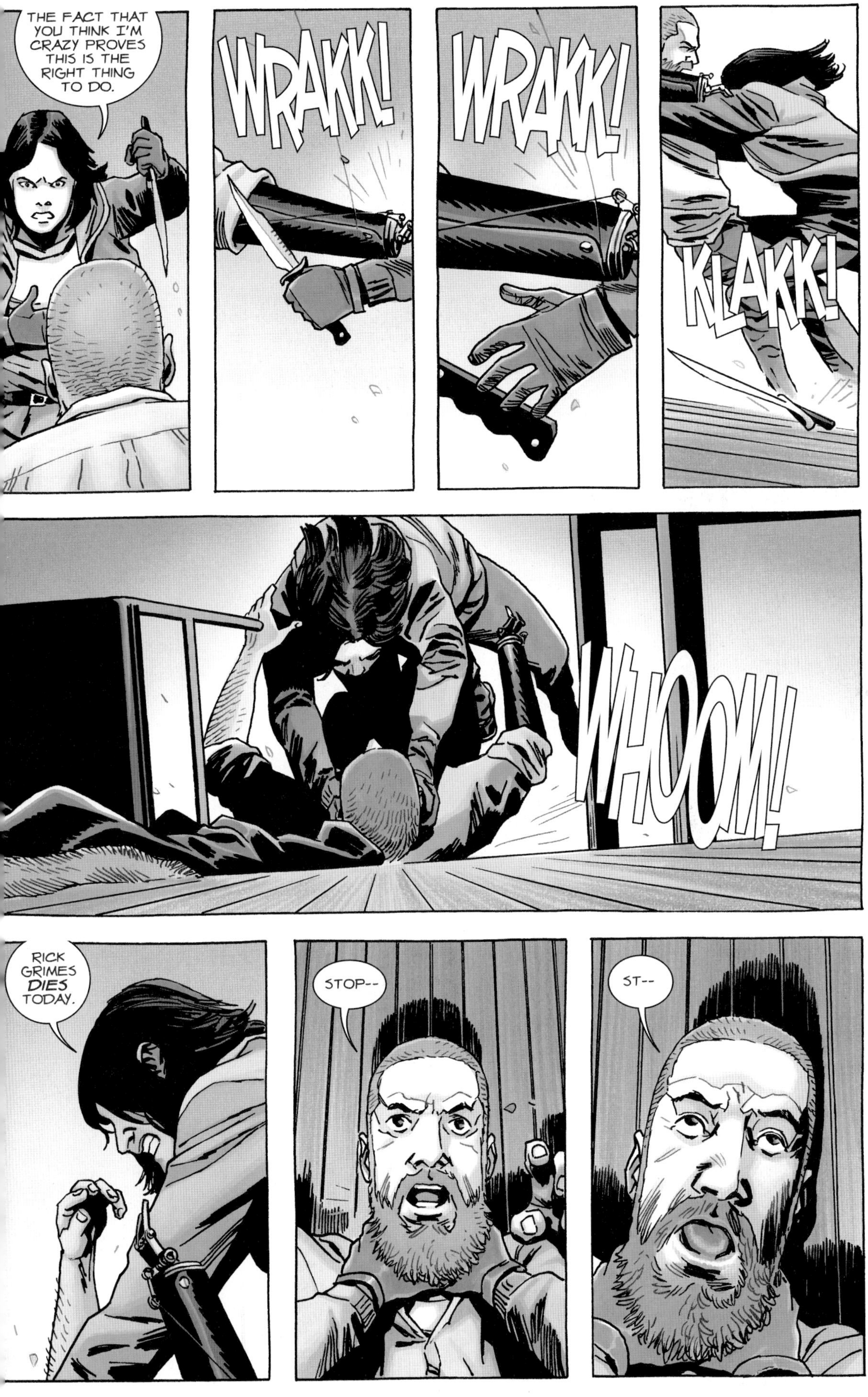
THE FACT THAT YOU THINK I'M CRAZY PROVES THIS IS THE RIGHT THING TO DO.
WRAKK!
WRAKK!
KLAKK!
WHOOM!
RICK GRIMES DIES TODAY.
STOP--
ST--

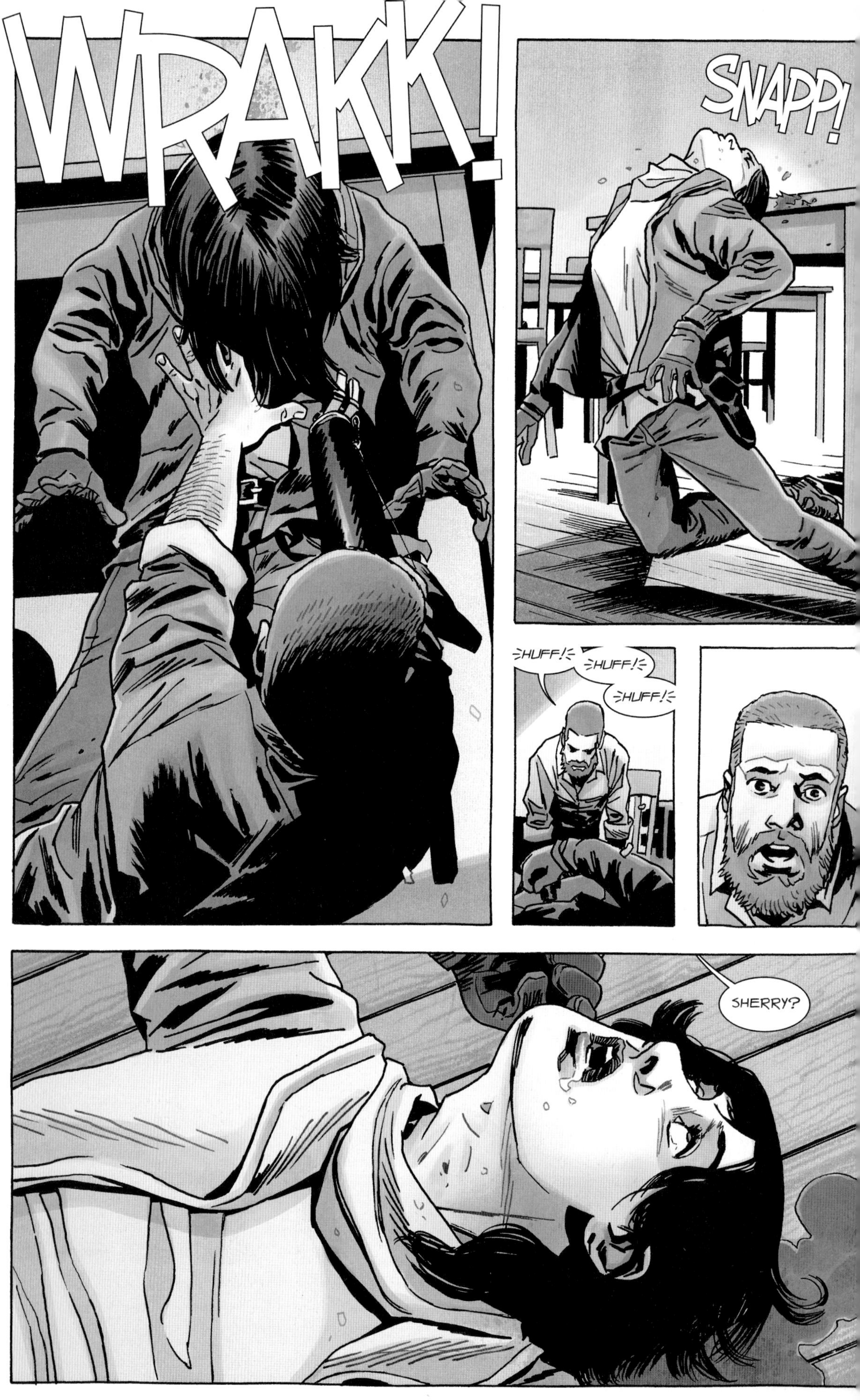
WRAKK!
SNAPP!
HUFF!
HUFF!
HUFF!
SHERRY?

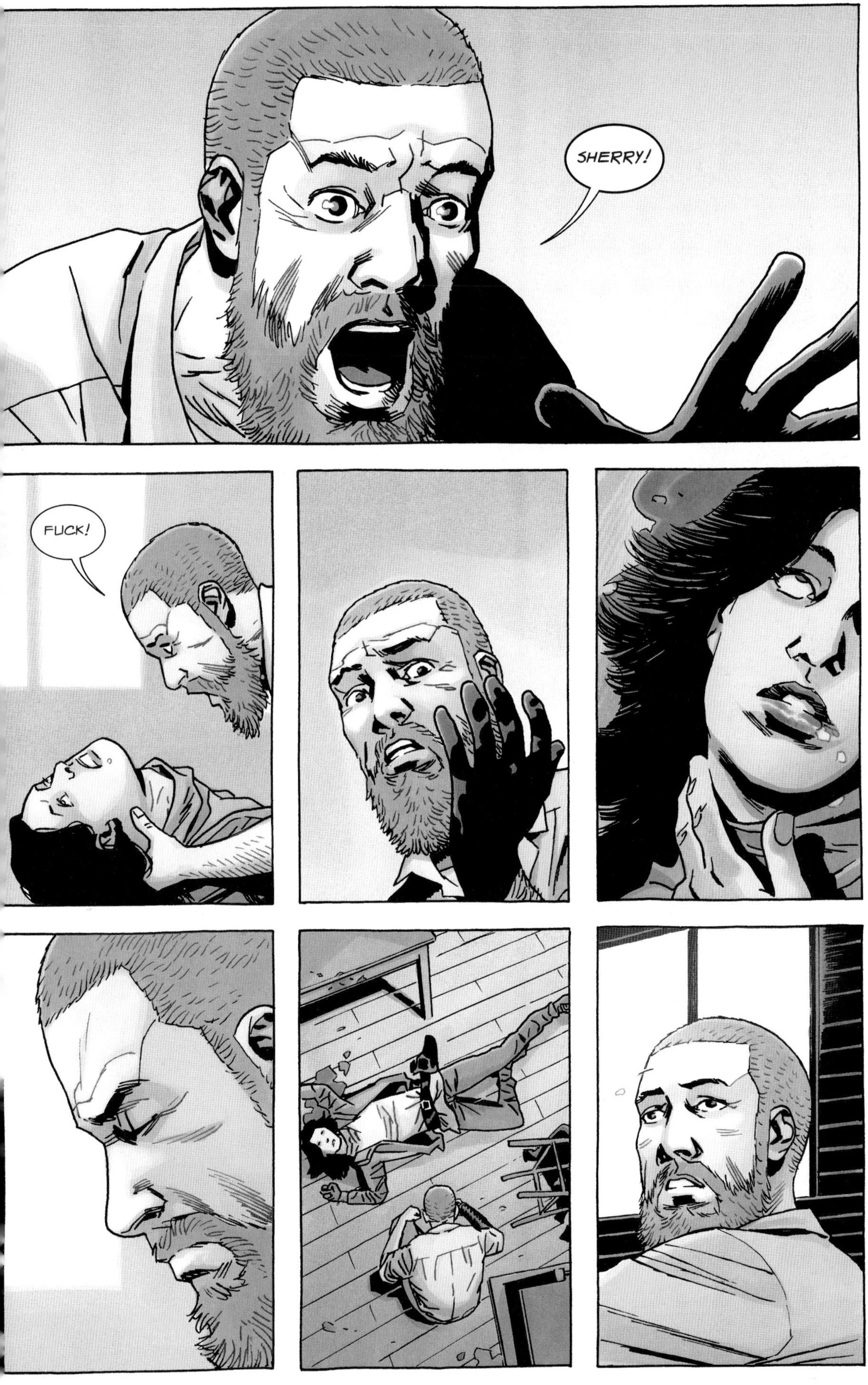
SHERRY!
FUCK!

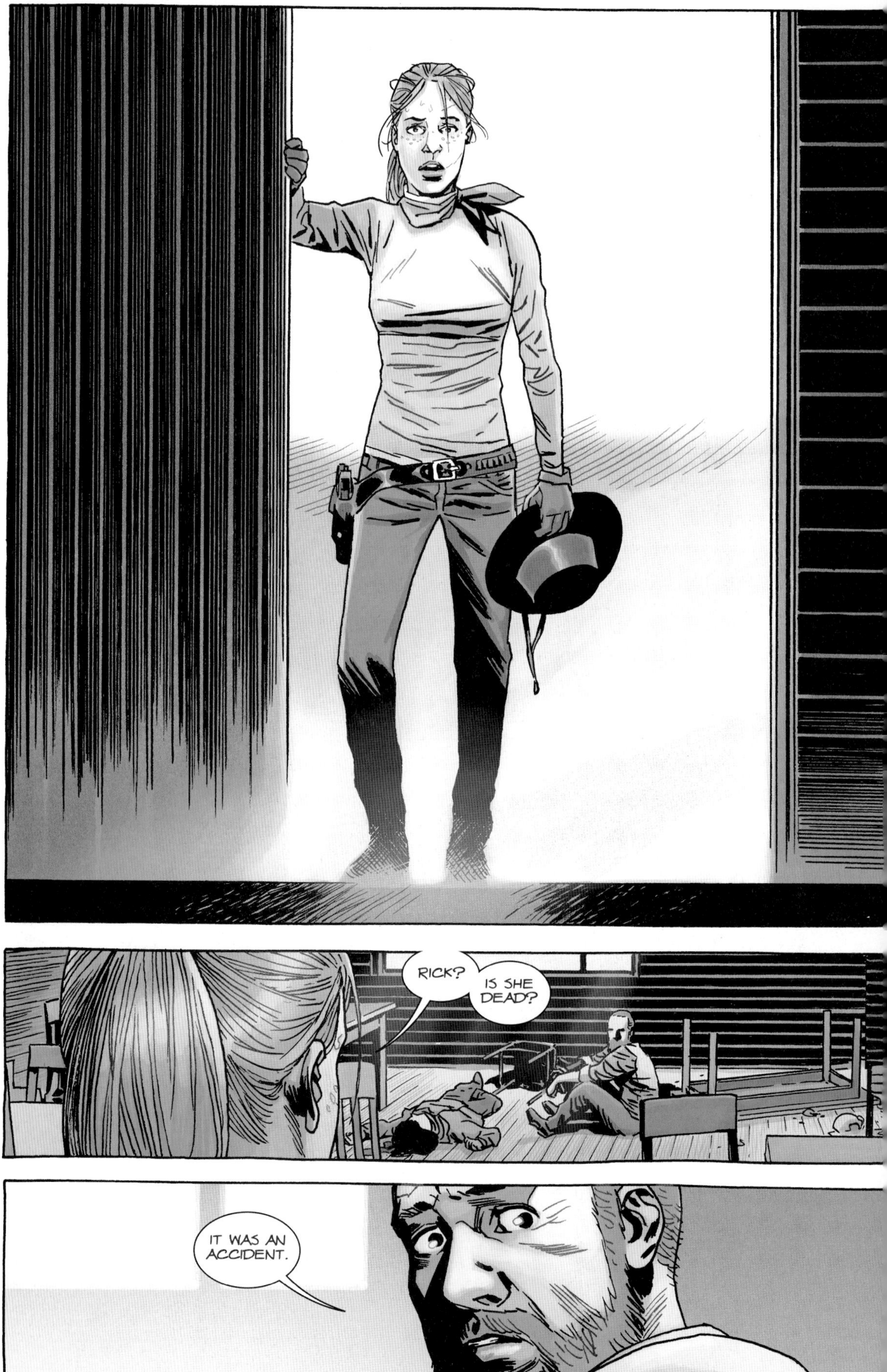
RICK?
IS SHE DEAD?
IT WAS AN ACCIDENT.

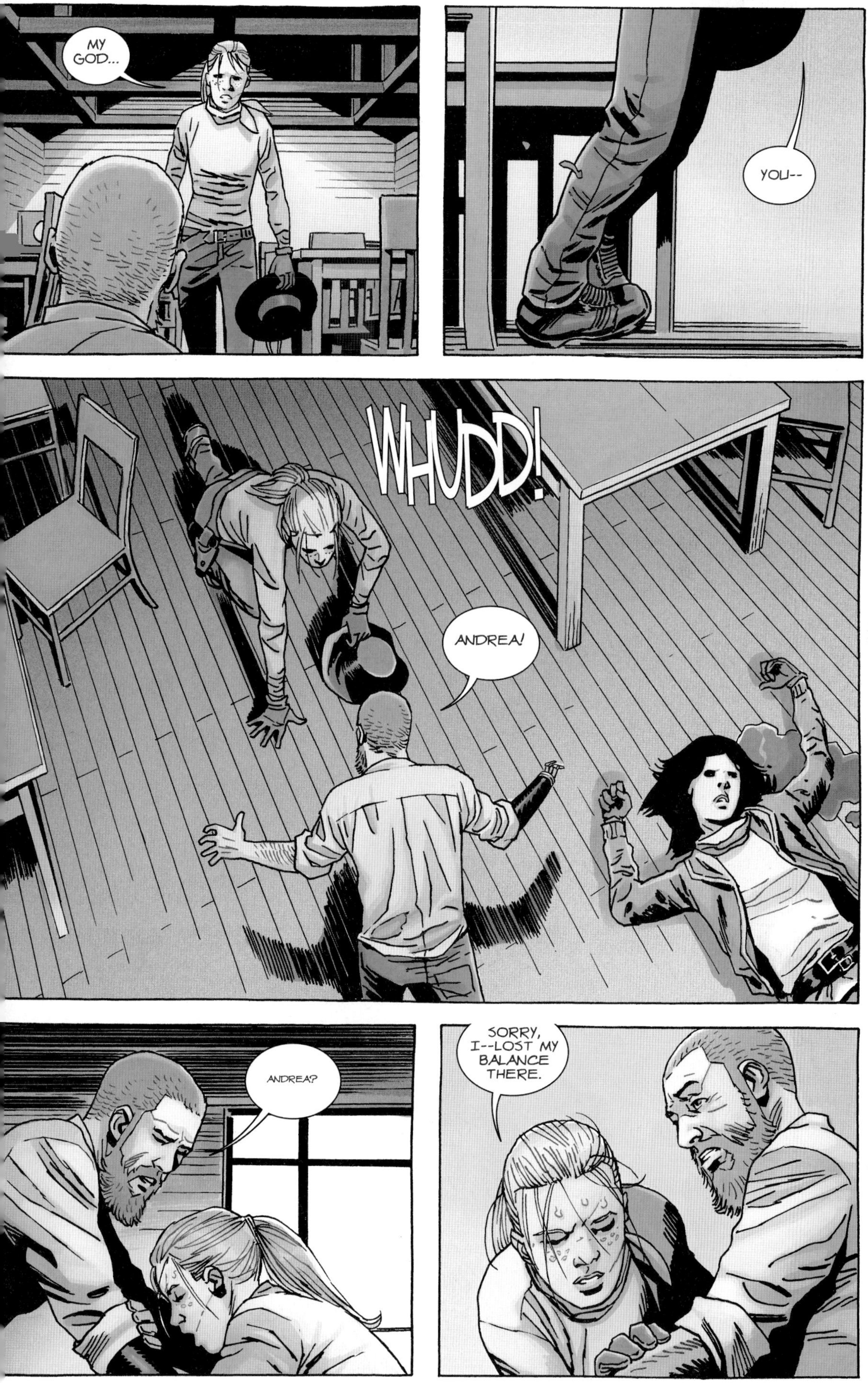
MY GOD...
YOU--
WHUDD!
ANDREA!
ANDREA?
SORRY, I--LOST MY BALANCE THERE.

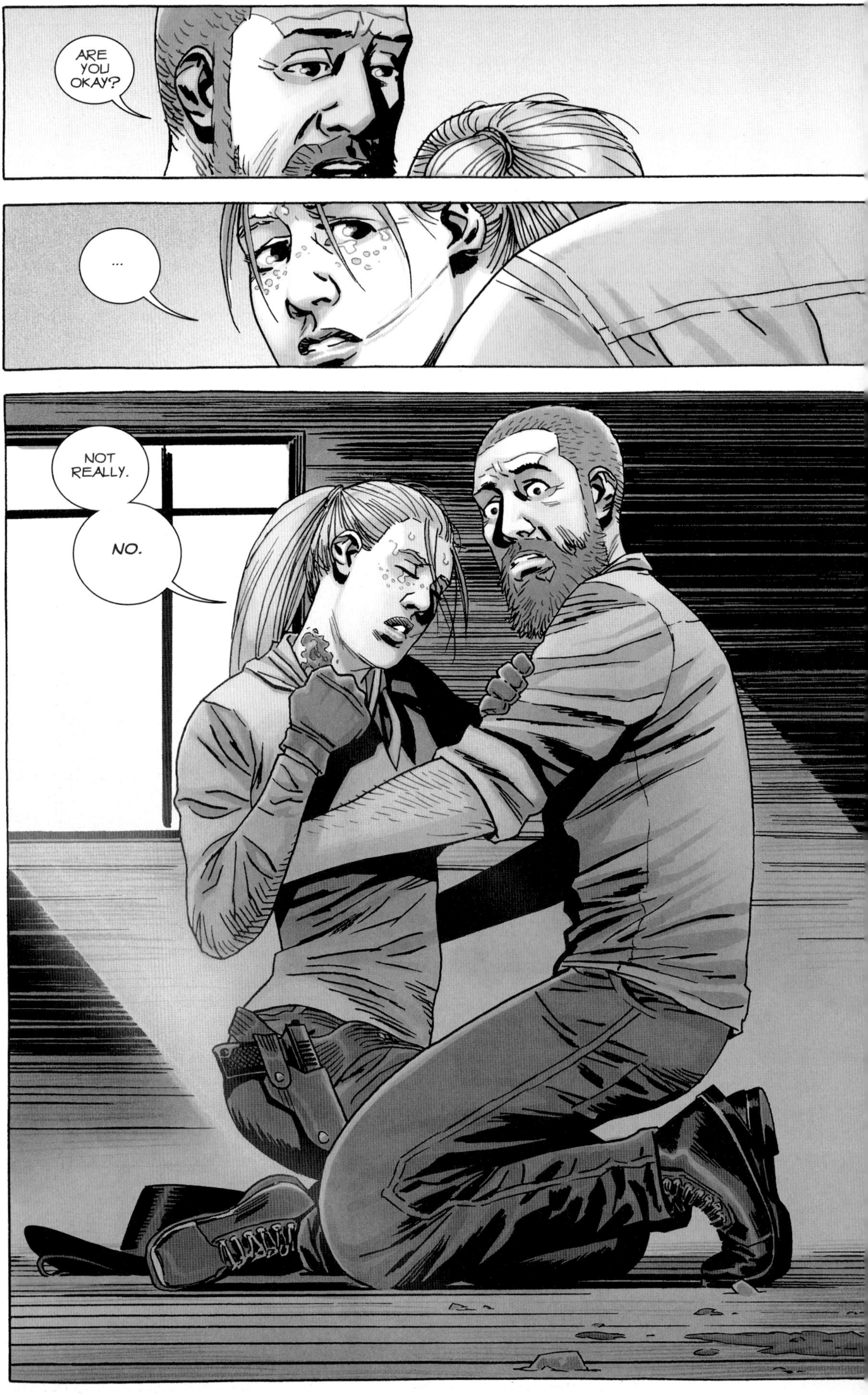
ARE YOU OKAY?
...
NOT REALLY.
NO.

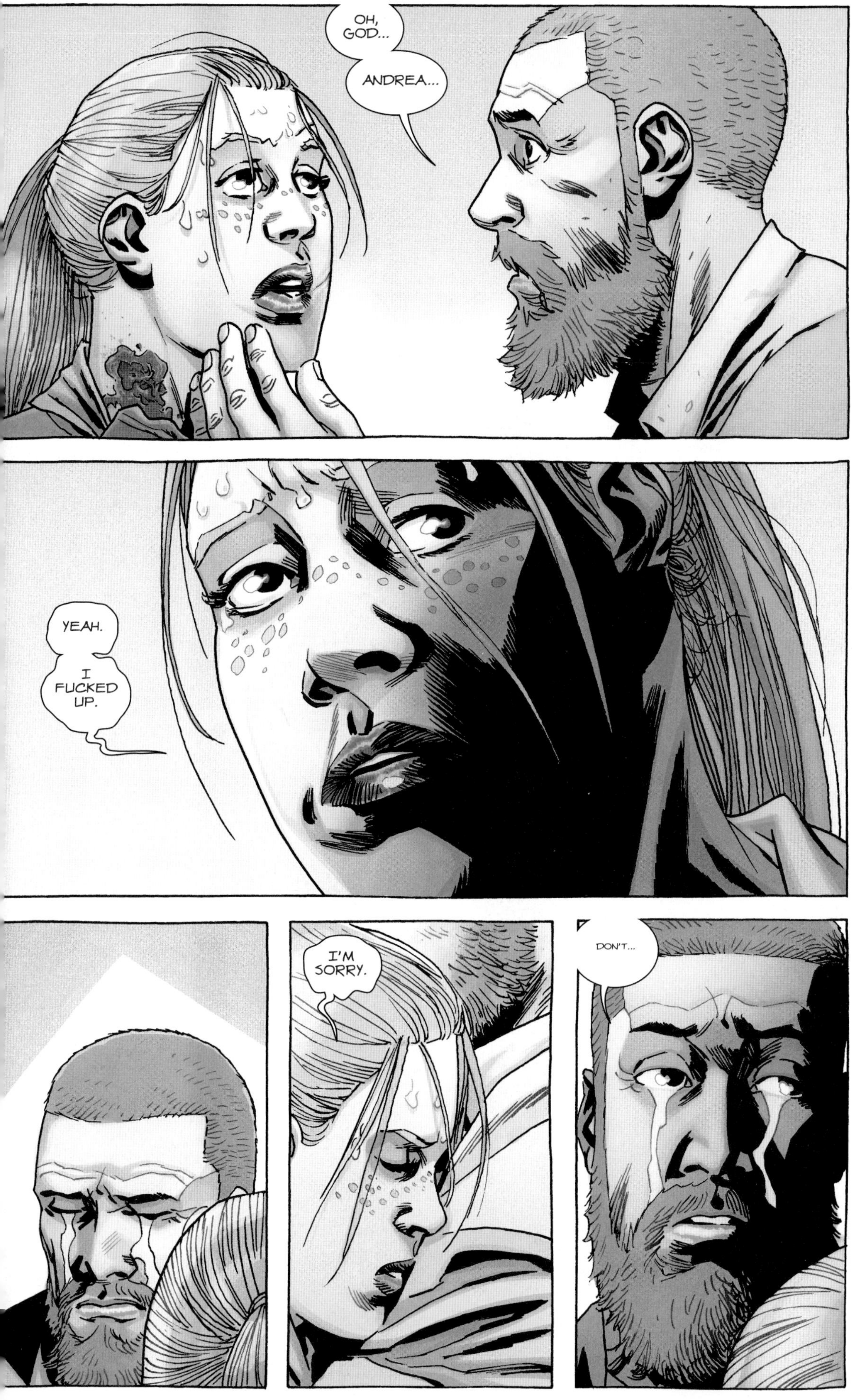
OH, GOD...
ANDREA...
YEAH.
I FUCKED UP.
I'M SORRY.
DON'T...

DON'T...

ANDREA?

ANDREA!

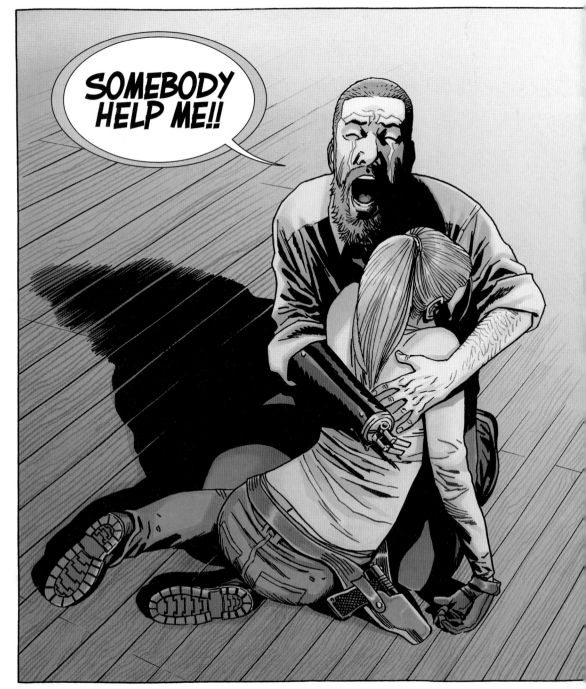

SOMEBODY HELP ME!!

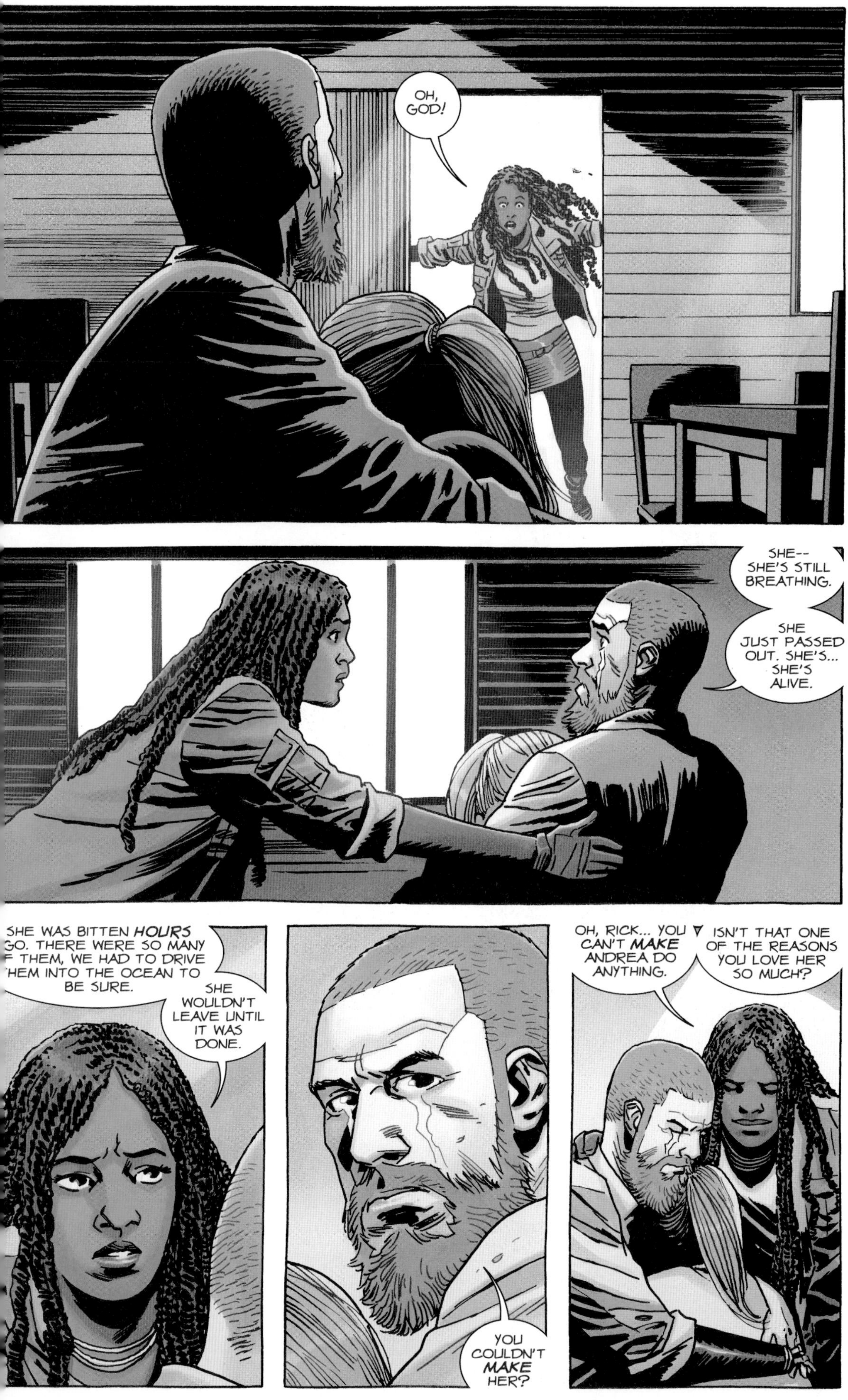
OH, GOD!
SHE-- SHE'S STILL BREATHING.
SHE JUST PASSED OUT. SHE'S... SHE'S ALIVE.
SHE WAS BITTEN HOURS GO. THERE WERE SO MANY F THEM, WE HAD TO DRIVE HEM INTO THE OCEAN TO BE SURE.
SHE WOULDN'T LEAVE UNTIL IT WAS DONE.
YOU COULDN'T MAKE HER?
OH, RICK... YOU CAN'T MAKE ANDREA DO ANYTHING.
ISN'T THAT ONE OF THE REASONS YOU LOVE HER SO MUCH?

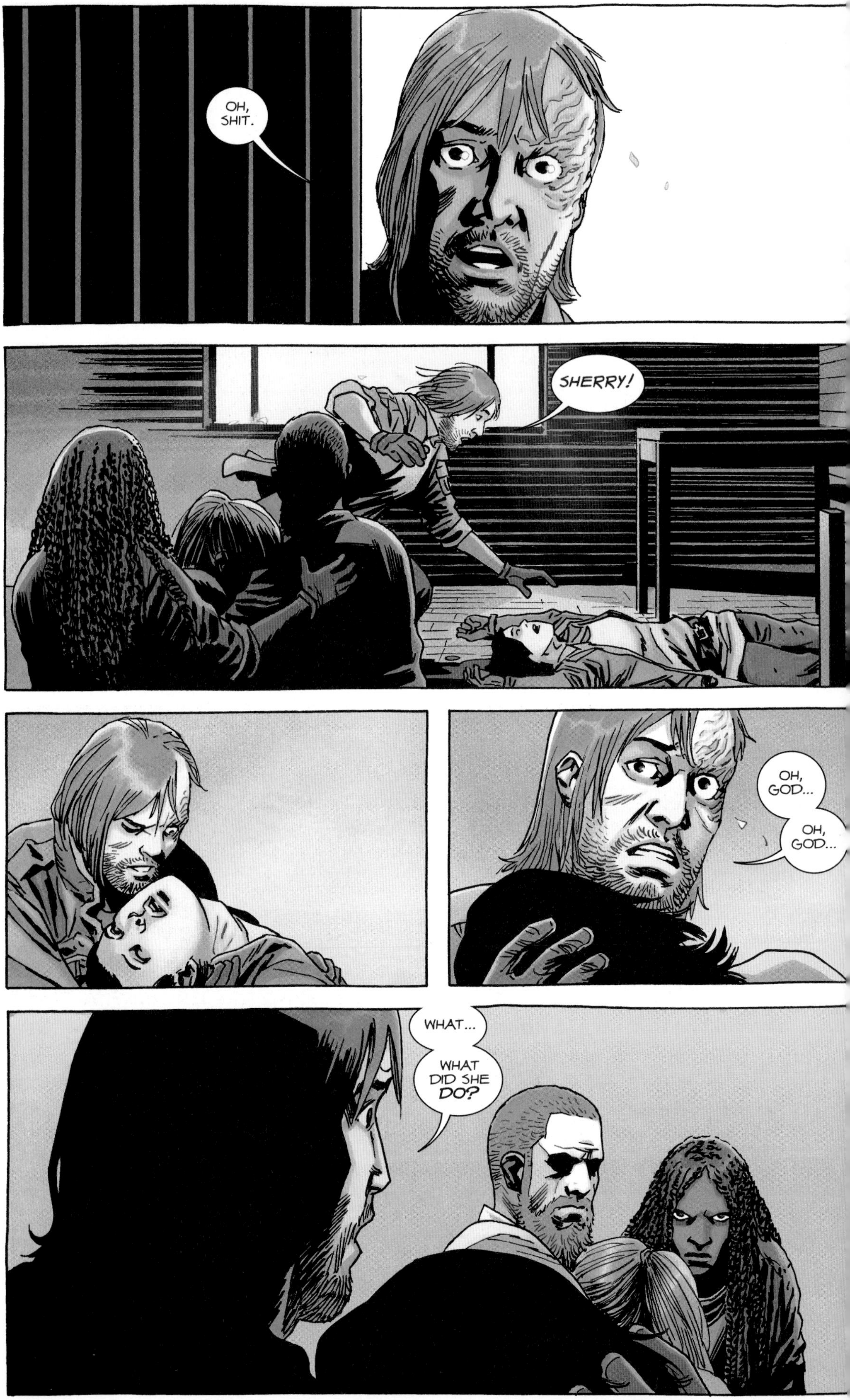
OH, SHIT.
SHERRY!
OH, GOD...
OH, GOD...
WHAT...
WHAT DID SHE DO?

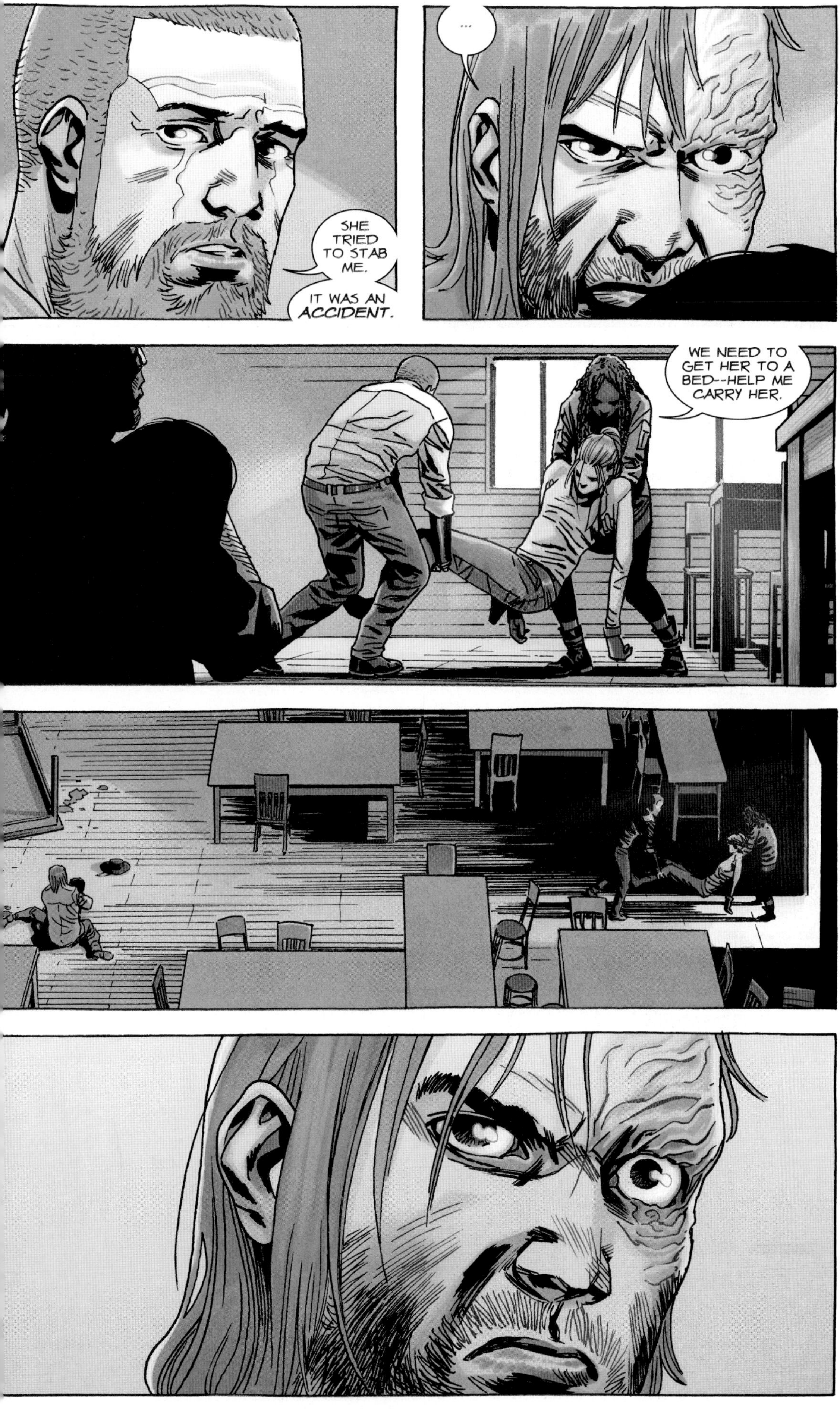
SHE TRIED TO STAB ME.
IT WAS AN ACCIDENT.
...
WE NEED TO GET HER TO A BED--HELP ME CARRY HER.

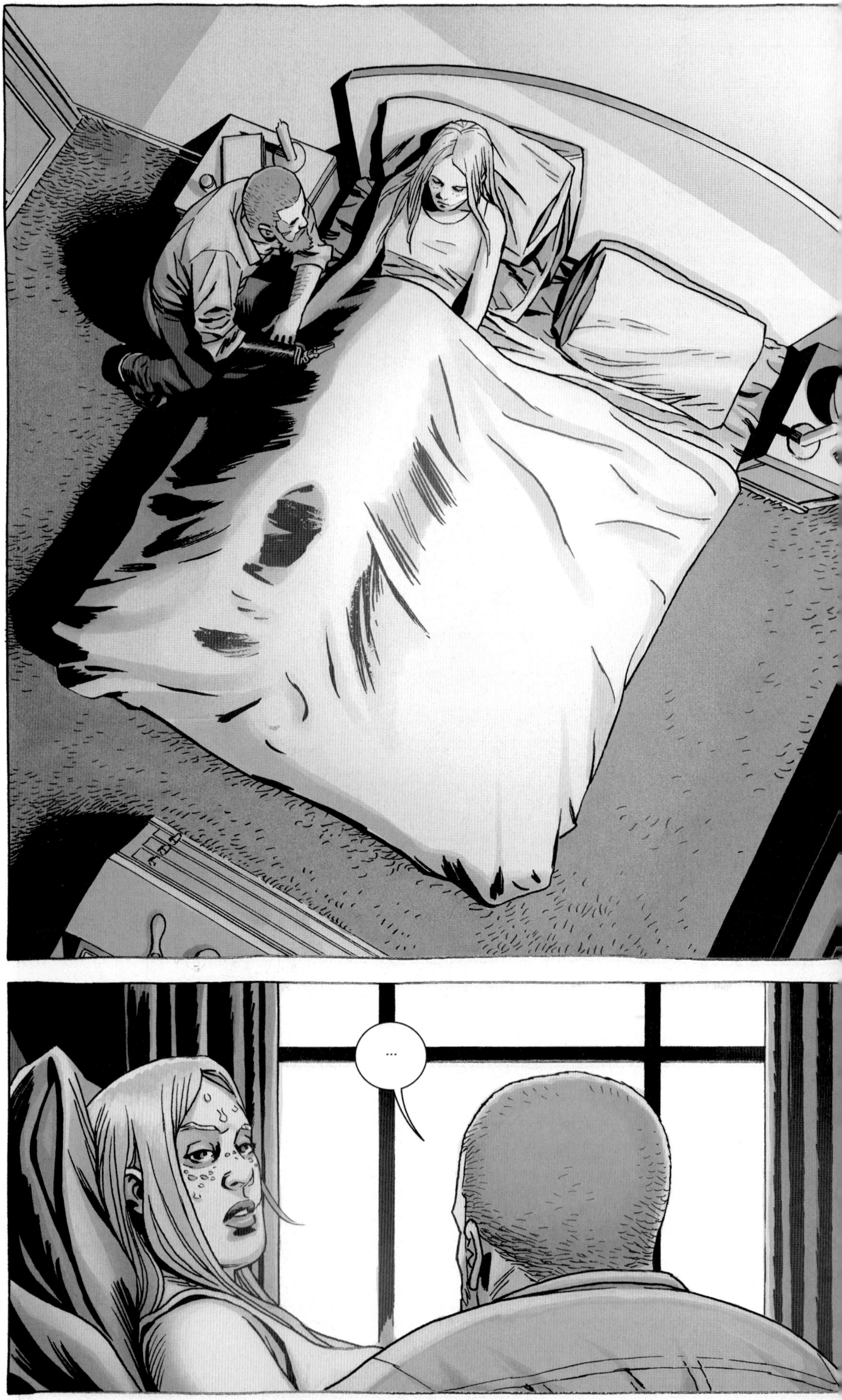
...

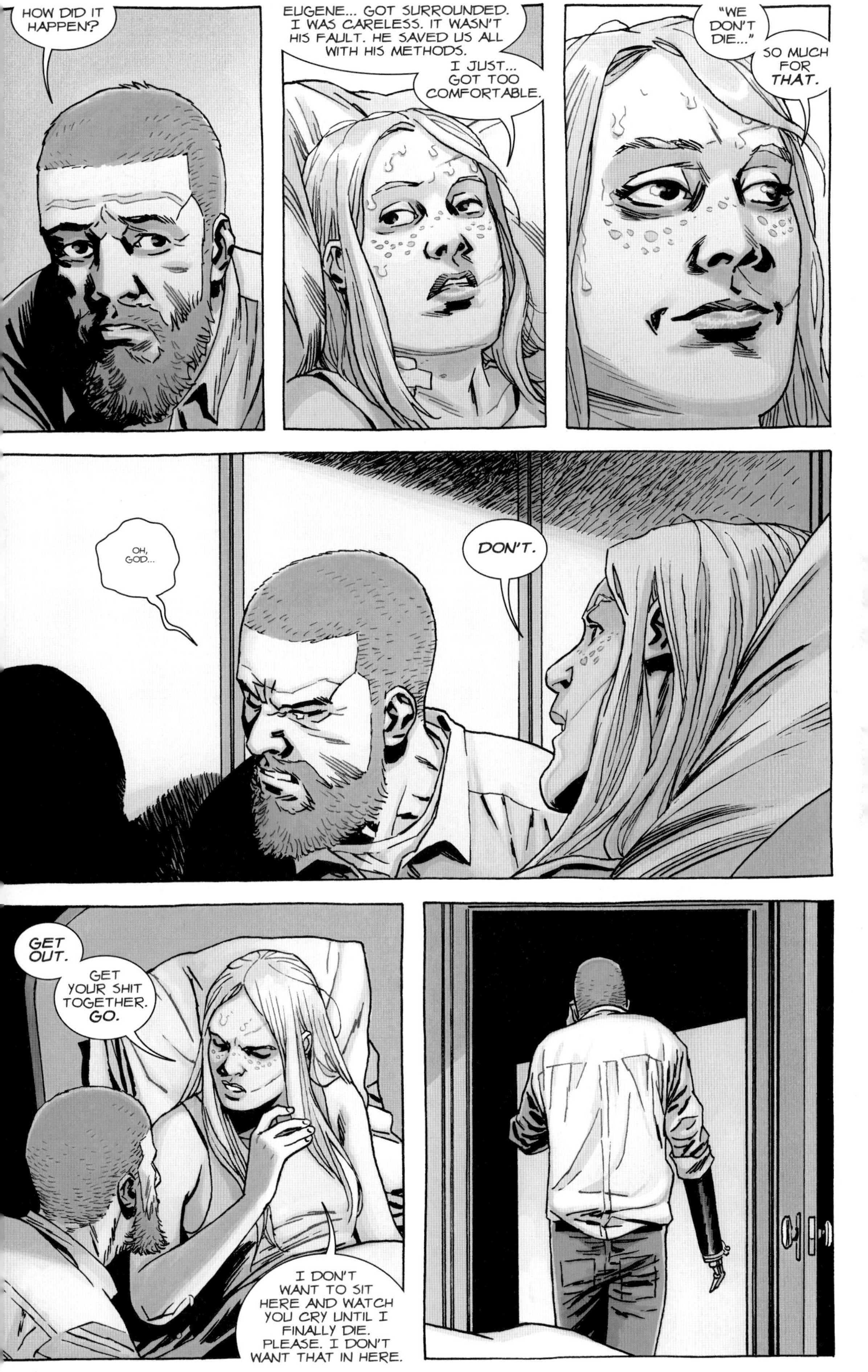
HOW DID IT HAPPEN?
EUGENE... GOT SURROUNDED. I WAS CARELESS. IT WASN'T HIS FAULT. HE SAVED US ALL WITH HIS METHODS.
I JUST... GOT TOO COMFORTABLE.
"WE DON'T DIE..."
SO MUCH FOR THAT.
OH, GOD...
DON'T.
GET OUT.
GET YOUR SHIT TOGETHER. GO.
I DON'T WANT TO SIT HERE AND WATCH YOU CRY UNTIL I FINALLY DIE. PLEASE. I DON'T WANT THAT IN HERE.

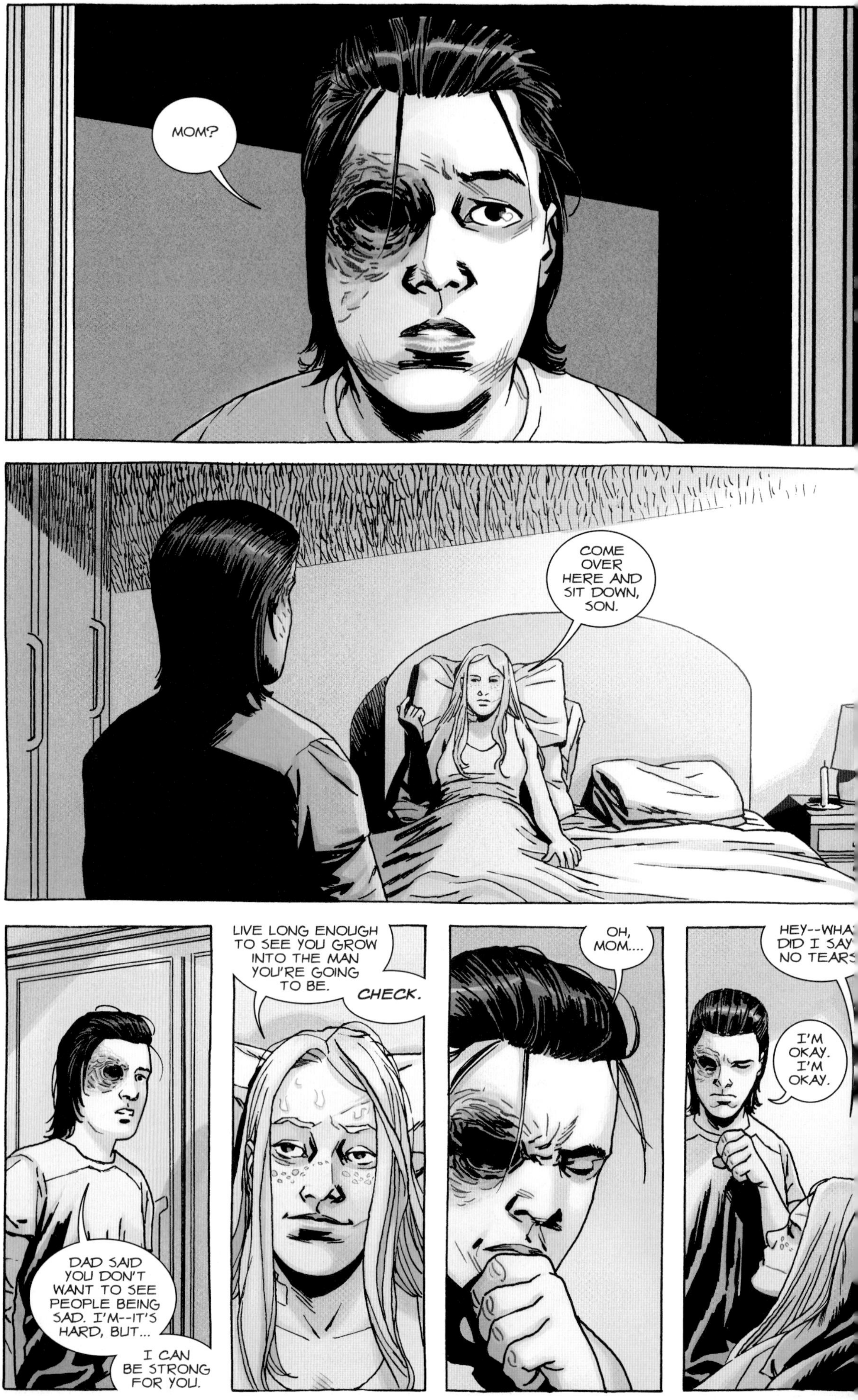
MOM?
COME OVER HERE AND SIT DOWN, SON.
DAD SAID YOU DON'T WANT TO SEE PEOPLE BEING SAD. I'M--IT'S HARD, BUT...
I CAN BE STRONG FOR YOU.
LIVE LONG ENOUGH TO SEE YOU GROW INTO THE MAN YOU'RE GOING TO BE.
CHECK.
OH, MOM....
HEY--WHA DID I SAY NO TEARS
I'M OKAY. I'M OKAY.

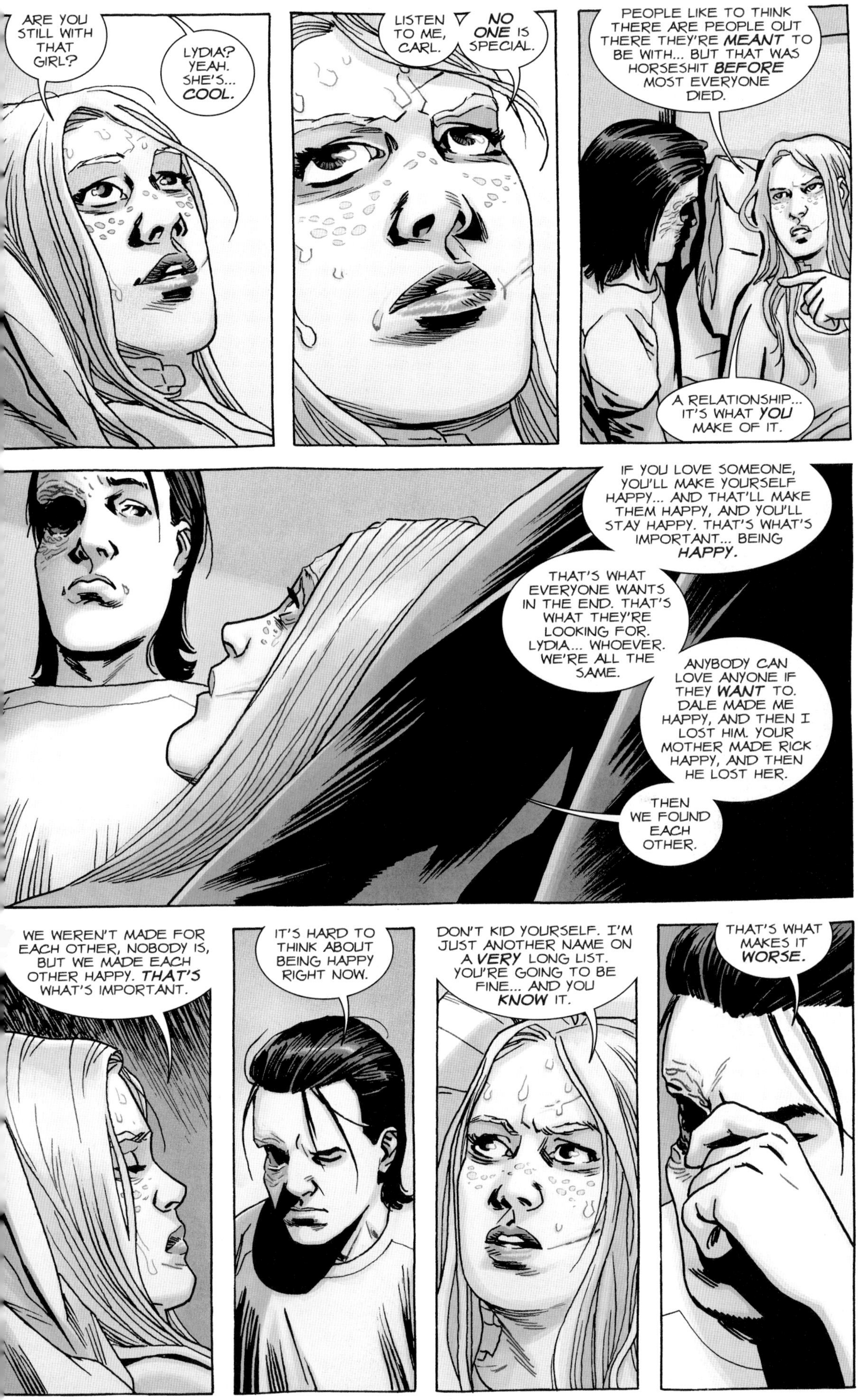
ARE YOU STILL WITH THAT GIRL?
LYDIA? YEAH. SHE'S... COOL.
LISTEN TO ME, CARL.
NO ONE IS SPECIAL.
PEOPLE LIKE TO THINK THERE ARE PEOPLE OUT THERE THEY'RE MEANT TO BE WITH... BUT THAT WAS HORSESHIT BEFORE MOST EVERYONE DIED.
A RELATIONSHIP... IT'S WHAT YOU MAKE OF IT.
IF YOU LOVE SOMEONE, YOU'LL MAKE YOURSELF HAPPY... AND THAT'LL MAKE THEM HAPPY, AND YOU'LL STAY HAPPY. THAT'S WHAT'S IMPORTANT... BEING HAPPY.
THAT'S WHAT EVERYONE WANTS IN THE END. THAT'S WHAT THEY'RE LOOKING FOR. LYDIA... WHOEVER. WE'RE ALL THE SAME.
ANYBODY CAN LOVE ANYONE IF THEY WANT TO. DALE MADE ME HAPPY, AND THEN I LOST HIM. YOUR MOTHER MADE RICK HAPPY, AND THEN HE LOST HER.
THEN WE FOUND EACH OTHER.
WE WEREN'T MADE FOR EACH OTHER, NOBODY IS, BUT WE MADE EACH OTHER HAPPY. THAT'S WHAT'S IMPORTANT.
IT'S HARD TO THINK ABOUT BEING HAPPY RIGHT NOW.
DON'T KID YOURSELF. I'M JUST ANOTHER NAME ON A VERY LONG LIST. YOU'RE GOING TO BE FINE... AND YOU KNOW IT.
THAT'S WHAT MAKES IT WORSE.

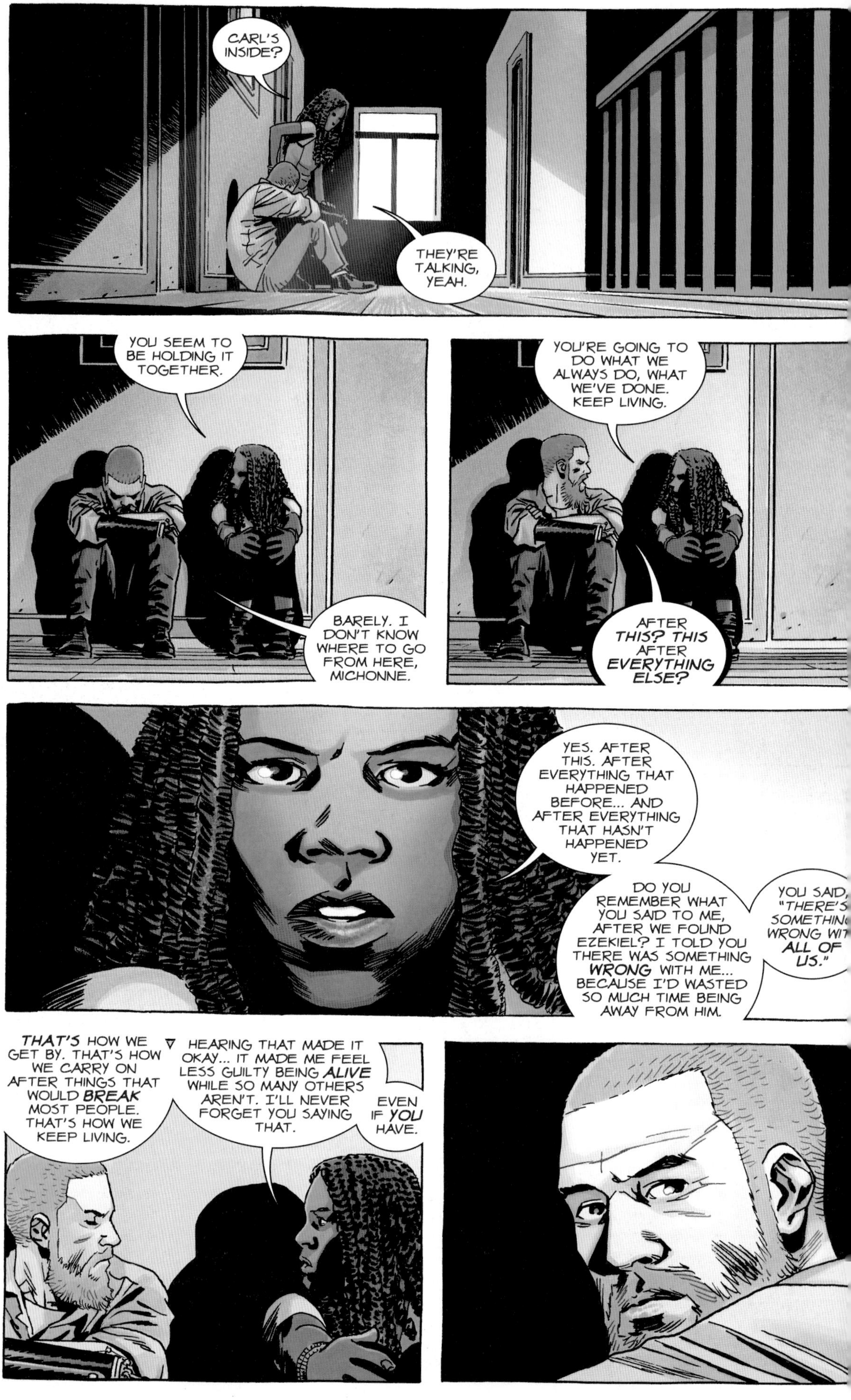
CARL'S INSIDE?
THEY'RE TALKING, YEAH.
YOU SEEM TO BE HOLDING IT TOGETHER.
BARELY. I DON'T KNOW WHERE TO GO FROM HERE, MICHONNE.
YOU'RE GOING TO DO WHAT WE ALWAYS DO, WHAT WE'VE DONE. KEEP LIVING.
AFTER THIS? THIS AFTER EVERYTHING ELSE?
YES. AFTER THIS. AFTER EVERYTHING THAT HAPPENED BEFORE... AND AFTER EVERYTHING THAT HASN'T HAPPENED YET.
DO YOU REMEMBER WHAT YOU SAID TO ME, AFTER WE FOUND EZEKIEL? I TOLD YOU THERE WAS SOMETHING WRONG WITH ME... BECAUSE I'D WASTED SO MUCH TIME BEING AWAY FROM HIM.
YOU SAID, "THERE'S SOMETHING WRONG WITH ALL OF US."
HEARING THAT MADE IT OKAY... IT MADE ME FEEL LESS GUILTY BEING ALIVE WHILE SO MANY OTHERS AREN'T. I'LL NEVER FORGET YOU SAYING THAT.
EVEN IF YOU HAVE.
THAT'S HOW WE GET BY. THAT'S HOW WE CARRY ON AFTER THINGS THAT WOULD BREAK MOST PEOPLE. THAT'S HOW WE KEEP LIVING.

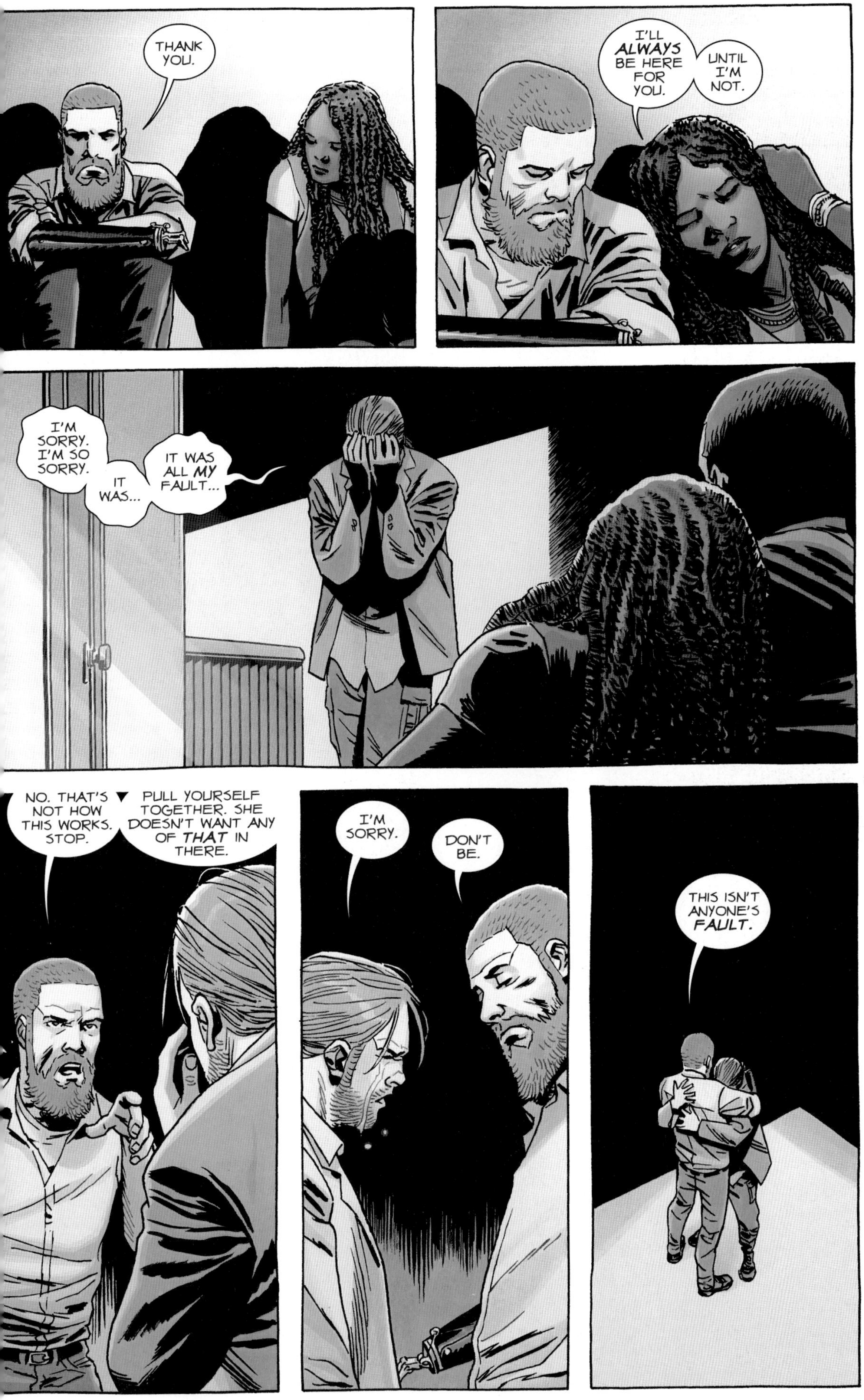
THANK YOU.
I'LL ALWAYS BE HERE FOR YOU.
UNTIL I'M NOT.
I'M SORRY. I'M SO SORRY.
IT WAS...
IT WAS ALL MY FAULT...
NO. THAT'S NOT HOW THIS WORKS. STOP.
PULL YOURSELF TOGETHER. SHE DOESN'T WANT ANY OF THAT IN THERE.
I'M SORRY.
DON'T BE.
THIS ISN'T ANYONE'S FAULT.

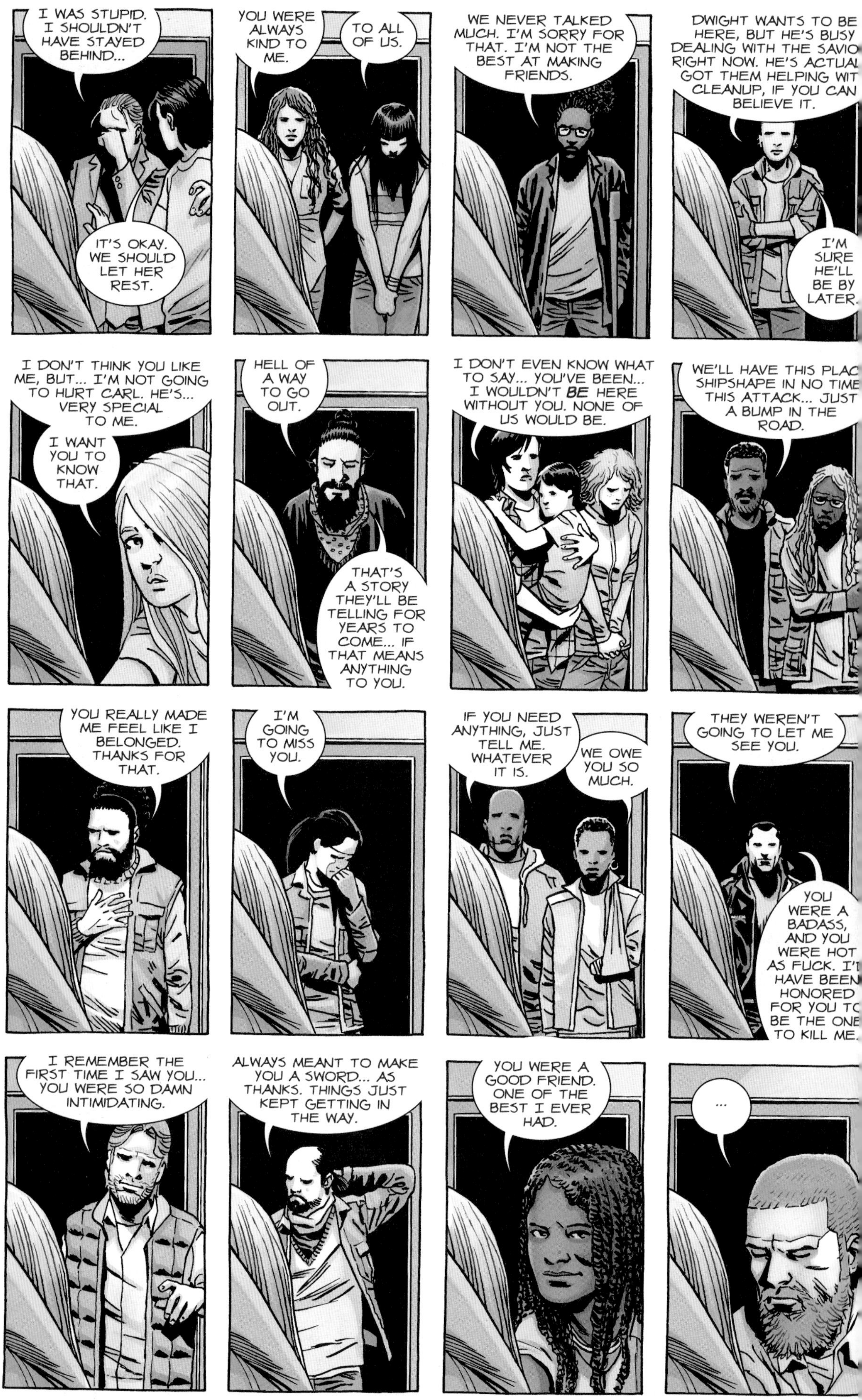
I WAS STUPID. I SHOULDN'T HAVE STAYED BEHIND...
IT'S OKAY. WE SHOULD LET HER REST.
YOU WERE ALWAYS KIND TO ME.
TO ALL OF US.
WE NEVER TALKED MUCH. I'M SORRY FOR THAT. I'M NOT THE BEST AT MAKING FRIENDS.
DWIGHT WANTS TO BE HERE, BUT HE'S BUSY DEALING WITH THE SAVIO RIGHT NOW. HE'S ACTUAL GOT THEM HELPING WIT CLEANUP, IF YOU CAN BELIEVE IT.
I'M SURE HE'LL BE BY LATER.
I DON'T THINK YOU LIKE ME, BUT... I'M NOT GOING TO HURT CARL. HE'S... VERY SPECIAL TO ME.
I WANT YOU TO KNOW THAT.
HELL OF A WAY TO GO OUT.
THAT'S A STORY THEY'LL BE TELLING FOR YEARS TO COME... IF THAT MEANS ANYTHING TO YOU.
I DON'T EVEN KNOW WHAT TO SAY... YOU'VE BEEN... I WOULDN'T BE HERE WITHOUT YOU. NONE OF US WOULD BE.
WE'LL HAVE THIS PLAC SHIPSHAPE IN NO TIME THIS ATTACK... JUST A BUMP IN THE ROAD.
YOU REALLY MADE ME FEEL LIKE I BELONGED. THANKS FOR THAT.
I'M GOING TO MISS YOU.
IF YOU NEED ANYTHING, JUST TELL ME. WHATEVER IT IS.
WE OWE YOU SO MUCH.
THEY WEREN'T GOING TO LET ME SEE YOU.
YOU WERE A BADASS, AND YOU WERE HOT AS FUCK. I'I HAVE BEEN HONORED FOR YOU TO BE THE ONE TO KILL ME.
I REMEMBER THE FIRST TIME I SAW YOU... YOU WERE SO DAMN INTIMIDATING.
ALWAYS MEANT TO MAKE YOU A SWORD... AS THANKS. THINGS JUST KEPT GETTING IN THE WAY.
YOU WERE A GOOD FRIEND. ONE OF THE BEST I EVER HAD.
...

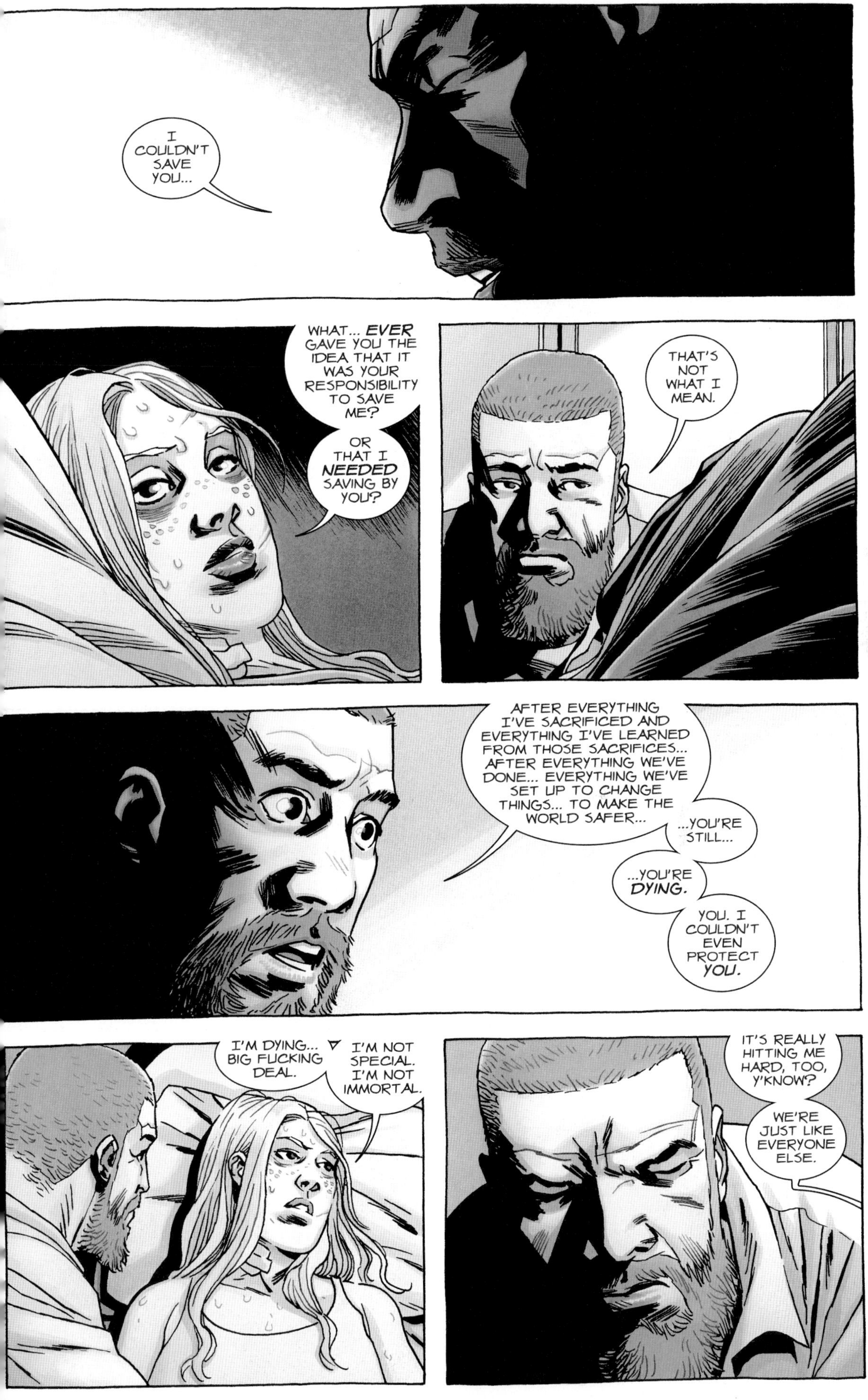
I COULDN'T SAVE YOU...
WHAT... EVER GAVE YOU THE IDEA THAT IT WAS YOUR RESPONSIBILITY TO SAVE ME?
OR THAT I NEEDED SAVING BY YOU?
THAT'S NOT WHAT I MEAN.
AFTER EVERYTHING I'VE SACRIFICED AND EVERYTHING I'VE LEARNED FROM THOSE SACRIFICES... AFTER EVERYTHING WE'VE DONE... EVERYTHING WE'VE SET UP TO CHANGE THINGS... TO MAKE THE WORLD SAFER...
...YOU'RE STILL...
...YOU'RE DYING.
YOU. I COULDN'T EVEN PROTECT YOU.
I'M DYING... BIG FUCKING DEAL.
I'M NOT SPECIAL. I'M NOT IMMORTAL.
IT'S REALLY HITTING ME HARD, TOO, Y'KNOW?
WE'RE JUST LIKE EVERYONE ELSE.

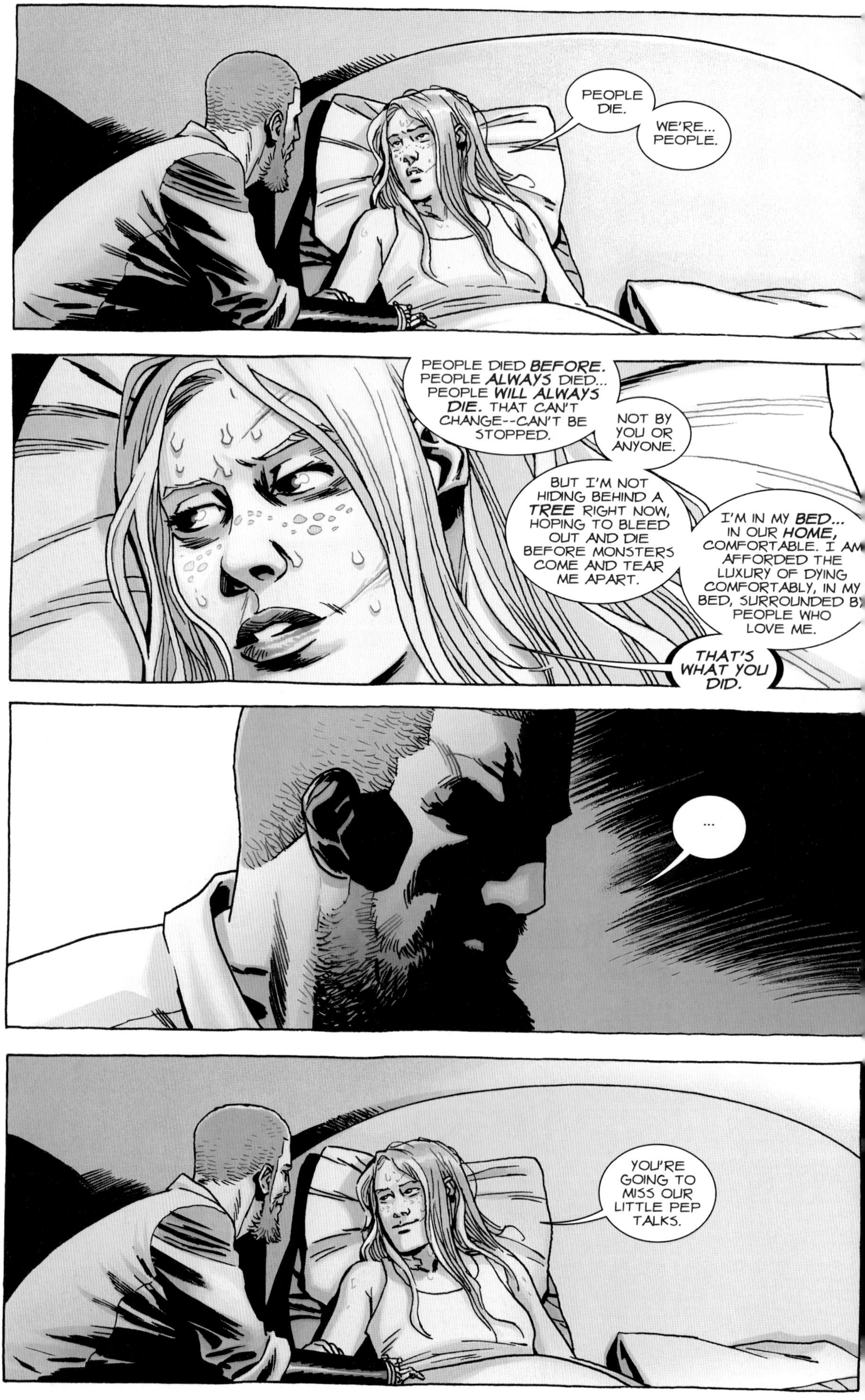
PEOPLE DIE.
WE'RE... PEOPLE.
PEOPLE DIED BEFORE. PEOPLE ALWAYS DIED... PEOPLE WILL ALWAYS DIE. THAT CAN'T CHANGE--CAN'T BE STOPPED.
NOT BY YOU OR ANYONE.
BUT I'M NOT HIDING BEHIND A TREE RIGHT NOW, HOPING TO BLEED OUT AND DIE BEFORE MONSTERS COME AND TEAR ME APART.
I'M IN MY BED... IN OUR HOME, COMFORTABLE. I AM AFFORDED THE LUXURY OF DYING COMFORTABLY, IN MY BED, SURROUNDED BY PEOPLE WHO LOVE ME.
THAT'S WHAT YOU DID.
...
YOU'RE GOING TO MISS OUR LITTLE PEP TALKS.

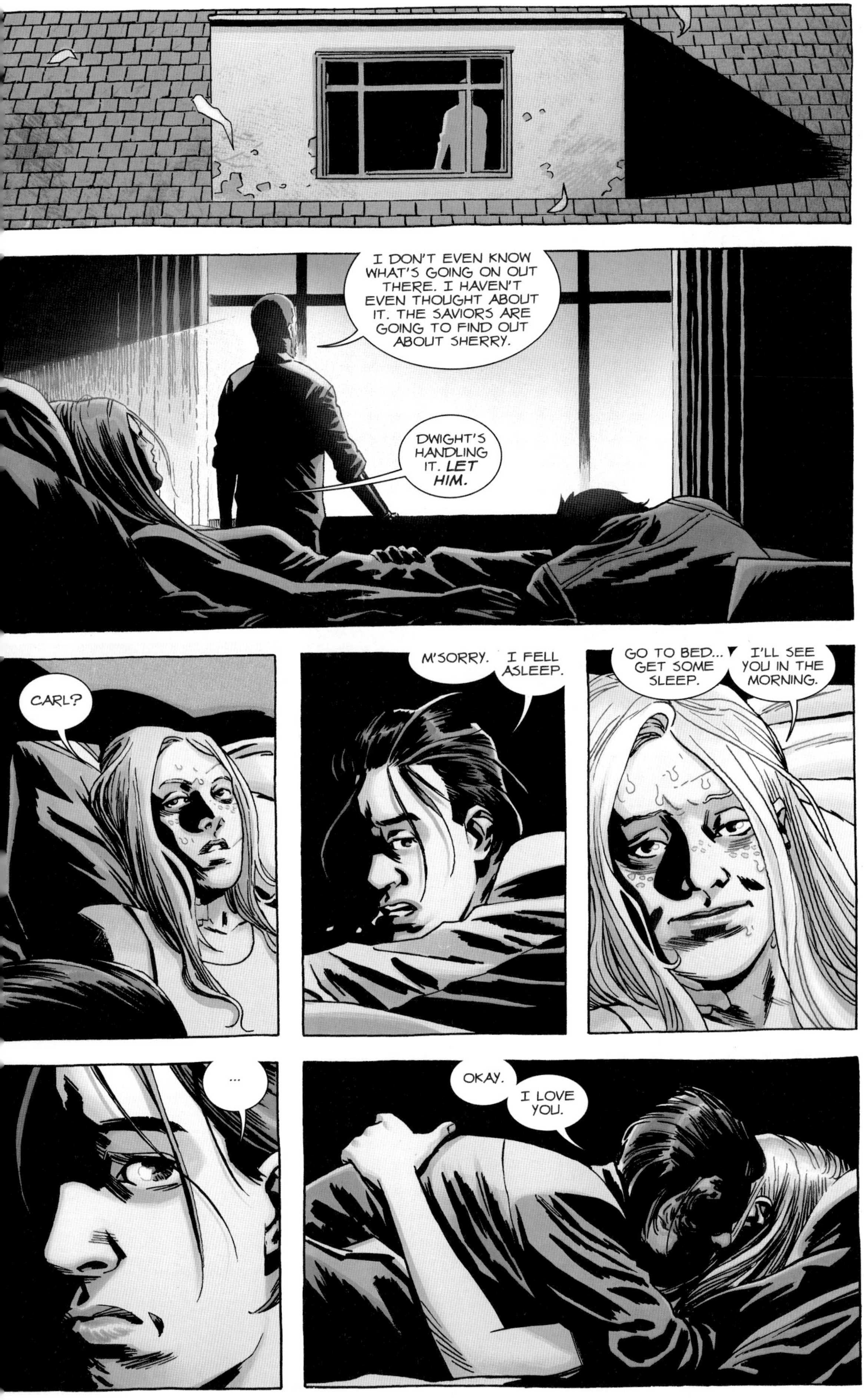
I DON'T EVEN KNOW WHAT'S GOING ON OUT THERE. I HAVEN'T EVEN THOUGHT ABOUT IT. THE SAVIORS ARE GOING TO FIND OUT ABOUT SHERRY.
DWIGHT'S HANDLING IT. LET HIM.
CARL?
M'SORRY.
I FELL ASLEEP.
GO TO BED... GET SOME SLEEP.
I'LL SEE YOU IN THE MORNING.
...
OKAY.
I LOVE YOU.

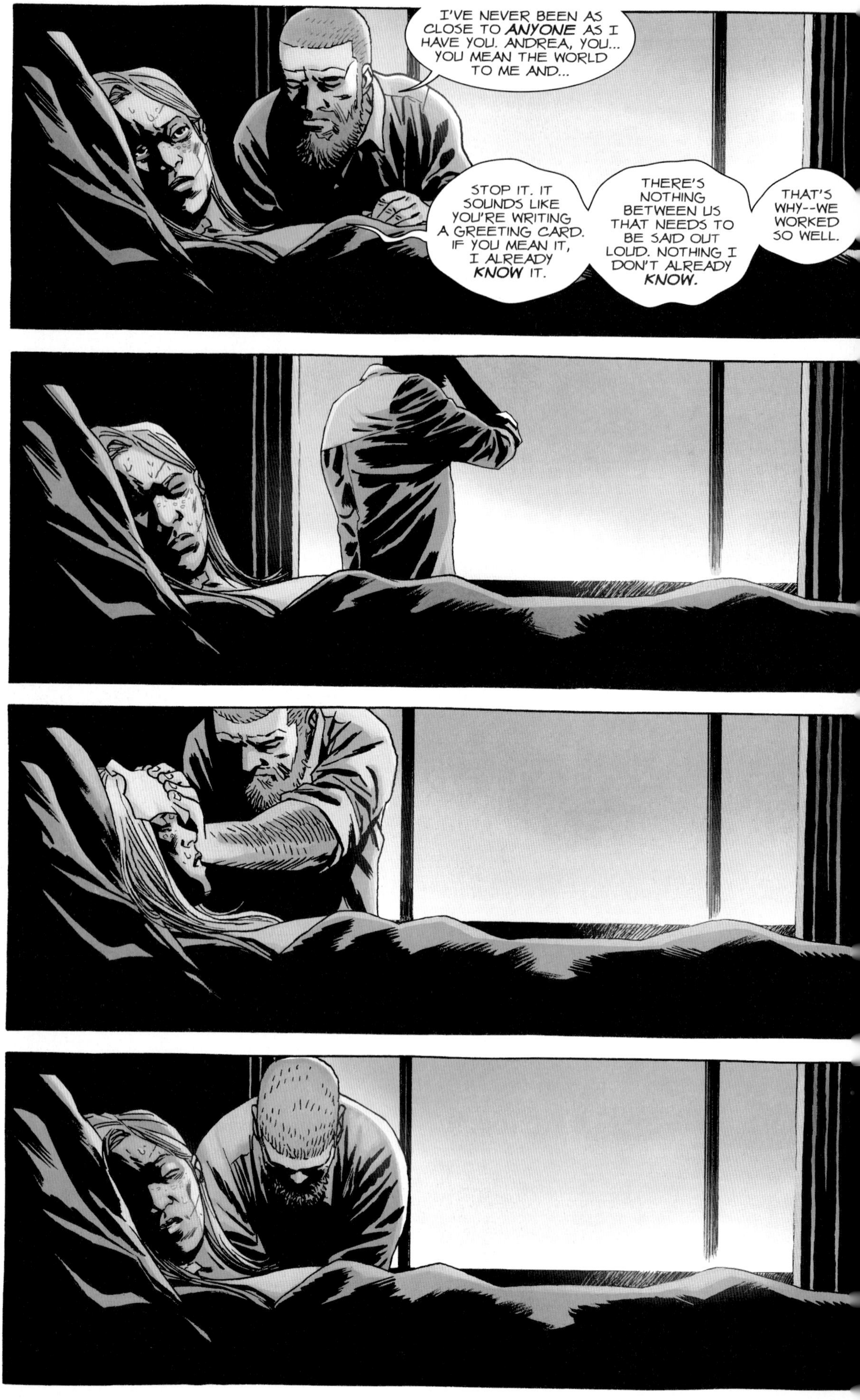

I'VE NEVER BEEN AS CLOSE TO ANYONE AS I HAVE YOU. ANDREA, YOU... YOU MEAN THE WORLD TO ME AND...
STOP IT. IT SOUNDS LIKE YOU'RE WRITING A GREETING CARD. IF YOU MEAN IT, I ALREADY KNOW IT.
THERE'S NOTHING BETWEEN US THAT NEEDS TO BE SAID OUT LOUD. NOTHING I DON'T ALREADY KNOW.
THAT'S WHY--WE WORKED SO WELL.

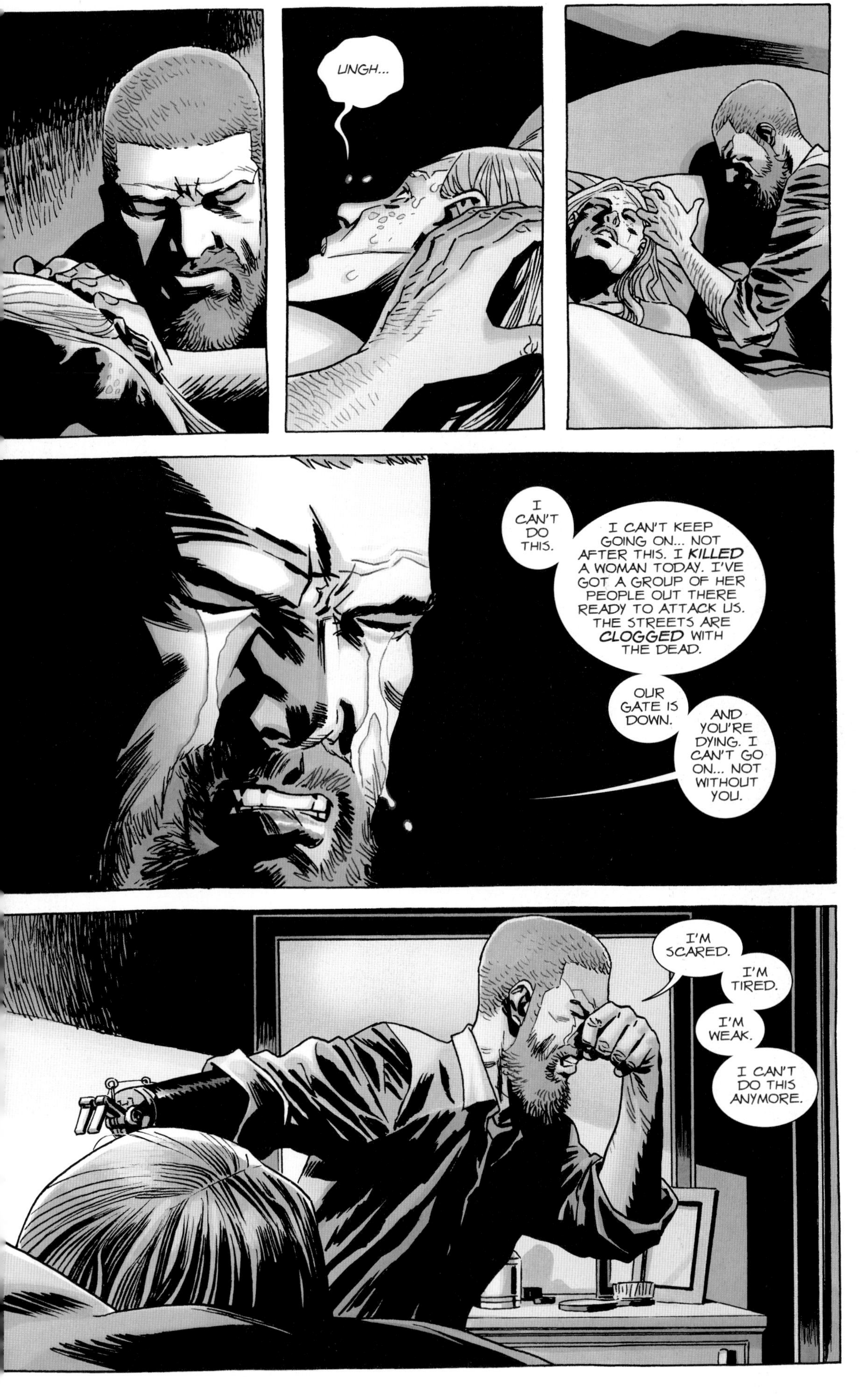
UNGH...
I CAN'T DO THIS.
I CAN'T KEEP GOING ON... NOT AFTER THIS. I KILLED A WOMAN TODAY. I'VE GOT A GROUP OF HER PEOPLE OUT THERE READY TO ATTACK US. THE STREETS ARE CLOGGED WITH THE DEAD.
OUR GATE IS DOWN.
AND YOU'RE DYING. I CAN'T GO ON... NOT WITHOUT YOU.
I'M SCARED.
I'M TIRED.
I'M WEAK.
I CAN'T DO THIS ANYMORE.

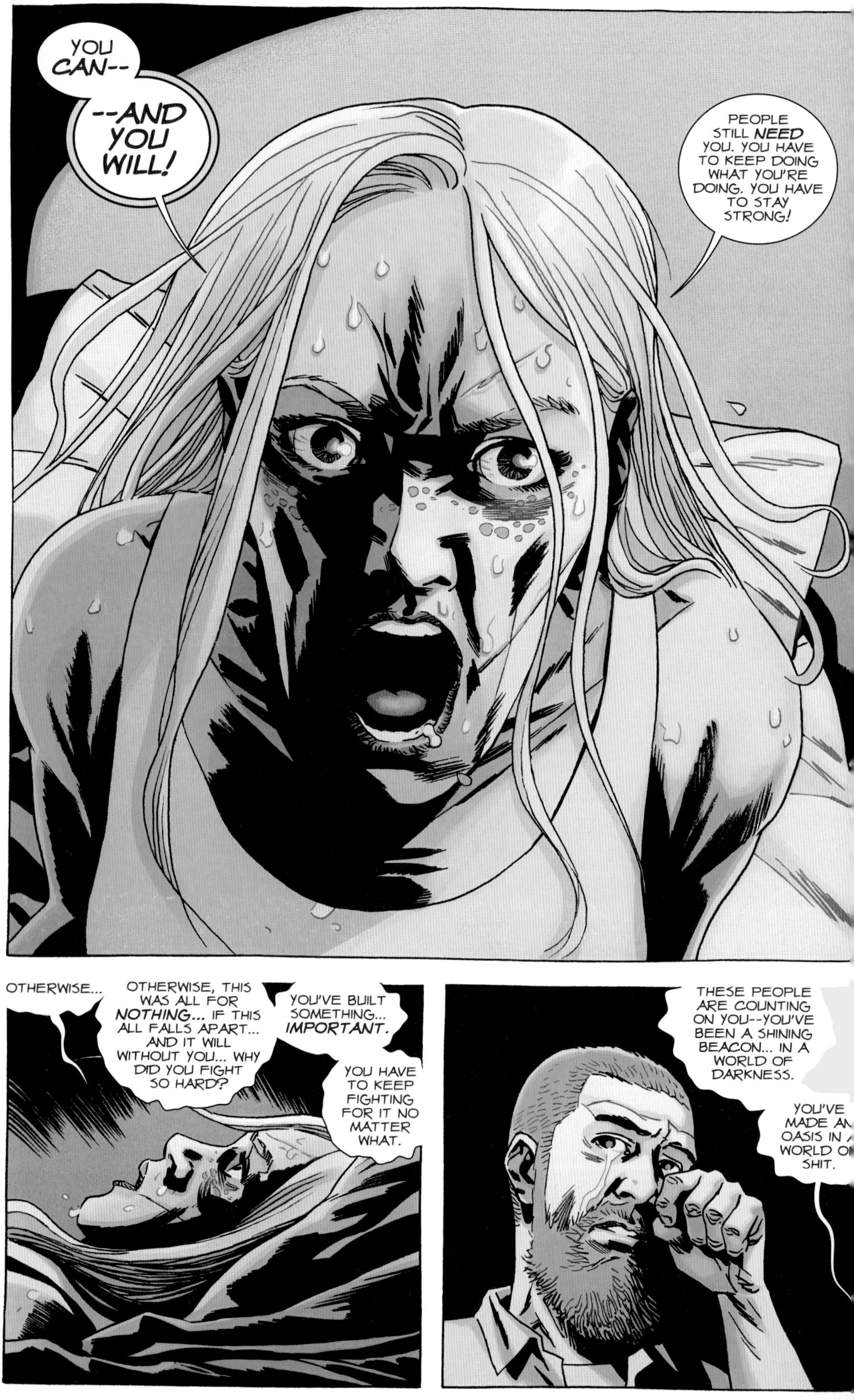
YOU CAN--
--AND YOU WILL!
PEOPLE STILL NEED YOU. YOU HAVE TO KEEP DOING WHAT YOU'RE DOING. YOU HAVE TO STAY STRONG!
OTHERWISE...
OTHERWISE, THIS WAS ALL FOR NOTHING... IF THIS ALL FALLS APART... AND IT WILL WITHOUT YOU... WHY DID YOU FIGHT SO HARD?
YOU'VE BUILT SOMETHING... IMPORTANT.
YOU HAVE TO KEEP FIGHTING FOR IT NO MATTER WHAT.
THESE PEOPLE ARE COUNTING ON YOU--YOU'VE BEEN A SHINING BEACON... IN A WORLD OF DARKNESS.
YOU'VE MADE AN OASIS IN A WORLD OF SHIT.

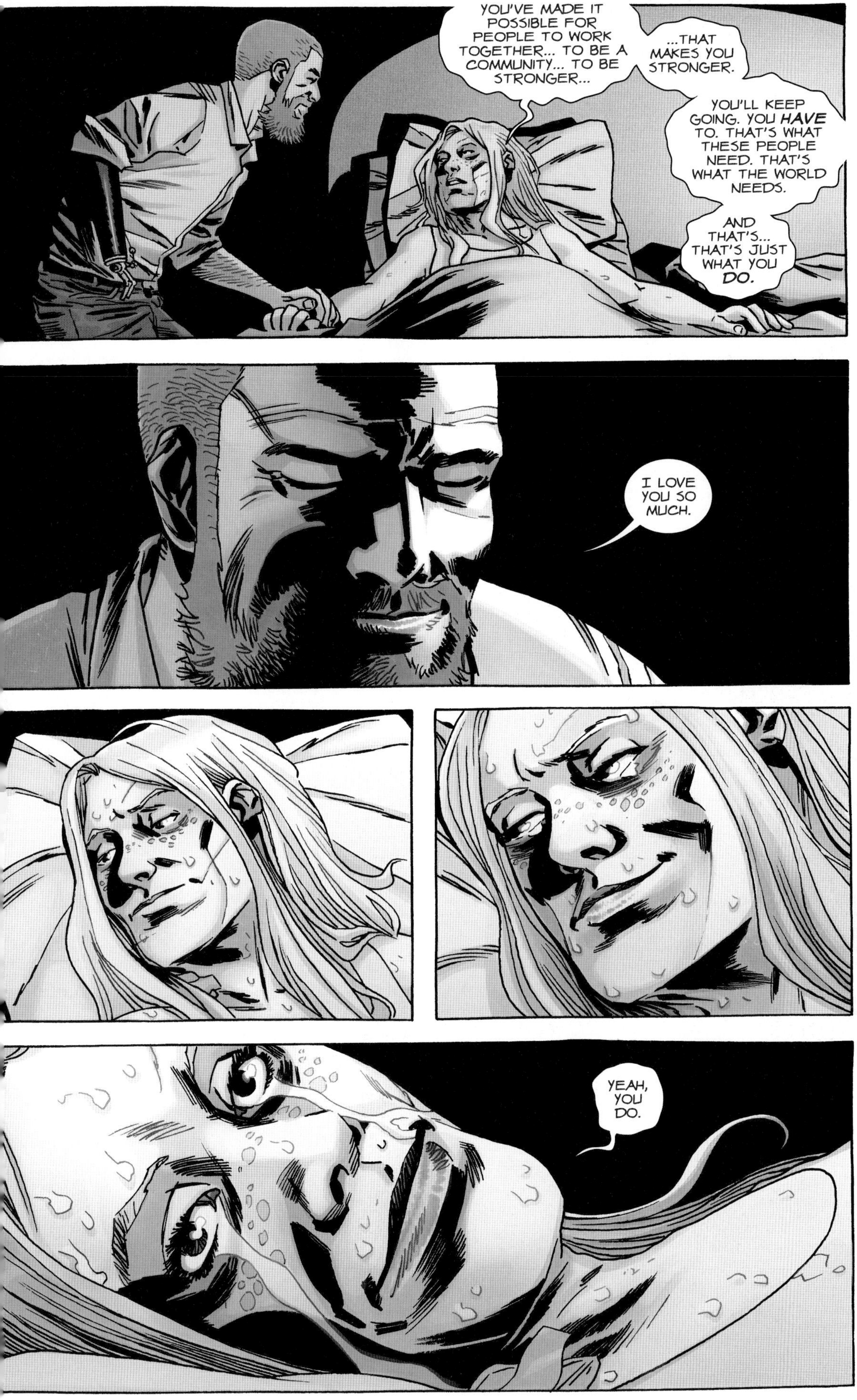
YOU'VE MADE IT POSSIBLE FOR PEOPLE TO WORK TOGETHER... TO BE A COMMUNITY... TO BE STRONGER...
...THAT MAKES YOU STRONGER.
YOU'LL KEEP GOING. YOU **HAVE** TO. THAT'S WHAT THESE PEOPLE NEED. THAT'S WHAT THE WORLD NEEDS.
AND THAT'S... THAT'S JUST WHAT YOU ***DO.***
I LOVE YOU SO MUCH.
YEAH, YOU DO.

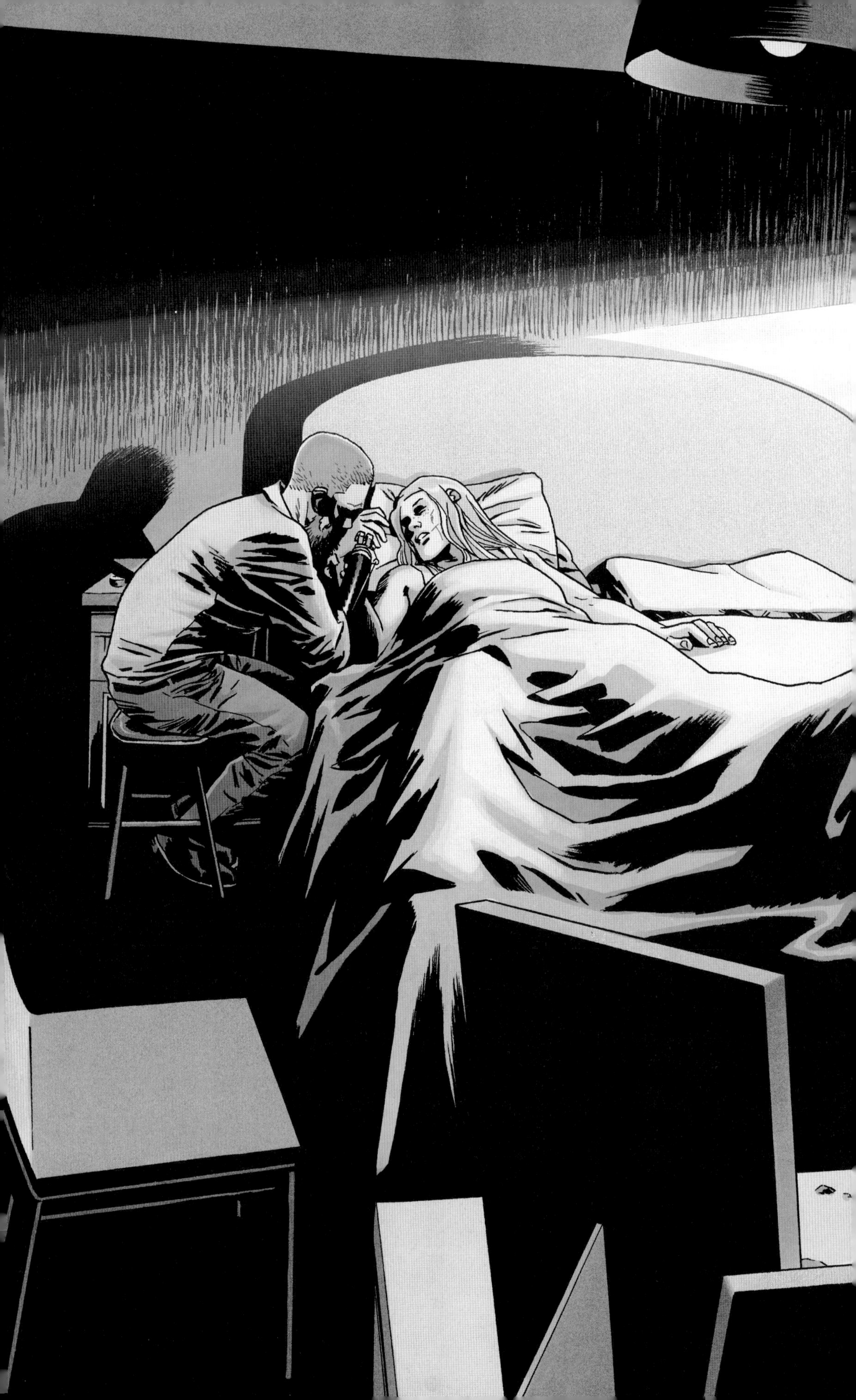

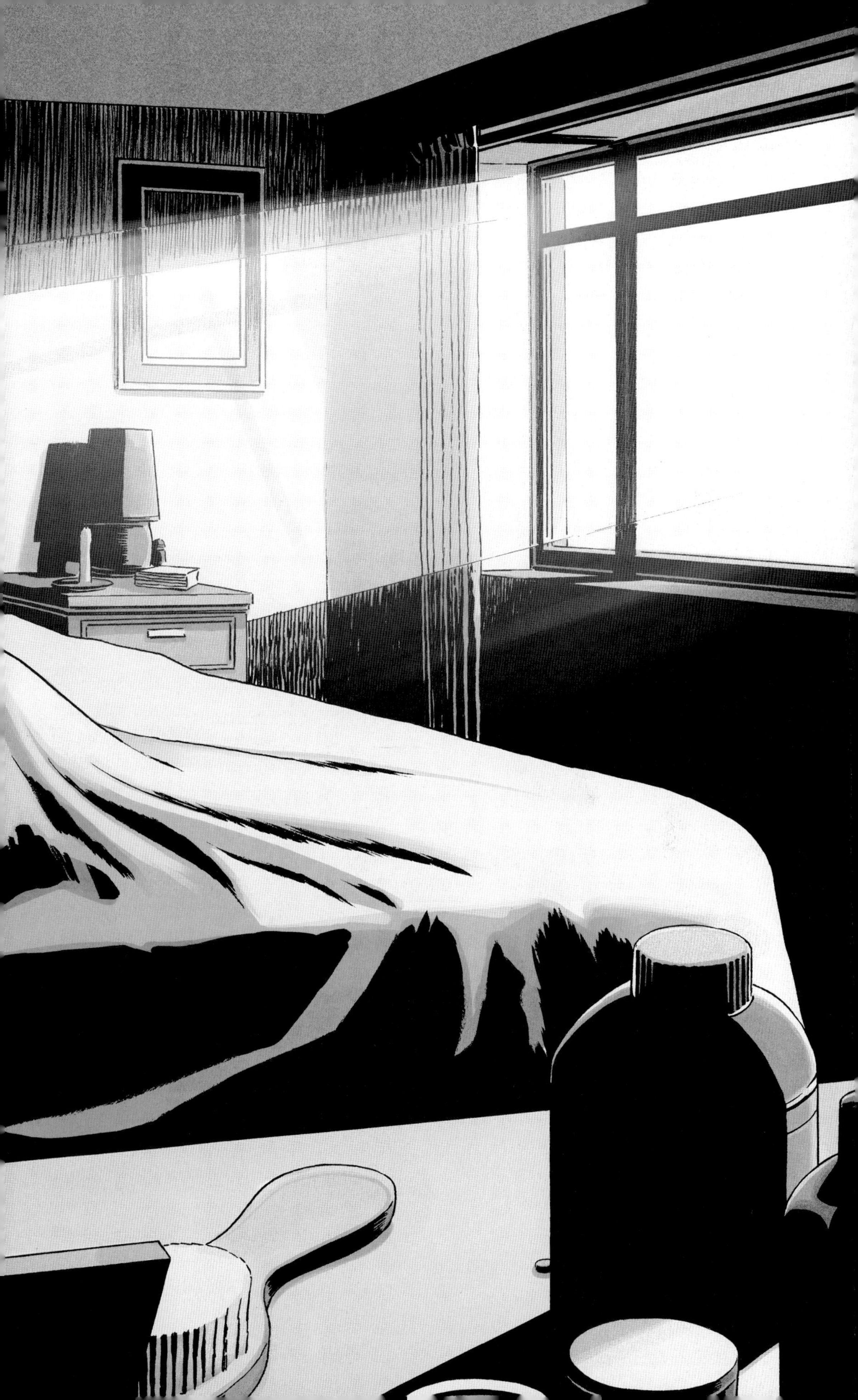

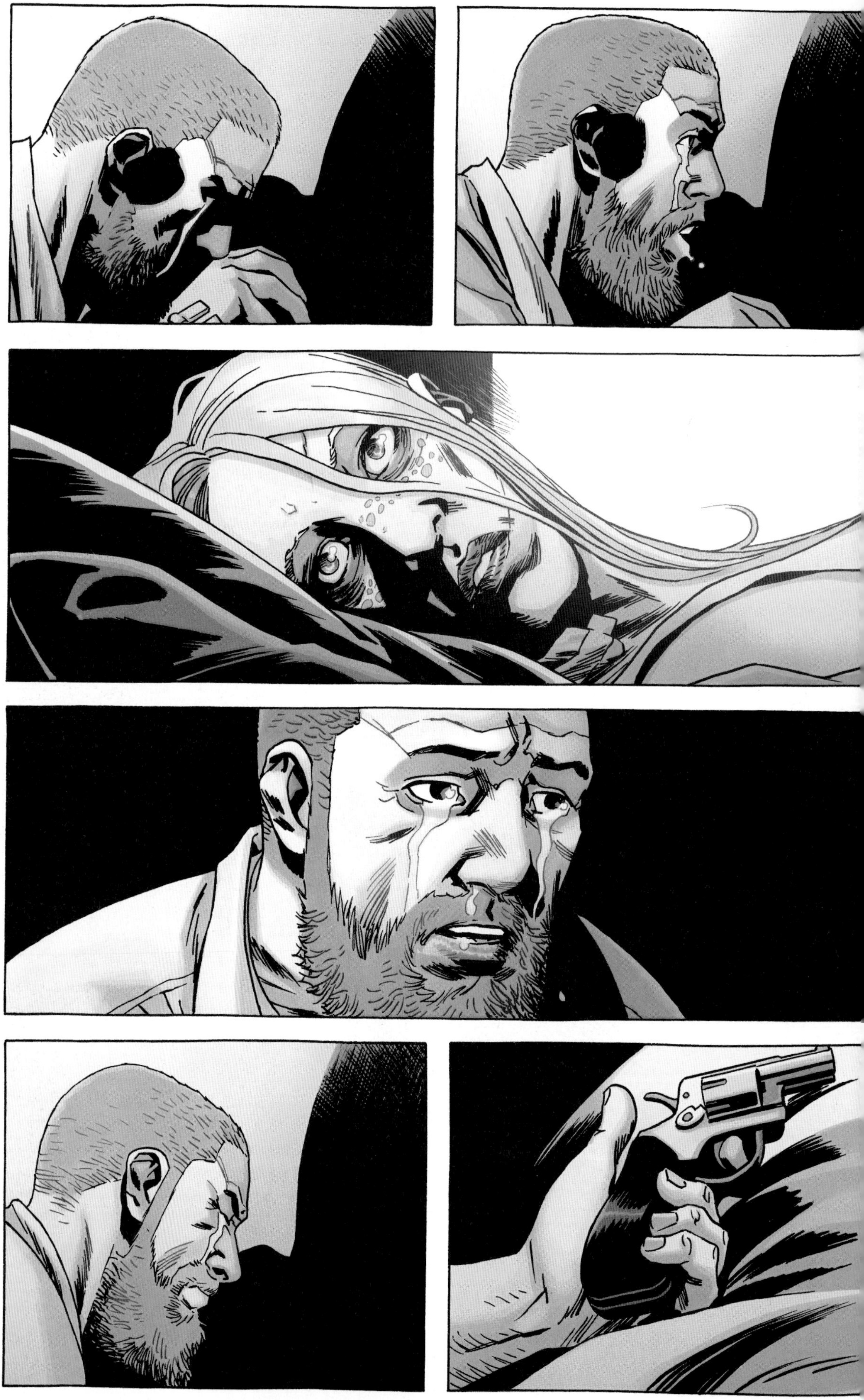

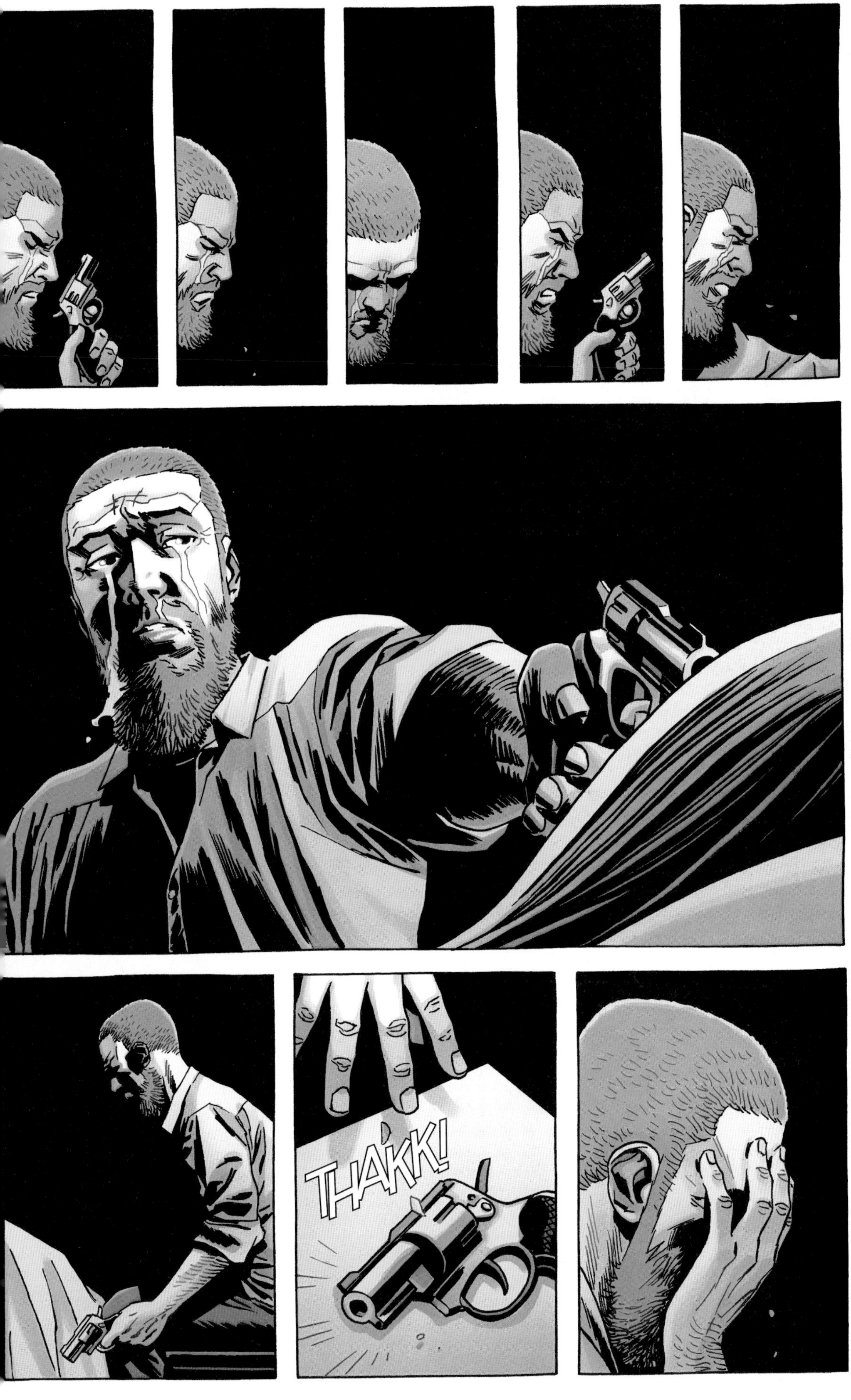
THAKK!

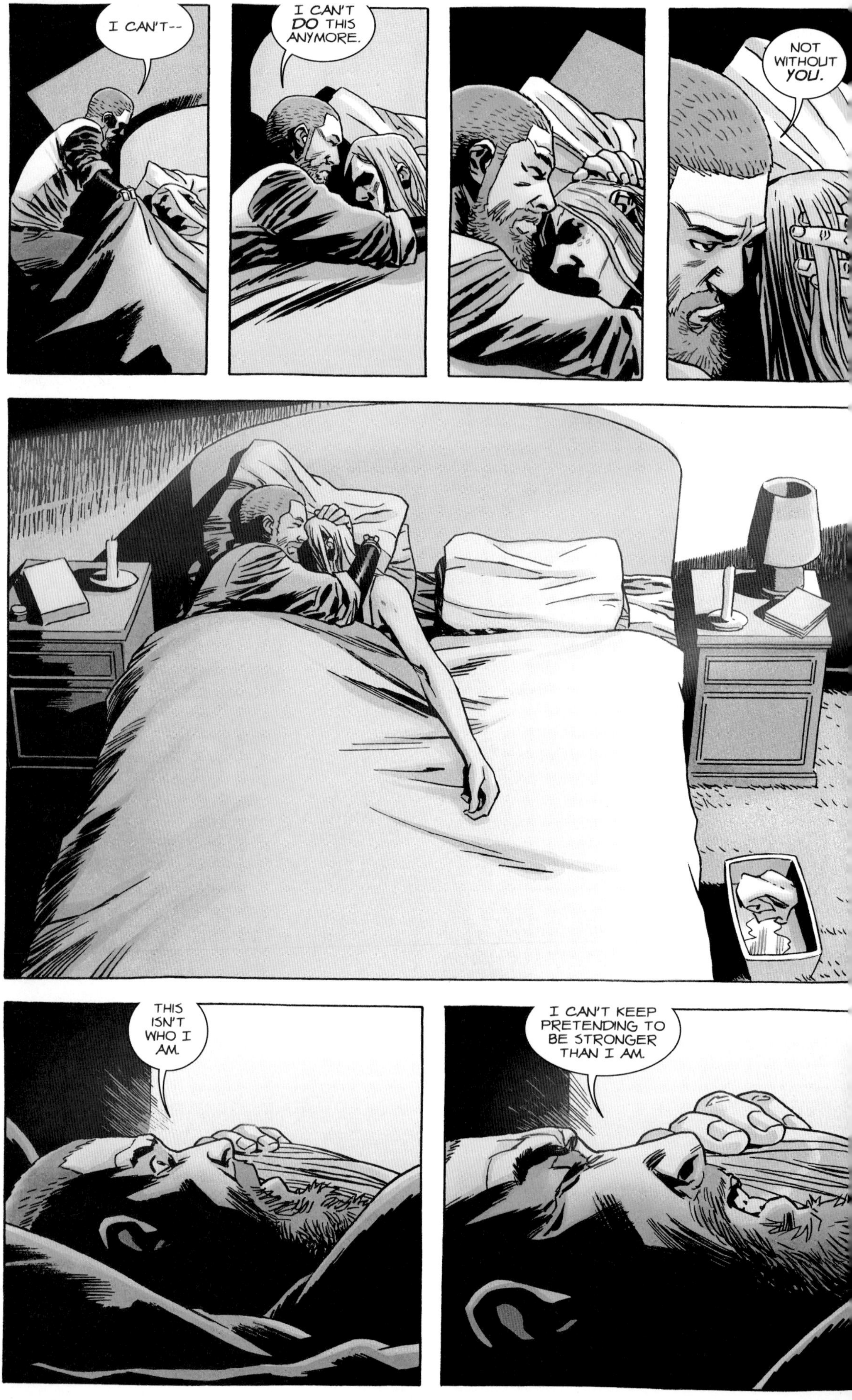

I CAN'T--
I CAN'T DO THIS ANYMORE.
NOT WITHOUT YOU.
THIS ISN'T WHO I AM.
I CAN'T KEEP PRETENDING TO BE STRONGER THAN I AM.

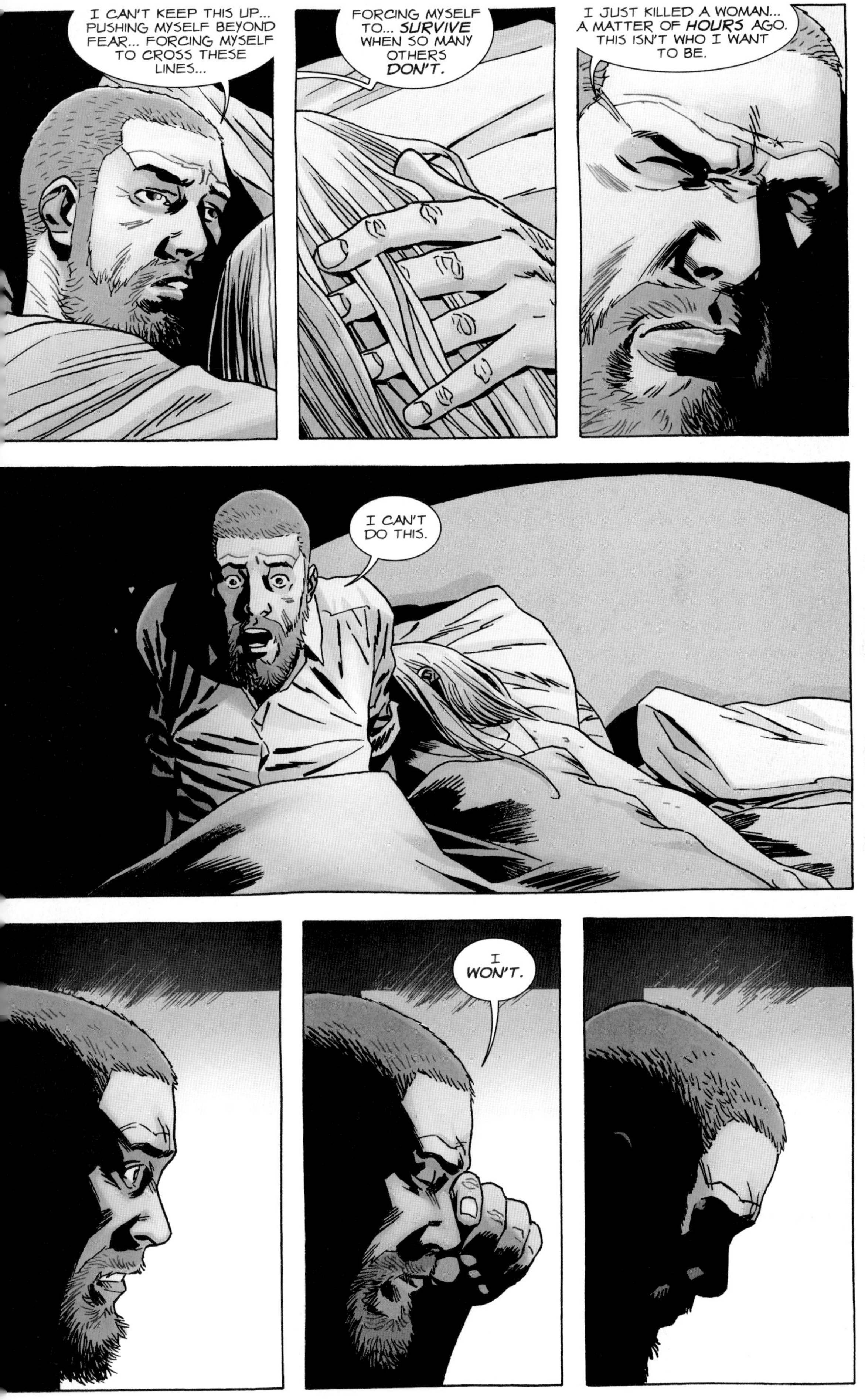
I CAN'T KEEP THIS UP... PUSHING MYSELF BEYOND FEAR... FORCING MYSELF TO CROSS THESE LINES...
FORCING MYSELF TO... SURVIVE WHEN SO MANY OTHERS DON'T.
I JUST KILLED A WOMAN... A MATTER OF HOURS AGO. THIS ISN'T WHO I WANT TO BE.
I CAN'T DO THIS.
I WON'T.

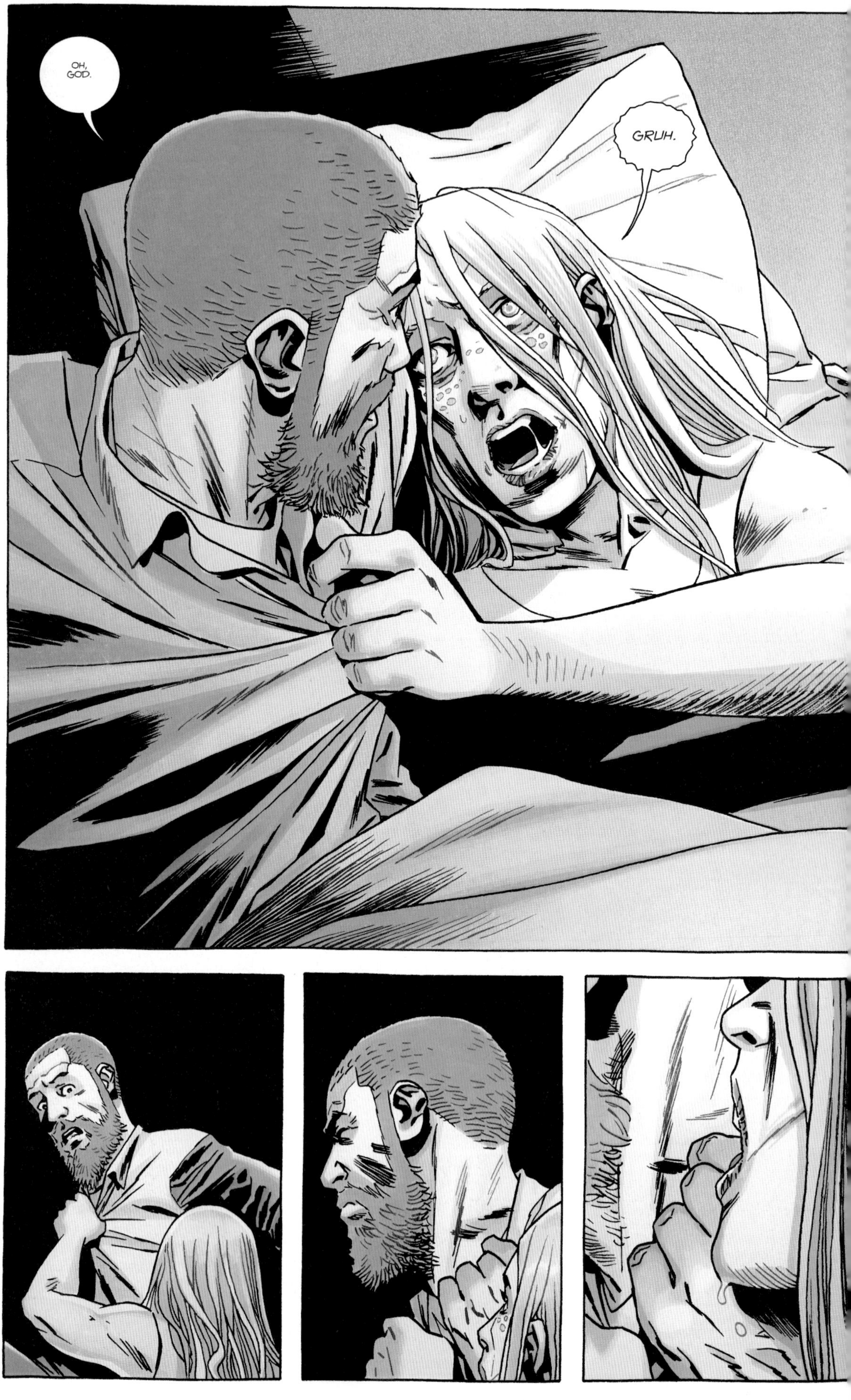
OH, GOD.
GRUH.

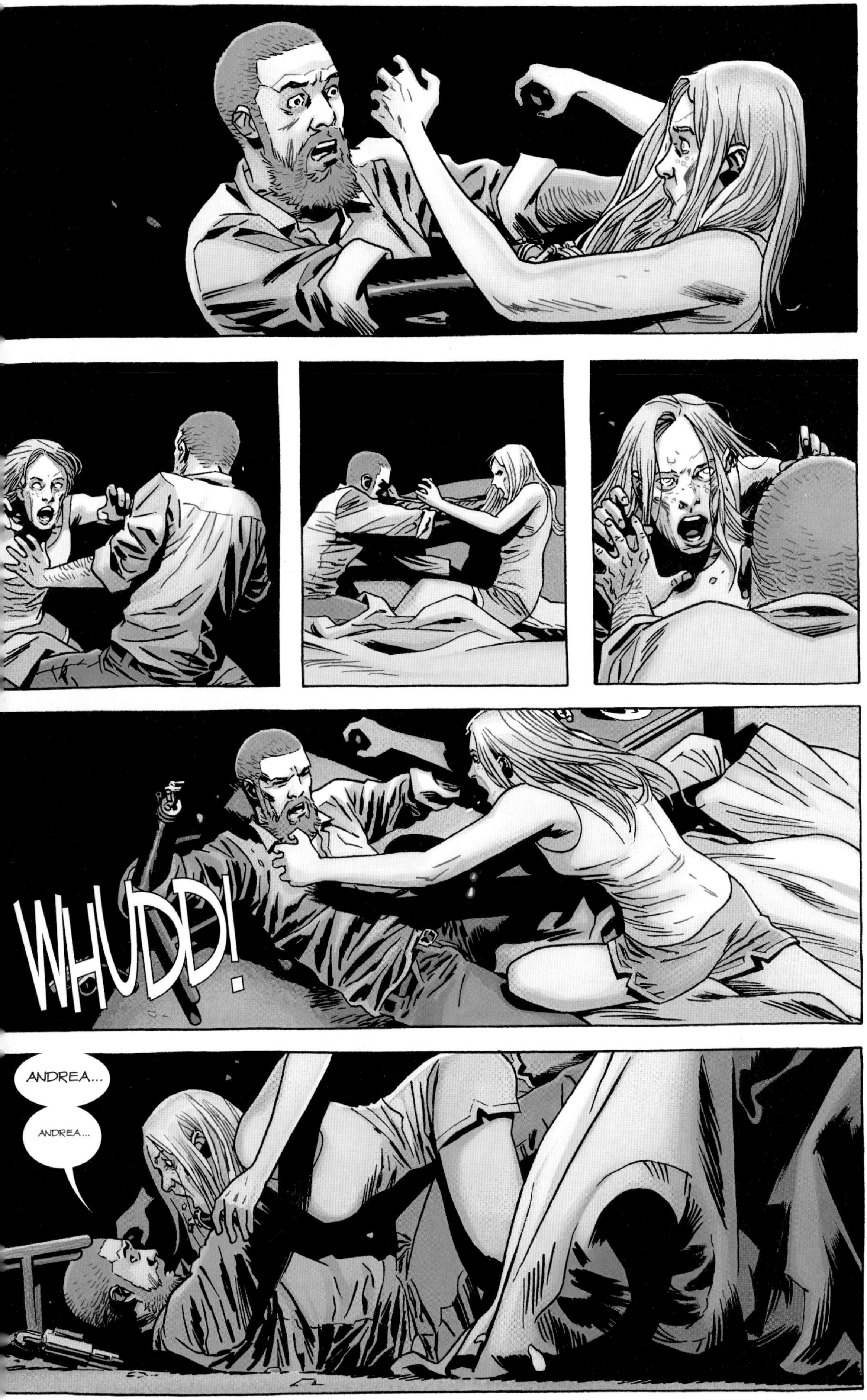
WHUDD!
ANDREA...
ANDREA...

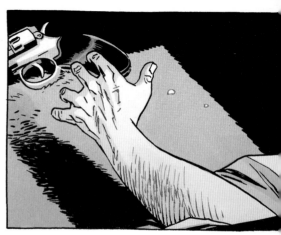

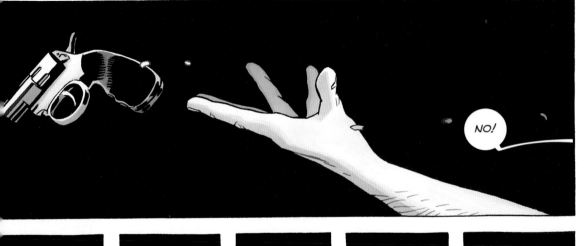

NO!

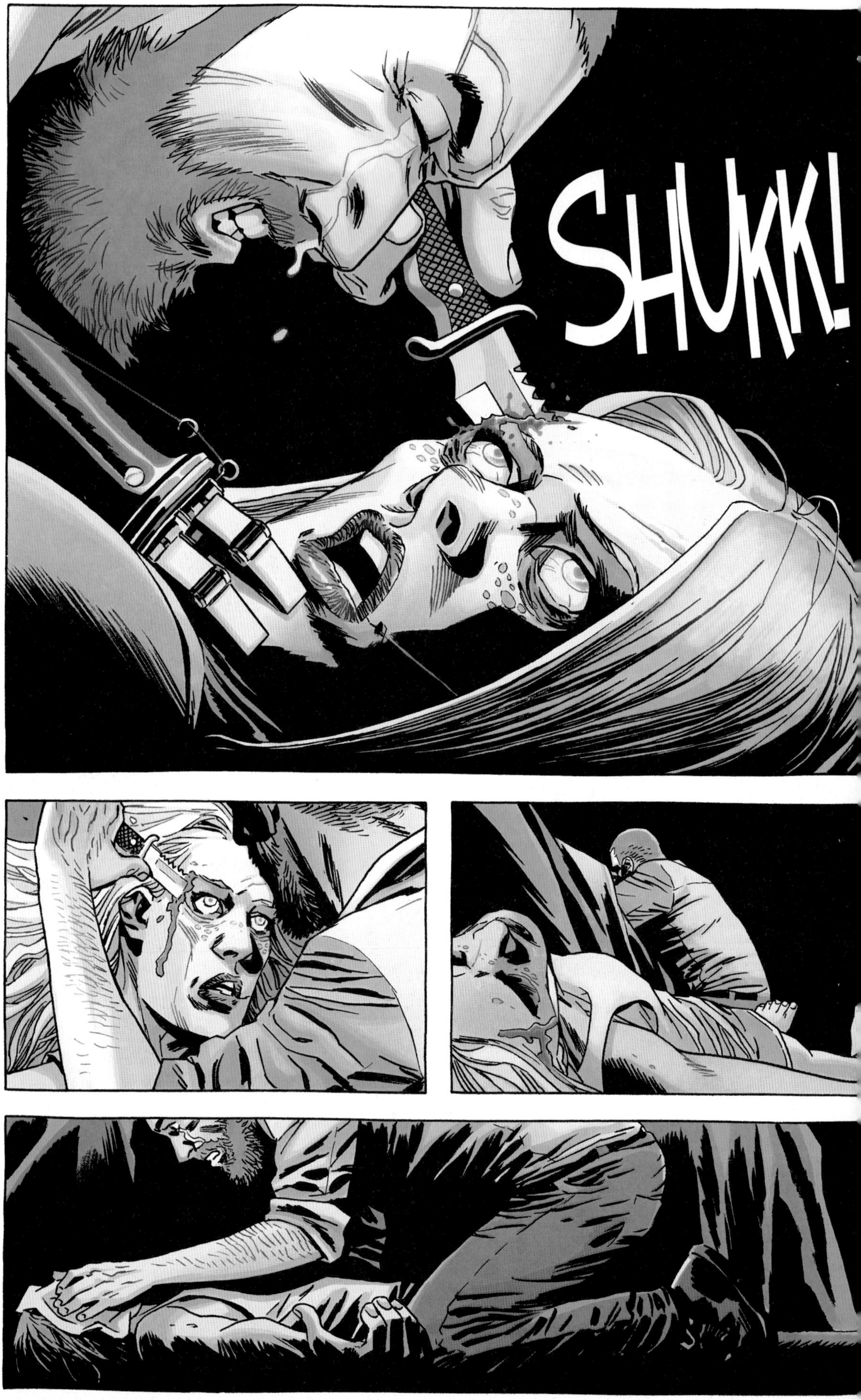
SHUKK!

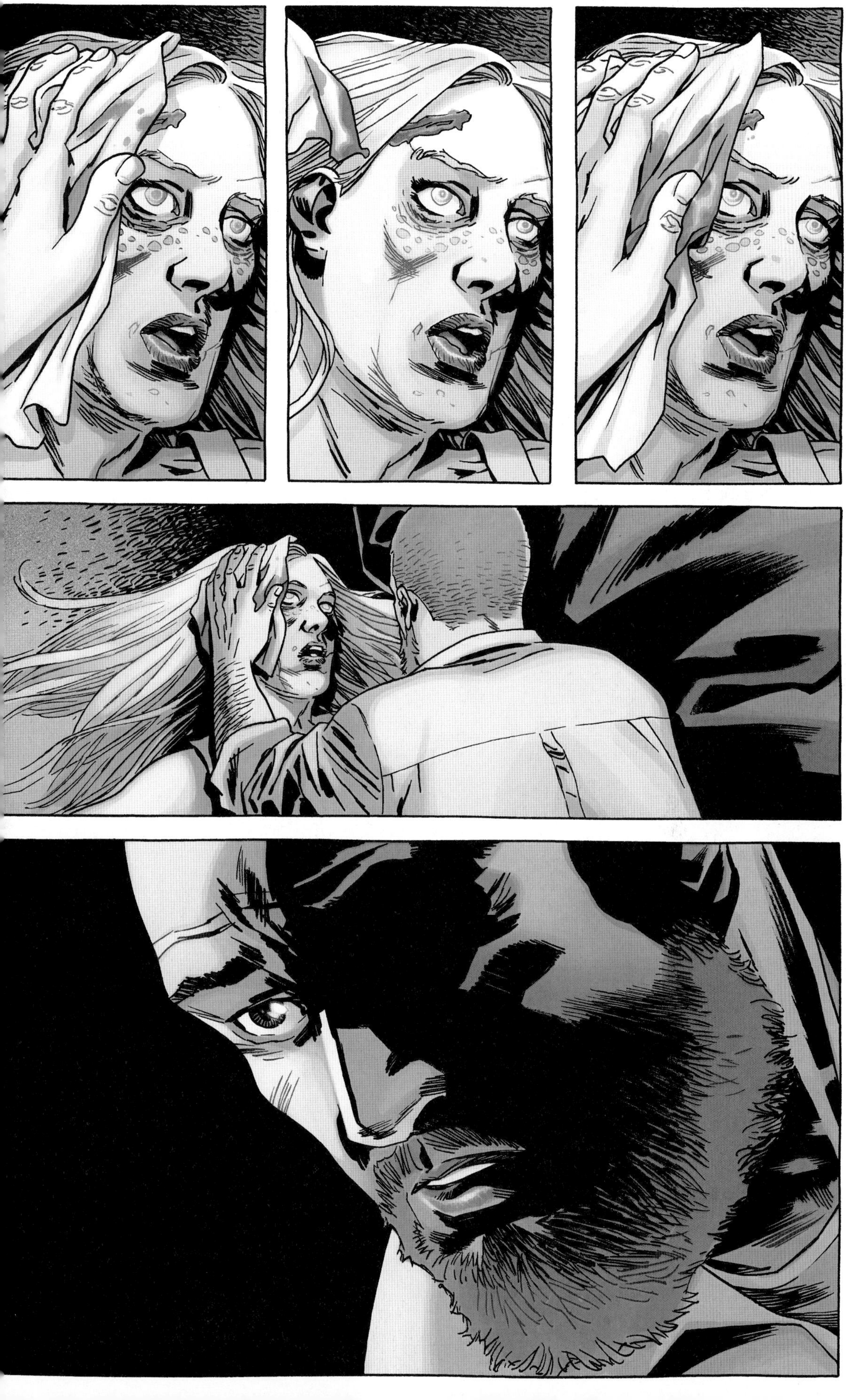

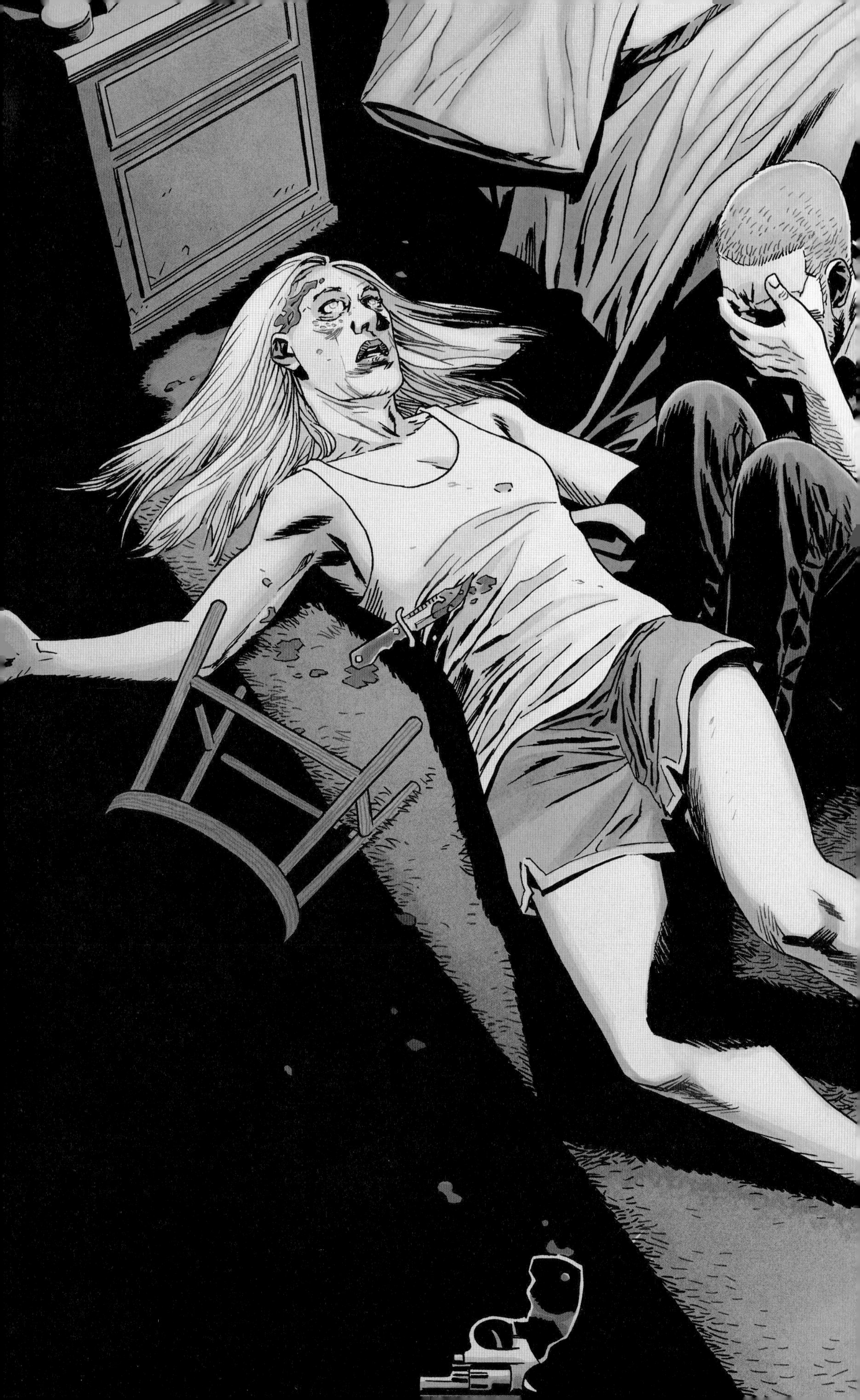

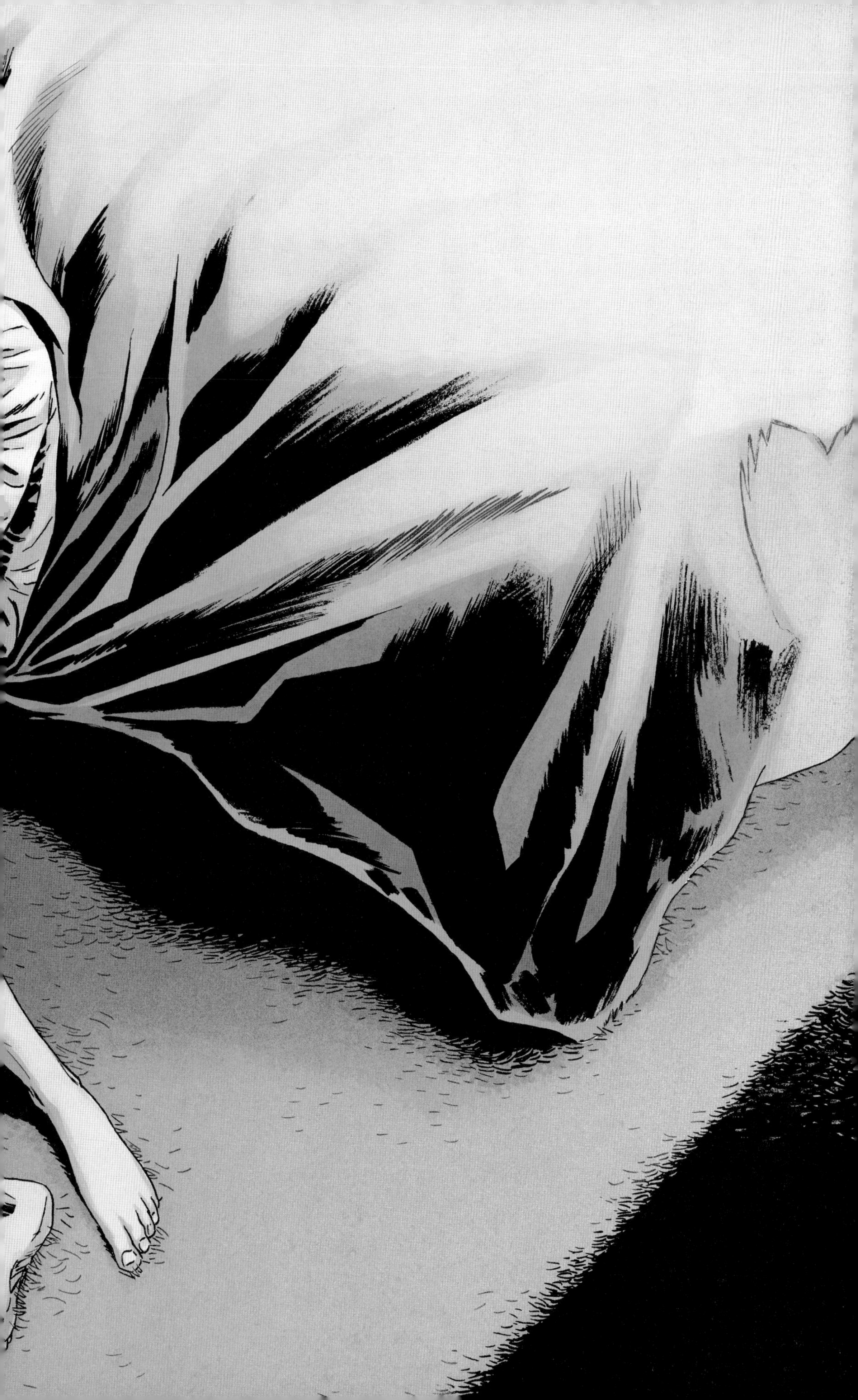

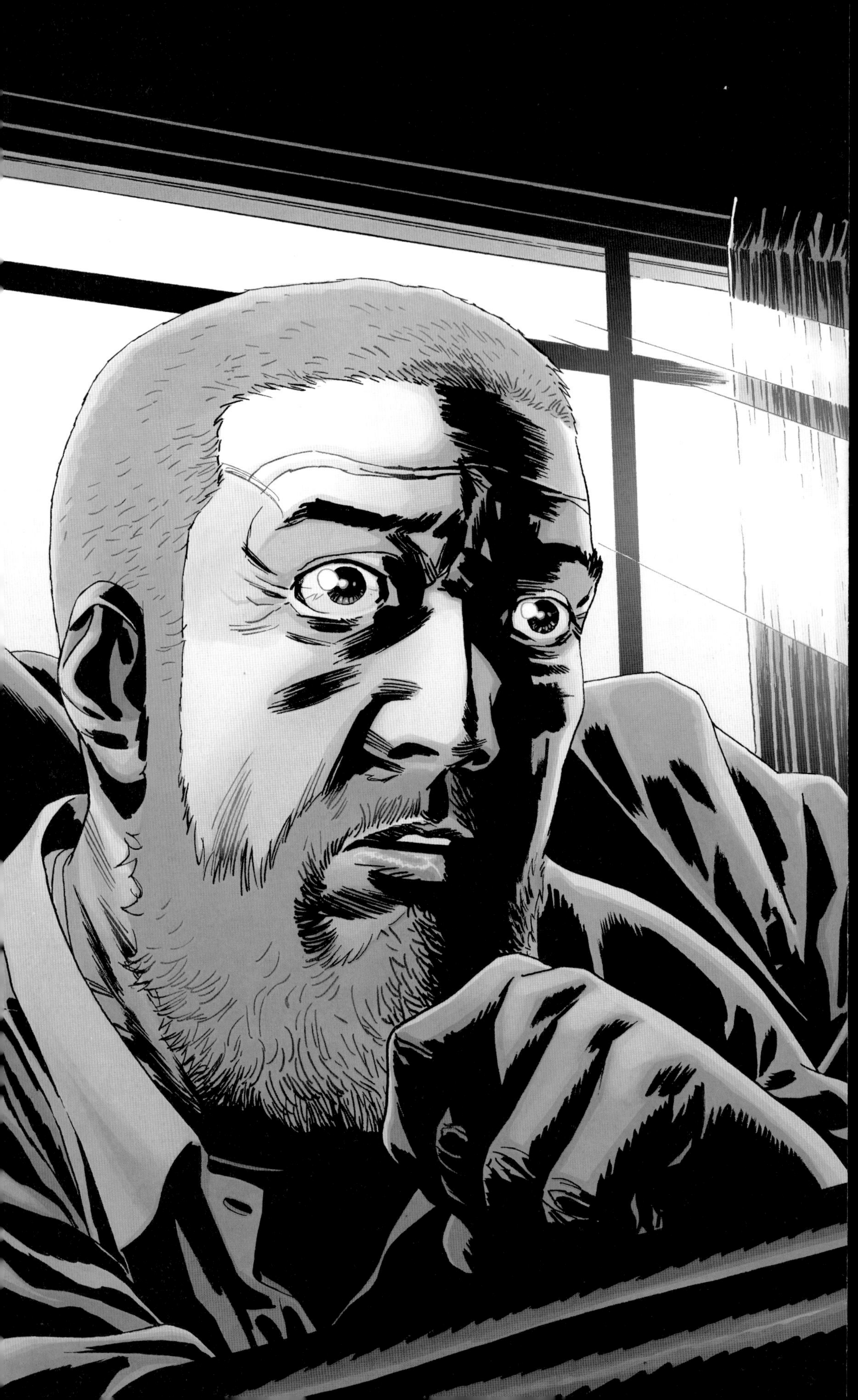

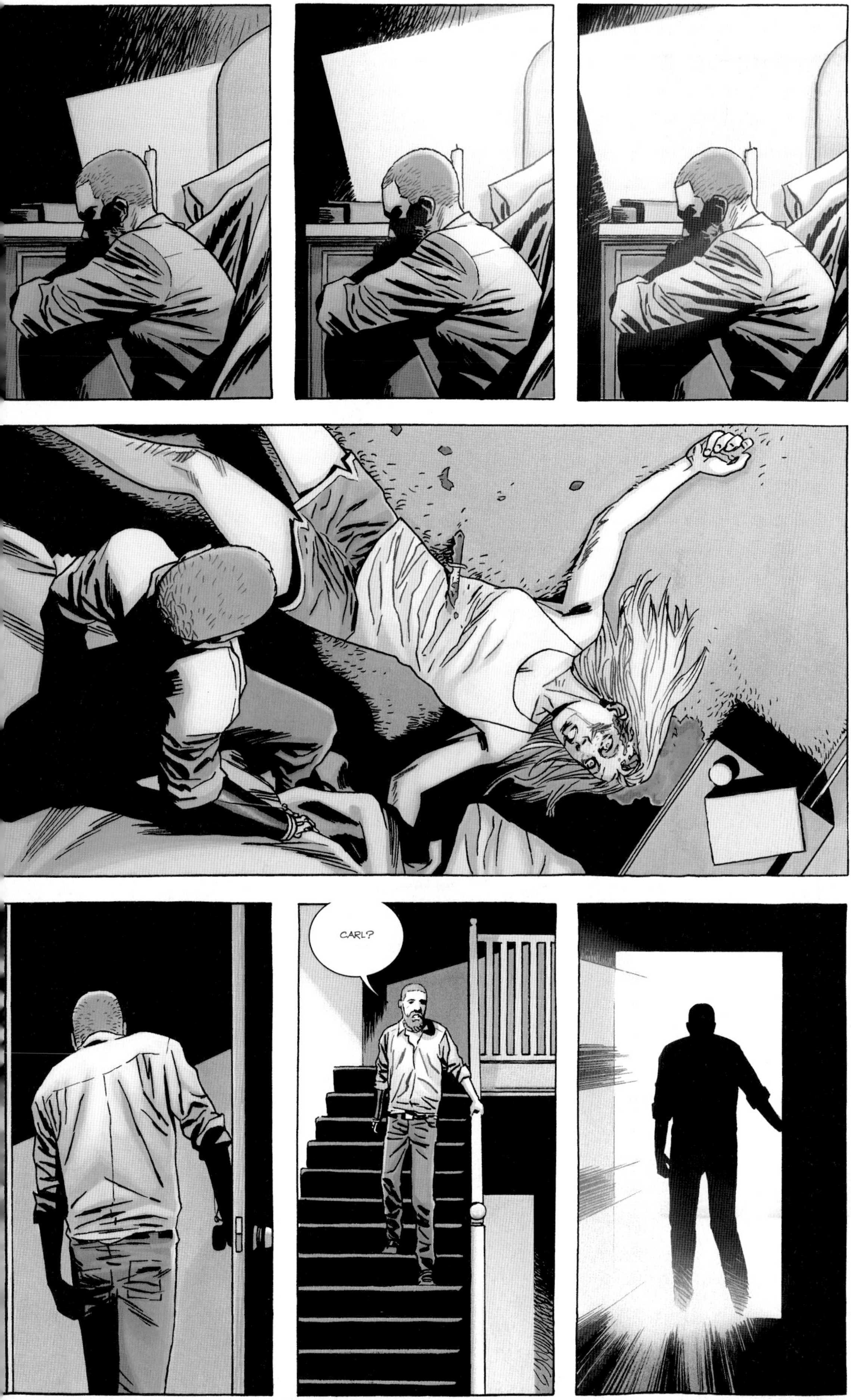
CARL?

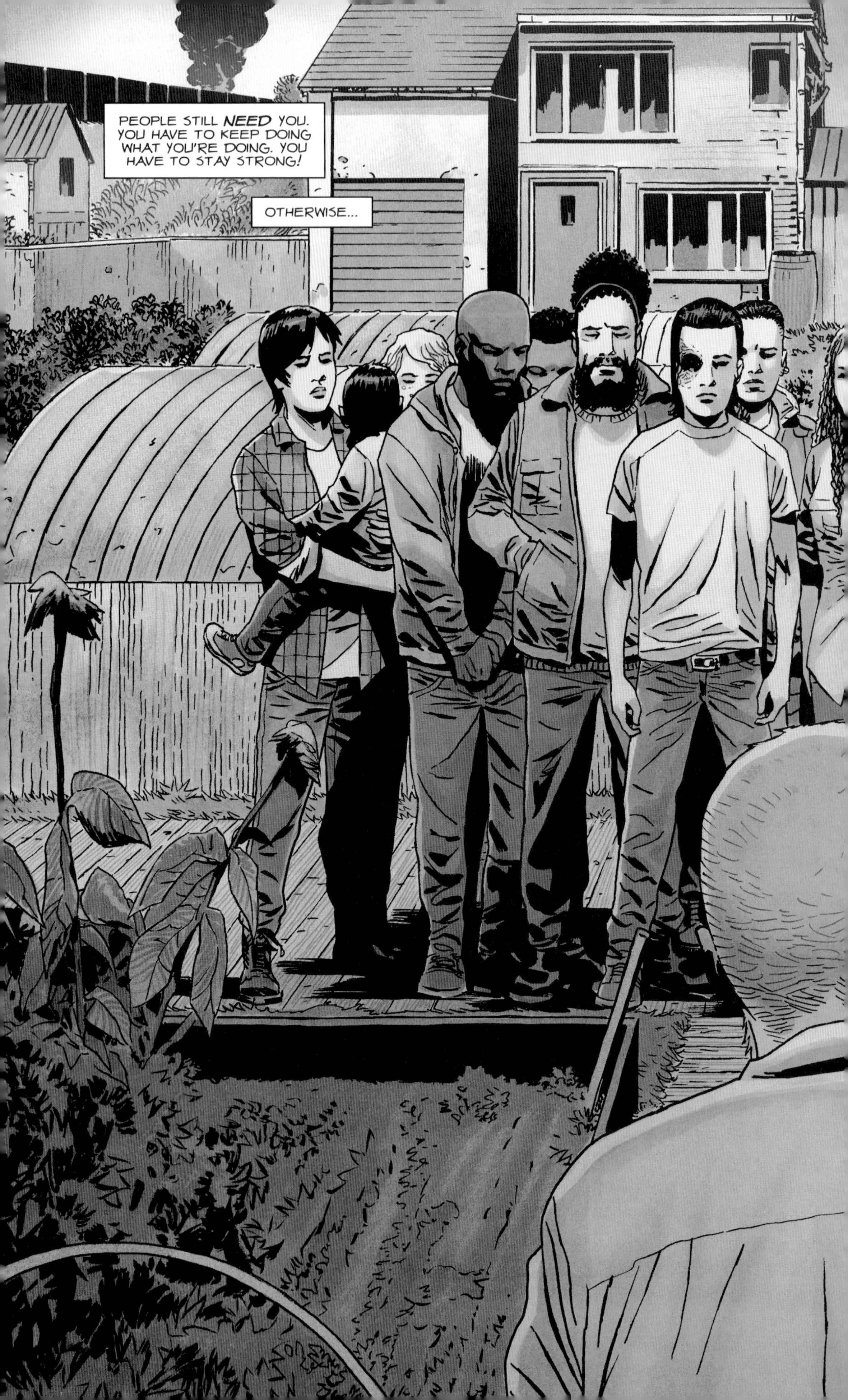
PEOPLE STILL NEED YOU. YOU HAVE TO KEEP DOING WHAT YOU'RE DOING. YOU HAVE TO STAY STRONG!
OTHERWISE...

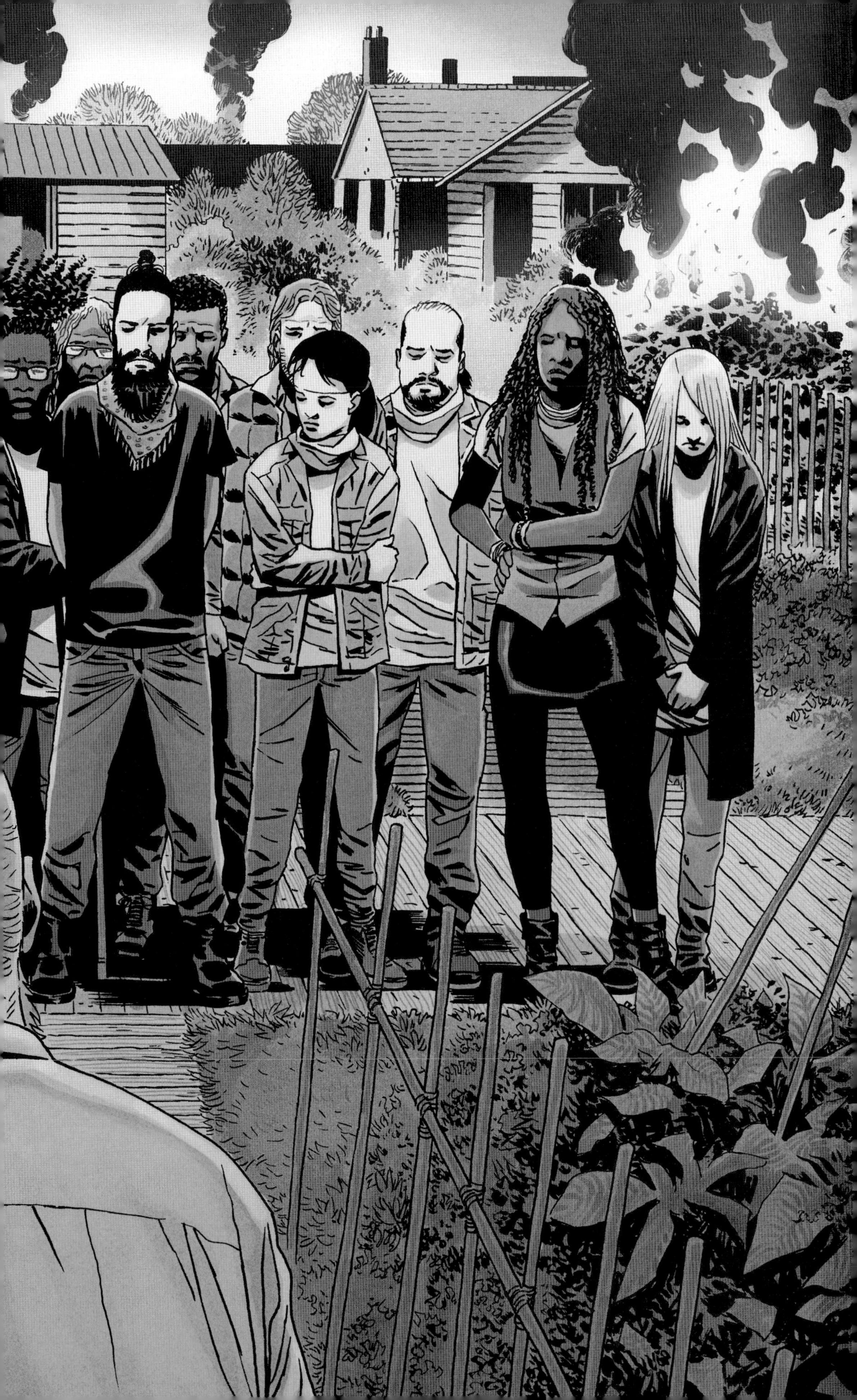

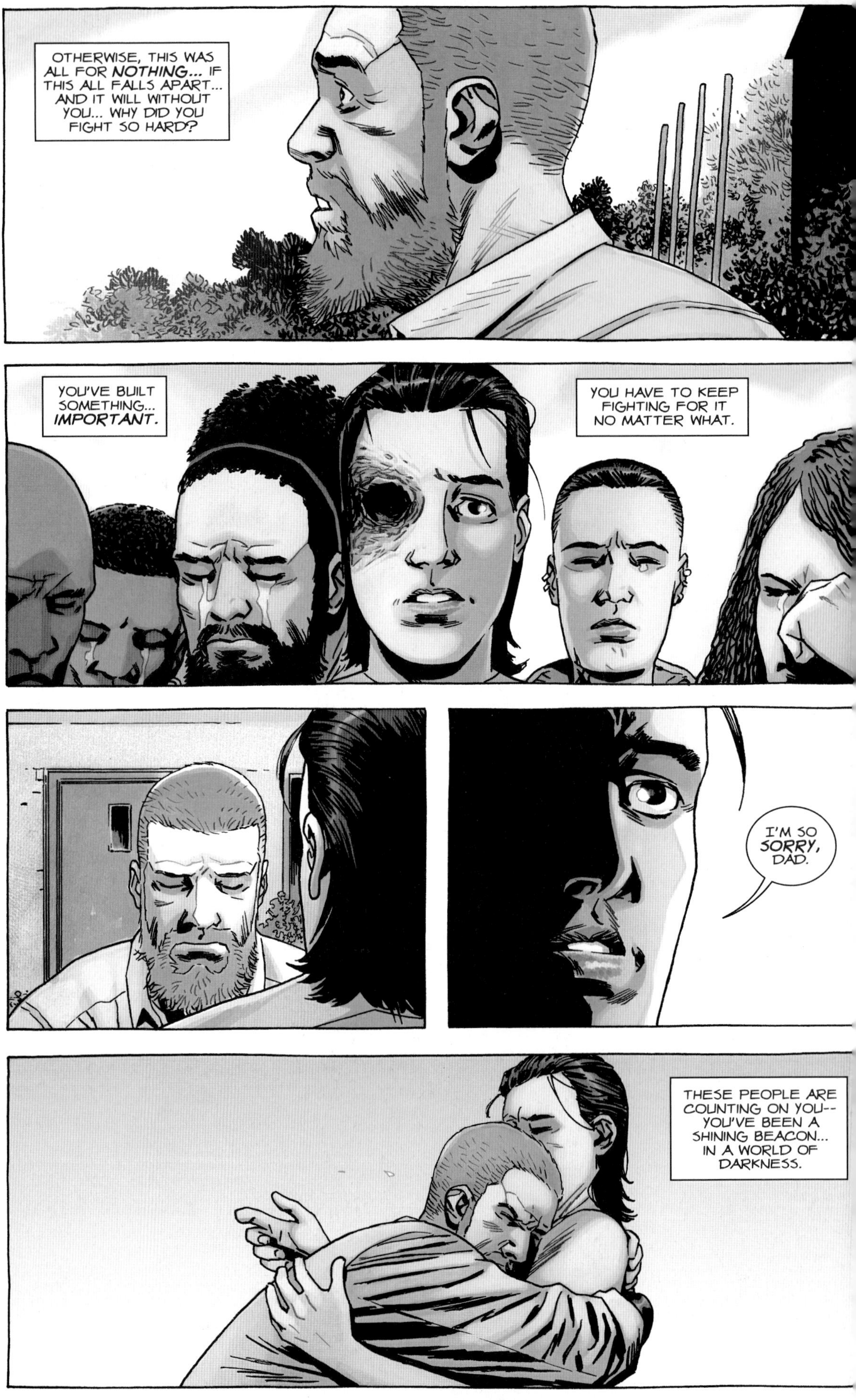
OTHERWISE, THIS WAS ALL FOR NOTHING... IF THIS ALL FALLS APART... AND IT WILL WITHOUT YOU... WHY DID YOU FIGHT SO HARD?
YOU'VE BUILT SOMETHING... IMPORTANT.
YOU HAVE TO KEEP FIGHTING FOR IT NO MATTER WHAT.
I'M SO SORRY, DAD.
THESE PEOPLE ARE COUNTING ON YOU-- YOU'VE BEEN A SHINING BEACON... IN A WORLD OF DARKNESS.

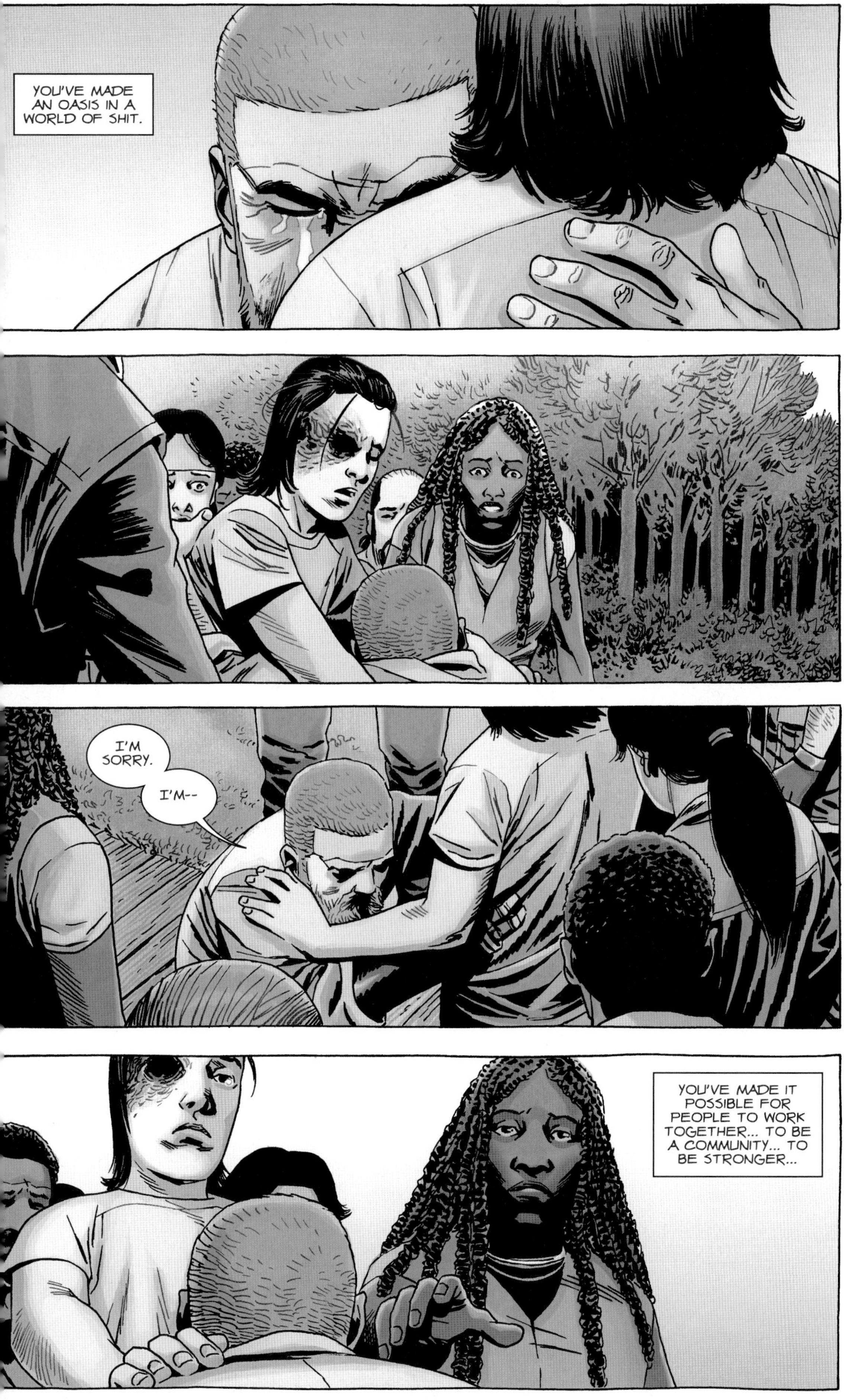
YOU'VE MADE AN OASIS IN A WORLD OF SHIT.
I'M SORRY.
I'M--
YOU'VE MADE IT POSSIBLE FOR PEOPLE TO WORK TOGETHER... TO BE A COMMUNITY... TO BE STRONGER...

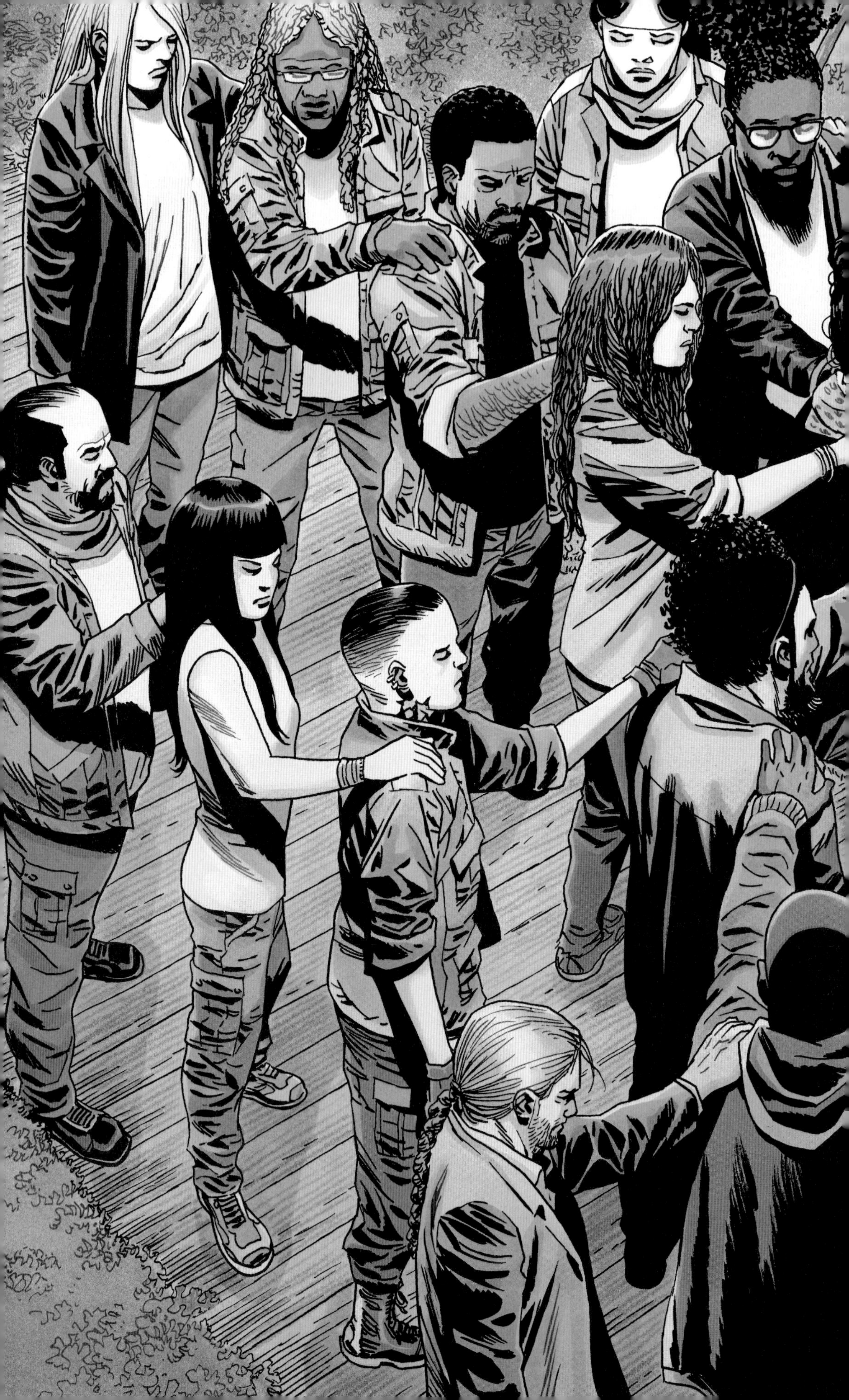

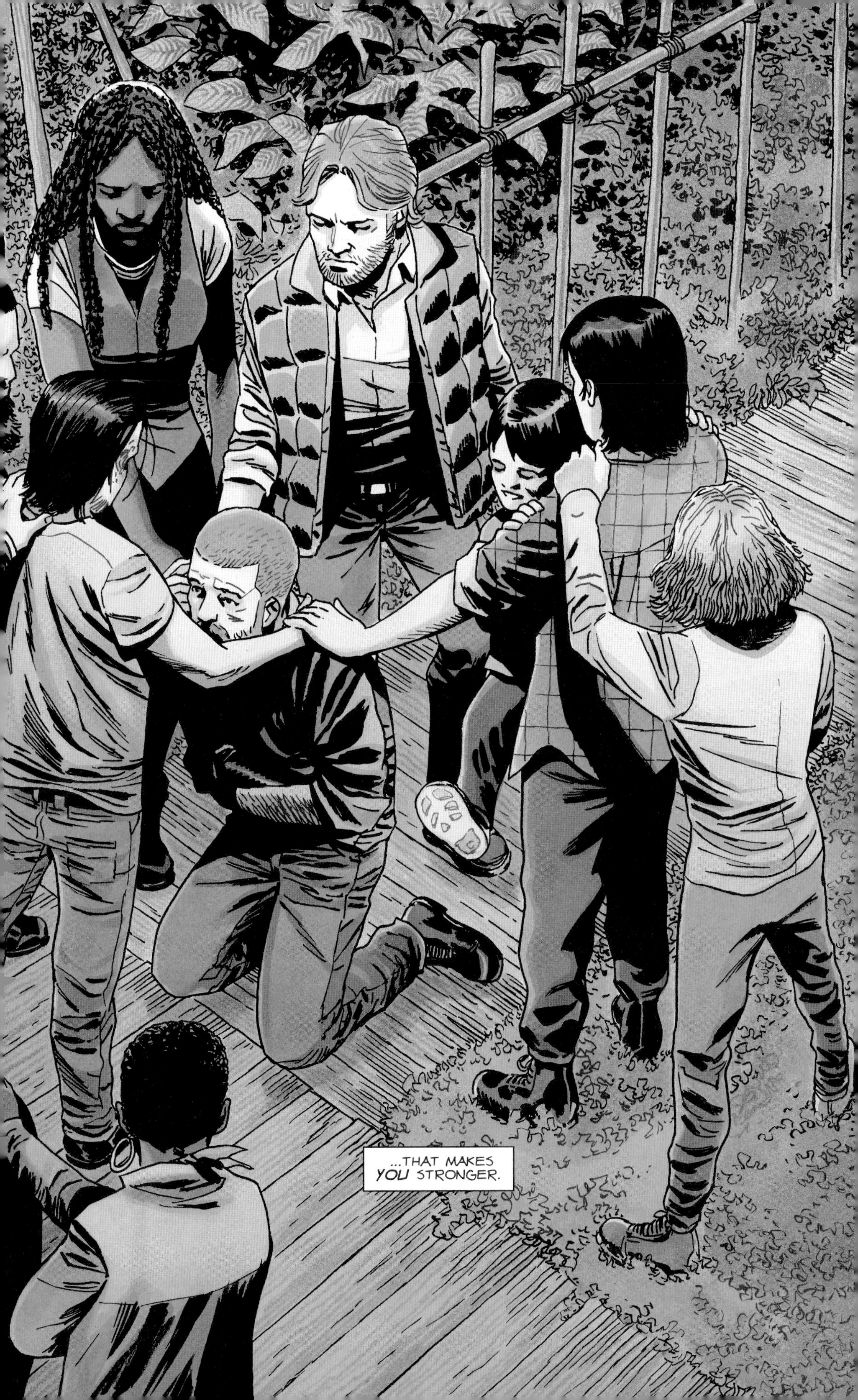
...THAT MAKES YOU STRONGER.

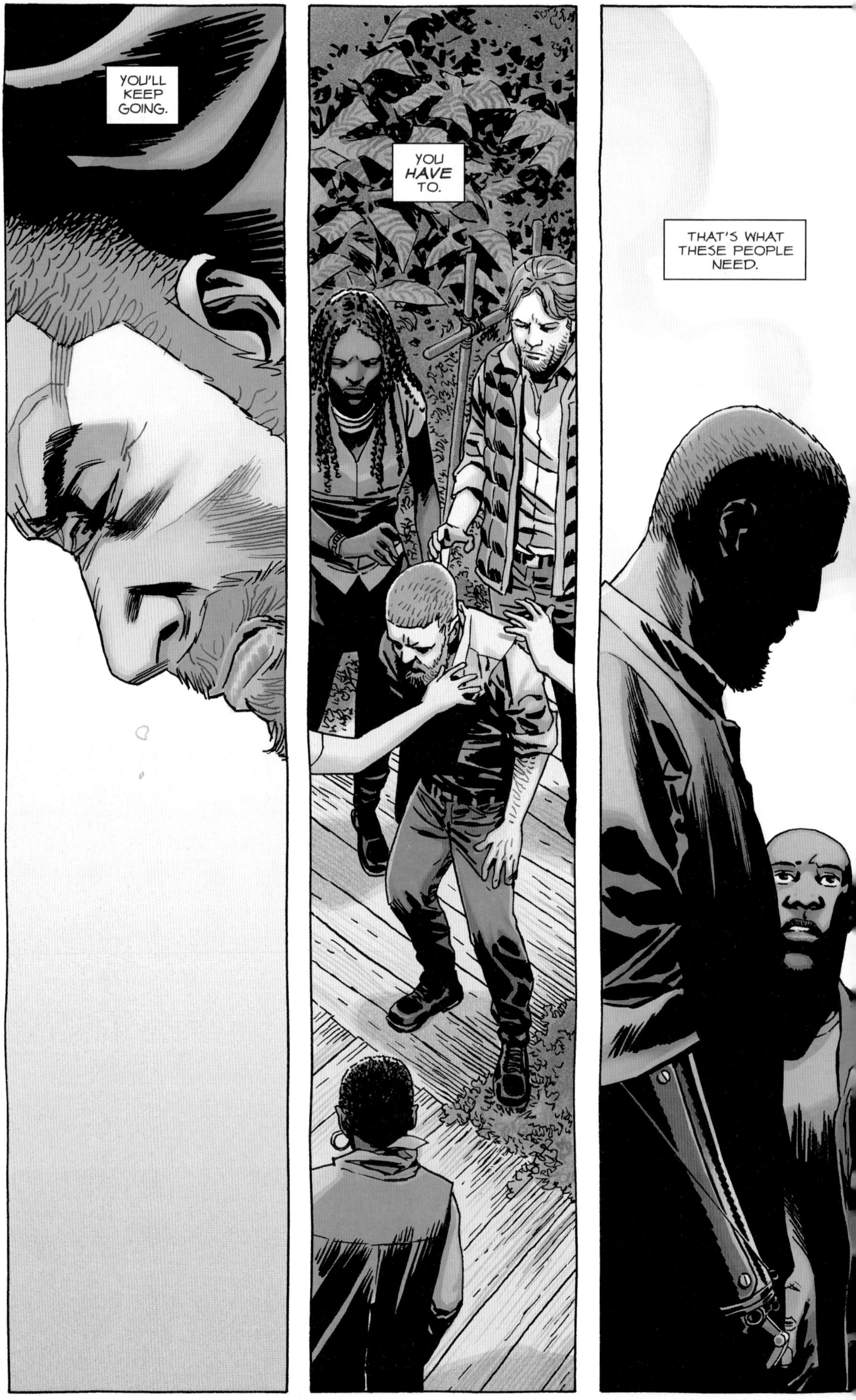
YOU'LL KEEP GOING.
YOU *HAVE* TO.
THAT'S WHAT THESE PEOPLE NEED.

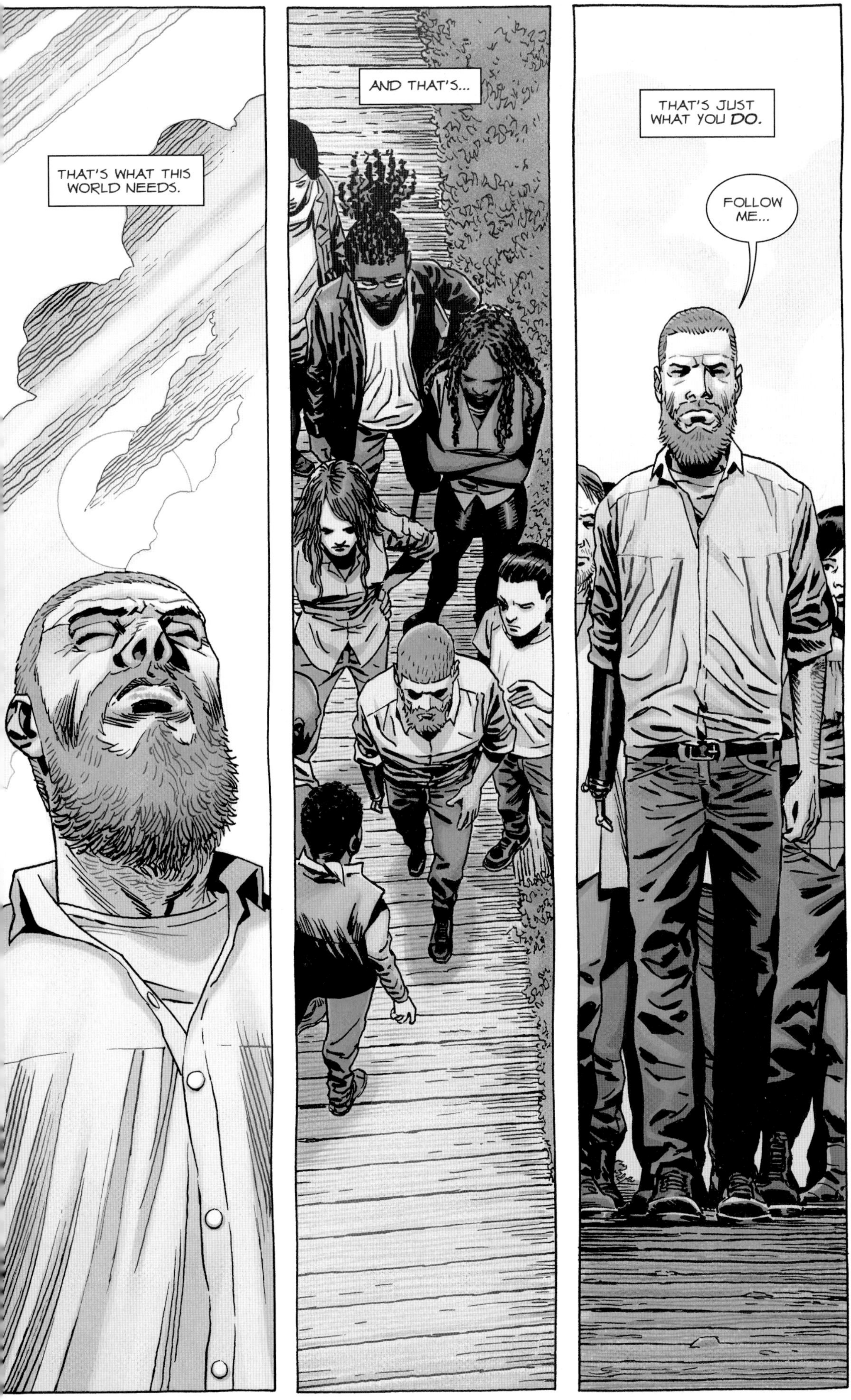
THAT'S WHAT THIS WORLD NEEDS.
AND THAT'S...
THAT'S JUST WHAT YOU DO.
FOLLOW ME...

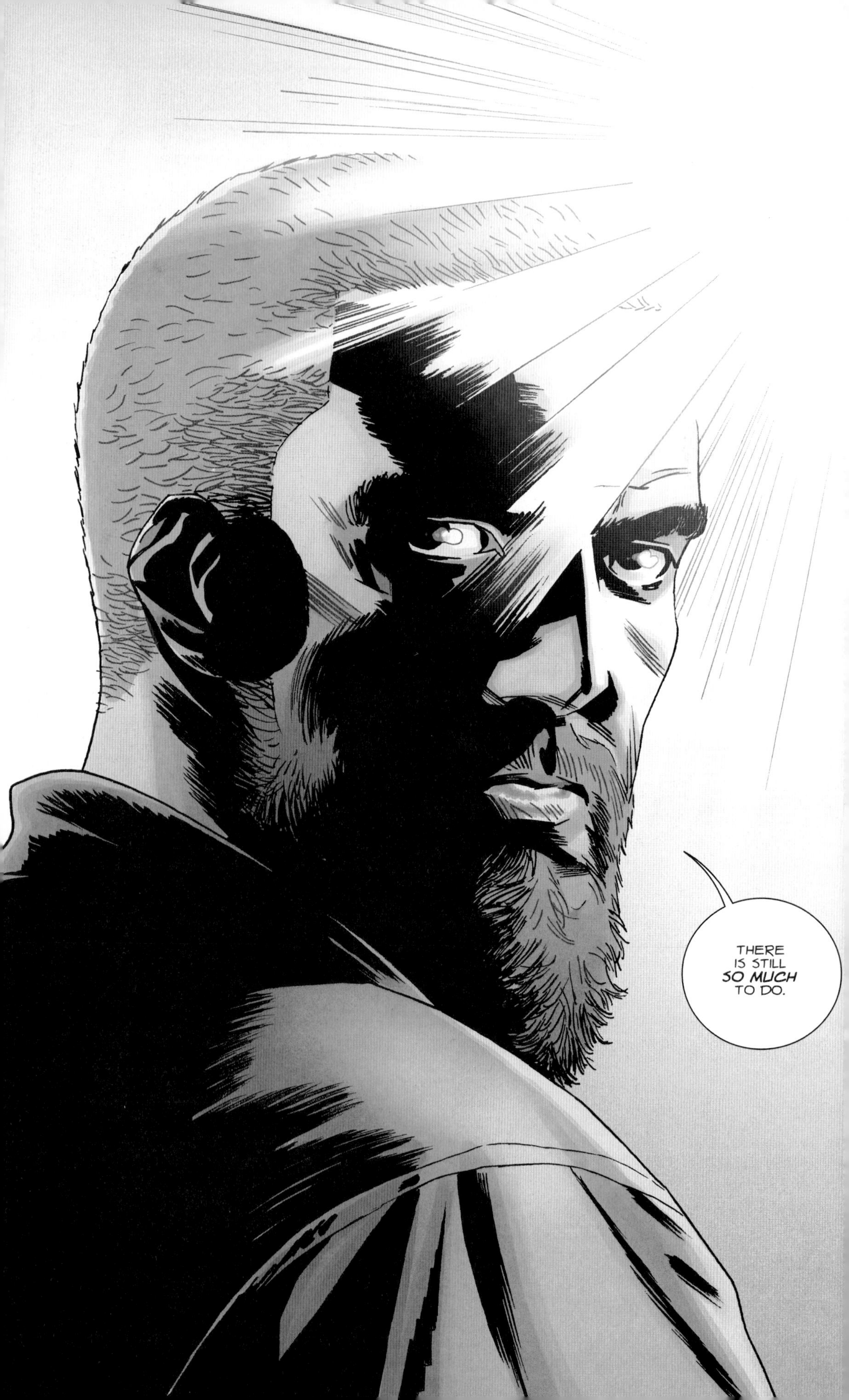
THERE IS STILL SO MUCH TO DO.

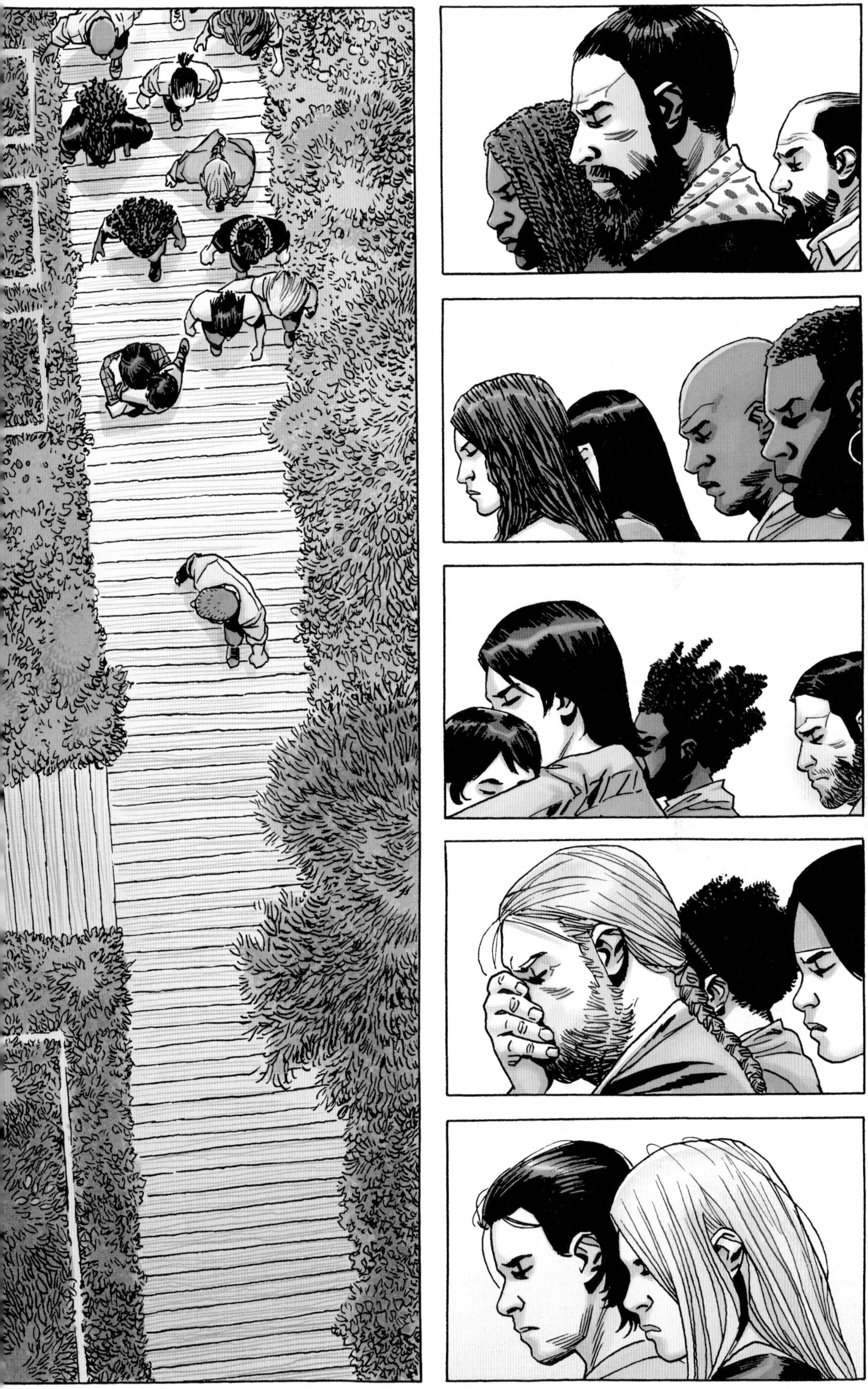

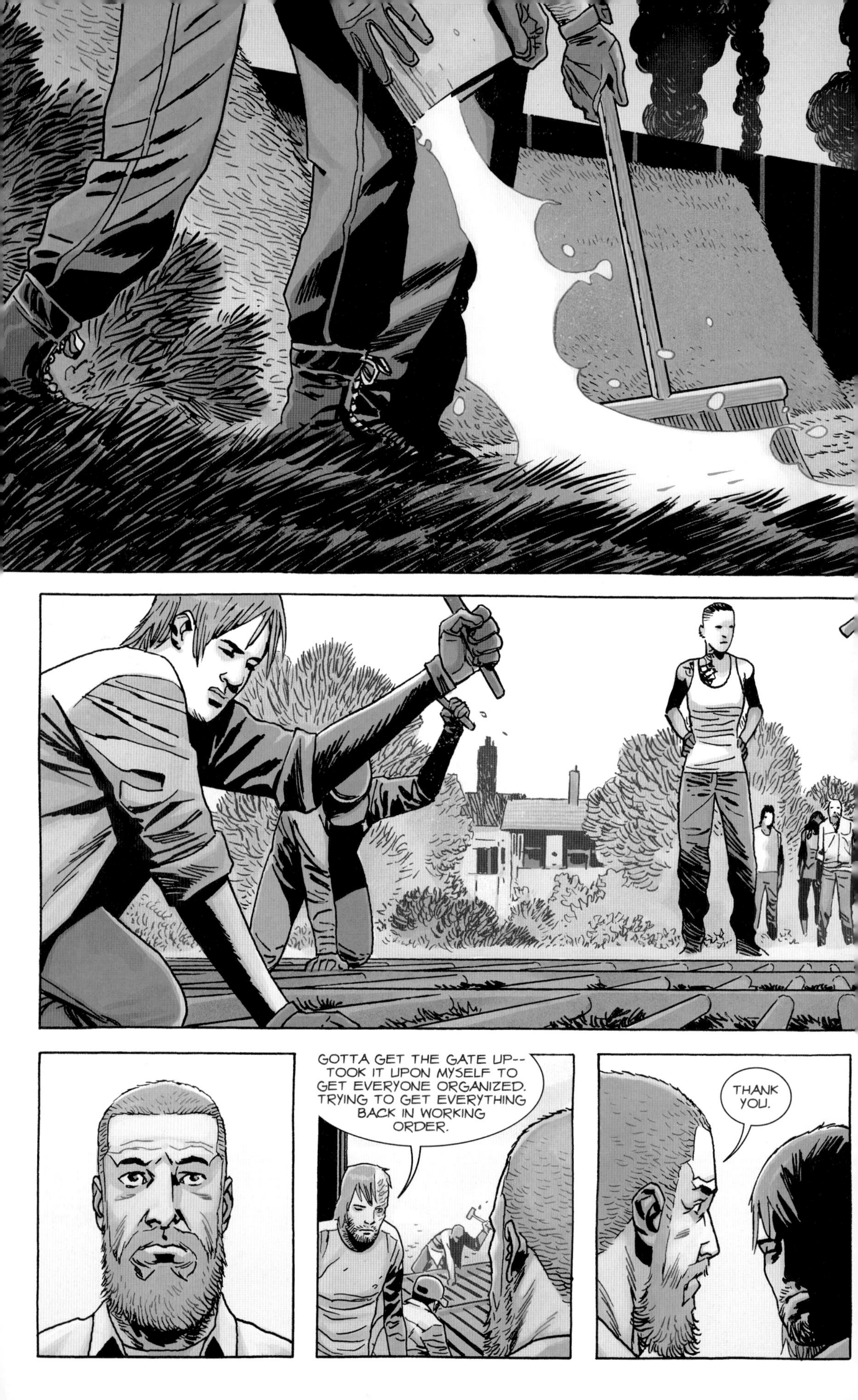
GOTTA GET THE GATE UP-- TOOK IT UPON MYSELF TO GET EVERYONE ORGANIZED. TRYING TO GET EVERYTHING BACK IN WORKING ORDER.
THANK YOU.

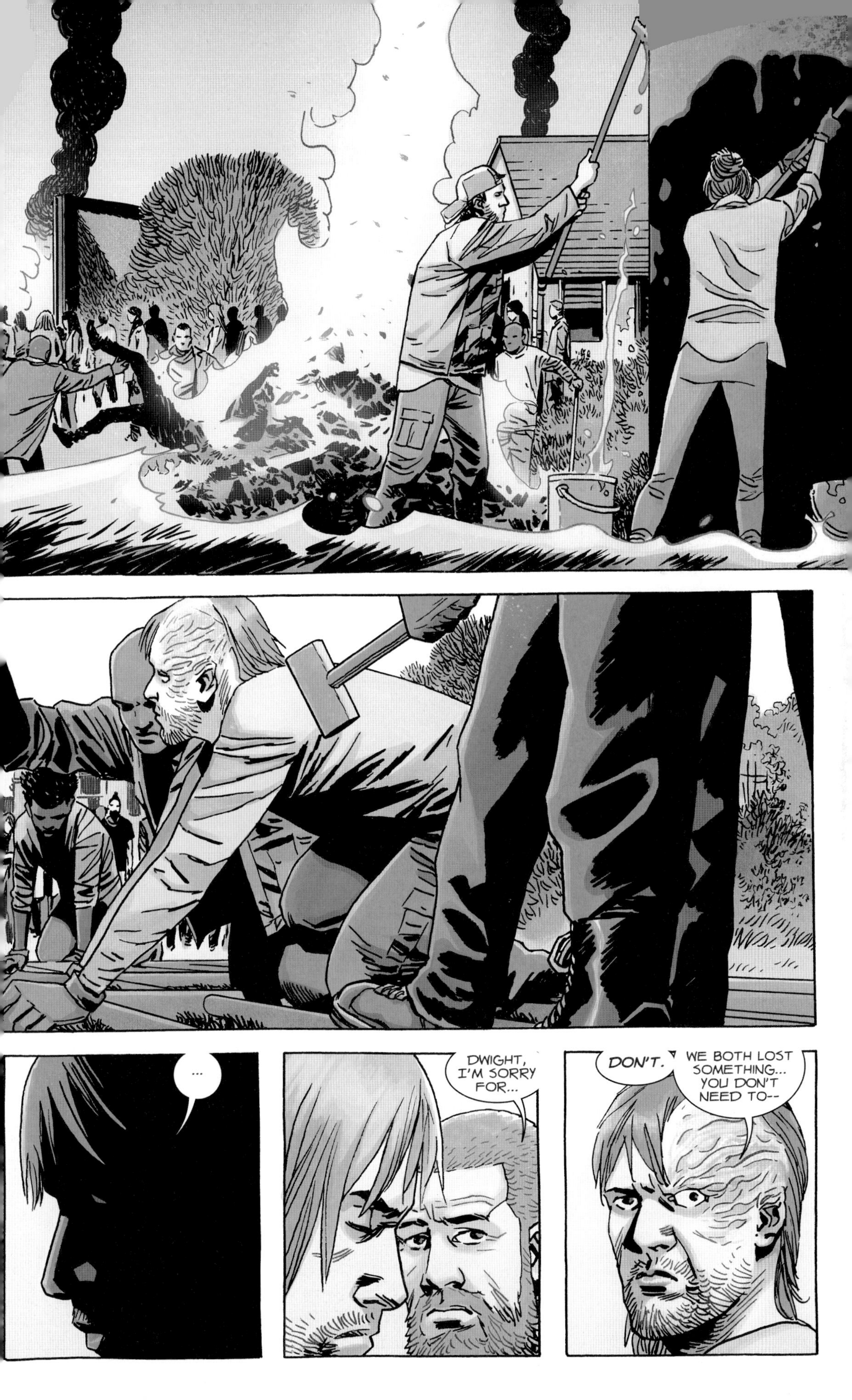
...
DWIGHT, I'M SORRY FOR...
DON'T.
WE BOTH LOST SOMETHING... YOU DON'T NEED TO--

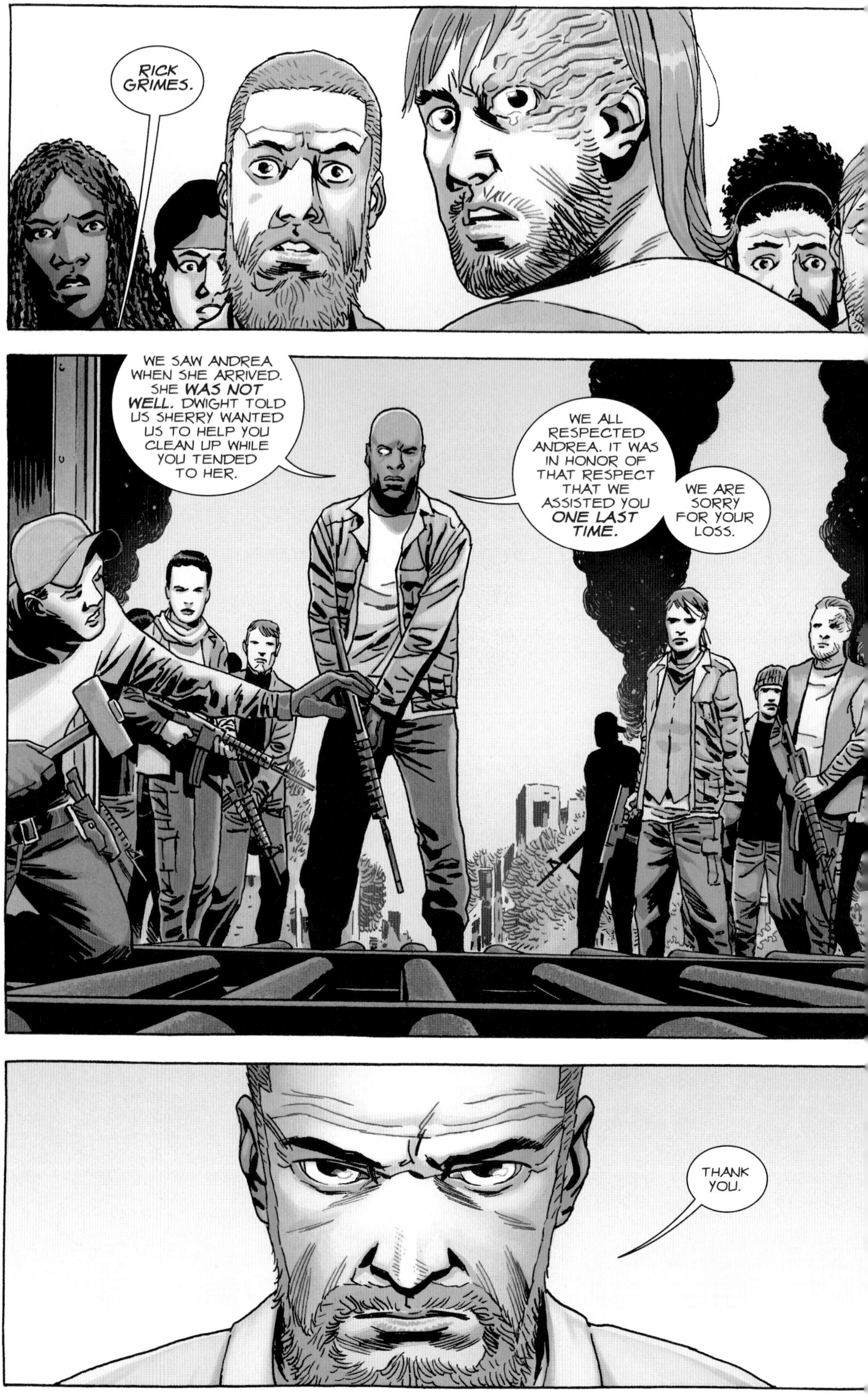
RICK GRIMES.
WE SAW ANDREA WHEN SHE ARRIVED. SHE **WAS NOT WELL.** DWIGHT TOLD US SHERRY WANTED US TO HELP YOU CLEAN UP WHILE YOU TENDED TO HER.
WE ALL RESPECTED ANDREA. IT WAS IN HONOR OF THAT RESPECT THAT WE ASSISTED YOU ***ONE LAST TIME.***
WE ARE SORRY FOR YOUR LOSS.
THANK YOU.

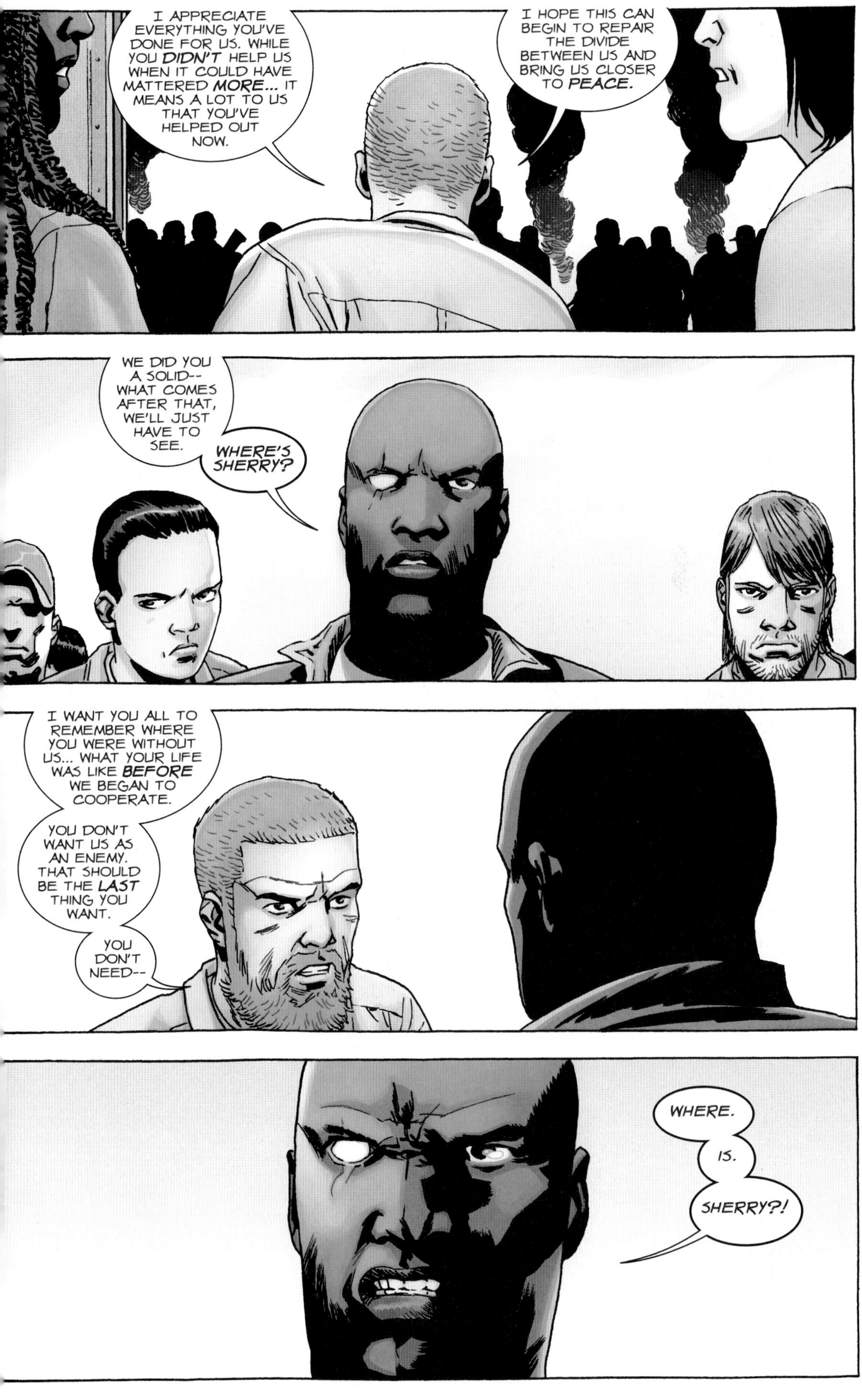

I APPRECIATE EVERYTHING YOU'VE DONE FOR US. WHILE YOU DIDN'T HELP US WHEN IT COULD HAVE MATTERED MORE... IT MEANS A LOT TO US THAT YOU'VE HELPED OUT NOW.
I HOPE THIS CAN BEGIN TO REPAIR THE DIVIDE BETWEEN US AND BRING US CLOSER TO PEACE.
WE DID YOU A SOLID-- WHAT COMES AFTER THAT, WE'LL JUST HAVE TO SEE.
WHERE'S SHERRY?
I WANT YOU ALL TO REMEMBER WHERE YOU WERE WITHOUT US... WHAT YOUR LIFE WAS LIKE BEFORE WE BEGAN TO COOPERATE.
YOU DON'T WANT US AS AN ENEMY. THAT SHOULD BE THE LAST THING YOU WANT.
YOU DON'T NEED--
WHERE.
IS.
SHERRY?!

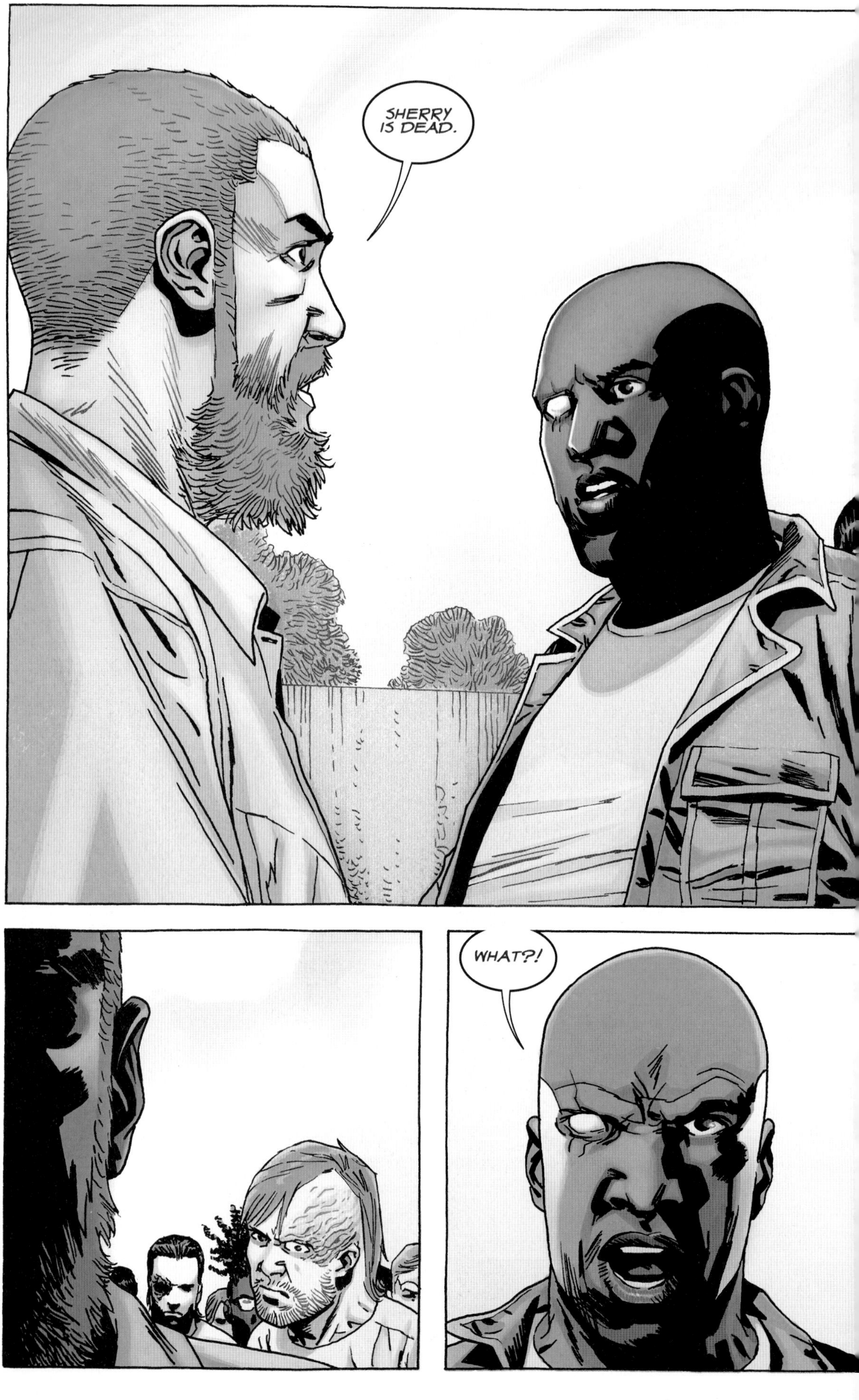
SHERRY IS DEAD.
WHAT?!

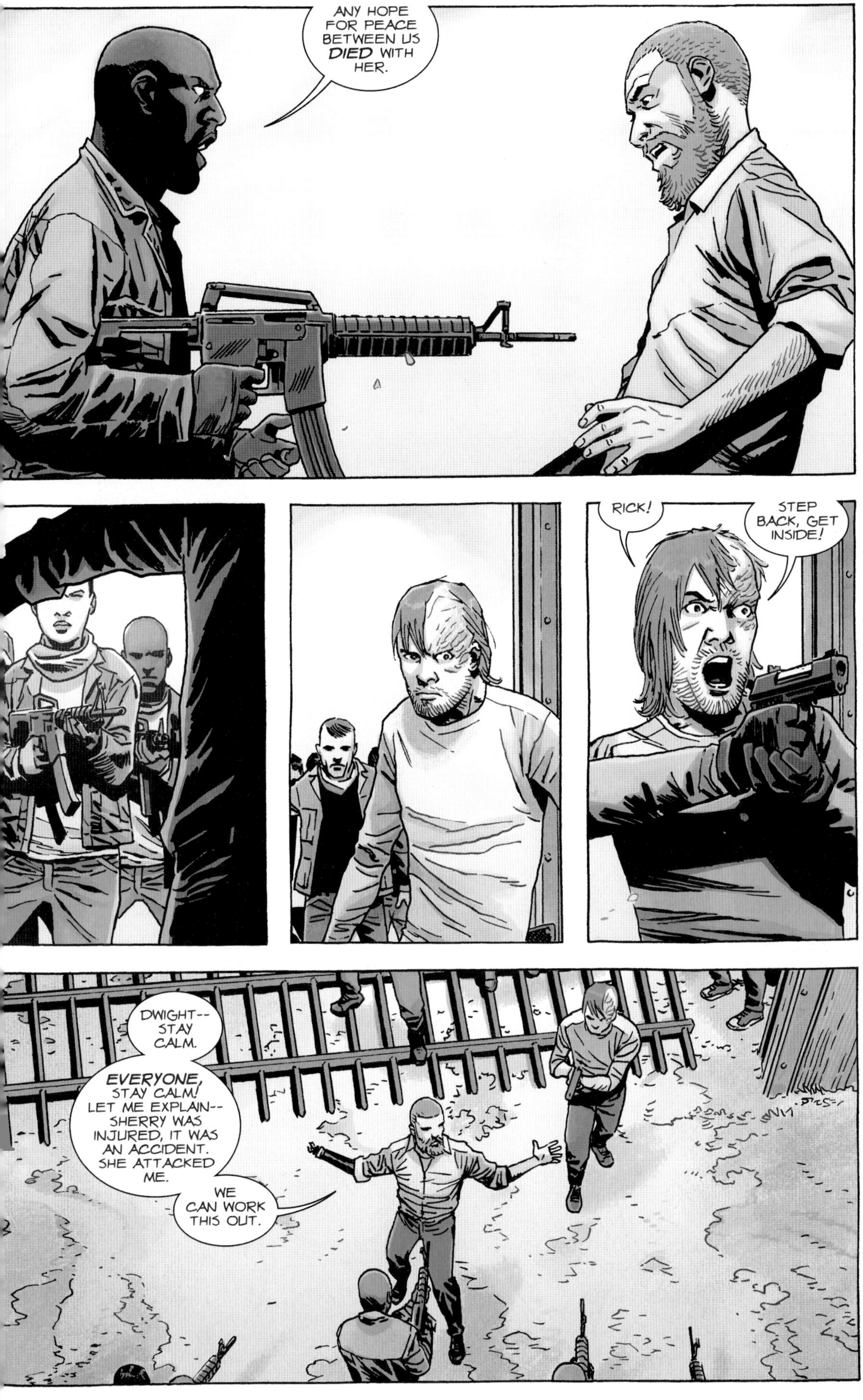

ANY HOPE FOR PEACE BETWEEN US *DIED* WITH HER.
RICK!
STEP BACK, GET INSIDE!
DWIGHT-- STAY CALM.
EVERYONE, STAY CALM! LET ME EXPLAIN-- SHERRY WAS INJURED, IT WAS AN ACCIDENT. SHE ATTACKED ME.
WE CAN WORK THIS OUT.

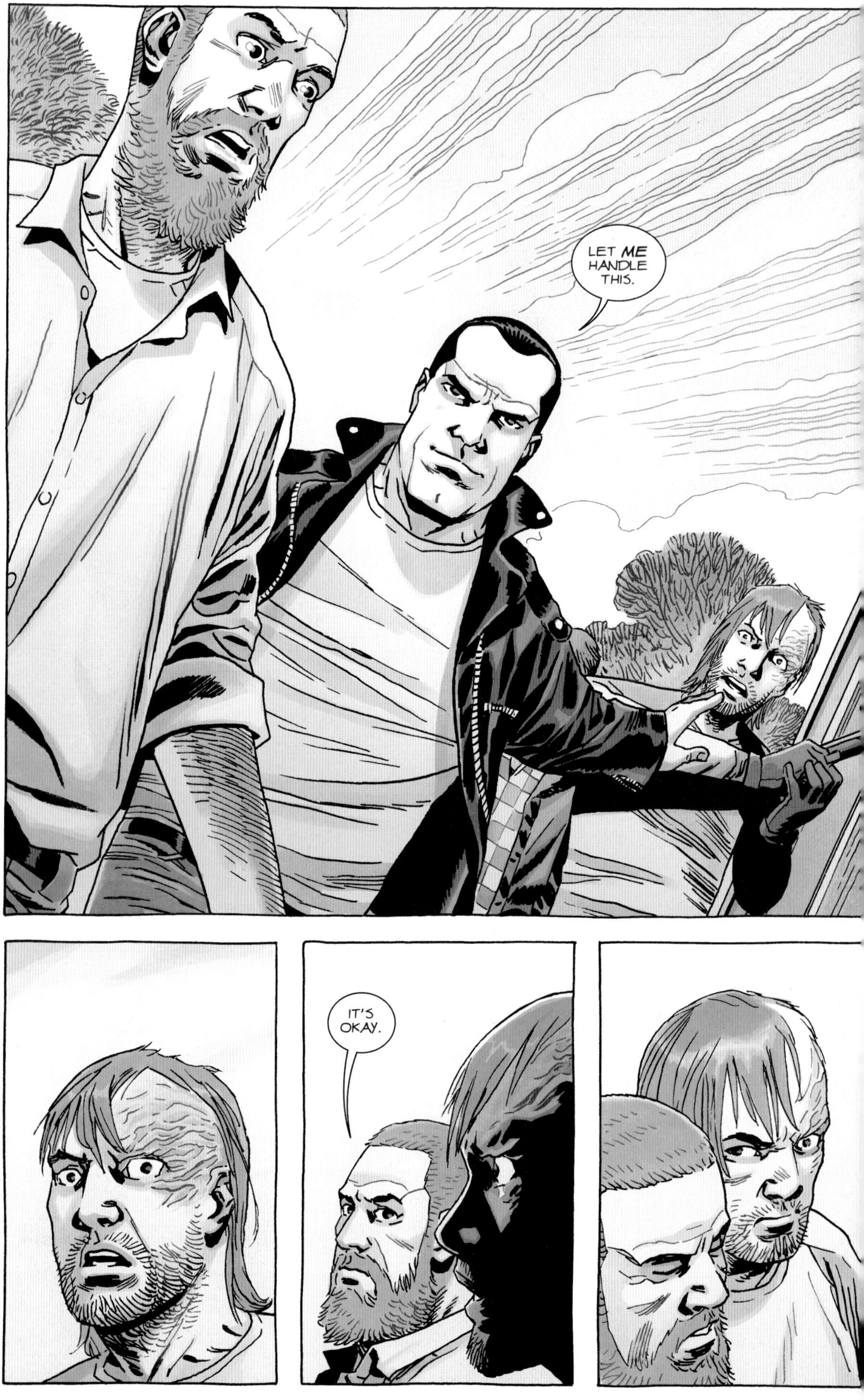
LET ME HANDLE THIS.
IT'S OKAY.

PUT YOUR FUCKING GUNS DOWN FOR A MOMENT AND LISTEN HERE, *YOU UNGRATEFUL FUCKS.*

YOU'RE ALIVE BECAUSE OF THE HARD, *BACK-FUCKING-BREAKING* WORK OF TWO PEOPLE.

ONE OF THOSE PEOPLE, OF COURSE... IS *ME.*

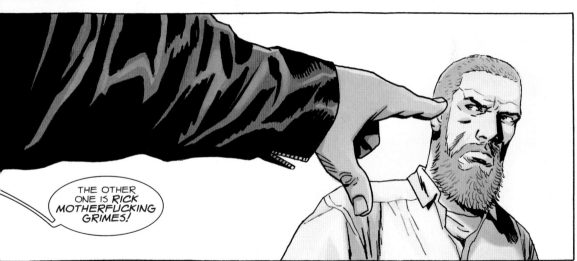

THE OTHER ONE IS *RICK MOTHERFUCKING GRIMES!*

I KNOW THE SCORE. YOU GUYS WANT YOUR FREEDOM AND NOW YOUR LEADER IS DEAD AND YOU'RE *ALL KINDS* OF PISSED OFF AND YOU FEEL LIKE THAT AIN'T GOING AWAY UNTIL YOU'RE BATHED IN BLOOD.

TRUST ME, I'VE BEEN THERE. *FUCK YES,* I HAVE. YOU CAN PROBABLY TASTE THAT METALLIC HINT OF BLOOD ON YOUR LIPS ALREADY.

YOU ARE SOME *BLOODTHIRSTY* FUCKING MONSTERS... TO RIVAL *LUCILLE HERSELF...*

...GOD REST HER WOODEN SOUL.

SO I HAVE A PROPOSITION FOR YOU. *READY?*

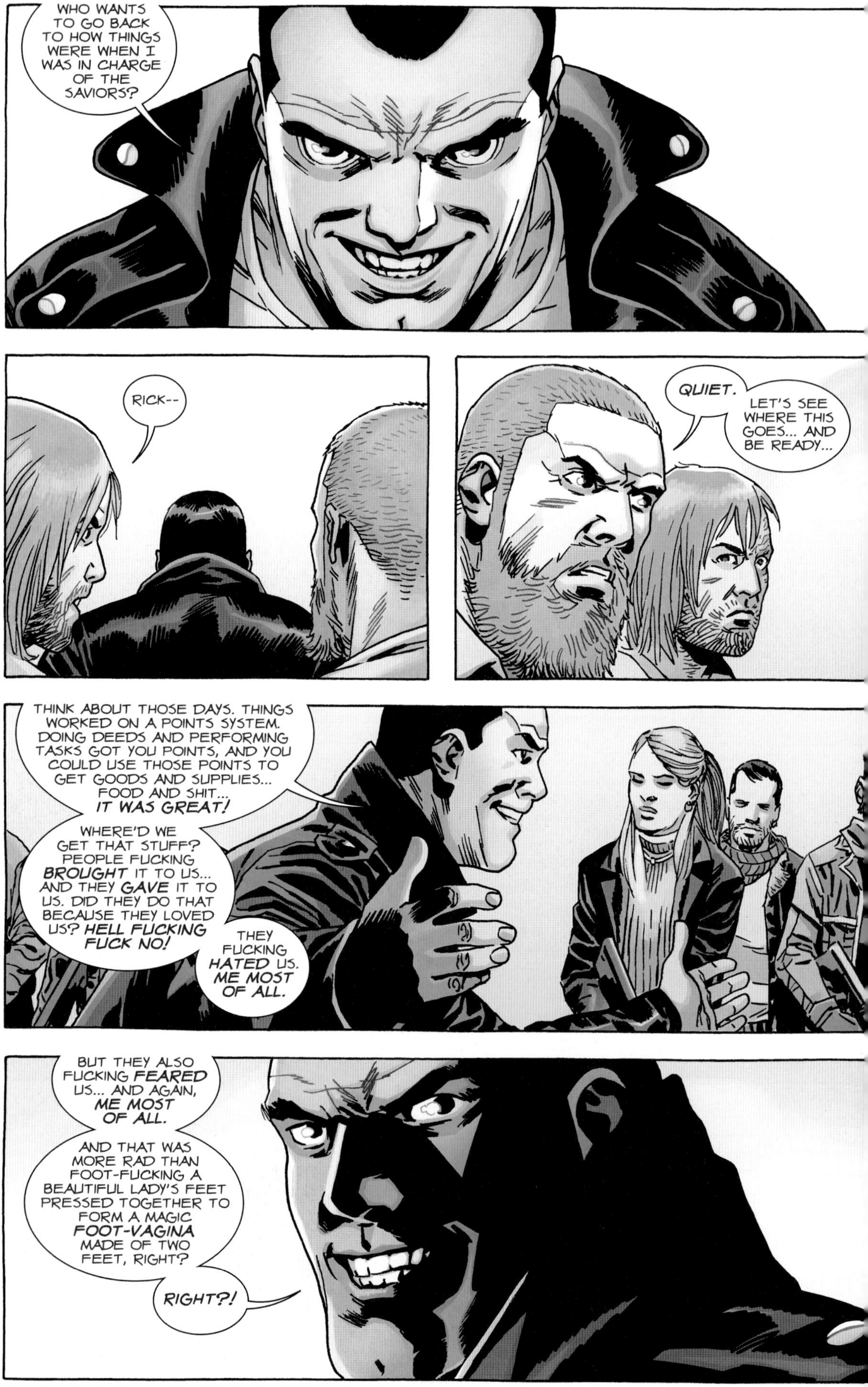
WHO WANTS TO GO BACK TO HOW THINGS WERE WHEN I WAS IN CHARGE OF THE SAVIORS?
RICK--
QUIET.
LET'S SEE WHERE THIS GOES... AND BE READY...
THINK ABOUT THOSE DAYS. THINGS WORKED ON A POINTS SYSTEM. DOING DEEDS AND PERFORMING TASKS GOT YOU POINTS, AND YOU COULD USE THOSE POINTS TO GET GOODS AND SUPPLIES... FOOD AND SHIT... IT WAS GREAT!
WHERE'D WE GET THAT STUFF? PEOPLE FUCKING BROUGHT IT TO US... AND THEY GAVE IT TO US. DID THEY DO THAT BECAUSE THEY LOVED US? HELL FUCKING FUCK NO!
THEY FUCKING HATED US. ME MOST OF ALL.
BUT THEY ALSO FUCKING FEARED US... AND AGAIN, ME MOST OF ALL.
AND THAT WAS MORE RAD THAN FOOT-FUCKING A BEAUTIFUL LADY'S FEET PRESSED TOGETHER TO FORM A MAGIC FOOT-VAGINA MADE OF TWO FEET, RIGHT?
RIGHT?!

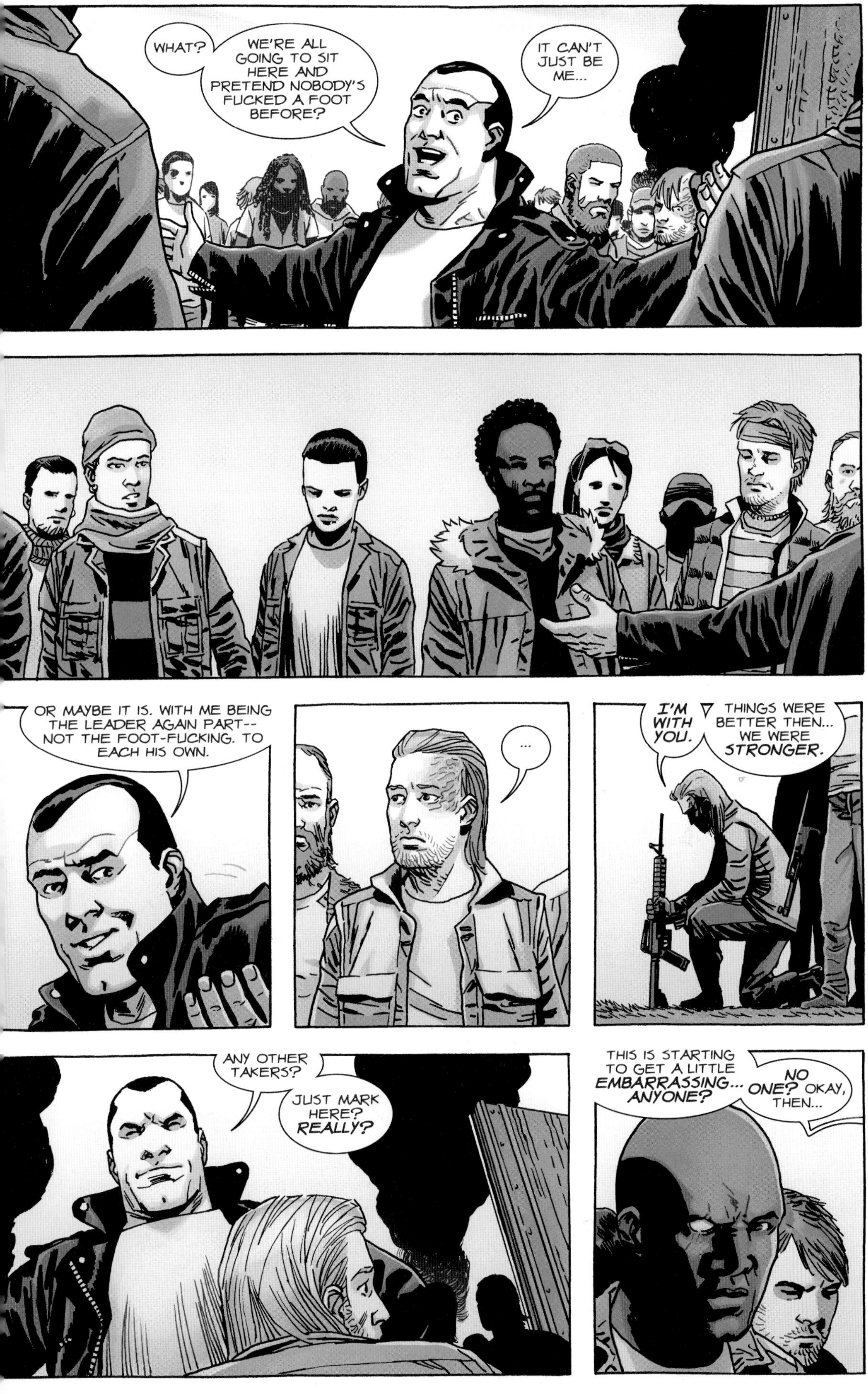
WHAT?
WE'RE ALL GOING TO SIT HERE AND PRETEND NOBODY'S FUCKED A FOOT BEFORE?
IT CAN'T JUST BE ME...
OR MAYBE IT IS. WITH ME BEING THE LEADER AGAIN PART-- NOT THE FOOT-FUCKING. TO EACH HIS OWN.
...
I'M WITH YOU.
THINGS WERE BETTER THEN... WE WERE STRONGER.
ANY OTHER TAKERS?
JUST MARK HERE? REALLY?
THIS IS STARTING TO GET A LITTLE EMBARRASSING... ANYONE?
NO ONE? OKAY, THEN...

YOU OF ALL FUCKING PEOPLE WANT TO GO BACK TO THE WAY THINGS WERE?!

I COOKED THE SIDE OF YOUR FUCKING FACE FOR FUCK'S SAKE, YOU FUCKING, FUCKED UP FUCK!

YOU WANT TO GO BACK TO THAT?! TO FUCKING FACE-COOKING WHEN IT WAS YOUR FUCKING FACE?!

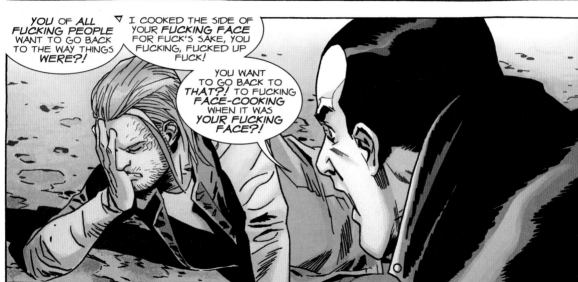

JESUS, MARK... YOU'RE A SPECIAL KIND OF SHEEP, AREN'T YOU?

WATCH OUT FOR THIS ONE, EVERYONE.

FUCK.

I DIDN'T... I JUST...

FUCKING HELL.

JESUS, MARK. PULL YOURSELF TOGETHER.

JOHN... FIRST OF ALL, KEEP AN EYE ON THAT KID... HE'S GOING TO FUCKING *KILL HIMSELF* OR SOMETHING AFTER THIS.

SECOND... I ALWAYS FUCKING LIKED YOU. YOU WERE A BIT OF A PRICK, TRUE, BUT THE TRUTH IS... YOU'RE A THINKER.

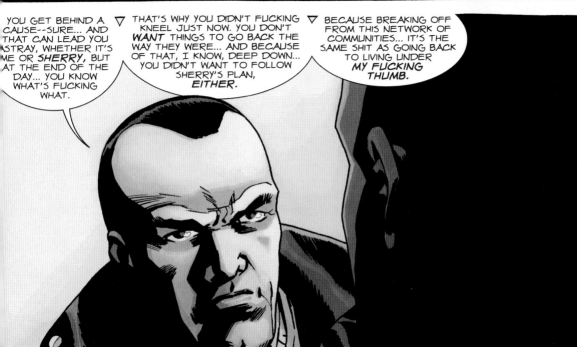

YOU GET BEHIND A CAUSE--SURE... AND THAT CAN LEAD YOU ASTRAY, WHETHER IT'S ME OR *SHERRY*, BUT AT THE END OF THE DAY... YOU KNOW WHAT'S FUCKING WHAT.

THAT'S WHY YOU DIDN'T FUCKING KNEEL JUST NOW. YOU DON'T *WANT* THINGS TO GO BACK THE WAY THEY WERE... AND BECAUSE OF THAT, I KNOW, DEEP DOWN... YOU DIDN'T WANT TO FOLLOW SHERRY'S PLAN, *EITHER.*

BECAUSE BREAKING OFF FROM THIS NETWORK OF COMMUNITIES... IT'S THE SAME SHIT AS GOING BACK TO LIVING UNDER *MY FUCKING THUMB.*

YOU KNOW RICK ISN'T A DICTATOR...

JUST LIKE I KNOW YOU AREN'T *REALLY* GOING TO AVENGE SHERRY... YOU DON'T *WANT* TO AVENGE SHERRY.

DEEP DOWN YOU'RE FUCKING *RELIEVED* SHE'S DEAD.

CAREFUL.

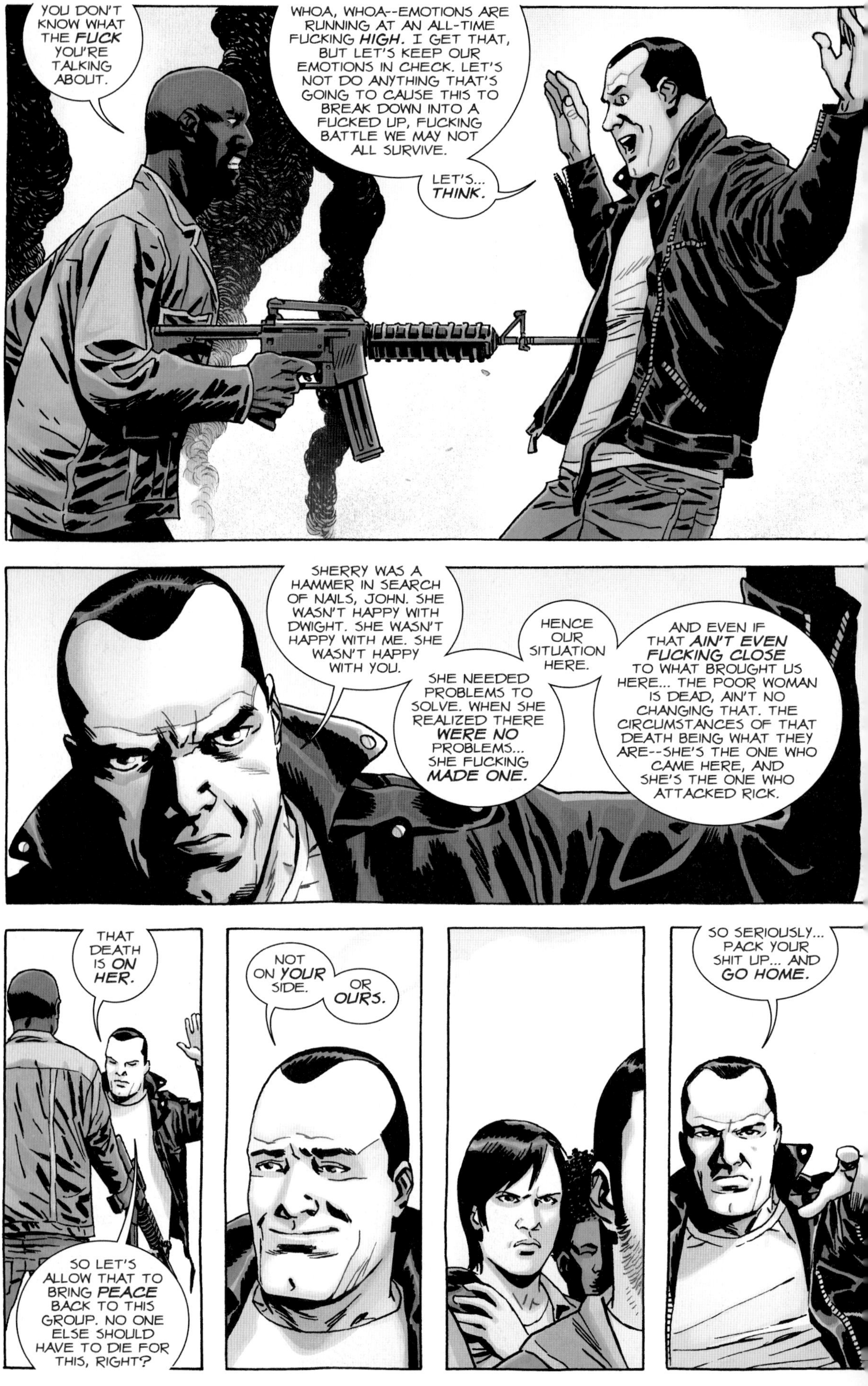
YOU DON'T KNOW WHAT THE FUCK YOU'RE TALKING ABOUT.
WHOA, WHOA--EMOTIONS ARE RUNNING AT AN ALL-TIME FUCKING HIGH. I GET THAT, BUT LET'S KEEP OUR EMOTIONS IN CHECK. LET'S NOT DO ANYTHING THAT'S GOING TO CAUSE THIS TO BREAK DOWN INTO A FUCKED UP, FUCKING BATTLE WE MAY NOT ALL SURVIVE.
LET'S... THINK.
SHERRY WAS A HAMMER IN SEARCH OF NAILS, JOHN. SHE WASN'T HAPPY WITH DWIGHT. SHE WASN'T HAPPY WITH ME. SHE WASN'T HAPPY WITH YOU.
SHE NEEDED PROBLEMS TO SOLVE. WHEN SHE REALIZED THERE WERE NO PROBLEMS... SHE FUCKING MADE ONE.
HENCE OUR SITUATION HERE.
AND EVEN IF THAT AIN'T EVEN FUCKING CLOSE TO WHAT BROUGHT US HERE... THE POOR WOMAN IS DEAD, AIN'T NO CHANGING THAT. THE CIRCUMSTANCES OF THAT DEATH BEING WHAT THEY ARE--SHE'S THE ONE WHO CAME HERE, AND SHE'S THE ONE WHO ATTACKED RICK.
THAT DEATH IS ON HER.
SO LET'S ALLOW THAT TO BRING PEACE BACK TO THIS GROUP. NO ONE ELSE SHOULD HAVE TO DIE FOR THIS, RIGHT?
NOT ON YOUR SIDE.
OR OURS.
SO SERIOUSLY... PACK YOUR SHIT UP... AND GO HOME.

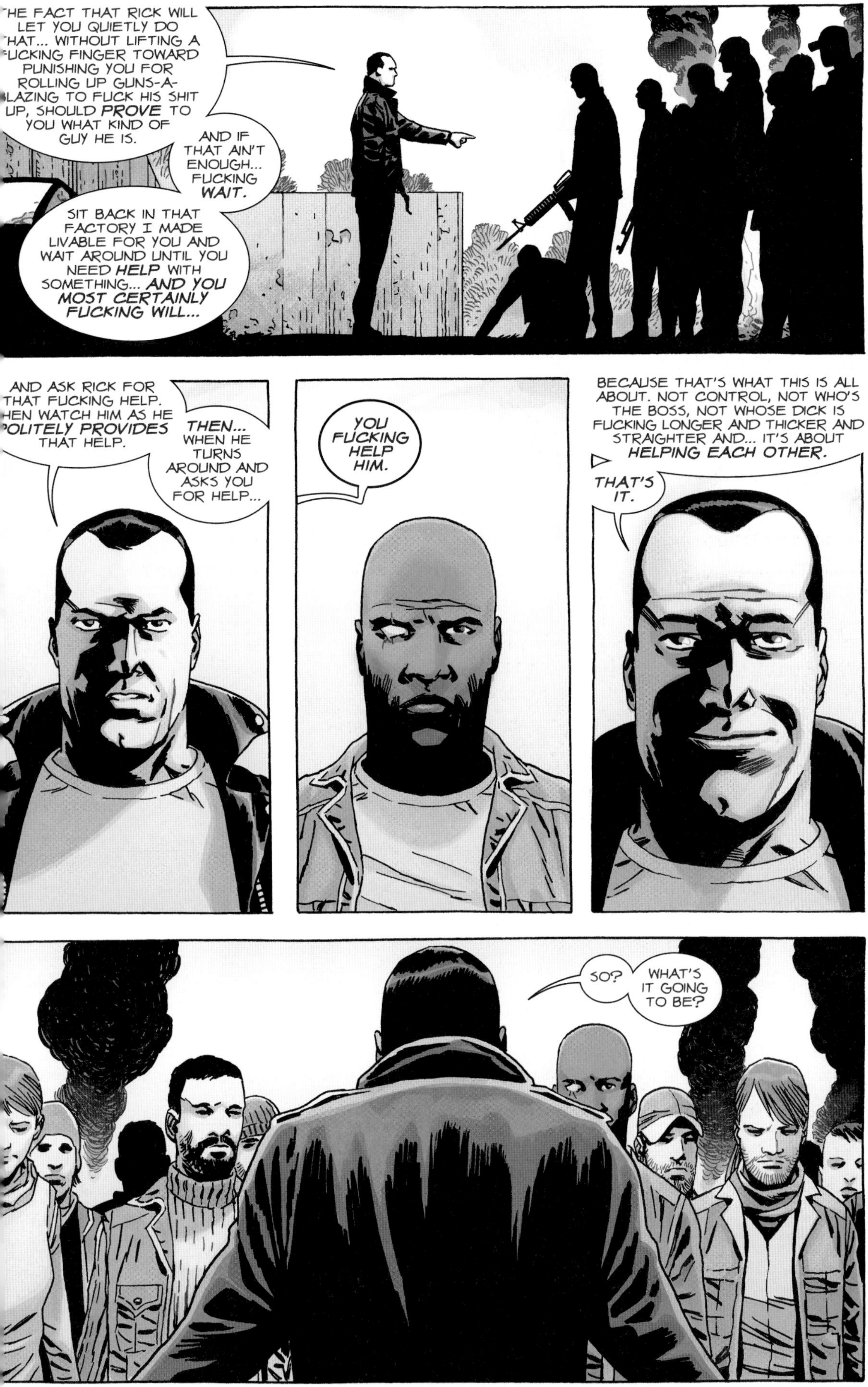

HE FACT THAT RICK WILL LET YOU QUIETLY DO THAT... WITHOUT LIFTING A FUCKING FINGER TOWARD PUNISHING YOU FOR ROLLING UP GUNS-A-BLAZING TO FUCK HIS SHIT UP, SHOULD PROVE TO YOU WHAT KIND OF GUY HE IS.
AND IF THAT AIN'T ENOUGH... FUCKING WAIT.
SIT BACK IN THAT FACTORY I MADE LIVABLE FOR YOU AND WAIT AROUND UNTIL YOU NEED HELP WITH SOMETHING... AND YOU MOST CERTAINLY FUCKING WILL...
AND ASK RICK FOR THAT FUCKING HELP. HEN WATCH HIM AS HE POLITELY PROVIDES THAT HELP.
THEN... WHEN HE TURNS AROUND AND ASKS YOU FOR HELP...
YOU FUCKING HELP HIM.
BECAUSE THAT'S WHAT THIS IS ALL ABOUT. NOT CONTROL, NOT WHO'S THE BOSS, NOT WHOSE DICK IS FUCKING LONGER AND THICKER AND STRAIGHTER AND... IT'S ABOUT HELPING EACH OTHER.
THAT'S IT.
SO?
WHAT'S IT GOING TO BE?

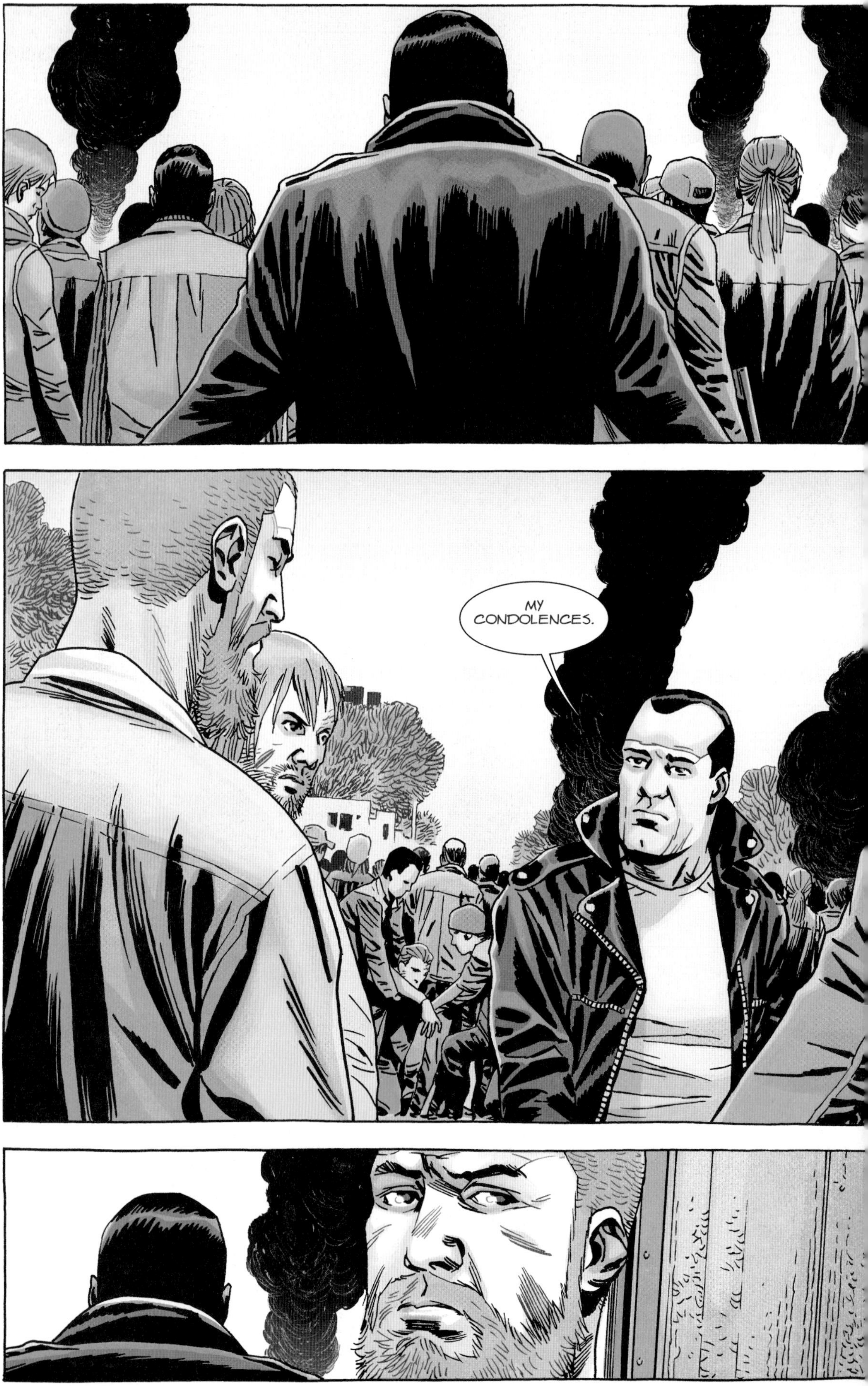
MY CONDOLENCES.

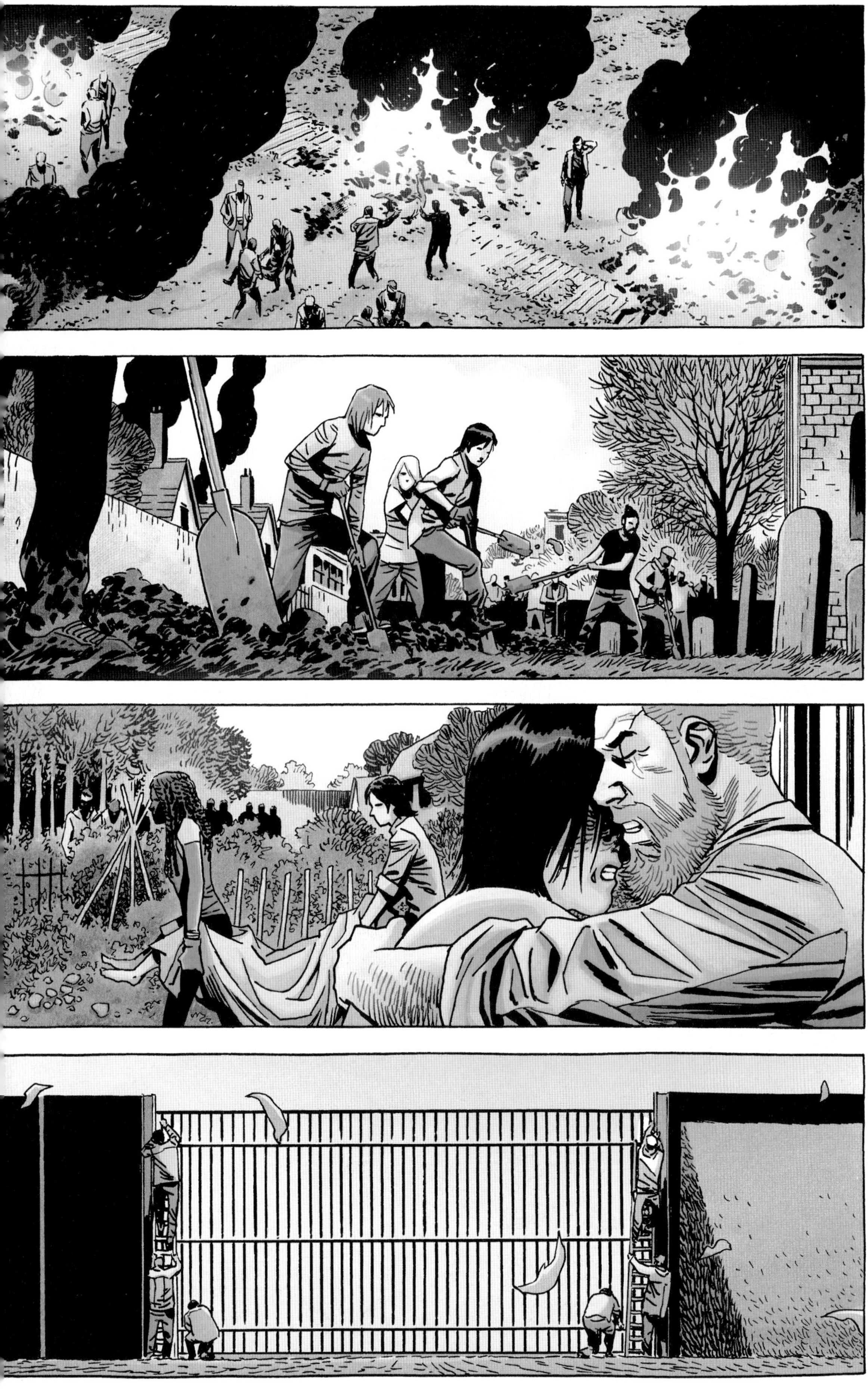

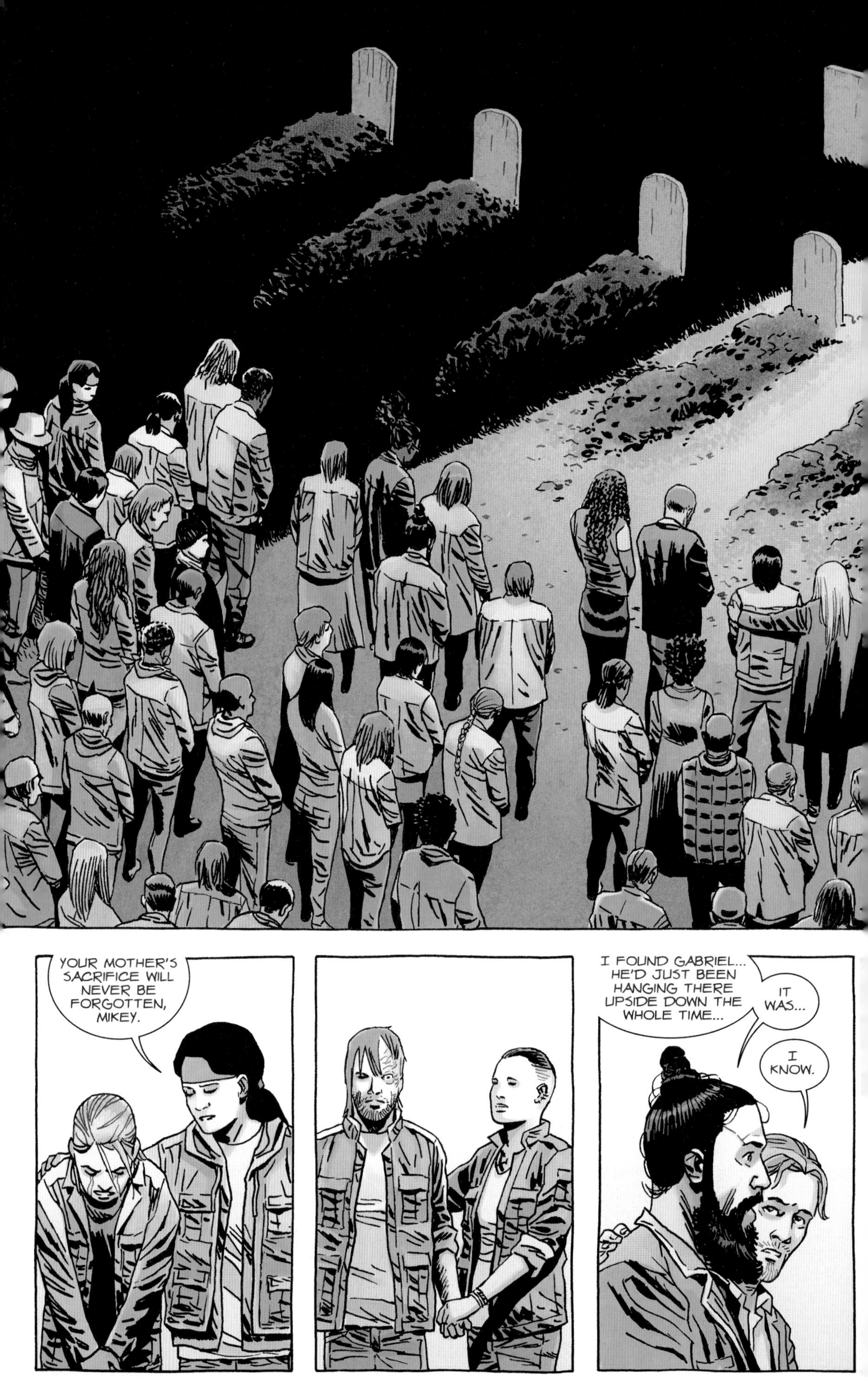
YOUR MOTHER'S SACRIFICE WILL NEVER BE FORGOTTEN, MIKEY.
I FOUND GABRIEL... HE'D JUST BEEN HANGING THERE UPSIDE DOWN THE WHOLE TIME...
IT WAS...
I KNOW.

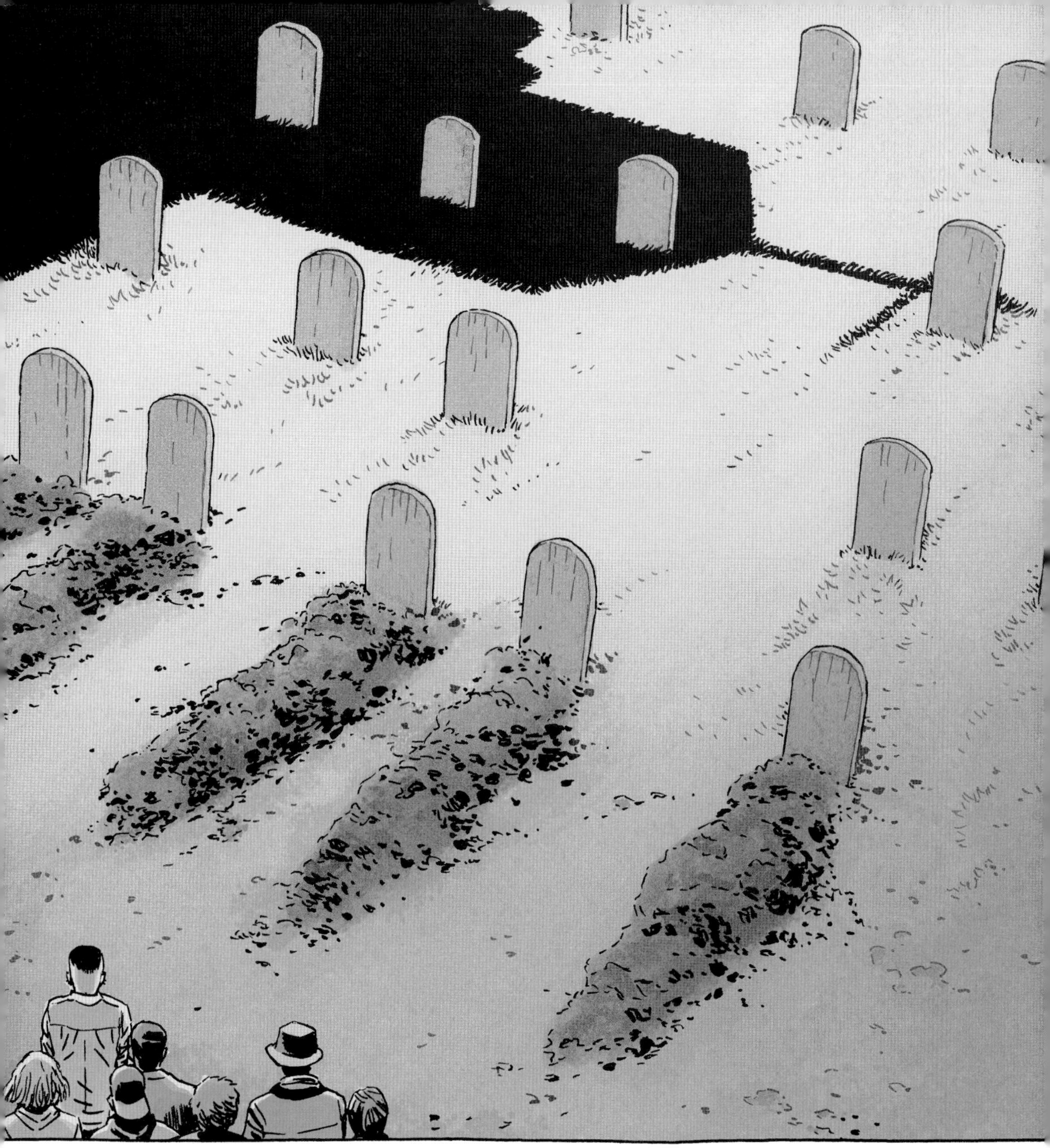

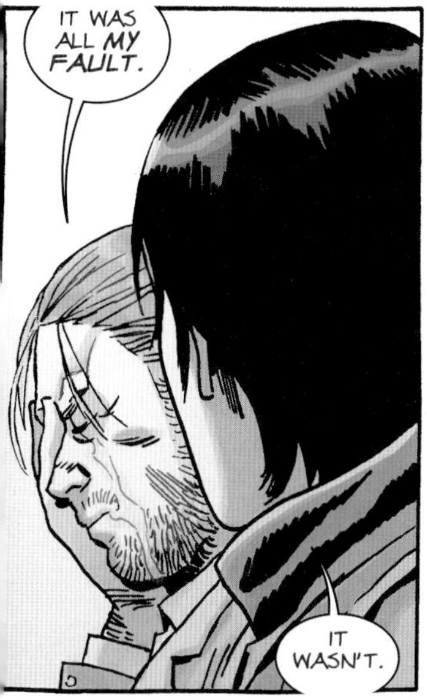
IT WAS ALL MY FAULT.
IT WASN'T.

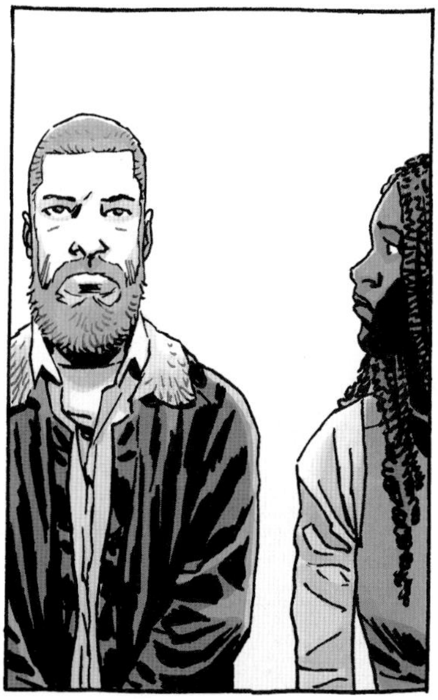

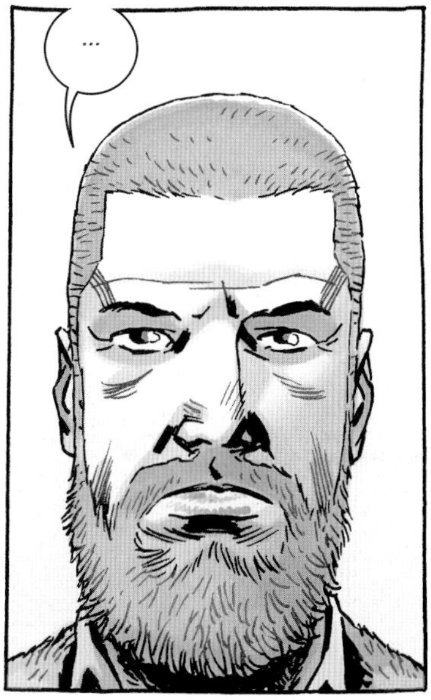
...

DAD, I'M SO SORRY.

DAD?

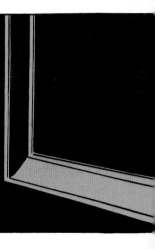

GOODNIGHT, DAD.

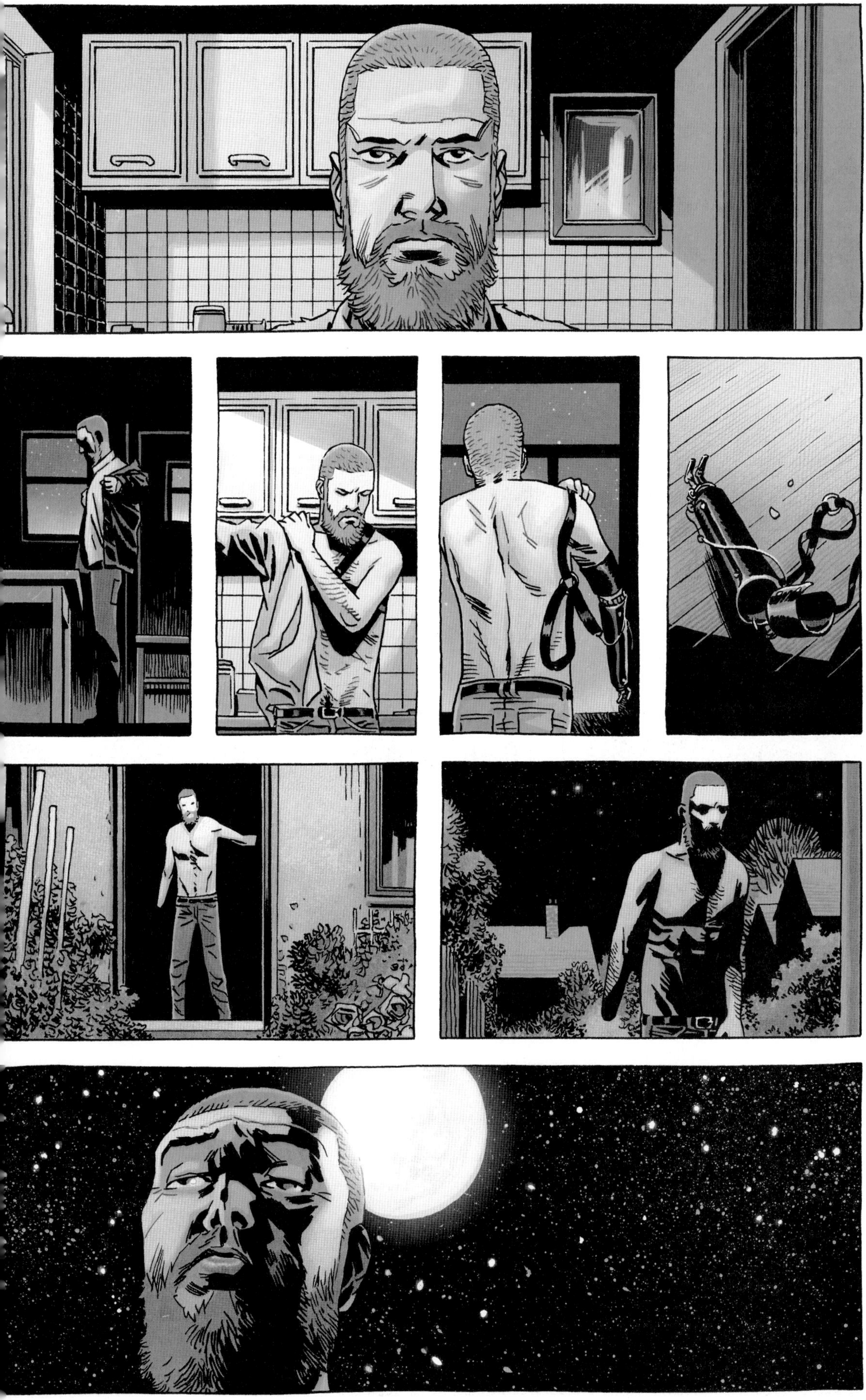

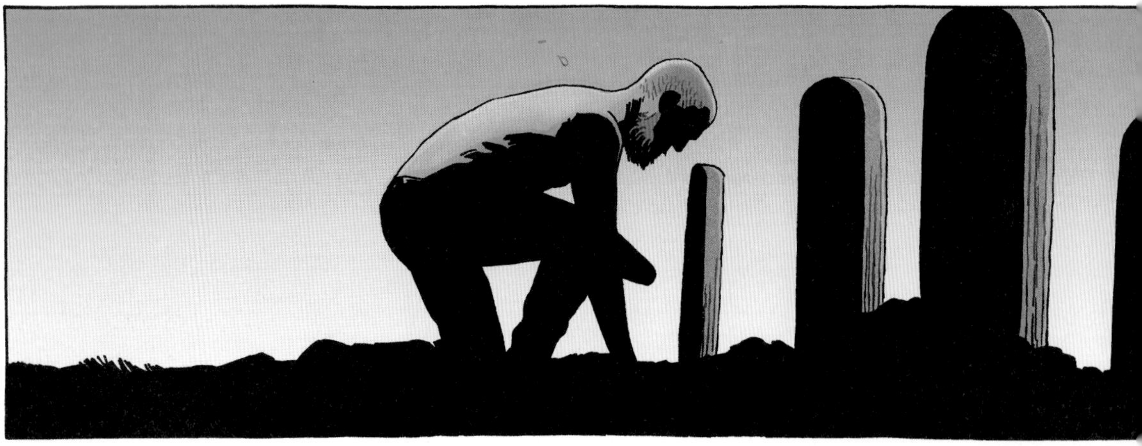

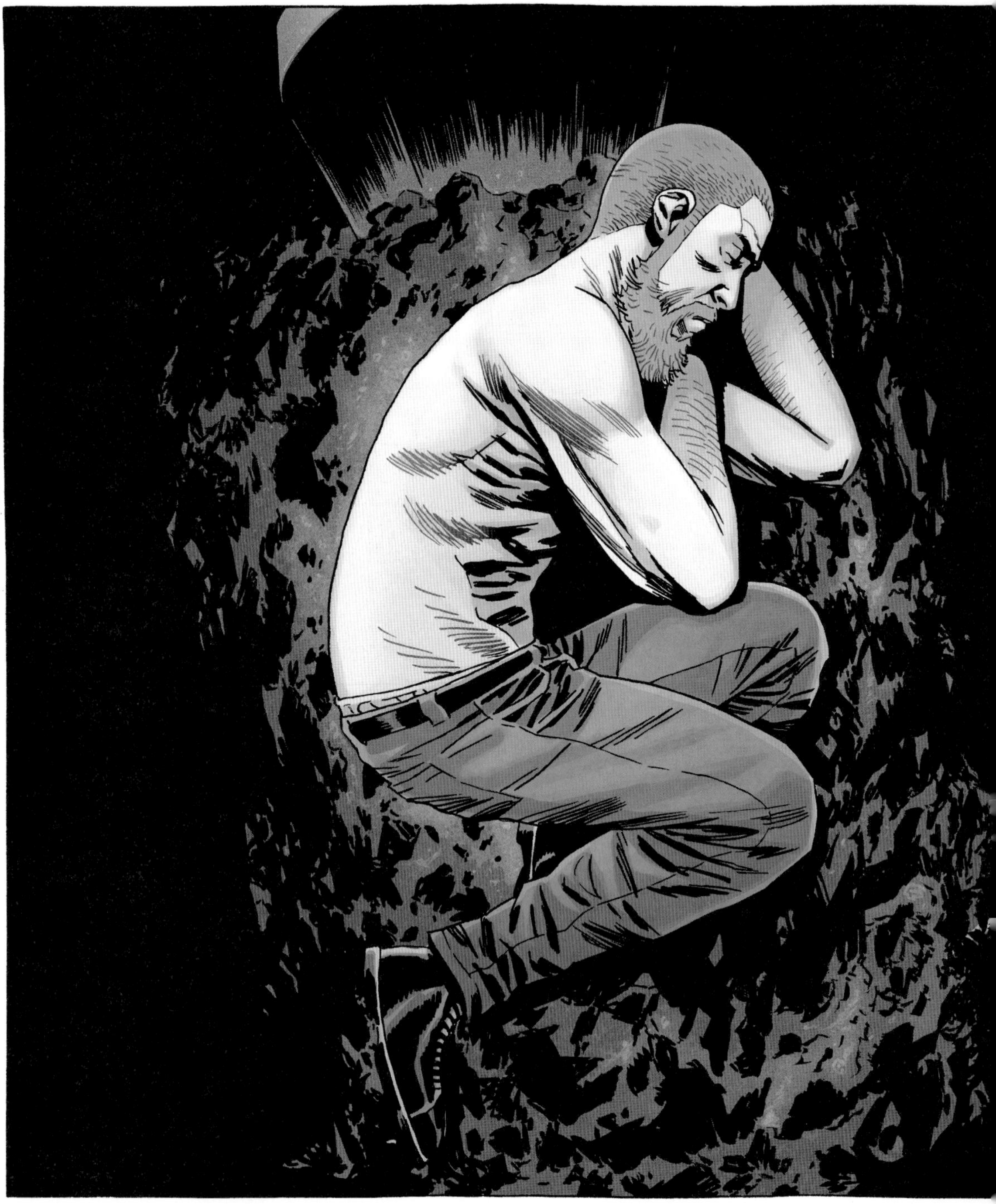

TO BE CONTINUED...

“THERE IS STILL SO MUCH TO DO.”

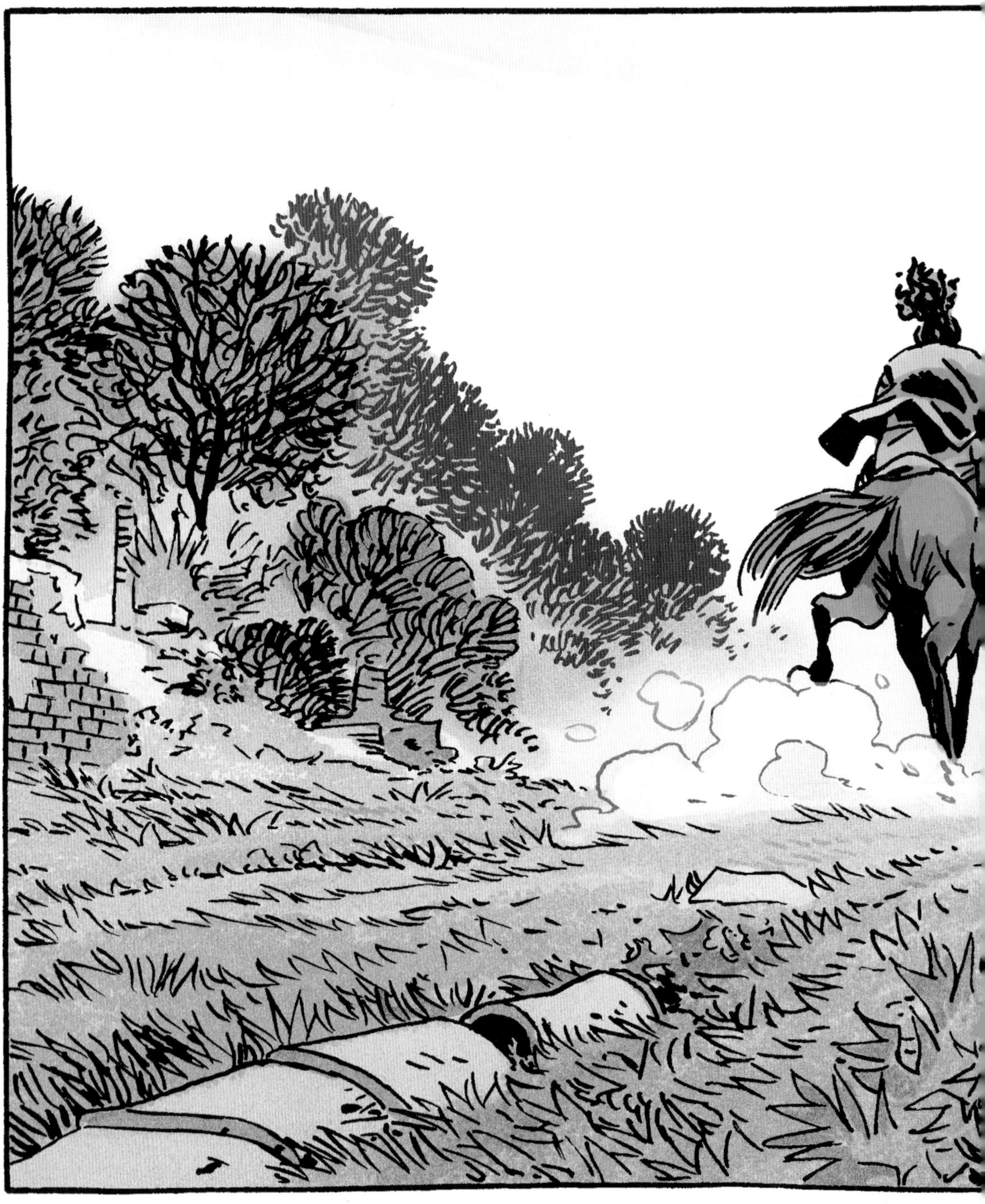

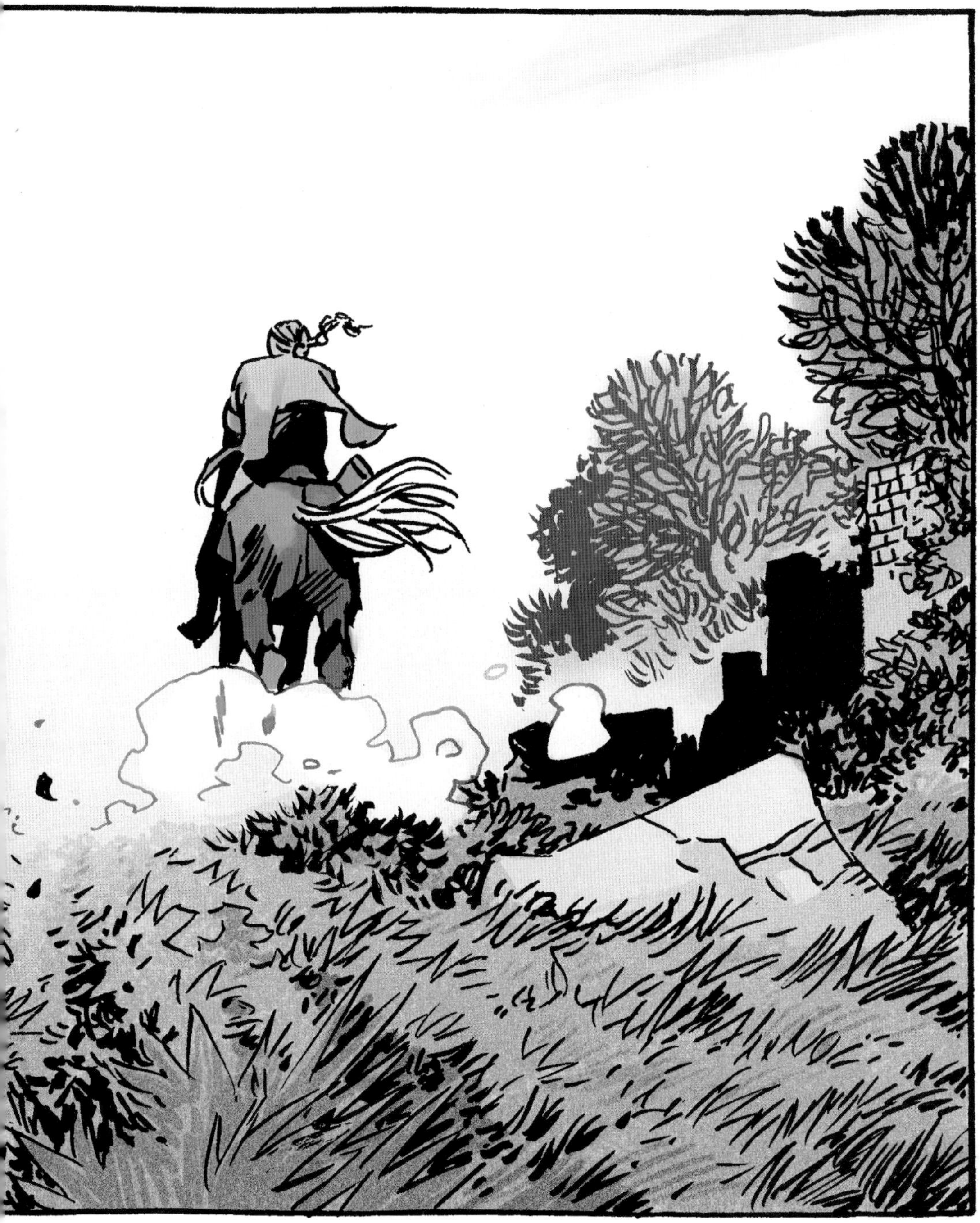

FOR MORE OF THE WALKING DEAD

TRADEPAPERBACKS

ROBERT KIRKMAN TONY MOORE
THE WALKING DEAD
VOLUME 1
DAYS GONE BYE

VOL. 1: DAYS GONE BYE TP
ISBN: 978-1-58240-672-5
$14.99
VOL. 2: MILES BEHIND US TP
ISBN: 978-1-58240-775-3
$14.99
VOL. 3: SAFETY BEHIND BARS TP
ISBN: 978-1-58240-805-7
$14.99
VOL. 4: THE HEART'S DESIRE TP
ISBN: 978-1-58240-530-8
$14.99
VOL. 5: THE BEST DEFENSE TP
ISBN: 978-1-58240-612-1
$14.99
VOL. 6: THIS SORROWFUL LIFE TP
ISBN: 978-1-58240-684-8
$14.99
VOL. 7: THE CALM BEFORE TP
ISBN: 978-1-58240-828-6
$14.99
VOL. 8: MADE TO SUFFER TP
ISBN: 978-1-58240-883-5
$14.99

VOL. 9: HERE WE REMAIN TP
ISBN: 978-1-60706-022-2
$14.99
VOL. 10: WHAT WE BECOME TP
ISBN: 978-1-60706-075-8
$14.99
VOL. 11: FEAR THE HUNTERS TP
ISBN: 978-1-60706-181-6
$14.99
VOL. 12: LIFE AMONG THEM TP
ISBN: 978-1-60706-254-7
$14.99
VOL. 13: TOO FAR GONE TP
ISBN: 978-1-60706-329-2
$14.99
VOL. 14: NO WAY OUT TP
ISBN: 978-1-60706-392-6
$14.99
VOL. 15: WE FIND OURSELVES TP
ISBN: 978-1-60706-440-4
$14.99
VOL. 16: A LARGER WORLD TP
ISBN: 978-1-60706-559-3
$14.99

VOL. 17: SOMETHING TO FEAR TP
ISBN: 978-1-60706-615-6
$14.99
VOL. 18: WHAT COMES AFTER TP
ISBN: 978-1-60706-687-3
$14.99
VOL. 19: MARCH TO WAR TP
ISBN: 978-1-60706-818-1
$14.99
VOL. 20: ALL OUT WAR PART ONE TP
ISBN: 978-1-60706-882-2
$14.99
VOL. 21: ALL OUT WAR PART TWO TP
ISBN: 978-1-63215-030-1
$14.99
VOL. 22: A NEW BEGINNING TP
ISBN: 978-1-63215-041-7
$14.99
VOL. 23: WHISPERS INTO SCREAMS TP
ISBN: 978-1-63215-258-9
$14.99
VOL. 24: LIFE AND DEATH TP
ISBN: 978-1-63215-402-6
$14.99

VOL. 25: NO TURNING BACK TP
ISBN: 978-1-63215-612-9
$14.99
VOL. 26: CALL TO ARMS TP
ISBN: 978-1-63215-917-5
$14.99
VOL. 27: THE WHISPERER WAR TP
ISBN: 978-1-5343-0052-1
$14.99
VOL. 28: A CERTAIN DOOM
ISBN: 978-1-5343-0244-0
$16.99
VOL. 1: SPANISH EDITION TP
ISBN: 978-1-60706-797-9
$14.99
VOL. 2: SPANISH EDITION TP
ISBN: 978-1-60706-845-7
$14.99
VOL. 3: SPANISH EDITION TP
ISBN: 978-1-60706-883-9
$14.99
VOL. 4: SPANISH EDITION TP
ISBN: 978-1-63215-035-6
$14.99

HARDCOVERS

THE WALKING DEAD
BOOK ONE
a continuing story of survival horror.

BOOK ONE HC
ISBN: 978-1-58240-619-0
$34.99
BOOK TWO HC
ISBN: 978-1-58240-698-5
$34.99
BOOK THREE HC
ISBN: 978-1-58240-825-5
$34.99
BOOK FOUR HC
ISBN: 978-1-60706-000-0
$34.99
BOOK FIVE HC
ISBN: 978-1-60706-171-7
$34.99
BOOK SIX HC
ISBN: 978-1-60706-327-8
$34.99
BOOK SEVEN HC
ISBN: 978-1-60706-439-8
$34.99
BOOK EIGHT HC
ISBN: 978-1-60706-593-7
$34.99
BOOK NINE HC
ISBN: 978-1-60706-798-6
$34.99
BOOK TEN HC
ISBN: 978-1-63215-034-9
$34.99
BOOK ELEVEN HC
ISBN: 978-1-63215-271-8
$34.99
BOOK TWELVE HC
ISBN: 978-1-63215-451-4
$34.99
BOOK THIRTEEN HC
ISBN: 978-1-63215-916-8
$34.99

COMPENDIUMS

THE WALKING DEAD
COMPENDIUM ONE

COMPENDIUM TP, VOL. 1
ISBN: 978-1-60706-076-5
$59.99
COMPENDIUM TP, VOL. 2
ISBN: 978-1-60706-596-8
$59.99
COMPENDIUM TP, VOL. 3
ISBN: 978-1-63215-456-9
$59.99

SPECIALTY BOOKS

THE WALKING DEAD
THE COVERS

THE WALKING DEAD: THE COVERS, VOL. 1 HC
ISBN: 978-1-60706-002-4
$24.99
THE WALKING DEAD: ALL OUT WAR HC
ISBN: 978-1-63215-038-7
$34.99
THE WALKING DEAD COLORING BOOK
ISBN: 978-1-63215-774-4
$14.99
THE WALKING DEAD RICK GRIMES COLORING BOOK
ISBN: 978-1-5343-0003-3
$14.99

OMNIBUS

THE WALKING DEAD

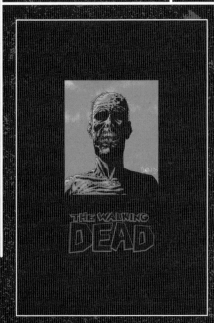

OMNIBUS, VOL. 1
ISBN: 978-1-60706-503-6
$100.00
OMNIBUS, VOL. 2
ISBN: 978-1-60706-515-9
$100.00
OMNIBUS, VOL. 3
ISBN: 978-1-60706-330-8
$100.00
OMNIBUS, VOL. 4
ISBN: 978-1-60706-616-3
$100.00
OMNIBUS, VOL. 5
ISBN: 978-1-63215-042-4
$100.00
OMNIBUS, VOL. 6
ISBN: 978-1-63215-521-4
$100.00